Mark

Of The
Two-Edged

Sword

By K. A. BRYANT

Thank you for choosing this book. Join the K. A. BRYANT Book Readers Club on kabryant.com with one click.

-K. A. BRYANT

Dedication

I am blessed to be afforded the time to write, the love to write,
And the support to write.
This came from God above, and my dear husband, Michael.
My Darling, I love you and dedicate this book to you for all
the times you looked at me with that flicker of faith in
your eyes as you encouraged me to finish.

My children, I love you. You are a gift from God, and I pray
this encourages you to achieve what God places in your heart.

Mom & Dad, you are perfect examples of what it means to be
fearlessly motivated, stepping into the unknown to fulfill your
dreams.
Thank you for seeing the gift in me and encouraging me
to reach higher. I am eternally grateful for all your love and
Godly guidance.

CHAPTER ONE

New York
Caleb Promise

The tree isn't wide enough, not nearly wide enough. It never is. Right now, being a man that is six foot two inches, isn't helping. My broad shoulders are sticking out. I can feel it. It will see me. Maybe if I crouch. It isn't finished yet. Not even close. The sound of my heart pounding seems louder than their screams, and it hears everything. That's how it found them underground in that muddy tunnel covered by the fall leaves.

They hid for weeks. A group here, a group there. Don't ask me how I know, I just do. Thin, rationing food for months. I can hear them praying as it holds them up like trophies in front of the government vehicle's lights. The agents, bored now, slump in their seats. The cold frost of their breath glows in the headlights.

Taller than any human, the face of a lioness and arms of a gorilla. That's all I ever see. It fades into shadows. No matter how hard I try, I never see all of it. Why am I always barefoot?

People that don't have this think it's cool, but it's not. Consciousness in a dream used to be fun. The ability to choose which way to go, whether to fly or walk and even to wake up or not. It's not fun. I don't truly rest. Ever. Especially in this dream. It has returned every night for weeks.

I've got to make it to that rock without it hearing me. From there, I may see it. All of it. There she is. The lady with the red hair. The creature turns around right after pulling her out. This is my chance.

I take one step. It's over. I felt the stick crack beneath my foot. My eyes close, praying it didn't hear me. But I know it did. I open my eyes. It's staring right at me.

It opens its claw, releasing her. It's coming. The ground vibrates with each step. I can't hear anything except my heart pounding. She's falling to the ground, but the drop encompasses me.

I jolt awake. Sitting straight up. My room is as cold and clammy as the dream. It's over, but the eeriness of the dream hangs in the air with the feeling that someone else was in that forest. Someone watches with a disconnected heart. Alive enough, but uncaring. Unaffected by what they saw.

A shiver runs up my back. The cheap flat coverlet in my grip lost its usefulness months ago. Now it only keeps the roaches from falling on my sheets.

I had no choice. This is where the orphanage arranged for me to live after I turned eighteen. It has been three years now living in this hotel-style living quarter. Wow, it seems as if I've been here much longer than that. I feel older than that. I don't want to get up yet.

I give in, flop back onto the flat dingy pillow and draw the cover up to my chin. My hair and full beard are soaked from perspiration. The rubber band I used to tie my hair back for work last night is now poking me in the ear.

It won't be long now. The shivering has begun and even with my eyes closed, the room spins violently. My head is pulsing.

"Shut up!" I yell.

The neighbors on the other side of the thin wall are always fighting. Every morning a blaring argument with their morning coffee about why he came home so late.

"You shut up!" She yells back with two bangs on the wall, making the cheap framed photo above my head jump.

The pulsing turns into a full-blown blinding headache. I must get up. I don't want to, but I have no choice. There it is, the chalky aspirin in the back of the night table drawer, right beside my keys and an unopened Gideon Bible. Flat soda works just at well at washing it down as a glass of cold water. I stagger into the bathroom. Funny, there's no heat, but the hot water in the shower works perfectly.

One advantage to being taller than average, I can reach the loose screws of the rusted vent in the wall easily. My hiding place. My fingers fumble around in the vent, searching for it. There it is. The dusty black sock guarding my life savings. The knot is smaller than last month. It started shrinking when my dream started shrinking.

I can't help but give it a squeeze right before I put it away, a sort of mental measurement of how much I need to put back if I ever regain hope of getting out of here. Where is the key? There, inside a fold in the sock, I feel it. A small gold-tone key. I rub its outline between my fingers. It is a lifeline to reality. I have a feeling I'll be needing it soon.

I started saving money the week I began work. I started work the day after the orphanage driver dropped me at the front door, a wide-eyed country boy gazing at skyscrapers.

Manhattan is full of lavish apartments with doormen tipping their hats as residents walk in swinging shiny shopping bags. Fresh out of the orphanage, I honestly believed that could be me one day, swinging those bags.

Hope. A gift from my parents. They always told me I could do and be anything. They told me I was smart and like any kid; I believed what my parents said. I never imagined the best I could be was the one holding the door. They never got to finish me. It's not their fault.

I can still remember the dress my mother wore to my fifteenth birthday party. It was just three days before she and my father were killed in the accident. At least then, I thought it was an accident. I can't think about that right now.

Housekeeping is coming today. Nothing spurs change like three police raids and a threat to be closed down. They knock on the door like the police. Hard and loud. When I open the door, if the housekeeper suspects nothing, she hands me clean sheets and towels. If she feels kind that day, she'll take the trash.

However, if she has suspicions, she does a thorough 'cleaning' of the room. I noticed a pattern. These were no petite housekeepers wearing uniform dresses and nursing shoes. They always wore jeans and were more muscular than most men, with a pistol bulging in the small of their back.

The press-board dresser with sharp corners holds the residue of every meal I ate for the week. I can hear the three knocks of the housekeeper getting louder as she approaches my door. I fold the pizza boxes and deli bags into the garbage can.

In the can's bottom, are my empty alcohol bottles. They clank in the can, telling my life's story. The faster I move, the more the torn linoleum snags the bottom of my socks. I can't help but look at the crack in the top right corner of the dresser mirror. It's not supposed to be there, maybe that's why it keeps catching my eye. It's the flaw in perfection. I thought of covering it, but it has a right to be there, just like the rest of the mirror.

I'm tired. At twenty-one, I'm tired. Tired of being the crack in the mirror. I've been mistaken for being in my forties. Tiredness makes you look old and feel old.

A flash of light outside of my window draws my attention. It is the 'C' in the cracked neon 'Vacancy' sign running vertically down the building. It wasn't lit yesterday. She's here. Three loud bangs.

"Housekeeping."

I knot the top of the full garbage bag, drop it on the floor beside the door, and open the door. Bare-face, she looks at me emotionless. I snatch the sheets off the bed into a ball and hold them out to her. She looks past me into the room. She scans me from head to toe but isn't taken aback by my lean undershirt-clad physique.

She pushes past me, glances into the bathroom, then drops the stack of clean sheets with towels on the bed. With gloved hands, she grabs the sheets from my hands and her icy stare reflects just how much she loves her job. One foot in the hall, she drops the sheets into the cart and grabs the garbage bag and walks out, leaving the door open behind her. A real ray of sunshine.

I look down at myself, sort of wondering why she wasn't in awe. I have a crease in my pants and everything. The cleaner's crease is always stiff and the pant bottoms are wide enough to go over my black boots. I walk to the door to close it.

Out of habit, I look left and right down the hall before closing the door. She pushes the over-sized cart to the next room. My sarcasm gets the best of me. After all, it has almost been a full five hours.

"And a Merry Christmas to you." I say.

As expected, she ignores me, rolling to the next room, but she pauses, she looks toward the floor to her left. What's over there? The cart passes revealing the hall prostitute with eyes dripping in makeup, knees drawn into her chest and back pressed to the wall of her pimp's apartment. A labored exhale.

I fell prey to her, once. Not the way most would. One glance at those glazed eyes, bleach blond hair and it all came back. My ignorance. She's about my age. I felt bad for her. That night, the hall was dark, hot and smelly and I still had my streak of naiveté fresh off the farm. I invited her in, offered her hot pizza and a cool breeze under my oscillating fan for the night. I gave her the bed and slept on the floor.

I woke to a boot in my gut and watched her willingly obey her large under dressed pimp to rob me of my last forty-five dollars. I know why she did it. It wasn't for the obvious reason. I look at it as payment for what she brought with her.

There she was, throwing those glassy eyes at me again. Slamming the door never felt so good. It even made the picture jump. Then I see it at my feet.

The white envelope with my name written on it in Jerry's child-like scratch. An eviction letter. I couldn't help but look at the blinking 'C' in the vacancy sign outside of the window. Jerry knows I don't have the rent money.

My five-dollar analogue clock is blaring the time. I stick the white envelope in my jackets' inner breast pocket. I don't have time to read it. At least that's my excuse to avoid making it a reality. I can't be late to work again. The benefit of being a consistent drinker is knowing exactly what my routine is.

Strangely, I'm neat, consistent. When I get back from drinking, I always lock the door behind me. I put my clothes over the back of the chair. Jeans first, shirt folded in half by the length, jacket on top, the same way, every time. My keys, the night table drawer, rear, left. Makes it easy when I'm racing to get to work, which is frequently. I can get dressed with my eyes closed the next day.

I can see Jerry behind the desk through the crack in the stairwell door. I don't take the elevator for two reasons; I don't like them, and well, it's broken. It's been broken since I got here over two years ago. The tape from the 'out of order' sign bonded to the paint on the elevator door and the sign has yellowed.

I can always spot a regular. They go straight to the stairwell. The new hopefuls drag their bags to the elevator door and smash that button at least three times before they look up and see the sign.

Come on, Jerry, go to the back. He's loud. Everyone in the lobby will know I got a notice if he sees me. The phone in his office rings. There, this is my opportunity.

I'll put my sweatshirt hood on, if he's not at the desk he won't even see me. So far, so good. If I can push the clunky metal plate on the door with my palm flat, perhaps it will not make a sound. I may get out without him seeing me. Almost there... I can feel the bitter cold air seeping in as I slowly push it open-

"CALEB."

Why me?

"Hey Jerry. Long time no-"

"Don't gimme that. You got your notice, right?" He shouts.

He's the only person I know who asks and answers his own questions. It's not even really a question anymore.

"Yes. I got it." I try to diffuse him.

I approach the desk, hoping it will get him to lower his naturally loud tone. I never asked him if he's hard of hearing because most people in New York seem to speak that way. No chance. He's not hard of hearing, he's just a skinny idiot.

"By six tomorrow. I'm not playing. Or you and your bottles are out-"

"I got it, Jerry, I got it."

"Forty-eight hours. Today, tomorrow, that's it."

"I can count."

"Yeah, then ya should have known ya were behind. I was gonna call you but you ain't got a cell phone number. Did I miss it? Do you have one?" He asks sarcastically.

He slides a pen and notepad through the Plexiglas slot to me. I just want to leave. Garbage picker.

"I don't have a cell."

He snatches the paper back.

"You don't have a cell? Who are you Ralph Kramden? Get a phone cheap-o."

I can feel eyes on my back. Everyone in the lobby is staring over their plastic chess pieces and reading glasses.

"I'm not cheap. Just don't need one."

"If ya had friends, you'd need one. Hermit weirdo." Jerry says turning toward his television.

"I can hear you talking, you know." I say.

"Good, then hear this." He turns to me again, pointing outside. "The sign's blinking. It won't take long to fill your room. Tomorrow, by six, no joke."

He turns around. I just got the hand in the air. Most New Yorkers don't end conversations. It's a hand raise, or just an 'all right, later', or 'it's all good'. It's a phrase that lets you know the conversation is over. An art, I mastered it. I like it. It's like me. To the point.

I know Jerry. The larger the audience, the longer he will go on. Work awaits. I'll figure out what to do about the money later. Can't ask Lou, not again.

This winter is far more brutal than last year and pushing that door let it rush in. The bitter bite of that Northern frigid air shoots straight through my brown leather waist-length jacket and the sweatshirt beneath it, and I've got four blocks and a bus ride to go. There's nothing normal about a New York block. Insanely long, I learned by almost being late to my first day at work. It was a more check-in than an interview. Father De'Vino arranged the job and room as soon as I turned eighteen. A gift from the old Monastery orphanage. Some gift. A job as a bus-boy. The bottom rung. I should be grateful. I know. I didn't want to be in an orphanage. I guess no one does. No kid wants to be stamped with the title of orphan. I heard most of us were just turned loose with some pocket change and a handshake.

I hated it there for the obvious. It was the reality that you have no one in the world. No one that could or willed to take you in. A perpetual loneliness hangs behind every stone wall. A reclaimed old stone Monastery in the middle of nowhere. It always felt damp. Funny, it's kind of like where I am now. I went from one cold, damp place to another. Maybe one day I'll feel warm.

The only time I considered going back was when I heard Father De'Vino was sick. Seventy-eight. His heart gave out before I could save enough money to buy the train ticket. When I first arrived at the orphanage and wasn't speaking, he talked to me. His voice reminded me I existed and was important to someone. When he ran out of words, he read to me. Sherlock Holmes mostly.

The day I turned eighteen, I put my bag into the trunk of the car with everything I had in the world. I could have held it on my lap. I was leaving. I climbed out of the car mid-roll and gave him a hug. He was the only one I hugged. Ever. I'm glad to have known him. I felt his stomach tremble as he cried deep inside while he held me.

The car drove me to New York three years ago and I never went back to that orphanage. I thought I'd be further along than this, but here I am three years later, still a bus-boy. Same routine. The line is blurring. If I didn't feel it coming soon... in my bones, I don't think I could keep this up much longer.

This cold finds every opening. Swims up my sleeve and bus-boy pants hold no heat. I watch people. Closely. The winter veterans pinch their sleeves, stick them deep into pockets, and tuck their chins into their scarves to keep their noses from freezing off their faces. I learned the technique from them. It works.

"Caleb. You're early again." Says Leo.

The liquor store cashier.

"Yeah, working late tonight. You guys close too early." I smirk.

Leo's laugh could make anyone smile.

"The usual?"

He rarely asks questions. I walk to my favorite brand, put my fingers on the third bottle from the front and pause. I walk my fingers to the fourth bottle and take it. I put it down on the counter. Leo pauses, staring at the bottle.

"Problem?" noticing his smile dropped.

He puts it into a small brown paper bag holding eye contact.

"No. Just... take it easy, okay?"

I snatch the bag.

"My mom's dead." I raise my hand to him as a goodbye.

I don't need Leo trying to 'mother' me. I just need him to bag it. I respect Leo, but I'm not in the mood. There's nothing exciting about clearing tables, and I think I would have left long ago if it weren't for Lou. I go in, do my time, grab my jacket from my locker with my waterlogged hands and clock out. It's dark.

Work was work. The chilly midnight air is refreshing after bumping around a busy hot diner kitchen all night. I'm a glorified dish washer. At least that's how it feels. I can't wait to get to my spot. Just a walk away.

Strangely, I prefer being in the kitchen to clearing tables and being around people. Lou's diner is one of the best on this side, meaning lots and lots of dirty dishes.

You get the rich post-Broadway-play gushing about the high-points of the show waving their little playbook. You get the drunks slash border-line-high ones with the munchies. More intriguing, the rendezvous. They try to look inconspicuous, which makes them more conspicuous. Then the texters. They don't even look at each other opposite the table. They don't speak and smile weirdly at their phones, oblivious to the human right in front of them. Funny, if you stay out of their way, they tip better. Liz hasn't learned that yet. Probably because she's Liz. I call her Liz. Her name is Elizabeth, pain-in-the-neck Harvard.

I unconsciously play everything back in my head. Just can't quit it. My father got me started on doing that. He said, if you don't find your mistake, you're likely to repeat it. He also told me never to trust anyone. Both seem to be excellent pieces of advice.

Let's see, I was late again. Maybe I shouldn't have told Liz she looked like a Pit-Bull after that last fight. Now, she's trying to get me fired but what's new. Jessie is flirting with me again. She must have had another fight with her boyfriend. I could have been a little nicer to her... hmm ... nope, can't play games.

I didn't like how Lou looked tonight. His cough is back, and his weight isn't helping. He really thinks he's hiding his pill bottle behind his computer screen. It's full, a new prescription too. The pills were bigger. Why is he trying to hide it from me? I know that's the real reason Liz hates me. She wants to be the right hand. I'll never forget the look on her face that night. She didn't know I saw her through the ambulance window when Lou wouldn't let go of my sleeve demanding I come with him to the hospital. He shoved a little black ledger in my pocket right before he lost consciousness. I never opened it.

Her face, blood red. I don't know why it's not enough for her to be the little rich girl-slumming it. Her daddy owns everything with an 'R' in it. But she always has to be the favorite. Liz plus jealousy equals trying to get me fired.

All right dad, I did my due diligence. I still don't trust anyone, except Lou. Yep, it's safe. The bottle's still in its brown paper bag. I wrap my hand around the brown paper bag in my jacket pocket.

It's against everything dad taught me. Everything he was. Stay in control. Think. Run your race, not someone else's. Think ten steps ahead or you'll find yourself behind.

When he was away on missions for the military, I spent my time after school and on the weekends sitting alone in his work shed. I 'felt' him there. I felt safe. I didn't want to be the 'man of the house' when he was gone. I wanted him home.

Wooden shelves displayed my ship-in-the-bottle projects, even the bad ones. He kept everything. He said that seeing my mistake reminds me not to make it again. I miss him. I miss my mother too, but I had more time with her. There's too much that is incomplete. Like an unraveled rope, we never tied up the ends.

He didn't get to teach me how to drive or dance with a girl. He didn't take me to baseball games. He missed my graduations, birthdays, first Flu. Thought I was going to die and prayed to see him one more time. No matter how hard I prayed, he couldn't come. Now, he expects me to use all that stuff he taught me.

I'm not strong like he was. I've never known him to break a promise. Once we went for a burger in a thunderstorm. Why? Because the day before, he said we would. "A storm can't dictate your actions," he said, "there will always be storms".

Here I am, at my favorite spot on the sidewalk beside the waist-high stone wall surrounding Central Park. I enjoy sitting back against the wall, facing the street and watching the traffic zip by.

I have a flat foam board I leave tucked on the inside of the Park wall. I reach over the wall to get it. I can't feel it, hold on, there it is. It's curved from me sitting on it night after night. I put it on top of a pile of snow drift.

Directly across the street is the toy store. The owner always runs the register, and he is usually alone. It's an old-fashioned register that rings when the metal drawer shoots out. He's probably got a dent in his gut from it. By now, the store is closed, but during Christmas, New York foot traffic is a goldmine. Fred won't close until he's so tired that his eyes cross. I gave him that name. He looks like a Fred.

And here she comes, right on time, into the money-pit. Like clock-work, just before closing time when she knows the register is full with her over-sized purse swinging from her arm and new high heel boots. Fresh from the beauty salon, her curls bounce behind her. What's this? She's broken out the mink. Figures.

The brick wall is cold against my back, but that won't last long. I've got a little friend that fixes all of that. I keep the liquor bottle in the small brown paper bag and just roll down the top, exposing the mouth of the bottle.

Quick inhale before every sip sets up my taste buds. I can't help but pause. Sip after sip. It always precedes. Guilt. I see my father's face. Disappointed, looking at me. I can feel my mother's hand on my shoulder, pulling at me, trying to tell me to stop, don't do it. If they were really here, maybe I would. I've never touched drugs. My only vice is drinking alcohol. Right now, I'm officially drunk.

"You left me!" I yell at the sky. "Wanna stop me? Come back!"

The tree branches covered with snow look beautiful against the gray sky. It slides down warmly and burns the back of my throat. That's it. Just a few more swallows will swirl reality away.

Fred is falling for it again. It's like watching a bad movie. The glass storefront window is trimmed with twinkling Christmas lights Fred put up alone. The poor sap. How many times will you fall for the same trick? Your wife doesn't need anything from the back-store room.

"S-She's in the r-register, Fred!"

Too bad. My snowball only made it to the middle of the street. Splattered on the side of a taxi. I hear his brakes screech. The driver looks pissed.

"Hey! Jerk!" he shakes his fist out the taxi window.

"Your momma!" I yell back. Even drunk, I couldn't resist. Whatever. Probably wouldn't feel it if he hits me.

"I won't f-feel it!" I yell at him.

"What? Stupid drunk." He says.

The taxi's wheels squeal as he pulls off. Already? The bottle's finished already? Leo sold me a small one. No, there is still some in there. I shake the bottle, listening to the liquid swish back and forward.

"That's right. Just dr-rive away. Take that!"

I look back at the toy store window. What's all that finger pointing? Oh snap. She's busted. Here we go.

"I can't... I can't read lips Fred! Not while I'm drunk."

I am drunk. Just hearing myself say it sounds alien. I never imagined it would pull me in this far. I felt invincible just six months ago, then; the line blurred. I must get back to 'him'. I can remember 'him'.

That part of me seems so far removed. I was the guy that smiled, that people loved to see coming. I loved waking up every day and stood up for people who couldn't stand up for themselves. I remember him vaguely. He had a vision and his missions were clear and pure. I liked him. I want him back.

Is this what they call the first step to a turnaround? Admitting you have a problem? I think it is. You know what, it feels good. And that's not the liquor talking. I do. I want him back. Are these tears?

Tears sting the corners of my eyes. Yes. I've heard about this and it is exactly as people describe. As I put the bottle down on the sidewalk in the snow, I tip it, purposely. The small amount of liquor still in the bottle slips out melting the snow. I exhale. That felt good.

What is that? I can't-. The lights are too close, too bright. What's screeching? I lift my arm and cover my eyes. I hear boots, someone big, coming close.

"That's him."

An unfamiliar voice says. I'm pulled upward. I can feel the toes of my boots drag on the ground.

"Wait! I can't see! Get off me! Who... ouch, my neck!"

Sounds like van doors closing. The screeching again. Even inside this black hood, I can feel the room spinning. I'm going to throw up. I feel like I'm on a boat. Rocking. I can't get up. This is what I get for quitting drinking. This doesn't feel like a new beginning.

My head bangs against the floor. Something wet and warm slides down my forehead into my eyes. Tiredness overtakes me. I let sleep take over. Everything goes black.

CHAPTER TWO

Washington, D. C.

Wilkes

The fresh snow that fell last night is already speckled with dirt. It truly is the harshest winter storm in D.C. in the last twenty-five years. I have lived long enough to know however, I will not be here for its climax.

I'm glad I decided five years ago to move to Woodbridge, Virginia. A stone's throw from Washington, D.C. However, the wind is no more forgiving on the Keystone Bridge in Northern Virginia. Thankfully Collins warmed the cabin of my stretched black government vehicle. This is my last ride into work and I'm delighted that the scenery is unforgettable. The heated seats erase the cold. I angle the lower vent toward my hip. At my age, heat feels good everywhere, particularly on this hip. It's a key motivator for what I've been planning for years.

"Collins, the scenic route, please. There's no need to rush anymore. At seventy, I find few reasons to rush."

"Yes, Sir."

The leather seat squeals as I reach for the television remote. For once, I want to hear what CNN has to say about me today. Muted, the CNN reporter, is smiling while she talks.

"They are smiling, Collins. They reserve those for important good deeds or for when they are burying someone. Agnes was right. They are definitely glad to see me go."

I can't help but chuckle to myself.

"Sir, coffee stop as usual?"

"Absolutely, at my age, small pleasures, Collins, small pleasures."

My name always looks good in big bold letters across the screen. At one point, they eliminated the John Wilkes and just gabbed away using 'The Secretary of Defense'.

I didn't mind, anonymity is married to a title, however, the absence of the man invites cruelty to slip in. A scrutiny unleashed and unchecked that drives nails at the man as much as at the title.

Here we go again. The same bone. They get their teeth into it and don't let go. I'm used to it, but I can't help but hope that my accomplishments would shine brighter than my mistakes. The panel bats my life's work like a ping-pong ball.

"He's done some good, right? You can't overlook those two soldiers coming home. If it wasn't for his decisive actions, they'd still be in that Afghan prison." Says a female commentator.

Jake Dapper, great.

"True," Says Jake, "however, the Secretary of Defense serves at the pleasure of the President and his handling of this project is suspect at best. If this were anyone else-"

"-suspect is a strong word." The female commentator intervenes. "You're basing your conclusion on a leak, a White House leak claiming that The Secretary of Defense, a credited war hero who survived horrific ordeals for his country, that his behavior was 'suspect'. We have yet to validate the facets of this leak."

One point for her.

"The facets of the leak don't overshadow this verified authentic audio recording of the Defense Secretary of the most powerful nation in the world giving directives that contradict his boss, who is The President. He is instructing others to continue a project that cost the American people twenty-three million dollars but produced no verifiable achievement. In the eyes of the American people, there is nothing left to validate. This is as cut and dry as it comes."

I hope you fall off your stool, Dapper. But to your argument, one point.

"We'll see. Today is the final day of his deposition." Says the female commentator.

Yes, it sure is.

"Ladies and gentlemen," the host interjects, "any predictions of the outcome?"

"He has a long hard run of it," says Jake, adjusting himself in his seat, "he's a war hero. I wish him all the best today and a well-deserved retirement."

Sorry I wanted you to fall off your stool.

"Agreed." Says the female commentator.

"Next, Breaking News from the White House..." continues the host.

The cell phone is buzzing in my pocket. It hasn't rung in days. Collins' eyes are glued to the road. I turn up the CNN news and take it out. Is it that time already? I answer it discreetly.

"Yes?... fine. (Pause)... Thank you. I'll be in the office in five." I say.

Collins' eyes are still glued to the road. Slip the phone back into my breast pocket and we are approaching the coffee stand. I will miss this. Mr. Fletcher's coffee. The best coffee stand in D.C. The only thing better is his genuineness. A rarity in the Washington, especially on the Hill.

"Get two." I say to Collins as he gets out of the vehicle.

"Yes, Sir."

He always waves. Mr. Fletcher. Even when the window is closed. He's happy. Another rarity. Happy fiddling around behind that long counter fussing over magazines and newspapers that people rarely buy anymore. There's something grounding about holding a good old newspaper in your hands. Black ink on your fingertips and the crinkling sound when you turn the page with your coffee at hand's reach. His hand goes up. As soon as the window descends, the cold floods in. It takes my breath away.

"The offer still stands." I say to Mr. Fletcher.

"Bricks and Mortar, not for me. They're talking about you're in the news again."

"Nothing new."

"It's good, my friend. If they stop talking, it means you're dead." Says Fletcher smiling.

Fletcher truly understands D.C. I lift my hand and force a smile. I have to close the window. Why is this happening? I've never been sentimental.

"Here you are, Sir. Two." Collins gets into the car and hands them to me.

"One is for you." I say.
"Thank you, Sir," Collins takes a sip, "oh, man. I'm hooked."

"I asked him, what makes your coffee taste so good? You know what he said?"

"No, what?"

"He said, 'I never wash the pot'."

Collins laughs briefly. Then looks at me through the rear-view mirror.

"What? Really?" He stops laughing and looks at the cup.

I almost threw up trying to hold in my laughter.

"No." I release a hearty chuckle.

The rest of the drive went quickly. I can't get the image out of my head. Every time I pull into the Pentagon parking lot, I see it as it was on 9-11. I don't think I ever want to forget. It reminds me of what I have to do here and why I don't care what they say about me in the news, I'm proud of what I did. All of it.

Every soldier has a war story. I have many, but I know the one they'll be asking me about today. The one that stabs me in the ribs at night and makes my hip ache. I knew they would save the most pressing questions for last.

I fought using it. Now, I appreciate the air of distinction it ends. It gives people pause when I enter a room with my cane. Guilty, I fought it, thinking it exposed a vulnerability   and announces dependence. I've matured realising it offers me strength, independence and balance. This hilt is perfect. It snugly fits into the palm of my hand. A gift from the President.

"Is there a queue, Collins?"

"Not for you, Sir." Says Collins pulling open the car door.

"I'm not so sure. No one bows to a dethroned king. They only look for the new one."

"Here you are, Sir."

I'll miss this briefcase, a gift from the Speaker of the House. Lately, I feel like a walking shrine. Just twenty years ago, I was a Captain in the Army with a blown out hip thinking life was over. Now, I have a sound retirement plan, a closet of shoes valued more than my father earned in a year and splendid memories of serving my country.

This building is humbling. The logistics and brilliant people who walk these halls. Where did all of this sentiment come from?

Most seem to have moved on, but I keep seeing the graves of the one-hundred and twenty-five people who died here. I watched on television. I didn't cry. I couldn't. Not one tear. Instead, anger burrowed into my heart and engraved itself in my bones. Whenever I step on these grounds I pause. My tribute.

I enter for the last time and hear the words that let me know I'm still on the throne. At least for one more day.

"Mr. Secretary, good morning."

Look at him. Security. The heart of this country's defense. New to the job. What is he twenty, twenty-two?

"First day, soldier?" I ask, lifting my chin.

"Yes, Sir."

A salute? I'm honored. He's short, wide-eyed and clean in heart. I know that shine anywhere. The shine of loyalty and respect for the country you are willing to die for.

I want to punch them in the face for laughing at him under their breath. The regulars standing behind him, peeking in purses and watching the scanners.

"Your name, Officer?" I ask, stepping through the scanner.

"Rodriguez, Sir."

I set off the metal detector. It's the metal pin the surgeons put in my hip. It will stay there for the rest of my life. I am accustomed to it. A gift from war. Unbuttoning my jacket is tricky with a cane.

"Mr. Secretary, Sir. You don't need to-"

"Rodriguez, every time. Everyone. Every single time."

My concern must be showing. His expression is scratching on fear.

"Even me. No one can be above your search. You're the front line for every life in this building. You trust no one. Got it?"

"Yes, Mr. Secretary. I won't forget."

He's got it. I can tell. Where is it? There it is. One last rub on the immaculate silver lapel pin. My United States Flag. It pierced every suit I put on for the last twenty-five years. I take it out.

"For you, Rodriguez. Today is my last day as being the Secretary of Defense for the greatest nation in the world," I can't help but smile, "just think, if I gave it to you tomorrow, it would have a weakened story. Enjoy."

Tears?

"Bite that, son." I say watching him squeeze it in his palm. "What's your goal, Officer?" I ask changing the subject. The other guards can't see him cry.

"One day, I want to be a special agent, Sir. Like my dad. My wife and I just had a little girl and moved to D.C. I want to show her you can be anything you want to be if you work hard."

"I think I can help with that."

"I really appreciate it, Sir. Thank you." Says Officer Rodriguez.

From the elevator, I could hear the other officers whispering to him.
"Rodriguez, don't hold your breath. They have short memories. They promised me a spot on the Emergency Response Team."

They don't realize that their murmurings just insured his promotion. If nothing else, I am a man of my word. I feel hope warming my chest. Rodriguez may never know what he gave me. Hope, that my legacy will go on.
The elevator beeps and the doors open just as I hear my pseudo name.

"Mr. Secretary."

I'd know that voice anywhere. Philip Cummings. I hear his steps quicken and he steps into the elevator with me, quickly pressing the button to make the doors close. He wants to speak to me privately. He's a capable agent but since that video leaked, he is a stretched rubber band. His nerves ready to snap. He never could just come out and ask me a straight question. He's irreplaceable as an analyst, but his greatest task is ahead of him today.

"Last day," says Phillip standing beside me.

Ah yes, the White House whisper. He's served me well and he's a skilled fisherman. I think he's more comfortable in his role of a fisherman than agent in the Department of Defense.

"I wanted you to know, they're bringing him in," Phillip says nervously watching the elevator numbers descend.

"Jason Jones?" I nod knowingly.

"Yes. We had no say. He's leading the deposition today."

"I thought he was on leave from his divorce?"

Phil wipes his forehead with his handkerchief. He always sweats profusely.

"If I were her," he says, "I would have left him too."

I throw him a look and he catches it.

"Sorry, Wilkes, I forgot how you feel about family." He says.

"It should be until the end, Phil, remember that. All of this politicking will go on." I loosen my jaw and take my eyes off his crooked tie and watch the numbers on the elevator.

"Well, they must truly think there's something to be heard."

"Is there?" Phil mumbles, stuffing his handkerchief back into his pocket.

I pat him on the back as the elevator dings and the doors slide open. I step out of the elevator and turn around facing him with both hands resting on the hilt of my cane.

"I'll see you at the gallows."
The elevator doors close.

"It's better if I know now," Phil hastens, "than later. Damage control and all that, you see. You need to be certain... or this will not end today." His voice fades as the elevator leaves.

My regular phone is buzzing. I received a text. I pause just outside of my office doors, reply to the text, and slip the phone back into my pocket. I give the wood carvings on the door a gentle brush, then open the door.

I feel reminiscent today. Just think, this is the last time Agnes will ever rattle off an itinerary to me. I think she is the only secretary that still swishes when she walks.

The new 'no stocking' fad came in and nicked the office formality that makes women look professionally polished. Agnes is a dying breed. She's got stockings and loyalty.

"Do they have Fritags today?" I blurt to Agnes.

"Good morning to you, Mr. Wilkes."

"Agnes, it is Mr. Secretary until six o'clock p.m."

She will not call me Mr. Secretary. She is the only one who doesn't and hasn't since our introduction. That is how I knew she was the right one for the job. Agnes has learned an art birthed by those that understood the beauty of serving. She knows when to serve the man and when to serve the suit, Secretary of Defense. Agnes gives the man a hot egg and cheese on a Keiser roll every morning, and briefs the Secretary after the man takes three bites.

I can rely on Agnes to not stroke my ego or pander. She gives it to me straight, like a mother with nothing to lose. I believe I have fired her about six times. Neither time did she even leave her desk.

She organized the Secretary during 9-11, the attack on the World Trade Centers in Manhattan, New York; but covered the man with a blanket before she left the office when he slept in the office for two weeks following the tragedy. I will never forget her but she doesn't believe in goodbyes, she says that they are too final and remind her of death.

"Fritags' Delicatessen opened an hour early to cater to you. Mr. Fritag wishes you well and says congratulations on not destroying the Country before you left."

"Send him a gift."

"Alright. Break the bank or just scratch it?"

"Last day, so break it."

"You got it." Agnes jots down a note on her pad. "In the meeting, do yourself a favor and remember, it was a courtesy that they came to you. They could have requested you go to them for the deposition. Which would have made you look- "

"Guilty." I say.

"As a fox in a hen-house."

"That saves their necks. Keeps it from looking like a trial. Yesterday, the food tasted like cardboard." I add.

"Jason-"

"I know Agnes, Jason Jones is closing it out."

"He will be direct, Sir."

I look at the photo on my desk of my old platoon.

"Every dog has a leash, my dear Agnes."

Jason Jones

Has it only been a week? Already, I appreciate my office in Langley at the Central Intelligence Agency. It's a viable constant. If she's like other people, and she is, she thinks I'm not listening. Contrary, what a person doesn't say is typically far more important than what they do say. I first met her, Director Barbara White, two years ago, briefly. She still seems undecided as to her posture. A fly stuck at the window, bashing its head against the glass, transfixed on the sun shining through the glass and its pseudo warmth. Drowning herself in masculine suits, not a trace of femininity in her office. No photographs of her children, that I know she has, her husband or personal affects.

The absorbent quantity of files on her desk, unnecessary but visually takes the place of what's missing. She's trying hard to 'fit in' in a typically male dominated position, thus her indecision reeks with perfume. It smacked me in the face the minute I opened the office door. She's still on her rant. Why? There is something here, I can smell it. She spent the last three and a half minutes nudging me into handling this with a level of sensitivity she knows I don't possess. Why? Is she afraid of an aftermath? Is she part of a conspiracy?

I need to throw her off balance.

"You changed your face powder." I blurt. "It makes you look dead. The other one was better."

She instinctively touches the base of her neck. That's her nervous tell.

"You said that out loud, you know."

I stand from the chair to increase the edgy feeling I've spurred. I'm not controllable and won't just comply by remaining in the seat she pointed me to.

"Director White, with all due respect, this is far from being put to bed. But you know that or I wouldn't be here."

"We will be in their wheel house, Mr. Jones. This man is NOT on trial and this office won't be accused of treating him as if he is. He's taking early retirement for health issues which we will not exacerbate in the course of this invest... I mean, interview. Remember, your presence is already raising eyebrows."

"You mean, an Agent of the Central Intelligence Agency."

"Exactly."

"Director White, you said it, you couldn't help yourself. It feels like an investigation because you still have questions. I intend to find out what happened in that desert. Only Secretary Wilkes knows the truth. Why dance around it? This is the last chance we'll have unless-"

"-unless you find something."

"Yes. You called me. You called me off of vacation for this. You wouldn't have, if you didn't want me to dig. So, take your hand off my shovel and let me do my job."

"It wasn't a vacation, Mr. Jones. Your wife left you. That's called recovery not vacation."

I remain silent purposely. How much of her femininity is still there?

"I'm sorry, Jason."

She fell for it. A man would never have apologised. She's touching her neck again. Why would she be sorry unless she empathises? Why would she empathise? I turn around slowly and face her. Ah, the mark of an absent wedding ring and her finger is red as if she tried to rub it away.

"I went too far. I'm sorry, Jason."

I smile purposely. Portraying the emotion necessary for the moment is so engraved after fifteen years of service, it has become my norm. I think before I smile, or move or frown. My ex-wife is right, I'm two toenails from being a robot. It is habitual.

"Did you? If I crumble that easily, I'd still be on vacation."

She sits in her chair. Trying to take her authoritative position behind that over-sized desk, however, it's a child running to momma's leg. A waft of her perfume fills my nostrils and she's uneasy about something. But what? In about fifteen minutes, I will have the answer to that question. I walk to the door and with my hand on the knob and she gives the matter an exclamation mark.

"I need to know you understand, Jason. This is not redemption."

"Redemption. Do you think I'm bitter because you pulled me from the Red case last year?"

"Yes."

"Well, you're right."

There is a new document on the desk peeking out from beneath a hastily tossed file. I need to get a glimpse. I walk to her desk, place both palms on it and lean forward.

"I could have solved it-"

"You were distressed because of your marriage issues and your judgment was clouded."

I lower my head, purposely appearing to yield to her explanation, but I can see that document clearly now. It is from the desk of Susan Letherby. She is one of the Presidents' advisers and it is dated with yesterday's date. That says enough. I turn around and return to the door and turn the knob.

"I am not done." Showing some firmness. Now I'm impressed. "It's not what you ask, it's how you ask it. I want you here to observe and listen. You've got a trained eye. You had your teeth in this one and well, I just want to see what you find. You're right, this is our last chance. I think you deserve that much."

"Thanks for the advice."

"Jason, change your shirt."

I couldn't help but look down.

"What? You don't like the pizza grease?"

I close her door behind me, stepping into the cold hallway. The stale smell of old coffee and wax is a rude awakening.

My temporary office centres on me. Samantha... Sam, my assistant arranged a hotel for the duration of my stay in Washington D.C. but why bother getting entangled in the traffic on Monument Avenue when there is a perfectly lumpy sofa in this cave? It won't surprise her that I never checked in. After all these years of working together, I don't think there is much I can do that will surprise her. But I'll never stop trying.

I open the door to my temporary office exhale and I get a surprise. Agent Philip Cummings. He is standing in my office. Not an act of respect. I purposely stack things in the seat opposite my desk. I don't like visitors. People don't stay long when they have to stand. No guest candy dishes, fresh coffee, all those office niceties. The leather sofa, conveniently draped with my clothing from the night before and a blanket. None of which anyone wants to touch. I intended it.

"Mr. Philip Cummings. I don't recall us having an appointment. In fact, some may mistake this as obstruction, at the very least, in poor taste. We all know who your fishing buddy is."

He extends his hand to me. His hand is too soft for my taste. I don't enjoy shaking hands with buttery lotion. Unless your name is Barbara. I slide my hands into my pockets and leave the door opened, purposely. He always over-plans, in my opinion. Sometimes you need to just hit the ball and play it where it lands.

"I'd offer you a seat but-"

"-no, it's okay, I'm not staying. I just thought we might have a word."

"Sure, yes. What's on your mind, Phil?"

I need him to relax. He's already swabbing his forehead with his moist handkerchief, and we haven't even begun speaking.

"First, how are you holding up? I heard about your... leave."

"You mean my divorce."

"Yes. Well, I heard it helps if..." Phil looks at my bedding on the sofa, "... you know, to separate yourself from the memories."

I think I will just keep clearing the desk and see how much pours out.

"Jason, I also wanted to make sure we were on one accord concerning this meeting. I know your method is to be aggressive, but he's not just the Sec. Def., he and I go way back and I just think we need a strategy going forward. I think it's important for us to be, well, civil and united. You know what I mean?"

He's expecting a rebuttal. I can tell by how he straightened his stance. He usually has a duck paddle stance.

"I agree, Phil."

"You do?" Surprised.

"I think we have things covered here."

Why is he floundering? Flipping about in the boat trying to decide if he should ask another question. I almost feel guilty sitting while he stands. Almost.

"Good... great. Look, we need to go fishing. I think you'd like it. We're a small group. Me, Wilkes, and Director White's husband."

" Okay. Does Director White know?"

"It's no secret. We go every year."

He spins his wedding ring.

"But does she know?"

"Yes. She knows. There's no conflict of interest due to a personal relationship, if that's what you're hinting."

He's squirming.

"I just thought it would be good for you, with your divorce and everything. Look, forget I asked."

He is genuinely trying to appear offended. I'll play along right as soon as his hand touches the doorknob. I'll speak in layman's terms and appeal to what he mentioned.

"Hey, I'm sorry, Phil. You're right. This divorce was tougher than I thought. It's got me... on edge a bit. Thanks and don't worry. The deposition is just a formality, like White said. Hey, what's her husband's name again... Dave... Henry-something?"

"Oh, Kent. Kent Covington. It's an independent woman thing. You know, she kept her maiden name."

"That's it, Kent."

He's reaching for the doorknob again, but looks happier.

"Hey, did we get Fritags?"

Laughing, snugly convinced he has accomplished his mission.

"It's a smorgasbord." He says.

"I love their liverwurst."

"Who eats that anymore? You're telling your age, Jason."

The door clicks closed behind Phil. Finally, I'm alone. I wasn't sure before. Now, I'm certain. I was hoping I wouldn't have to make this call. At least not now. I have no choice.

I pull a small burner cell phone out of a secret compartment in my duffel bag and dial the number. It rings. There's no answer. There isn't supposed to be. I leave the message.

"It's time." I say.

I hang up the phone, remove the back and pull out the tiny SIM card. It cracks easily in my rough fingers and it feels good to smash something, even if it is only a phone. I tap the bridge of my glasses with a flick of my right middle finger and rock back in the leather chair letting my head rest.

Wilkes

On the surface, it looks like a conference room with amenities. However, I know better. The windows are tinted and I can hear the snow beating against the glass and the whistling wind getting stronger.

I've been privy to a fair share of questionings. Tying up loose ends, as some say. This room is a subtle interrogation room. Yet, at its core, it is just that. Unlike the ones in the seedy police stations, it has windows, decorative pieces concealing cameras giving those in the dim-lit room behind the two-way mirror visual angles. There is a team manning computer screens, watching my every breath.

Instead of being handcuffed to a cold steel table, I get to drift over to the full tea and coffee service bar with a variety of herbal teas. Being the Secretary of Defense, at least until the end of the day, has privileges even when being suspected of a crime.

That is what this is all about. But they have nothing. If they did, this wouldn't be in this conference room, it would be in a courtroom. Nevertheless, that coffee pot has eyes.

The carpet ensures sound quality for their recordings but isn't deep enough for me to catch my cane on. They took Agnes's memo seriously. They lay the buffet table with Fritags Artesian Deli sandwiches, potato salad and seasoned olive and pimiento mix.

It's a science I practiced in the field. Give a man what he wants to make him talk. You fill the belly and loosen the tongue. If you give a man what he needs, you will have gained his loyalty. My hip is bothering me. The weather is horrendous and as much as I don't want to show any form of weakness, I can feel my weight shifting heavily onto the cane. I need to leave quickly but clean. No follow-ups or subpoenas. There's only one-way I can do that. Tell the truth. Deep breath.

"Mr. Secretary. Good to see you."

Benjamin is a square head. He is balanced. A good neutral ear. He holds no bias to party and looks with a clear eye. Every time. Few men have that after being in politics as long as he has been. I don't think they mean to, but they get tainted over time. It's almost inevitable. You make a friend, their friends become your friends and instantly, you have taken sides. Benjamin eats alone. Talks to his wife mostly and is free. A title most of us in the political game don't hold. It is easy to extend my hand to him. He gives me a neutral handshake with no dominant undertones.

"Ben, how's your wife?"

"Still shopping. Are you all right?"

He is observant. His question is coming from genuine concern. He must have noticed my limp intensity. Unlike the cavalry standing in front of their seats on the other side of the table. Philip Cummings, an empty seat belonging to Benjamin and Jason Jones beside him. The cavalry rises. Except one.

"Mr. Secretary."

Phil reaches over the table, extending his hand.

"Phil. Good to see you."

"The privilege is mine."

Jason nods at me. "Mr. Wilkes," he says.

Jason has already stripped me of my title. He had no intention of standing. There is a stack of files beside him, only him. All the file tabs are turned toward me. The entire room is staring at me now, awkwardly trying to make small talk. I smile and ignore it. He is in character. I shall take the lead.

"Mr.-?"

"Jason, Special Agent Jason Jones, Internal Affairs."

"Any field-time?"

I already know the answer to the question. He headed his class as a strategist and an expert in analysis but never saw the field.

"Desk jockey."

I couldn't resist glancing over at the mirror. A silent dig at the Director who is standing behind that glass.
"Mr. Secretary."

Phil gestures to his chair. It is upright and all metal. It is loaded it with sensors embedded into its beveled dips. I pause and stare at the chair with unease.

"Gentlemen, could I impose upon you, this old wound... I had them bring in my chair. I know we will be some time. If I may?"

I imagine Dir. White's words were 'let him have it' because of the awkward two-second pause before Phil says:

"Of course."

Phil couldn't have moved any quicker. I adjust myself, lean my cane against the table, take out a pill from my small silver pill box and send it down with the frosty glass goblet of water at my seat. I glimpse his clear ear-piece slipped deep in the canal of his ear as he stands from fixing my chair.

Time moved quickly. At least it felt like it. Benjamin was good. He laid the tinder wood. The small brush of twigs that the large logs sit upon. It catches fire and burns long enough to get the wood engulfed in flames. Benjamin asked the minor questions whose answers I will later be challenged on. Inevitably, they will pick my answers apart for contradictions, and thus we have the flame of an indictment lit.

"Afghanistan. 1997," Benjamin continues.

"Yes."

I keep my calm. Leaning back in my chair and holding a placid look on my face. Not mockingly joyful, yet not looking overly concerned or worried. Jason is trying to read my face. This must drive him mad.

"What can you tell us about that mission? Anything at all."

"May I have some water, please?"

Phil places the refilled goblet in front of me.

"Thank you." I take a sip. "Dread was my gunnery. He was in charge of all of our ammunition and guns. Rolly was the technical specialist. Picker was our sniper. Fletcher, the best navigator I ever had. Doc was the medic. This was his first mission. And Officer Promise, my first officer and key strategist. I was their captain. They were Secret Operation Soldiers. But we… we were family. We did deep cover within the forces. That night in Afghanistan, we were ambushed half-way to our destination. I was wounded. When I regained consciousness, we had been captured. Officer Promise and I were in the same cell. I was told the others... were killed."

They paused respectfully. And I truly appreciate that. I have never spoken of that night after they debriefed me.

"Do you know why they were killed, so quickly?"

"I was unconscious. If I had to guess, these weren't the kind of guys to go down without a hell of a fight. No soldier over there wants to be taken alive. They all know what that could mean."

"Please explain for the sake of the record."

"Torture. Public execution."

"Why didn't they kill Officer Promise?"

"Prom was different."

Agent Jones lifts his pen, pausing from writing his notes and interjects. His tone is curt and somehow it makes the memory fall into a cold reality and the other gentlemen sit back in their chairs and silently watch as if not wanting to get hit by stray questions themselves.

"Different how?" asks Jason.
I have to answer his question with logic.

"He was a strategist. Again, I was unconscious, but if I had to guess, he probably convinced them there was a reason to keep him alive."

"From what I hear about how they handle captured American Soldiers, that's quite a negotiation skill. Why didn't they keep you? Why didn't they kill you? A captain is a prize."

Jason's question is as cold as his stare. I can't get drawn into responding defensively, which is exactly what he wants.

"My guess is they didn't know I was a captain. You know, on a mission, we don't wear distinguishable titles."

He's not convinced. I can see it in his eyes.

"What was the purpose of the mission?"

"That's classified."

"Who were you going to meet?"

"Classified."

"Did this mission have anything to do with the Project?"

"To answer that would require classified information."

A loud gust of what sounds like hail splatters against the window. The storm is whipping itself up outside and the questioning is whipping in here.

"Your answers are not answers, Wilkes. You can't hide behind the redundancy of 'that's classified'. If it were a valid answer, we wouldn't be here right now. There are valid non-speculative reasons yourself and Officer Joshua Promise were the only two men that got out of that confrontation alive and I want to know those reasons."

My hip is throbbing. The storm outside seems to coincide with its increase in pain.

"Mr. Secretary, do you need a break?" asks Phil.

"I think we are on a good roll here, Phil, if I may," Jason interjects. "Let's get back on track. Okay. So, everyone's dead, yourself and Officer Promise are alive, how did you get out? What negotiations transpired? They just don't let people walk out of Afghanistan prisons without a purpose or promise. What did you promise them, Mr. Wilkes?"

"Your tone is questionable, Agent. I don't know. I lost consciousness several times and was heavily sedated with pain killers. For me to speculate on something that will be on an official record, would be negligent of me. Do you want me to say something I'm not sure of, to satisfy your itch? The only thing I remember is waking up on a military chopper on my back with a shattered hip and the bullet still lodged in my pelvis."

He is not the agent to show his frustration, but if I had to guess, his toes are wiggling a hole in his socks right now.

"Surely you and Officer Promise spoke afterward. He would have filled you in on the events you missed. You said he was a good First Officer, didn't you?"

"Yes."

"Then, wouldn't a good first Officer update his captain who was his, and I quote, "family", after the event?"

"I don't recall that. I do recall both of us being grateful to be Stateside. Family, that we were, son. We didn't think very much about ourselves. We were busy. We went to all five funerals. I couldn't sit, so I had them push me on a stretcher from an ambulance."

I can't help but grip the hilt of my cane. That day came back to my mind when the words left my mouth. I feel my chin tremble and all eyes are on Agent Jones opening the next file.

"You led your men into an ambush."

I feel anger rising within me. Any captain would behind that statement, and Agent Jones knows it. Behind those glasses, his eyes are searching for a reaction that I can't give him. However, if I show no reaction, I'm guilty of leading them into an ambush because they will assume that I didn't truly care about them.

"As insulting as your comment was, I appreciate you trying to do your job. However, there is no captain who feels about their men the way I felt about mine, that would lead them into an ambush. Please consider the fact that I went into it with them, and though I came out, it was not without penalty."

I raise my cane for them all to see. Jason is biting his jaw. Now he will try to clean it up.

"I'm just trying to understand what happened in the desert. Officer Promise's statement of accounts upon his return is redacted down to a stack of 'buts' and 'the's'. No guilt for that day?"

I lower the cane to the floor and squeeze the hilt. The arrogance of Jason is appalling, yet his dedication to his purpose refreshing. I think if he really knew my purpose, he might be on board.

"I live with regret. There is not a day I do not wish I didn't take that mission. But guilt is for someone who did something wrong. I followed orders. I did what I was supposed to do, Agent."

I'm surprised. Jason Jones takes his glasses off, rubs the bridge of his nose at length and lets Phil lead the next round of questioning. Phil didn't fail me.

"Tea?" Phil asks me nervously.

"Mint, please."

I stretch the blood back into my legs and Phil places the steaming cup beside me. I can feel Director White holding her breath behind that mirror as Jason puts his glasses back on and roughly snatches a file out from the bottom of the pile. He clears his throat. I can't resist asking him.

"Mint tea, Agent Jones?"

He ignores my question and proceeds.

"The BST-10 Project was the brainchild of your successor, correct?"

"Yes."

"A successor and mentor."

"Yes."

"So, this project means a great deal to you."

"Meant. It no longer exists."

"Right. Let us go back a bit. Initially, you were tasked, by your predecessor as you put it, with security for the entire facility, no? A man who is thorough, cares about his men, cares about this project, but it all burns down. 'Your' men, your Officer Joshua Promise, just got back from a four-month tour. Exhausted, yet you put him in charge of the facilities security. Is that correct?"

"Yes. Officer Joshua Promise was in charge."

"How did that happen... on your watch? Why didn't you put fresh men on this twenty-seven million dollar project? Officer Promise had a wife, a son, and a house with two mortgages on it. You knew all of this, yet you choose him to bear such a burden."

I grip the hilt of my cane.

"Agent Jones, do you know how hard it is for active duty servicemen to find work between tours? I'm sorry, I forgot, you wouldn't. Well, it's hard. Very hard. My men had families. People depending on them to bring home a pay-check. They had the clearance level and showed up on time, every time. The fire investigation proved inconclusive-"

"-because of all the flammable material used, yes. So, what happened?"

"I wasn't there. I don't know."

"I do."

Benjamin and Phil look in my direction.

"Twenty-seven million dollars of research, logs, hard drives and all back-up material went up in an explosion in the middle of the Brazilian forest."

I relax my grip on the cane.

"That sounds right."

"Why wasn't the laboratory on U. S. Soil?"

"I inherited it, remember. I had no say on its inception."

"Let's back up. You inherited this project from the former Secretary of Defense. It was an ongoing project you only had to get funded for. That's over ten years of research and nothing to show for it. Why did he pick you?"

"How can I possibly answer that?"

"There is a record of the former Secretary of Defense having given you eighty-seven thousand dollars. What was that money for?"

I didn't want to, but I felt my eyes lower and stared at the base of my water goblet.

"If you're having difficulty recalling, it went into your personal bank account. Why would a Secretary of Defense give you man eighty-seven thousand dollars?"

"Because he was a good man."

"A good man buying silence?"

Something fell in the room behind the mirror. Director White may have just fainted.

"I was re-assigned in the desert. Just got my new platoon. I was still grieving over the men that were lost in Afghanistan. It was then my wife found out..." I swallow hard, "... it was too far gone, but we had to try. I had to watch her through a computer screen. I could not put my arms around her. Radiation and chemotherapy were expensive and came with no promises. But we hoped it would give her more time. She died in my arms, vomiting a quarter of her body's blood."

I stare directly at him. I purposely looked deep into his eyes. I wanted this to get under his skin. The wind outside pelts at the window and Phil can't stop clearing his throat. It didn't seem to bother Agent Jones. He continues coming at me.

"So, the money was for medical bills."

He ignores me completely, holding the floor.

"I went back to work. What else would a man do? If it weren't for his kindness, I would have lost my house, my car, and probably my mind. But we fought. She was the toughest soldier I ever met. You will not find what you are looking for."

"Just what is that?"

"Dirt. This isn't a dirty story."

"So you say. Tell me about the Beaston Project."

It's time to sway the pressure onto his shoulders.

"All those files and you don't know?"

"These files have the logistics. They state it was a project 'Intended to produce weapons for the United States of America.'"

"Exactly. So how is it different from any other of the thousands of weapon projects we have worked on?" I ask.

"Mr. Wilkes, the others have something to show for ten years of work other than a burned-out bunker. Fast forward, you become Secretary of Defense. You've got over a decade of active duty service to your credit, and you inherit the project. You're vested. You know it inside and out. You were angry. You were angry when the President said the project would not be re-funded. Correct?"

I can hear Director White yelling at him through his ear-piece. He ignores it completely. Agent Jones taps his pen on the table three times. An old signal, meaning increase the heat on the thermostat by three degrees. It is intended to keep the 'heat' on me and increase my discomfort. I won't tell him that at my age I welcome the additional heat. He taps his pen again. I'll answer his question after this sip of water.

"No. The President had his reasons. Budget cuts, election coming up."

"So, you say, that politics killed your project. Cancer killed your wife. You're angry about that, Mr. Wilkes, understandably. Aren't you?"

Phil had to intervene. "Jason... Agent Jones, I think we need a break here. It's been two hours."

"I think he should answer the question."

There he goes. Three taps. Something hard hits the window of the room.
"BREAK!" I hear Director White yell into Jason's ear-piece.

He pulls the ear-piece out of his ear and slams it on the desk beneath his cupped palm.

"Mr. John Wilkes, why did the President of the United States kill this Project?"

"I have tolerated your insolence long enough! Address me as Mr. Secretary or don't address me at all."

"Sure, I can address you as that," he glances at his watch, "for the next nine hours." Says Jason.

Jason turns over a piece of paper and shoves it across the table at me. It stops at the base of my water goblet.

"The President found and I quote 'Unethical Practices inconsistent with U.S. values.'

Four taps. Everyone but me adjusts their tie.

"What unethical practices did he mean?"

"You've just crossed from question to accusation, son. An accusation I take very seriously."

"Every project turns in intermittent reports. Where are yours? I've been through every file." He slams his open palm on the top of the pile of files and continues. "Nothing. What is visible in the BST-10 Project file is so heavily redacted is not of substantive. Why is that?"

I expected Phil, and here he comes.

"Jason, the DOD does redactions-"

"That he is head of. Why Mr. Secretary?"

Agent Jones doesn't loosen the grip of his stare. Benjamin is still. A statue. There, observing. He is more intimidating than Agent Jones. With Agent Jones, I see the gun and the bullet.

With Benjamin, you see nothing. The danger of what he may deduce is far more threatening.

"Why are you looking at Phil? I asked the question."

"You're about to ask your last question."

I can feel my knuckles turn white from squeezing the hilt of my cane.

"Is that a threat?"

"I haven't decided which you have insulted more, my integrity or my loyalty."

"You're the one with the answers. Everyone — everyone who had a hand, foot in the BST-10 Project is dead. Everyone except you. Why is that, MR. SECRETARY?"

Director White is yelling. His ear-piece is vibrating beneath his hand. He looks directly into the mirror and answers her. "After he answers the question!"

"Listen to your Director, Agent Jason Jones. If you want to have a job when you rise from this table."

He looks like a bloodhound who has picked up a scent and can't get it out of his nostrils. Agent Jones did what any man with a car payment and mortgage would do. He reluctantly pushes his seat out and goes to the room. I release my cane and inconspicuously rub my palms on my trousers.

Jason

Some thing's not right here. I step into the dark observation room. Computer screens and monitors are lit and the three technicians manning them turn and look at me with total fear in their eyes. Director White's jacket is thrown over the back of a chair and her sleeves are rolled up to her elbows.

"I'm pulling you!"

"No. That's what you called me in here to do. Isn't it?"

"I called you in to listen, observe. We were clear. You have racked up a list of offenses subordinate at best and all of it leads back to me."

"This case-"

"It is not a case! This is not a trial and you can't grill the Secretary of Defense like a defendant. You're out."

"You didn't want to find out the truth, did you? You called me in for the record. Didn't you? You wanted your tidy report to say you had Agent Jason Jones question the Secretary of Defense and even he found nothing. I never pegged you for slimy."

"Watch it, Jason. You're treading on dangerous ground."

"No, Barbara. You are. I could write a report on the multiple times you tried to 'guide' me away from doing my job effectively. You ever try to muzzle a dog in attack mode? It doesn't end well for the one holding the muzzle."

"You weren't ready for this. I should have known. You should have stayed on leave."

"You won't be using my name on this debacle. I hereby formally withdraw from the panel. All of you are my witnesses. I'll clean up first."

I pull the door knob gently. The technicians look as baffled at how quickly I change my demeanor.

"Mr. Secretary, I owe you an apology. Especially for the mention of your wife. I was out of line. I lost my mother to cancer. Don't know what I would do if someone brought her up that way. Anyway, I'm just a desk jockey that was trying too hard to do my job. Do you forgive me?"

I know he's relieved. He'll relax. His eyes have a creased squint in the corners as if they are always smiling. His mouth shows what he really feels. It's turned down. His gray mustache and perfectly trimmed beard frame his mouth. He reaches for his cane. Is he going to leave? He goes for a club turkey and cheese sandwich. The entire room is watching him eat. Is this some sort of punishment?

"I'm disappointed," he says, then takes a bite and chews. Slowly. A sip of water and he clears his throat and speaks. "Today, I wanted evidence. Evidence that I was leaving this department ready for what lies ahead. This country is at war. We are one attack away from a code orange. You all are the front line of defense. You are a weak man, Jason. I had hope for you in the beginning. You drove strong. But when you yielded, you dropped the ball. No one — no one can be above the law. What if I was disgruntled with the President with knowledge of the ins and outs? You're his front line of Defense. It's YOUR job to find the hate, the bitter, the glitch. You buckled. Telling me about your mother dying. No one gets that! Not from a United States Agent. Men died in my arms and everything I do is to keep that from happening again somewhere else in this world. So, I apologize to you. Because somewhere, somehow, I failed to do my job."

His eyes trace over everyone in the room.

"So..." He wipes his mouth with the cloth napkin. Stands, braced on his cane, tugs his suit jacket downward and walks toward the door, then turns, facing everyone. "I apologize to you. All of you."

Wilkes raises his tone. "Director White, I will issue a statement regarding the BST-10 Project so you can tie up your ends. I'm no threat to this nation or the President. I love it like I loved my wife. You see, loyalty is steady."

My cell phone rings in the case we all deposited our phones into. I can tell by the ring tone. I open the case and look at it. Oh, perfect. I answer it.

"No need to apologize, Mr. Secretary," I say to him as he turns away from us, heading toward the door.

"Hello Mom." I say.

Yes. I lied. He stops, turns his head slightly to the right, huffs, and leaves. The automatic glass doors shut behind him, but I get a feeling that I will see him again.
"No, Mom, I won't forget the milk."

I hang up the phone. White comes out of the glass room with a sea of faces staring through the door. Benjamin picks up the last file I read out loud to Wilkes.

"You tried it," Benjamin says, looking at the open file.

"Blank!" Leave it to Phil to be dramatically outraged. "You are unbelievable. What if-?"

"But, he didn't. Do you know why? Because the statement didn't surprised him. Know why?"

Benjamin fills in. "Because there were practices that were unethical and inconsistent with American values."

"Exactly."

Benjamin is expressionless. I expected that. But why is Phil's lip almost bit to bleeding? He is unusually flustered. What is it? Is he scared of the Secretary of Defense? Or is he involved? Time will tell.

"That," Phil points to the blank piece of paper, "is unethical."

Benjamin writes a note, shuts his file. Phil can't spin his ring much more before it burns into his finger. The swinging paneled door opens and Director White's hand is on her hip. Her smart black pant suit is the perfect color for the moment. Secretary of Defense told the truth about one thing, Fritags' ham and Swiss cheese is great. I put another one on my plate. I was hoping to fly home tonight, but from the sounds of the storm outside, flights are probably still grounded.

"Director White, shall I go back to my office or back on... vacation?"

She crosses her arms. She knows as well as I, that my report, littered with the multiple times she attempted to dissuade me from asking the tough questions, will not read well for her. In this respect, her positional insecurity serves me. She'll just have to go back to her office and pop one of those pills she has in her pocket that she thinks no one knows about. If her trousers were a half a size larger, they would hide their lumpy outline. Her silence was my cue to exit and go to the office. I was right to make that call. It *is* time.

CHAPTER THREE

Caleb Promise

I hate that clock. Not sure how long it's been going off. Funny how we keep things around just because they're there. My head is throbbing, that's not unusual. Why can't I see? This isn't right. Something fell. Was that the lamp? I'm in my bed. I can tell by the familiar squeak of the mattress springs. Maybe if I push my hair backward, I'll be able — Nope. Wait. The last thing I remember was being grabbed.

I need to see. I need to know if I'm really in my bed or on a cheap prison bed. Am I a hostage? That's a viable possibility. Maybe it was just a dream. Even worse, maybe I'm still in my dream. It's happened before. In the past, I have dreamed that I've woken up from a dream later to realise; I was still in it. Only one-way to find out.

Sitting up, I grab the bottom of my shirt and rub my eyes with it. Relief. I'm not blind. Things are blurry, but I can see. Okay, I am in my room. I am not dreaming. But, how did I get here? I know that someone took me. I felt it. But, why would they let me go?

My boots are off, I step on the linoleum floor and feel my way to the bathroom holding the wall. Maybe if I wash my face. Cold water feels good on my face. That's better. Still a little blurry, but it's probably the headache. My head. I hit it on the floor of a van. I part my hair on my forehead. Nothing there, not a drop of blood or scratch. Not even a tender spot. It felt so real.

Was it just a drunken dream? Was my mind trying to make me feel more important than I am? That must be it. Who would take a broke drunk? Then, take all the trouble of putting him back in his room. I hope they took the eviction notice.

Here comes my reality. I am the crack in the mirror. They didn't keep me. No one would have need to.

"Shut that thing up!"

I'm amazed she took time out from yelling at her husband to yell at my clock. I walk back to the bed and slam my hand down on it. It turns off. The room is cold. Nothing odd there. Everything is where it usually is. My clothes, laid across the back of the chair. My boots, at the side of the bed. Is that the time? Work. I need aspirin and a shower. Pulling the drawer open the aspirin is where it always is. Where are my keys?

They wouldn't know how I put my things away, where I put my keys. Typical men put their keys in their pocket. Jeans pocket where it can't fall out. I don't. I never do. If they took me. That's where they'd be.

I squeeze the pockets of the jeans. They are not in there. I tug the drawer open again and the keys slide forward exactly in the spot that I usually place them. Strange. I almost feel disappointed. Only a desperately lonely person would feel disappointed to not being abducted.

Dressed and full of aspirin, I lock the door behind me. I feel the buzz. Sunglasses, even cheap ones, work when you've got a hangover the size of New Jersey. The hall prostitute isn't there. She must have had quite a night too. I look half decent in my man pony tail and combed beard. Lou told me I look twenty years older with all this hair, but I figure, why bother? Razors, shaving every day, it makes no difference. No one spoke to me more or less with or without it. I hold my breath going down the urine splashed stairwell.

"Caleb. Today by 6:00. Or else." Says Jerry pointing to a new box of black garbage bags.

"I got you, Jerry." I say passing him.

"Yeah, right."

I would tell him to shut up if I weren't in the financial situation that I'm in. The metal plate on the door clicks and I get an eye-opening blast of cold air. I hate to do it, but I will have to ask Lou for an advance on my pay-check. I'm a modern-day indentured servant already, though Lou never takes the money out of my checks. I got a solid two blocks before... Rachel.

"Hey, Caleb."

Why is she always so happy? She greets me like we're a couple that share a kid together or something. I don't lead her on, but she's so nice every time she sees me. She's decent looking and really doesn't have to chase me. That guy that works with her doesn't tire of throwing me the hate-look.

"Rachel, hi."
"In a rush?"

"Ah, yes. You know, work."

She wraps her knit sweater around herself tightly. She looks cozy. Like someone you would want to hold. Someone... but not me. Small talk. Make small talk.

"Flowers look good."

"Thanks. I got a new shipment this morning. You know me, if it blooms, I've got it."

Did she just hit me with a sales pitch? Do I look like the kind of guy that buys flowers. Maybe before, but that was a long time ago.

"Yeah, they're nice."

The wind has died down, but the cold seems more frigid. We are both squinting.

"Hey, how about dinner tonight?"

No.

"I'd like to but I think I'm doing a double shift."

I'm lying and I think she knows it, so why does she look down but keeps smiling? Maybe she remembers that's the excuse I gave the last three times.

"Next time, okay? You know where I am." She points to the window above the flower shop. "Caleb, if you need anything, ever, just let me know, okay?"

"Thanks. See ya."

For the first time, I'm glad to be at work. Inside from the cold. The glance from Tina, the hostess, warns me there's a storm brewing in the back that is probably about me. Liz isn't on the floor. I hate her. No, I hate all she takes for granted. She's got everything. I'm not talking about the fact that she's rich. She has her parents. The other bus-boy gives me a warning.

"Before you go back there, soldier-up." He whispers.

I can hear Lou coughing while her nasal voice rings through the kitchen. I shut my locker quietly and tie my black apron on. It's not exactly an employee break room. A row of rusty twenty-year-old lockers on a wall and employee only bathroom.

Turning the corner, I can hear them. The entire kitchen can hear them.

"Lou, Caleb is a drunk! He hangs out all night-"

I step right into it. Let's get this over with.

"What I do after work is MY business."

She rolls her eyes and shoves her hands into her apron pockets.

"Speak of the devil."

"No. We're not talking about your daddy, Liz."

Yeah, I said it. Her face can't get any redder. I needed to draw her attitude to me and off of Lou. He doesn't look good. Of course, she's oblivious to that. This needs to end fast.

"Immature idiot! See." She points at me with an open hand. "This is exactly what I'm talking about. He strolls in here late, looking like a billy goat and no one says anything to him but Scott gets fired. For what?"

Lou coughs and responds to her.

"That's between me and Scott."

Lou's raspy voice is troubling. His black land line phone rings. It's an old dial phone. He just can't let the past go. 'Some things should take time,' he told me when dialing the circular dial making a phone call. He answers the phone.

"Lou here. What? Yeah, I got that, hang on."

He fishes around on the desk and I put my back to the doorway, blocking Lou's view. I lean in toward Liz.

"You can come at me all day. I don't care, but Lou doesn't need this right now. Open your eyes, Liz. He's not doing well."

"He's the boss. He asked for the job so he should do it and do it right. I see a dozen code violations and quite frankly, one phone call can end this debacle."

That was low, even for her. I couldn't help but rear my head back and look confused. What would she gain? Ah. .

"Earn your little legal street credit somewhere else. He gave you a job-"

"He gave me a job because of my dad. He's not mother Theresa."

"What do you want?"

"You, gone."

"Or?"

Glancing over my shoulder, I can see Lou still on the phone. He closes a file.

"I've got the health inspector on speed dial."

I want to punch her square in the face. Haul off and nail her one good one. Not for me. For him. He's a fair guy. He works this diner day and night to leave it for his kids who don't even call him anymore. But, because of my mother who taught me better, I won't. For Lou, I won't.

"Really? You would do that to him?"

I hear Lou go into a coughing fit and his pill bottle rattle.

"In a New York heartbeat. Caleb. Today."

"Fine."

Surprised, her eyes widen and for a split second I think her human kindness kicks in. Then my hope smashes. A smug glow falls on her face and she folds her arms in satisfaction.

"Just so you know, Scott got fired because Lou caught him stealing tips. Your tips. I do this my way. Walk away."

Even she knows I'll keep my word. I may not have money, but I have my integrity. Lou's chair screeches as he turns toward the doorway, and sees Liz walk away.

"Don't worry about her, kid, I can manage her."

This wooden chair is more comfortable than it looks. I've sat in it many times after work and just talked to Lou.

"No, no need for that."

"You look terrible. Caleb, that bottle sucks the life out of you, I told you-"

"You don't look so hot yourself and you don't drink."

There's a hospital identification band on the desk, freshly cut off. "Yeah. They changed my prescription again."

"You need to rest, Lou. Joe can keep an eye on things."
"Joe's butt is glued to that stool. That's where he belongs. This is where I belong."

The office is nestled behind the kitchen. No windows, stacked with papers.

"I just came in to tell you something. I got another job."

He's smart. He looks at me from head to toe.

"You came in to tell me that. Where?"

"What?"

"Where's the new job?"

"Across town at a restaurant."

"What's the name? I'll give you a reference."

He doesn't believe me.

"It's new... the... gourmet something-"

"You come in dressed for work to tell me you have another job."

"I - I didn't want to leave you without notice."
He shakes his head. "Cut it out. You're not going anywhere."

"Yes, I am. Tonight's my last night."
I couldn't help but look up to see Liz staring at us through the glass wall with that smirk on her face. Lou catches it.

"No. Because of that? No. Caleb, she's a sour kid blowing off smoke. You can't let her win."

He's flushed. His breathing is short. Losing this Diner would kill him and I know it. Losing me won't.

"You've always told me to be my own man. This is my decision. I'm sorry."

Standing from that chair was the hardest thing I've ever done. I didn't want to leave. I put my hand out to shake his, just like he did for me on my first day there. He knows I won't go back on it. I have said it. Once I say something, I will stick to it. That's why I never told him I would stop drinking.

He knows he can't change my mind. He grips my hand, then covers it with his left hand. The sting of tears in the corner of my eyes makes me blink.

"Here." He says hurriedly, digging into his pocket.

"No, Lou. I'm okay. Really."

If I stay one more second, tears are inevitable.

"Bye, Lou." I turn to the door.

"Goodbye, son." He says.

That word stopped me mid stride. My back to him, I can't turn around. Keep going. This was my toughest shift, and for once, I didn't want it to go fast. I did it in a blur, knowing it was my last time. Liz didn't say a word but I caught her gloating glance from time to time. We finish our shift at the same time.

As usual, she hails a taxi. As usual, I put feet to the pavement to walk home. I watch her taxi pull off through the diner window.

I have no one I need to say goodbye to. No one that will ask me if everything is alright. So, I step outside and hear the bells ring on the diner door as it shuts behind me for the last time.

The winter storm knocks the warmth of the diner away. It's unbearable although the thirty mile per hour winds are broken between the tall city buildings. My reality is as bitter cold as the storm. Lou was my only semblance of family. A father figure I looked forward to seeing.

I could have left that job a long time ago. Manhattan is full of opportunities. However, Lou's kindness held me there. And mine let him go. Thanks to my new small bottle, I can fix this. A mouth full. This seems to be the bottom of the barrel. Why not? Tonight, Liz and I are equals. I lift my hand. A yellow taxi stops. So this is what it feels like.

I tuck the bottle into my right pocket and open the taxi door. Taxi seats are black leather and springy. Thick cloudy bullet proof glass separates the driver's front seat from the rear. It makes me feel like a fish. It's only the second time I've been in a taxi. It's a luxury I can't afford and rarely need. The driver slides open a small door in the bulletproof glass.

"Where to?" asks the taxi Driver.

"5th and East 96th Ave. park-side."

"You got it," replies the driver.

I settle back in the seat. In luxury. A small soda can rolls around, bumping my foot. My last luxury. Everything in my pocket couldn't pay for this ride. The radio is loud. Most New York taxi drivers don't like chit-chat. At least that's what one told me while I cleared his plate at the diner.

"New York, brace yourself. They have issued extreme winter storm advisory. Temperatures plunging to five degrees below zero so snuggle up with your loved ones and grab that cup of cocoa. Stay inside, stay warm, and check on your elderly neighbors. You don't need to dream of it, but we're playing that all time Christmas favorite, White Christmas. Stay tuned for more updates on airport closings."

"Can you turn that down?"

The driver looks at me from the rear-view mirror.

"No."

I'm not offended. New Yorkers don't leave you guessing about what they feel. You always know where you stand with them. Total opposite of the Southern hospitality I was taught since birth.

The tall buildings roll by quickly. Way too quickly. My little glass friend blurs them all together. The wipers swipe furiously but can't keep the falling snow off of the windshield. I can feel the car bracing the gusts of wind.

In this part of town, the streets are empty. I don't come here often. Occasionally, a person stepping quickly out of a private car or taxi then rushes through large doors held open by a suited and gloved doorman. There is no doorman where I live- well, lived. It's well past six p.m.

The bounce and sway are comforting. Unlike riding in the crowded subway or bus where no one wants to close their eyes, this was a safe place. The dark night vanishes and the glow of a warm sun rises behind my closed eyelids. I see rows of deep green fields and can smell fresh rain coming in the distance. Now and then, I catch the aroma of home-cooked meals from farmhouses that dot the countryside. I can't manipulate things here. The memory is so perfect I don't want to.

There is a worn wooden church and a lake. Not a huge one, but big enough for a boat. The boat dad and I refurbished all summer last year. It's docked, bobbing in the water behind our house. It must be Sunday because mom has the front door open and the screen door I promised to fix is unlocked. There she is. Mom walking past the window holding a serving tray waiting for the Pastor, his wife and the love of my life to come over after church. This feels real. I know it's a memory breathing in my cold reality, but I want to stay in it.

I want to see us laughing at the dinner table. I want to see my mother brush back the strands of hair that slip from her Sunday French twist. I want to see my father sipping her perfect lemonade, making jokes. The feeling in that moment is perfect. Safe. I truly want to stay right here. No chance. What's that tapping?

"We're here. Hey, buddy, we're here. Wake up."

The driver knocking on the glass divider. I purposely picked this street in Manhattan because I knew it was right beside an entrance to Central Park.

"Okay. All right."

"Twenty-seven fifty."

He's looking at me through the rear-view mirror. I start fishing in my left pocket.

"Oh, yeah, it's in this pocket."

I act as if I'm reaching into my right pocket but I pull the door handle hard and lean into it expecting it to open. It doesn't. He's reaching for something.

"Just give me my money! Pay!"

I saw this in a movie. Hopefully, it works. I hit the door panel just beneath the lock with my elbow. The lock pops up. It worked.

"Sorry."

The falling snow gets in my eyes. I can feel my boots slide slightly. I can't stop now. An opening to Central Park is right across the street. I can see it.

"THIEF! THIEF! Police!"

I hear a car door shut and screeching wheels sliding in the snow. A few more feet. No car entry into the park means I'm in the clear. A cop car. Coming in the distance. I have to cross the street right in front of it. Slow down. I pull my hood on and hunker into my thin jacket. Wearing my hood pulled this far down is not suspicious on a night like this. The taxi driver is on a one-way street. He has to circle around the block. That's why I chose this drop-off point.

There he is, coming up to the Police car that is heading my way. This fresh snow! I can't run. I have to hurry. A few more feet to the park entrance. I put one foot on the curb.

"Hey!"

I don't want to turn around. If I don't, it may be worse.

"Hey, you! Let's go."

Reluctantly, I turn. A homeless man covered by a tarp is on a subway grid with steam rising from it.

"Too cold for that tonight. Go to the shelter." Yells the police.

Now entering the park entrance, I hear the taxi driver yelling for to the officer.

"T-eeef! Police!"

The police car turns his spotlight into the park.

"No."

The elements are on my side. Blinding snow, trees and lots of darkness. It being two degrees below zero helps too. My adrenalin makes up for my thin coat. My hood is soaked. I run until the cold air hurts to inhale. I see light in the distance. Is it a cop car? I can't tell, but I can't spend the night out here. Already, I can't feel my nose. A sip. That's what I need. Ironic, how eerie a place intended to be occupied can be when it's desolate.

Tonight, the night before Christmas Eve, people have family or friends to be with. No need to be in an empty park. Tree by tree, I inch into the light. Traffic is a welcoming sound compared to the silence of the park. Standing beneath the streetlight, I feel warmer.

I made it. No cops in sight. I can't help but stare. I don't come here. It's the other side of Manhattan, separated by Central Park.

There is a huge white large brick building. Elegant, entreating. Long windows from ceiling to floor framed with expensive curtains swooped open by large tassels. Twinkling Christmas trees in some, Tiffany lamps perched on cherry wood tables in others. It's something... familiar. In one window, a large television's playing Christmas shows, a husband, a wife, snuggled on the sofa wearing thick white robes holding steaming mugs. I can't help but smile at the two brothers bouncing from present to present, shaking them roughly. It was home. Family. Love. Everything I don't have right now. That question, the one I hate that I can't get out of my mind. Was my parent's death really an accident? I can't let it go until I know for certain. A deep swallow.

The cold vanishes, each window tells a story. I feel snowflakes fall on my open lips and my running nose. These buildings loom above, a beacon for New York new arrivals with visions of 'making it' into the wealthy elite class. Tonight, it taunts me. It represents all that I miss and will never attain.

I tap my breast pocket and hear the paper crunch. It's still there. The eviction notice. It may as well be for millions. My debt is their pocket change, a tip they leave on a restaurant table. A flickering fireplace catches my eyes. Three adults, two elderly and one young, rushing to decorate a tree. Rushing so little Johnny won't catch them. How cute. I used to be little Johnny.

I wish I had photos of my family. My memories burned in the mysterious orphanage fire. The Monks were accustomed to young boys coming in silent, depressed and struggling to leave their old life behind them. The stone walls of the Monastery aren't like these stone walls. There was no warmth within them. No family. But, usually after a few weeks, meals and outdoor play, tongues loosen and kids assumed normalcy. I didn't. I didn't speak for a year. That's when Wallie broke through.

I found one thing behind those icy walls. A brother. He talked. I listened. We connected in my silence. His mother died in child birth with him. His father, a long lingering death. Cancer.

I liked listening to Wallie's stories. Tales of summers on his father's yacht and winters skiing in Vermont with dignitaries. Tea with royalty.

I thought he was lying, of course. It didn't matter. They took me out of where I was. A dark place. I didn't care about revenge on the drunk driver that ran my parents off the road. I was angry that I had to keep living, alone. It's easy to get lost in open windows. Watching snips of lives in motion. They were like Wallie's stories.

Police sirens? You must be kidding me for taxi fare? A group of loud party goers. Perfect. Slip into the group and a few blocks up, I'm in the clear. I have a few blocks to figure out how to get into my apartment.

The cold has gotten down into my bones. I wish I had a scarf. The air is frigid. Finally, I reach the building. I hope that's not my stuff in the new black garbage bags under that fresh snow in the alley. The glass on the building door is foggy, but I can see Jerry right there at the desk.

I look up, catching a face full of snow. The fire escape ladder is gone. I guess I'm not the only one who thought of that. Wait, who is that? Great, she saw me. Why isn't she in the hall where she belongs?

The wind is gusting so hard I can barely stand still. I press myself against the building so Jerry can't see me. I lean my head forward to peer through the foggy door. Is she ratting on me?

Why is she talking to Jerry? No one willingly talks to Jerry. What's she doing? She's laughing with him. She must be drunk. Wait, she's waving me past. Merry Christmas to me.

The bells on the door. He'll hear them. I stop with my hand on the door when an elderly man still holding his plastic chess piece appears in the door, looking right at me. He grabs the bells while

I push the door gently. I look straight at him and he smiles with his gray beard stubble. I duck and make it to the stairwell.

"Hey, Reggie. What-r you doing'?" asks Jerry.

"Need a little fresh air. You don't want me kicking the bucket down here, do you? That'd be quite a mess to clean up."

"Very funny. As I was saying, my dear, I have a bottle of wine in the back and-"

She must have seen the stairwell door close behind me because their conversation ends abruptly.

"Look at the time, Jerry, I got to go. Bye."

I hear his salty reply.

"Hey, forget you."

I can't believe I made it to the room. I stick the key in, praying silently. The lock isn't changed yet. Good thing it's close to Christmas Eve, Jerry probably couldn't get a locksmith. All the time I've complained about this place, but right now, I can't help but feel grateful I have a place to go tonight. Especially with this storm. The money. It's still here. Forty, fifty, seventy... one-hundred and sixty. Jerry's crooked. That's assured. It's not enough for the rent, but it might be enough to buy Jerry off for a few more day's stay.

It feels good to toss my jacket on the back of the chair. I need a hot shower to chase this cold from my bones. In the morning. I'm too tired. I collapse backward on the squeaky bed and pull the blanket over me.

It was a long day. Eviction notice, fired, chased by police... what next? I spin the little gold key between my fingers and shove it and the sock of money into my jean pocket. I feel sleep slipping in faster than usual and I will not fight it. I'll just get up early, shower and leave long before Jerry can get up here.

Normal people sleep or celebrate on Christmas Eve day. But Jerry is not normal. I must get up early.

CHAPTER FOUR

Wilkes

"Tonight, guests are out in their finery to celebrate the retirement of the United States Secretary of Defense. The air is electric and tender moments reflect his service. Even standing here in the lobby of this fine hotel, there is a somberness from those who will miss him and his dedication dearly."

Newscasters breathe for moments like this. I'm ready to go home. My retirement dinner is polished. This phase is over. The next phase has already begun. It is amusing that even my enemies will smile in photos with me now. It is part of the political game.

"Wilkes," says a general who second-guessed me for years says, "if there's anything you need, please call me."

The flash bulbs flare and we shake hands for a photo. I resist the urge to hit him with my cane. Diplomacy wins.

"Keep the torch burning, General."

"I will. Don't worry."

My successor. Soon to be announced. Tastefully, he should have stayed away tonight and allow this old relic the ability to shine alone. But that kind of tact is dead. I still don't like the flash from cameras. Most of us who have seen combat do not. They evoke memories we try hard forget. Focusing on my walk, cigar, anything, helps. My therapist told me to let my anxiety finds its way onto the hilt of my cane.

The President's absence did not ruin my evening. His presence would have put to bed some rumors, but I am not surprised. Re-election campaigns are already being planned. My full-length London Fog coat was a good choice. It goes perfectly with this tuxedo and hangs on at the shoulders well.

"Oh, Wilkes."

A cheeky embrace and sultry smile from an attractive woman. She clings to my arm for a flurry of camera flash bulbs. I draw her into a friendly embrace. The article will never say that I don't even know her name. At this point, I don't even care. She'll gush on social media about how much she'll miss me. Who knows, it may be the highlight of her life. Oh good, my ride is here. Reporters on the hotel steps stand shivering in the snow. I feel for them.

"Sir? Leaving so soon?"

"It's been a lovely evening. You all go inside and get yourselves a drink."

"Thank you, Mr. Secretary."

I touch the brim of my hat as the chauffeur closes my car door. That always makes for a pleasant picture.

"Tonight, is the last night you will drive for me, Collins. How long has it been?"

"Since we have we been delivering Christmas Presents to the families of your men? Eight years, Sir."

"Quite a run. They deserve it. One always thinks about those who died, during Christmas. It's inevitable. These presents make them feel like their dad or husband gave it to them directly. I owe them that."

"It wasn't your fault, Sir. It's the price of war."

"It's always your fault, son. Remember that."

I notice Collins smiles when we stop at each house as he pulls the gift from the trunk and hands it to me while I make my way to the front doors. It's almost midnight, but I will not stop until we deliver every last one.

The sharp pain in my hip deepens as the night passes. Vestibule after vestibule, it still takes me back to see their youthful photos in their military uniforms hanging in the hallways.

We finish and Collins pulls in front of my home. The evening well spent, the front doorway to my D.C. townhouse well-lit by my wrought-iron pole light. I step out of the vehicle. My hip is throbbing. I have at least seven steps in front of my four-story townhouse. I can bear it one last time.

"It's been a real pleasure, Sir."

His suit and hat always look as if they belonged to another. Collins looks out of place suited, but I'd never tell him that.

"For me as well."

"I want to tell you, thanks for giving me a chance. Given my past… well addictions… it's not easy to get a job. Especially one like this. They say I'd be pushing up daisies in Greenfield right now if it weren't for you. I mean, you could've picked any of those other posh drivers, but you picked me. And well, I - I just wanted to say thank you. I appreciate you recommending me to drive for that senator. I start Monday. I know you don't like to take gifts, but if you would." Collins hands me a present. "From me and the Mrs."

"Thank you. The pleasure was mine."

That phone rings again. Collins turns away and lowers his eyes. I answer it.

"Give me two minutes. I'll call you back." I slip it into my pocket.

"Shall I see you in, Sir?"

"No, I'm fine. You go on home and tell your wife 'Merry Christmas'."

Lifting his gift. I thought it crazy to have interior decorators ten years ago. To be honest, they did a good job, but I'll never tell Agnes that. Standing in here for my last night I recall telling them, do as you will but keep my favorites in the seating area. Cigar case, ashtray and heating pad for my hip. The rest impressed visitors more than me. It was the home of a single man. Neutral colors and no flowers in ornate vases. There it is, greeting me at the door for the last time.

It was the first frame I bought my wife after our wedding. Young, cheek to cheek, her veil nothing more than a lace tablecloth pinned to the top of her head. Yet, she was the most beautiful woman in the world. The front hall table is its home. When I leave, I purposely angle the picture frame to face the door so it is the first thing I see when I walk in. I then turn it the other way so it is certain to be the last thing I see when I leave. I never noticed the slight scratches on the wood table that give away my secret habit.

It's quiet. An advantage to living alone. It is always quiet. Hot shower, heavy monogrammed robe and a Cuban cigar. A deep draw and I sink into my worn leather chair in front of the gas fireplace, and watch the flames flicker, swirling a glass of brandy. It interrupts my wonderful moment. That phone rings again. I answer it.

"Yes. Now, what's so imp-... When?" I put the glass down harder than I thought. "You have everyone on it?" I listen. "Keep me posted." I hang up the call.

There's nothing I can do about it. That is what my men are for. Bed. I have an early flight.

Jason Jones

The weather shut down every airport just as I thought it would. Rushing home was superficial anyway. There is no one at home to rush to. Not since she walked out. She had to leave. I can hear a pin drop five offices down. The usual skeleton crew is here, and then there is me.

It's still in my teeth. The grit of Director White trying to use me to add accreditation to her fraudulent report. My true motivating factor is none of her concern. If she didn't stop me, I would have found out what I came to find out. I needed more. I thought for sure something more would have surfaced, but Wilkes proved more clever than I first anticipated. He's calculating. The one thing I am sure of, it is now or never. I had to give my man the signal. I had to let him know it was time. Did I do it prematurely? No. I can't second-guess my decision. Knowing him, it's probably too late any way.

My cell phone is ringing. That could only be one person. My trusted assistant. She's the only one who would call me right now. Sam. Through thick and thin together.

Holding the last file in my left hand, I answer the phone with my right and sit down on the lumpy sofa. I have the lamps lit and the shadows in the office seem to be creep closer.

"It's me," I say, answering the phone.

"I called the hotel," she says, chewing. "You never checked in. Typical. It's Christmas Eve, Jason. You can't stay away forever. You will have to go home, eventually." Sam sips a drink.

"All the flights are grounded," I say. Let's see if she buys that? "You are in D.C. It's an hour and a half drive."

No chance. I trained her well.

"Did you ever watch geese cross a street?" I ask her.

"What? Has your brain frozen?"

"Geese. I visited a town in Virginia and everywhere there was a lake, there were geese. They cross the street just like they walk, in a line. There's always one that goes first, I noticed that it is usually the biggest one, taller than the others. It sticks its head way up and looks around, then it takes one step off the curb and stands there for a while. They just don't rush into the street like squirrels or deer. It stands there then takes one step at a time very slowly, advancing. At first, I watched them anxiously and I kept wondering..." I flip through files.

"Wondering what?" Sam asks.

"I kept wondering why they didn't just fly over the street or make a run for it fast. But that big goose was big because he lived a long time. He lived a long time because he learned how to stand there long enough for the cars to see him standing there, and when the cars slowed, the other geese followed. If only one stepped out, it increased the chances of the one being killed, visibility. They move as a group and it insures the likelihood of survival." I pause to let it sink in.

"And you're telling me this because..."

"Sam, I think the big goose is moving."

There it is, the internal ah-hah. Wilkes is moving and it won't be long before the other geese stick their heads out and waddle into the street with him. Sam didn't get it. Maybe it's better if she doesn't. I like to keep her clear so she can think about the things I need her to focus on. She doesn't puzzle things together. She analyzes the full picture.

"Okay, Jason. Right. There is something you need to look into. Immediately. It just came in," she says.

"How did you know I don't have plans?" When all else fails, turn to sarcasm.

"You told me to tell you if anything big showed up within the next forty-eight hours, well, it hasn't even been nine hours but something popped up. A homicide," she says. I can hear her clicking on the computer keyboard.

"Where?" I ask.

"New York."

I sit straight up and drop the file on the coffee table. Now I'm curious.

"Why did this shine to you?"

"Steve Harvard. His daughter Elizabeth Harvard was found dead a few hours ago in a taxi in front of their building. It looks like a professional hit."

"Steve Harvard, billionaire Steve Harvard? Heavily invested in overseas tech, Steve Harvard?" I say hanging on her next words.

"Yes. Suspected drug cartel investor, Steve Harvard. If that doesn't shine, I don't know what does. The higher ups think you should go too."

"Why would they send me? Why not the Federal Bureau of Investigation? They rarely handle a dead body unless there is money wrapped around it. This killing may have illegal dollar signs all over it. Why Central Intelligence Agency?" I ask her. She pauses. Our 'read between the lines' signal.

"There's no mistake, Jason."

"Get me the-"

"-next thing moving out of Washington D.C. Done. A driver is waiting outside. Standard black government vehicle. You can't miss it. I'd go with you but, you know..."

"You have a life. I know. Thanks, Sam."

"God help New York." Murmurs Sam.

"I didn't hang up the phone yet."

I hear her laugh and then a click. Anything that significant in New York means it truly has begun. The first goose has moved and the line is forming.

Road trips don't appeal to me. I don't like to talk much when I'm working on a case and most drivers want to talk. Except Fernando. I am hoping Sam arranged for Fernando to drive. The only thing he likes to do on road trips is listen to his rap music. I pull open the back door and hear rap music blaring. I smile. I have proved capable of sleeping through that. Also, he drives faster to music.

The five-hour drive went quicker than I thought. I fell asleep during most of it and woke to Fernando bopping away. Manhattan, New York is beautiful during Christmas. But this storm, it's almost at its climax and draped itself over the city. I have never felt cold like this. It's like the end of the world. Fernando pulls into the front of a hotel.

"No. Take me straight to the site."

"Yes, Sir."

He rubs his eyes. I can't blame him. Staring at the barely visible street through thick falling snow. I need to get there while things are fresh.

We pull up in front of Steve Harvard's building and I open the door before the vehicle comes to a full stop. I get out of the car quickly, eager to see the site. A New York Police Officer approaches me. I didn't realize I was only in my suit jacket.

"You need a coat." He says.

"You deduced that all by yourself, did you?" I say flashing my badge and a smirk.

He smiles. That's one thing I like about New Yorkers, they don't bruise easily.

"Here big-wig. That is, if you don't mind wearing a N.Y.P.D. I keep an extra one in my car. You are?"

"Jason. Thanks," I take the jacket, "proud to wear one."

"What? No mile-long title?" he says sarcastically blowing into his cupped hands.

"I'm just Jason. Thanks for the jacket."

A good detective disappears, blends in and watches. His gesture just helped me more than he realizes. I can't help but look straight up at the penthouse balcony. Wind freezing my face off. On the penthouse balcony, a woman's night robe flows in the wind. She is as white as snow except her red lips. She must be frozen. Must be the victim's mother. A large diamond wedding ring on her finger catches the morning light. When you can see a rock ten stories up, it's a gem. Her eyes fixed on the roof of the taxi cab below. A police officer yells at the other officers on the street.

"Get these people back!"

Press? Of course. He looks like he's been out here for a while. The perfect person to ask.

"Why hasn't the body been moved yet? It's been hours." I ask the officer.

"The storm. Harvard's men are just five minutes out. All I know is, we wait."

The coat breaks the cold from my back.

"Harvard's men?"

"The victims, father. A call from the Mayor tied our hands. Figures."

"Where's the Captain?"

"What are you writing a book? Security room. There's video. They've got a suspect."

"Really." I feel my livers freezing. "Thanks, hey, you need to go inside and warm up."

"Nah, I'm used to this. Besides, I'd rather be out here with the guys."

He gestures to the other officers outside, directing traffic, holding back the crowds. They are doing what it takes to secure the scene. I can respect that sense of unity. As I walk inside, I hear him talking to the reporters.

"Sorry, you know I can't tell you anything. Please move back."

"Officer," a young eager-eyed brunette reporter begins, "judging from the amount of police presence and the fact that the chief himself is standing right there, this must be related to Harvard, come on, give me something here."

"Sorry, you won't be impressing your editor tonight. Please move your crew back," says the Police Officer.

There is a barricade curtain draped a few feet from the crime scene taxi. A futile attempt to block photographers. All the taxi doors are open. It's eerie. I never liked the stillness that creeps in with death. Alright. I must look at this deductively. The driver's head is turned to the right as if he were speaking to the passenger. Bullet entry to the back of the head, exit through the forehead. He never saw it coming. This wasn't a personal or emotional murder. Who went first? The dead taxi driver's shoulders shrugged with lifeless drop. His eyes open, staring with total unexpectedness. No opportunity to pray, beg for his life, nothing.

He's a family man. A creased color photograph of a smiling woman holding a young boy is taped to the dashboard with a crucifix hanging from the rear-view mirror. At least he was a Christian. A half-eaten sandwich in its wrapper on the passenger seat beside a book, "Home Buying for Dummies". This guy was going places. He had plans and probably not likely to mix himself up with the wrong crowd.

The girl saw it all happen. Her bullet came from the side of her left temple. Both her hands are on the door handle and one foot is outside of the taxi. She tried to get out. Her eyes are still open. She saw her killer. The absence of breath is obvious. And a sparkling frost has formed over them.

Any footprints have been filled with the freshly fallen snow. No shell casing for the two bullets fired. This wasn't a spray or shower of shots. They were direct intended hits by someone who got close.

There is a camera mounted on the outside of the building pointing directly at the entrance. Curious. The person was disguised or didn't care. Not a robbery. Her purse is still there, and his tip reservoir is full of fives and singles. I'm curious about what is on this tape.

"May I help you, Sir," asks the doorman, dressed in a traditional red long-tailed jacket with top hat. He is comfortable in his suit.

"The Captain?" I ask.

"Yes, of course. He's in there. It's the security office."

I can hear a squabble in full swing. Inside, it's interesting. The Captain is a tall man. He's dressed in a suit and full-length dress coat as if he just came from a function. His strong jaw bones are bulging like the veins on his temples. Why is he yelling at this man in black discreet tactical gear with no identifying badges on his clothing?

"That video is evidence! New York Police Department is leading this investigation. Any side-investigation Mr. Harvard wants to do, is up to you. Now he may have pulled some favor with the Mayor, which is the only reason I haven't snatched that video out of your hands, but you will not obstruct the course of this investigation. My men will run facial recognition in our labs."

"The Mayor said-"

"Don't tell me what the Mayor said! You own him, not me... look, I'm willing to cooperate with you as he stated, but we need to get this to the lab. The faster we identify this man," he taps the screen, "the greater the likelihood we have of catching him."

While they bicker, I glance the room over. There are all kinds of muddy footprints on the floor. The security monitor shows a frozen screen of a man in a hood, short jacket with hands in his pockets standing, staring at the building but his face is obscured by the snow and the shadow cast on his face because he is standing directly beneath the streetlight. I squint and lean in closer. It can't be.

There is a thin man in glasses sitting at the table clicking away on his laptop while they argue. What is he doing? A detective interrupts.

"Sir, we have something."

"Hang on, detective." He turns to the thin man. "Give it, now."

The thin man ejects the CD, slips it into a cover and hands it to the Captain. He puts it into his breast pocket. I don't think the Captain realises that it's a copy, or worse, an altered copy.

The Captain exhales and pushes past me. I forgive him for bumping me like a piece of furniture. There are three elevators. Two for residents and one with an engraved 'P' on it with a code pad beside it accessible by fingerprint. The Penthouse floor.

"Tell me."

I don't even have to introduce myself. I just stand here and everything will come to me.

"Hey, outside. Control that scene."

I spoke too soon. I just stand there and look at the Captain. His deputy is more observant than he is because he has broken rule number one. Always stay calm.

"Captain, he's not ours."

"What makes you say that?"

"Those shoes."

His deputy steps outside to take a call.

"Who are you? One of Harvard's?" the Captain asks me, rudely at that.

"No. Central Intelligence Agency. C.I.A."

A surprised response. Typical when those three letters are put together.

"This case gets odder by the minute," the Captain says shaking his head   now trying to decide whether to divulge his information to me.

"Let it out, Sir. I'm here to help. Despite the shoes."

He's stretched. This will be easier than I thought.

"Yeah, yeah. Elizabeth Harvard, aka Liz, was coming home from work-"

I didn't intend to stop him, but I have to ask.

"Work?"

The Captain fills me in. "Street credit, she was studying law. Part time, gives her something to talk about, you know. Okay, so she takes a cab as usual, it stops and just as she's about to pay, pow."

"Any eyes?"

"One. The doorman. He hid when he heard the shots. Get this. He saw the shooter come inside and go into the security office."

"What did the guard say?"

"Nothing. Lucky for him he was in the bathroom at the time. Bad egg salad for lunch. Door man says the guy was in there at least a minute."

"Did he get a good look?"

"No. Too scared to look. He's from England, nice guy, Edward, just scared. I call him Sir Edward."

Things are adding up quickly and the Captain knows it. What happened at work? Why tonight? Why here? If this was from Harvard's dealings, there's a million discreet ways to do this unless it's a message. I need to get to Harvard. His dealings are international, but he kept his daughter local. Let's see if the Captain makes the right call. This is his wheel house. He does. The Captain calls his deputy over and slips him the security video disk.

"First, get this to the lab. Tell them I need it, stat. I need an identification on that face before Harvard's men can get one. If they get to this guy before we do, we'll probably never find his body. Second, we need to get Sir Edward out of here and fast. Take an officer with you. He doesn't leave your sight until this is over. Harvard won't take kindly to knowing that his first line of defense that could have stopped his daughter's murderer is still living."

I couldn't have done better myself. He continues speaking into his deputy's ear. "Use your car and get that bleeding red doorman's coat off of him. Use the kitchen exit."

I am impressed.

"Take him to the station?" his deputy asks.

"No. Harvard has pull with the Mayor, we don't know where else he's got eyes. You know where to take him. I'll check out the Diner she worked at and see if there's anything there," says the Captain.

I love this guy.
"Right. I'm on it." His deputy says leaving.

With the Captain wanting to go to the Diner, I rush to the elevator and press the Penthouse button. Instead of the elevator doors opening, a panel slides open and a glass number code pad appears.

"I need to talk to Harvard." I say to the Captain.

"He's in residence. I've got to follow this lead to the Diner." Says the Captain.

"I don't need you to hold my hand. I just need an intro to get past that." I gesture to the keypad at the elevator.

He smiles and takes out his phone just as a black windowless van reverses behind the taxi. The doors open and a team dressed in black cold weather suits emerge with white kits. Four of them covered in disposable coverings. Their shoes and hair covered, and surgical gloves on their hands. The leader steps out of the passenger seat wearing an expensive leather overcoat, leather gloves. He stands waiting for his go-ahead. Harvard's team leader nods, then moves into the perimeter and boldly says

"Excuse me" to replace the police forensic team and foot officers at the crime scene.

"Hey! Who do you think you are?" says an N.Y.P.D. Police Officer, pushing the guy back.

A rumble of disagreements erupts into a shoving squall between the Police and Harvard's men. The Captain rushes over to quell it. The elevator arrives, some residents, probably Harvard's friends, step out dabbing tears and I step in, leaving all the noise of the lobby behind. The elevator doors close. I take off the coat and hang it over my arm.

The elevator ascends to the Penthouse and opens to opulence. I am not taken aback by his marble floors and fine paintings bought with dirty money. He has his hand so far in the drug money cookie jar you can barely see his elbow. Tonight, he is a grieving father and I will treat him as such, unless he is a goose. He seems genuinely distraught, but more so, angry. His wife, the woman on the balcony, seems on the border of insanity. I don't think he appreciates my presence, perhaps afraid of the light this shines on his dark dealings overseas. Guys like him can tell the difference between a boot and a suit at a glance. The murder isn't my concern. Who did he piss off to get his daughter killed? How is he connected to my man on the phone? How may this all impact the U.S.? That's my concern. He is issuing a statement to someone.

'My daughter's a saint, no enemies', the usual. He wants to get to her killer first, I can feel it. His head team leader, the guy in black that went toe to toe with the Police Captain, comes out of the elevator and walks right up to Harvard. The Detective taking Harvard's statement immediately stops speaking and steps aside. The man in black says what any father that just lost his baby girl would want to hear.

"We identified him."

He opens his mouth to speak further, but Harvard puts his hand up, stopping him, and looks directly at me.

"Who are you?" asks Harvard.

"Jason-"

"C.I.A." he says flatly.

"Yes." I extend my hand. "I am here to assist you in any way I can, Mr. Harvard. Sincerely sorry for your loss."

It diffused him. He shakes my hand modestly.

"Thank you." he says.

His floor length breasted robe just brushes the tops of his monogrammed velour bedroom slippers with leather bottoms. His hair is freshly cut. I can tell by the sharpened edges of his taper behind his neck and the manicure is new as well. He stills smells of aftershave so he must have just gotten home or freshened himself for the evening.

"Please, don't let me interrupt."

I step backward and clasp my hands behind my back, turning away from him and his man in black. In actuality, I am turning my ear toward them and offering the illusion of privacy by looking as if I am not paying attention to them. I need to hear who the murderer is. Sure enough, the man in black continues to speak to him. Nothing of substance. I walk over to his wife. She looks drugged.

"Madam, my name is Jason, I am with the C.I.A. and I want you to know I will do everything I-"

"GET OUT! No more, Steven! No more people. Tell Lizzy it's time for dinner. See, I made her favorite."

I step backward, surprised at her dazed outburst. She looked so calm.

"Hey, it's okay, dear... shh, it's okay. Jason, what did you say to her? I think you should go."

I hold my hands up, showing my palms out of respect and leave. Downstairs in the lobby, an officer is speaking on a cell phone. He is looking around and then sees me.

"Yeah, I got him. He's here." He hands me the cell phone. "Are you Jason?"

"Yes."

"Captain wants to speak with you."

I take the phone with my right hand and shove my left arm through the N.Y.P.D. jacket.

"It's me." I say.

"Listen, less than ten minutes before the shooting, there was a taxi fare hopper that ran from the West Central Park entrance toward the building. Park surveillance shows him heading toward the Harvard building. The video in the park and the person standing under the streetlight matches. The guy in the park is the guy standing under the light pole. Guess where the cab picked him up?" asks the Captain.
"Where?"

I stop juggling the jacket onto my shoulder.

"The Diner Elizabeth Harvard worked at. I just spoke with the owner. He didn't want to say anything, but she had an argument at work with him, tonight. Wasn't the first either. The hostess told me Elizabeth was bragging about how she got him fired. She left happy, she left then he left angry... in a taxi. That's motive."

"You buy it?"

"Buy it? It's clear-cut." The Captain says with certainty.

"Solved before the New Year. You get a gold medal."

"What are you trying to say? Keep that up and you're out of the loop."

"Captain, I'm saying it's too easy. I'm no homicide detective-"

"That's right, you're not." He snaps.

I can hear him honking his car horn trying to move the traffic.

"-but just think about it." I say. "Why hop a cab, draw heat to yourself and then kill someone in front of a camera and doorman? Even an idiot murderer wouldn't do that without a death wish."

"Maybe he's got one."

"Maybe he's not our guy."

"Think what you want. I've got a home address on the suspect and I'm in-route now. An accident. Great."

I hear car horns honking in the background of the call.

"All right, who is this amazing murderer?"

"A twenty-four-year-old drunk as I hear it. A bus Boy Caleb. Caleb Promise."

I feel the coat slip from my shoulder. I think my heart just stopped.

CHAPTER FIVE

Jason Jones

I take a deep breath and my wheels are spinning. My suit jacket flapping in the wind behind me, I race back to the S.U.V. Fernando sees my facial expression in as I approach the vehicle. The sun is rising. He stops tapping on the steering wheel and turns the radio off. I open the trunk, pull a new burner cell phone out of my duffel bag. I hand dial the number. No answer.

"Call me."

I hang up, run back into the lobby and grab the N.Y.P.D. jacket off of the floor and race back to the S.U.V.

"Where to?" Fernando asks me.

"Across town. What's the fastest route?"

Fernando looks at the traffic satellite device attached to the vehicle.

"It's Christmas Day. Traffic's a mess in every direction. Grid lock from multiple accidents. Probably from the storm."

"Get me as close as you can."

I pull my seatbelt. My hand sanitizer is almost empty. So quickly. I just bought that bottle. I thought she would call, shall I say, I hoped she would call. My personal cell phone shows no missed calls. There must be someone else in her life. Our split was very public, although we were in our own kitchen. Nothing is private when you endeavor to be a C.I.A. agent. Your home is littered with audio surveillance, probably even video, and they question every action. Those watching us could understand the strain on our relationship. It was obvious. Sleeping in my office for convenience left her alone night after night. Everything about us was visible. My therapist said I was engulfed myself in cases instead of her. The vehicle stops. I look at my watch.

"We will be here a while, Sir."

A long line of vehicles and taxis with brake lights lit are ahead of us. There's no time. I turn the N.Y.P.D. jacket inside out, put it on and get out of the vehicle. Fernando turns around and throws his hands up. The wind hit me right in the face but decreases as I descend the steps of the subway opening, humming the song in my head. I glance at the train map behind a glass display, tap it and run to catch the train I hear rumbling into the station. The ride is swift and I exit the train with three other passengers. Slowly, I ascend the stairwell, walking backwards, rubbing hand sanitizer into my hands. As soon as I reach the step elevating me to see the street, I stop. I can see the man who rode the train with me pulling the Police Captain with his left hand and pointing down the subway entrance behind me. He's doing what I paid him to do. I can hear him speaking to the Captain.

"She's down here. She said she's gonna jump. Throw herself on the train tracks. Something about he cheated on her... I don't know."

The Captain keeps looking at the cheap hotel across the street with the Vacancy sign blinking. Finally, frustrated, he gives in and goes down the subway steps with the man. I run into the building as soon as the top of his head disappears down the stairwell. My heart is pounding. In the lobby, I go to the elevator and see 'OUT OF ORDER'. I pull out my cell phone while running up the steps, trying not to touch anything. Still no answer. I reach the dismal hallway. From the window at the end of the hall, I can see the Captain coming out of the subway opening.

"Which room!" I can hear the Captain yelling downstairs. He lost it again.

"What am I? A mind reader. Whose room?" says the clerk.

"I want a team in the rear and one in the side alley!" the Captain yells. His voice carries up the stairwell.

"Caleb's room, now," the Captain asks.

"Caleb who?" says the desk clerk.

"The Caleb that's will get you arrested for obstruction if you don't tell me where he is. Want me to come back there?" the Captain says, gesturing to the desk.

"302. But he's not there. Evicted yesterday. Ain't been back since."

Captain's heavy footsteps echo up the stairs. I didn't see her at first. There is a prostitute sitting in the hall. She bumps the wall twice with her elbow. Why would she do that unless she's warning someone? But her eyes are glued to the room in front of her. That's the one. I turn the N.Y.P.D. jacket to its right side, showing the emblems and the police radio on the shoulder. She rolls her eyes. I put my fingers on my lips for her to be quiet and point her down the stairwell. She goes, but not before another eye-roll.

The Captain's steps are loud. He is almost here. I put my ear to the door and hear the shower running. I turn the knob. The door opens. I step inside. The room is empty, but the bathroom door is cracked with steam pouring out. Captain pushes past me and rushes into the room with his weapon drawn. He goes straight to the bathroom, disappearing into the steam. A brown leather jacket is thrown across the top of the chair. I hear the captain pull the shower curtain open hard. I look calm, but my heart is in my throat. Does he have him? The Captain emerged alone. I exhale.

"He's still here! Lock it down!" he holsters his gun.

The officers' pound on every door. The Captain holsters his weapon and uses a pen to pull open the drawers. He looks at the brown leather jacket thrown over the chair and smiles, nodding his head.

"Still think I was jumping to conclusions?" the Captain asks me. I'll let him gloat. Then, a funny look comes over his face. He turns to me. "How did you know the location?"

I look at him and a my training engages.

"Everyone knew the location."

"Not everyone. I didn't tell you. When I called you, I told you I was on route, I never said where it was. How did you know?" He places his hand on his holster.

Perfect.

"What?" I cross my arms. "Are you questioning me? You think I'm in on it? You're so new."

How long can I hold him here? Let's see.

"New?" he asks.

"As a newborn baby. You are looking in all the wrong directions." I say.

"How did you know, Jason? If you aren't dirty, tell me. How did you know?"

I flip the switch on the Police radio attached to the New York Police Department jacket on my shoulder and we hear the Officers' communication in progress.

"The roof! He's on the roof!" an officer yells.

"Fair enough," the Captain says, then runs out of the room yelling into his Police Radio. "Double the men in the alley below."

I head up the opposite stairwell to the roof. "EMERGENCY EXIT ONLY" boldly on the door, 'Alarm will Sound'. The door is ajar. I push the door open and step out onto the roof. The wind is whipping loose snow like a whirlwind. Mixed with the blinding sunrise, I squint, but I see him. He's standing a few feet away. Blue jeans and a hooded sweatshirt. The snow, swirling around his head. Why is he just standing there? I open my mouth to yell to him, but I hear the steel door on the other side of the roof open behind me with a bang. The Captain and his officers.

"Caleb Promise! Freeze!" Yells the Captain.

Caleb doesn't look back. He runs. He's going to jump to the next roof. The alley gap is too wide! He won't make it.

"NO!" escapes my lips before I can think.

Caleb's foot leaves the ledge and he is airborne, arms flailing. I hold my breath. Gunshots! What! The bullets whiz past me. I stoop. More shots fired. Then, silence. I stand. Did he make it? He's down. I see his sweatshirt poking out of the snow heap on the next roof, but I don't see movement. I step out from the doorway into their line of fire, holding my hands up, facing the Captain and his men.

"Hold your fire! C.I.A. ON THE ROOF!"

"Get out of the way!" The Captain yells aiming his gun at me.

I pull out my badge and hold it high. I bite my jaw and stand firm. They lower their weapons. I lower my hands and turn around. Caleb is gone.

"No!" I hear the Captain yell and kick the snow. He speaks into his Police Radio...

"Next building. Next building. Shut it down NOW! No one in or out. Detain everyone!"

The Captain stomps through the thick snow toward me. He's angry, but this isn't my first confrontation and I am sure it won't be my last.

"I wasn't sure before," the Captain begins, "but I am now. I don't care whose side you are on and what your real agenda is. This is mine. My jurisdiction. Despite you, Harvard and the Mayor, I will find the man who murdered a taxi driver and Elizabeth Harvard in cold blood and why. You get in my way again, I will have you arrested. You got that?"

"And bring him in, dead or alive? Which one is more important?"

"That's my business."

I step forward into his personal space. His eyes are piercing and his voice deeper and more intimidating than mine. But this man is intelligent enough to know that it is not physique that holds power in this game.

"Captain. Are you familiar with stippling?"

"Your point?"

"It's a painting technique that builds a picture using colors subtly. It takes time. There are no long strokes. Taps of a stiff bristle brush, just taps."

"I don't have time for this."

The Captain turns to leave.

"What? You don't think your men can lock down a building without you?" He stops, crosses his arms.

"The artist has to step back, far back from the painting, to see the big picture as it builds. There is always a big picture that can't truly be appreciated when you are standing too close to it so-"

I step so close to him our noses almost touch.

"You are standing so close, there is paint on your nose. My view, way back there. I am paid to be way back there, then watch the artists tap... tap... tap. I tell YOU when you are going off sketch. You ever feel the need to threaten me again, do yourself a favor, and smile afterward. I just may take it the wrong way."

He snickers. I expected as much. He turns and runs down the stairwell. Tap... tap... tap. That should have gained Caleb some time.

CHAPTER SIX

Caleb Promise

My sweatshirt is wet. The snow on the roof still clinging to me. Can't catch my breath. Not now. Who's that? He is standing right in front of my exit. I can't read him. Snitch? Saint? His hand is on the fire alarm, but his eyes are locked on me. At his age, I could just shove him out of the way. He may not even be able to get up afterward. But that is not my style. Even drunk I wouldn't hurt anyone. Especially an elderly man. I can hear the officers teaming into the front door of the building and running past the Chinese restaurant straight up the steps to the apartments above.

Standing in the Chinese food restaurant's busy kitchen, our eyes lock. This is his restaurant. His kitchen. I don't belong here, nevertheless, his eyes are kind. Turned downward. When all the officers are up the steps. His eyes trace upward. My brow drops, confused. My beard wet and water dripping onto my sweatshirt. His hand still grips the fire alarm handle. He looks at me, smiles and pulls it.

Above, frantic residents clamor into the halls, profanity rolling off their tongues for the interruption of their Christmas routine. He looks at the chefs in the Chinese Restaurant, stirring hot woks, and nods at them. One glances over his shoulders at him and drop five egg rolls into the rolling hot oil. They keep cooking as if nothing is happening.

The doorway to the apartments upstairs opens and people rush onto the sidewalk, cursing and waving their arms in the cold air. After, they do what any New Yorker with common sense would do; they go into the Chinese Restaurant and order an egg roll while they wait it out.

"You got to be kidding me!" an officer says.

My heart is pounding. The elderly Chinese man takes keys from a nail beside the door and waves me through the back kitchen door to the delivery van in the back of the restaurant. An elderly woman eating noodles with chopsticks, perhaps his wife, locks the door behind us and I can hear her seat bump against the door. I climb into the van via the driver's side door and slip into the passenger seat; he points me to the back. I huddle between some boxes and squat down.

"Stop," an Officer standing in front of the van says. That's it. I'm caught.

"Open it."

"Huh?" the man replies as if not understanding English. I hear a paper bag rustle. He lifts it, insinuating he's making a delivery. Then speaks Chinese angrily. He squeezes out a few words in English.

"I late... food cold."

Then keeps ranting. The back door opens. The cold rushes in. I inhale and hold it. The Officer glances in. The door shuts.

"Go ahead. He's clear."

Exhale. The Chinese man throws up his hand in frustration instead of thanks. Smart. An authentic response. The van bounces and jolts. He drives through the delivery alley to the next major cross street. If he didn't, we probably would have been stopped again. The next cop may have searched more thoroughly.

"Come."

No cause to not trust him. Yet, I do. He's wearing a faded New York Yankees baseball cap. The adventurer in him hidden by aged smile lines in the corner of his eyes, but betrayed by his quick thinking and the rebel's sparkle in his eyes. I don't know where we're going. I've seen him only a few times and barely said hi. Now, I wish I said more. He stops in front of the train station and starts reaching into his pocket. I know that reach. He hands me a fist of ones, probably tips.

"No... no thank you. I can't take your money. I owe you." I shake my head.

His eyes are dancing. I feel, if I don't take it, I'm robbing him of the moment. I won't rob him. I exhale.

"Thank you," I say, take the money and step down from the van. Just before I close the door, he reaches over the seat and grabs my arm.

"Sta-t ova," the elderly gentleman says.

He turns his arm outward, revealing his inner wrist. There is a Chinese Mafia tattoo on the inside of his forearm.
A lump forms in my throat. He smiles. I won't ever forget that smile. I pull on my hood and nod at him. A car honks its horn impatiently.

"Come on! Move it!" a voice yells.

"Hold ya horses! Will ya!" he yells back in a perfect New York accent.

I smile shake my head and jog into the train station. Fists in my jeans pocket, I fiddle with the small gold key between my fingers. I don't get it. Why all this? For rent? Can't be. Jerry is a jerk, but that's even overkill for him. Hard to think looking over your shoulder. Subway? No choice, but there are cops even in the subways. I have to chance it. The streets are crawling with Police. I'm missing a piece to this puzzle. I've got to get to Lou. I've got no choice.

I wait for a crowd coming out of the subway and ease in with them and walk amid them to Lou's Diner. The gate is down, locked. Why? No sign, and no one around. I have never seen it shut. Lou always stays open during the holidays.

"Caleb?"

Judy. Owns the hair salon next door. I'd know her voice anywhere. Right next door but always requested me, personally, to deliver.

"Caleb? Is that you?" She looks deeply into my eyes. "What have you done to yourself? Come in here, you'll catch your death."

I walk into her empty beauty salon and she makes me a hot chocolate from her guest bar.

"Drink this, sunshine. Now, tell me, how is Lou?"

I stop raising the cup to my lips. My hands are blue and wrapped around the heat of the cup.

"Lou?"

"Yes... wait, don't you know?"

She tilts her head in the other direction and fiddles in her mini fridge. She pulls out a packaged sandwich. I put the cup down and run my fingers through my hair. My beard dripping from the melted snow.

"Know what?"

"Sweetie Lou had a stroke last night,"

I feel weak. My heart must have skipped five beats. I just let her finish. She couldn't tell.

"Last night, some cops came in and told him about Liz." She can tell I don't know about Liz either. She continues. "She was shot, Caleb. Last night. She died. I think it was too much for him. They've got him in Mt. Sinai Hospital. That's all I know."

I feel like I will pass out. No. Not here.

"Can I use your bathroom?"

"Sure. Straight through there," she points down the hall.

The sink is holding me up. I wail silently and punch the wall once. My eyes look fifty years old and my beard and hair look like one. Too much. That's why the police were there. They think I killed Liz. I have to let Lou know that it wasn't me. The room is spinning. I need a drink, badly. I take the money the elderly man gave me and my black sock and zip them into the inner breast pocket of the coat. The gold key, I leave in my jean pocket. Never put all your valuables in the same place. If a robber finds the money, they won't bother hunting for what is truly valuable. Deep breath and I walk out of the bathroom.

"Thanks, Judy. I've got to check on Lou."

"I tried. No visitors allowed until tomorrow. He's in the Intensive Care Unit. Tomorrow, they will move him to recovery. First thing in the morning."

"Okay. I'll go tomorrow."

I reach for the door but my hand is shaking so much I can't grab it.

"Wait, Caleb." She hurries behind a wall in the back of the shop, swirling a breeze of sweet perfume in the room behind her.

"I kept this, it was my husband's. I keep it in the back room just where he hung it. Said it was the warmest coat he ever bought. Now and then, I hang it by the front door. You know, so people won't think I'm here alone. I still wear the ring too. Put it on. Perfect fit."

It is too big, but warm.

"I'll bring it back in the morning."

"No, sunshine, it's yours." Smiling kindly. "Don't you say a word. Just give Lou my love when ya see him, tell him don't come rushing back. I'll keep an eye on the place for him. All right?"

The coat feels good. She was smiling as I walked out, but I glimpse her reflection in an angled window and see her smile drop abruptly. I need to get out of site. There are cameras everywhere. Mounted on buildings and inside of stores, searching for shoplifters. I'm soaked. It's snowing again. Who doesn't dream of a white Christmas?

The train is warmer than my room. I lost track of the time. I tuck into a corner and change train lines when I see Police coming to do their rounds. Too many cops. I can thank the increased alert for that. After all everyone wants to blow up New York. After all, it is a status State.

It should be dark by now. Shifts are changing. There's something earthy about this place that grabs me. Maybe that's why I never tried to go back home. Who am I kidding? I never went back because I didn't want to face the past. Sounds strange, but I miss 'me'. I see myself in the bank window and don't recognize myself. I don't even think the same. It has been too long. I walk into the bank, use the bathroom and end up getting shoved out by the security guard with a firm warning. Bitterness sets in.

I'm on the street. I don't know where, but it's dark and when you're wanted, that is a good thing. The only bad thing about getting a break from the cold is that going back outside, the cold feels even more extreme. I haven't walked two full blocks and can feel myself starting to shiver. I see light flickering in the darkness. It is under an overpass. Is that a fire? Yes. A large one. All the stores are closed and I can't go back to the subway. Not yet. I move closer to get a better look. It's a barrel on fire. Are those men?

"Step up," someone says to me.

An invitation? I'm hesitant but I'm out of options. It's as if I'm a part of some unwanted breed. I've only been homeless a day and already, they can tell. Being embraced by the unwanted is confusing but humbling. In a matter of hours, it launched me into this mysterious society that no one wants to be a member of. I have no choice. I dried off in the train, but I'm soaked again. Though I miss my leather jacket, I can't chance going back to the room to get it. It stuck to me closer than a friend.

Standing shoulder to shoulder in the circle of three large men around the flaming barrel, the beard is serving me well. I appear older than I am. I want to return to the above-ground land of the living. The land where you didn't feel you have to hide.

Now, people lower their eyes when I walked by. Once one crosses that line, can one cross back? If not, what is down this rabbit hole? A life of survival? A life of hardship and hiding?

What is its end? I think I know. I can't go for a job. Not looking like this. No address. No phone. Wanted.

"Better put-em up before ya catch frost bite. There's no saving them after that."

He's twice my age. Weather-beaten. How long has he been out here? The heat feels good. My palms warm up first. Barely feeling the heat on my fingertips, I put them closer.

"Not too close. You'll burn them. Look here."

He backs his hands up from the fire and I imitate him cautiously.

"Let him figure it out. What are you, his daddy?" says the man beside me. The knuckles on his left hand have deep scars.

I'm tall, but not very muscular. This coat helps. Suddenly, stature is everything. The scarred man is bigger than both of us. I can tell the older man fears him. There's a strange eye exchange going on. The nice guy shakes his head no and lowers his glare to the fire.

"Nice coat." Grunts the scarred man.

Somehow, I don't think that's just a compliment. The older man confirms it for me.

"Come on, he won't last long without it. Tomorrow, I'll get-"

"Mind ya business!" he yells at the old man.

A burning rises inside. I squeeze my fists. The older man eases away from the barrel and gestures to me to leave with a shift of his eyes as he slips into the shadows. Not a chance. I'm done running. The traffic rumbles overhead and the scarred guy steps up to me.

"Take it off," says the man, lowering his hands from the flame. "I'll take it with holes in it if need be." He pulls out a knife. "You deaf? I didn't stutter!"

"Just give it to him!" yells the old man from the shadows.

I step away from the blazing barrel and two men grab my arms. The dirty blade pressed on my cheek. With a flick, he cuts off a piece of my beard. My hands still bound, I take a punch to the gut. The air is knocked out of me. I buckle over and he pulls the coat off of me. Then it begins. Kicks and punches to my ribs, head, and back. It feels like it is going on forever. Finally, they stop.

"Nice fit!" says the scarred man.

I'm in the slushy mud. Soaked to the skin. A dull heavy pain between my shoulder blades. Snow mashes into my nose and eyes, then, a tug on my leg, someone's trying to take my boots. I hear a zipper open. My life savings. But the little gold key, that's still in my jean pocket. Far more important than the money. I stay still.

"Jackpot!" He says.

There is no one rushing to my rescue, no feeling of release from the weight of the massive man on top of me. I see the older man huddled against the bridge wall rocking, humming to himself.

Rage. A piece of the old me shows up. I hate seeing people bullied, victimized or just afraid. I'm more enraged at what ever he did to that old man to in-still fear into him, than I am for what he just did to me.

I push my body up as hard as I can and the scarred man falls off of my back. I grapple the ground and find a chunk of ice. I hit him. Again and again. I feel no urge to stop. The two other men completely ignore the fact that I am beating him and grab the money he dropped and run into the shadows. Faces peek at me from tents and boxes watching with no emotional reaction at all. Witnesses. I stop. I get up. The bloody man groans. I spared him. I didn't hit him in the head. Just the face, neck and chest. I can't recognize him. Most importantly, he'll never forget me.

"Go," whispers the elderly man, still rocking.

He looks like a man trapped within himself. The bloody man starts to get up. I walk away. I head back toward the street and shops. It's safer there. I would rather be ignored than killed.

I smell fresh pizza from an all-night pizzeria. A few party goers, bar hoppers are out. I'm trembling. I look in the reflection of a closed glass store front and try to fix my hair. There is mud and blood on the front of my sweatshirt and on my face. My thoughts aren't rational. I need a drink. My hands are trembling and it's not from the cold. It's withdrawal. Someone must have a heart, at least tonight. Christmas night. I'm going to ask. I have no money. I have to ask. At least if I can get something to eat I may feel better. My thoughts will be clearer. I pull open the door of the pizzeria. Before I get three steps in the door, the clerk yells across the room.

"Can't you read? No Vagrants."

I turn and see a sign. 'NO VAGRANTS'.

"Please, I've been robbed," I say, biting every bit of pride I have.

"The Police Station's up the block!" he says in frustration flinging his hand in the air then continues to cut a pie.

Jail even sounded good. Wait, I'm wanted for murder. I leave the shop with patrons staring at me. The door shuts behind me and I walk to the large steel street garbage can on the corner. I can't believe I'm doing this but a white paper plate creased, with a greasy napkin stuck to a partially eaten pizza crust looks good. Without hesitation, I reach into the garbage and grab it. I bite it and start walking up the street as fast as I can. Embarrassment wells inside me with each bite. My eyes fill with tears and there's no need to fight them back. No one looks at the crack in the mirror.

I pass a store with television monitors playing. Pictures of the winter storm setting in tonight. Warnings for people to stay inside and keep warm. I have to get indoors or I'll freeze to death. The churches are filled with people going to mass. I can't. A vacant building. Raw stone rubble scattered floors. Why not? I have nothing for anyone to steal. At least some windows are boarded up. I look for a viable room on the first floor. Easy escape. Lightly pushing the unlocked doors. They are all occupied by families. Every room tells a story.

Children huddled between their parents. Couples lying on bare mattresses. Some drug addicts eight to a room, half naked but they can't feel the cold, anyway. This is a dark place. No choice, up the urine-covered steps, disturbing rats and unknowingly kicking cans on the dark steps. A rustling sound. Just a dog. I continue down a long corridor on the second floor with doors staggered on each side. Empty studio apartments stripped of all their contents. The broken tile beneath my feet, crunches and cracks with every step.

A door is slightly open. It's empty. After my last experience, the absence of people is more comforting than the presence of them. The room across the hall is also empty, but this one has a mattress on the floor. Ripped pale blue strips of wall paper flap in the breezes slipping through the spaces in wood slats nailed in front of a broken window. I ease down on the dirty blue mattress and lean my back against the wall. I have a blinding headache. I just curl up. I just need to shut my eyes for a moment.

Green fields. Rolling hills and covered by warm rays of sun. I see my house. I am going up the front steps and can see mom holding the serving tray of baked chicken. The screen door is open with the little rip in the side I promised to fix but never got to.

"What the hell! Get out! This is my house!"

Someone is kicking the side of the mattress.   For once, I would love to just wake up peacefully.

"Stop! Stop kicking me, you crazy..."

"I'm not CRAZY! You're on my bed you freak!"

"You can have it."

I scoot to the end of the mattress and try to stand. The room spins violently. The wall. I need to lean.

"Hey, hey..."

She steadies me, holding my arm. I snatch my arm away.

"Don't touch me!"

"How long has it been?" she asks.

"Long for what?"

"You're kidding me, right?"

I close my eyes but feel myself shaking my head. Now mistaken for a drug addict. Great.

"I'm not like you. I'm not a drug head."

"Whoopee-doody. Well, whatever you are, you look terrible. And I'm clean. Seventy-three days and counting."

Where's the door? I need to get out of here.

"You won't last long. Not with that cough."

She's right. It started last night. Besides, where am I running to? The hospital. Lou.

"Headache? I have something for it if you want. A good friend gives me stuff and talks to me when I'm lonely. If you don't want, it's all good, I'll save it."

"Yeah, alright… alright. Thanks."

"It's aspirin."

I recognize those chalky circles anywhere.

"No brand name, but they work even expired. Just take a few more. What's your story?" she asks.

She looks clean and has put several large tote bags on the floor beside the bed. One deep blue plastic tote has a fluffy comforter inside. I'm not answering questions.

"Cool. I didn't want to talk at first either. Been on streets three years yesterday. Got hooked in high school. Dropped out and left home. The usual."

She's rambling as if she hasn't spoken to anyone in a while. Barely pausing as if she is accustomed to no one else speaking. She reminds me of Rachel. Just a few days ago, I didn't like being around people and avoided conversations as much as possible. But now, this alien voice acknowledging me is soothing. Her rambling fills an empty space. I run my hand through my damp oily hair trying to rub the headache away. My beard is clumped with dirt and my hands are filthy. Dirt under my fingernails and I have small cuts on the back of my knuckles from the fight.

It's the first time I take a moment to assess myself. My socks are soaked. Can't do anything about that and my sweatshirt is too. I ram my fists in my jean pockets. It's still there. Good. The little gold key.

"Yeah, behind the pharmacy when the companies come to get the expired ones, you can get what you need. The key is to not take much."

She pulls things out of her large tote bags like a tenant moving in adding touches to the room. A small vase of fake flowers like something won from a cheap street carnival. She puts it on a broken cabinet. A long poster, she rolls out and tacks to the wooden boards covering the cracks.

"... I can get most things you need. The key is, you got to look clean. Don't stink, that's a dead give-away." She stops and looks at me. "No offense, the bathroom's there."
She points down the hall to a thin door at the end of the hall.

I'm surprised there's running water in the building. Half-way up the hall, she rambles on.

"Keep your hair combed... alright, alright, I got you. I'm coming."

Approaching the bathroom door, I'm still listening to her and wondering who she is talking to. Her conversation is confusing.
There's an odor coming from the bathroom. I push the door. I'm not seeing this. Bloody bare footprints are on the floor. They were dark burgundy and dried. The bathtub is stained with blood pooled around the drain. Bloody hand prints are on the wall beside the tub as if someone braced their full weight on it.
She's still talking. What's going on? I back out of the bathroom slowly focusing on her chatter. She sounds like a mother comforting a child. I tip toe back into the room and see the large comforter opened neatly on the bed and she is holding what seems to be a doll over her left shoulder with a blanket over it. I hope it's a doll. She's bouncing and rocking it. The bundle in the blanket does not move. It is stiff.

"Is that better? Good, see, I told you we'd get the gas out. We have company, yes, we do. I want you to meet my daughter Chemise. She's just three weeks old. I know, I look good for someone who just had a baby."

It can't be. Maybe it is alive. She walks eagerly toward me, leans it back gingerly showing the baby's face. I look and close my eyes. I put my fist in front of my nose and mouth. The stench.

A small round-faced infant with darkened eyes shut tightly and lips blue and slightly agape is bundled and swaddled in layers of blankets, making the face look even smaller.

Lifeless, no color or sign of life. Its temples sunken in and skin wrinkled. This tiny body decomposing and the pungent odor of it rushes up my nose. I back out of the apartment hearing her yelling after me.

"No! You're my friend! Her father! Come back. You can't just leave me again!"

I run down the stairs and out of the building hoping to run long and hard enough to run the memory of what I just saw out of my mind. I need to get to Lou. That's what I have to focus on. Hospital. Lou is normal. Lou is a center of gravity. He may be home. No. The stroke. He's still in the hospital. What's happening to me? I can't think clearly. Were those really aspirin or is this just from not having eaten in two days?

'EMERGENCY ROOM'. Finally. I look like an emergency. Through the glass walls, I can see it is full. Good. I need to get cleaned up. Lou can't see me like this. Are those... yes, Police officers near the door talking. I walk to a side brick wall where I don't see any video cameras. I can hear the chatter inside the emergency room and people complaining about how long they have been waiting. Think. I didn't come all this way for nothing.

"I will kill you all! I have a bomb inside of me."
Perfect. Thank you, New York.

"Officers!" yells the registration nurse.

Amusingly, she doesn't seem startled as if this is an everyday occurrence. Thank you, crazy person. The automatic doors slide open and I slip in, going straight for the stairwell. I'll use a bathroom on the second floor. I wash my face and see muddy water splash in the sink. I got cut right by my hairline. Didn't even feel it. I have to ditch the muddy sweatshirt. I shove it into the bin marked 'soiled robes'. My shirt is wet, but it's not filthy. I can get away with it.

"Louis De'Marco's room, please." I say discreetly to the woman at the information desk.

"Room 307. Elevators right there."

That gum pops so loudly. She shouldn't do that to people.

"Thanks."

She picks up the phone. Why? It didn't ring. She locks her eyes on me. I choose to take the stairs.

I hurry imitating a returning visitor who knows exactly where they are going. The doors of the rooms are open. Beeping machines and clear tubes stream from IV poles. The antiseptic smell is everywhere. I inadvertently meet eyes of a few patients sitting listlessly in their beds waiting for their visitors who will never come. It's Christmas day.

Second to last room on the left. There it is. Directly across from a door marked "Employees Only." It looks like the forgotten room, so far from the nurse station. I wonder if they placed Lou there because his condition isn't severe enough to warrant a position directly in front of the nurse station; or was he so far gone that proximity to it doesn't matter?

A heavy black marker hastily scrawled the paper sign with his name is stuffed crookedly into a silver metal frame. His door is open. A pale printed curtain blocks everything except his feet that are covered by the white hospital blanket. A clear plastic bag on a bright green chair in the corner in front of the window, shows his wallet and keys. Police and ambulance sirens sound faintly in the background. I'm scared. I don't know why. I'm afraid of what he'll look like. Afraid of what he'll think of me. I stand at the foot of the bed. His eyes are closed. He looks so calm. His mouth slightly open. He's asleep. An excessive amount of tubes are coming out of him. His eyes are closed tightly, an oxygen mask strapped tightly to his face, and his machines beep rhythmically. I didn't expect this. I pictured him sitting up and smiling saying, 'Hey, Cae'. My spirit feels broken. I am taken back by the gray tone of Lou's face. My heart sinks into my stomach. I did this. I broke his heart. I shouldn't have quit.

Lou's right arm is turned outward displaying an IV securely taped. The wrinkled pale blue hospital gown draped on him with blankets tucked around his waist. Hesitantly, I touch his hand. I lower my head and fight the tears swelling in my eyes.

"Hey, Cae."

What? I hear his voice and it all gushes out. I try to stop them but cry uncontrollably. I can't... everything I held in is pouring out in a river of tears of joy to just hear those words again. Those familiar words. That familiar voice. I abandoned myself so long ago and Lou was the only one I could let the old Caleb breathe around. With an exhale, I lower my forehead to the back of his hand. This is no time to be selfish. I can't make him sad. Come on. Lighten it up.

"You trying to scare me to death?" I say wiping tears away.

Lou shuts his eyes slowly, but where is that smile?

"No, son."

His voice is so weak. That bold deep raspy voice that bellows over the kitchen noise is not there. I can hear the oxygen going on. He coughs. A dry wheezing cough, uncontrollable. Lou's face turns red and his chest trembles uncontrollably, trying to catch his breath. Composing himself, Lou struggles a smile.

"Caleb, it is ... serious."

I lean in and place my left hand on Lou's arm. I hate what I feel. He is freezing.

"Pull those up for me, Caleb." Lou glancing down at the covers on his stomach. I look back at him, puzzled.

"Can't move, Caleb. Little gift left behind from the stroke. Listen to me, Caleb..." He glances toward the door, sees the drawn curtains and looks at the floor to see if there are any feet beneath it. There aren't any. Lou continues. "... there's something I have to tell you. I will not make it-"

"Why are you talking like that? Stop it. Come on, don't do that-"

"-listen! There's no time."

"No time? What are you talking about? Did they give you something?" I ask.

"I got so much I want to tell you." Tears flow from his eyes into his ears. "First, there is one thing I didn't do, Caleb. I didn't get out and live. I made that office my life. Time moved on, but I didn't go anywhere, see anything. Caleb, I want you to live."

I swallow hard. He's speaking a little over a whisper and so am I. I pull my chair closer and lean both elbows on the bed and cup my hands with my thumbs lightly touching my lips.

"I'm good.   Lou, two jobs lined up, should hear something tomorrow."

Lou turns his head, looks at me closely.   His eyes stop at the dirt around my neck.

"What's going on, Caleb? Tell me," Lou says, looking into my eyes.

"It's all good, really."   I hate lying to him.   "You just think about getting better."

I fiddle and pull the blanket up around his neck.

"Caleb... the police (cough)... they came to the diner last night. They said they wanted to talk to you... they wanted to talk to you about... Liz," Lou says in a whisper.

"I didn't do it, Lou. You know that's not me-"

"I know. I know who did. There's something else-" Lou glances nervously at the still curtain again. With an urgency he shirks his head for me to come closer to him.   "I've made a mistake. Caleb, I'm sorry..."

A nurse appears. How long was she standing there? The metal rings clank from her rough shove of the curtain.

"Mr. De'Marco? Time for your medicine."

Her uniform freshly creased straight off the rack.   Her blond streaky hair in a neat bun and stethoscope shining around her neck. Lou looks at her as the imposing force that she was. Lou doesn't finish his statement and doesn't feel comfortable speaking in front of her.

She snatches the covers down revealing his arm and places two fingers on his wrist taking his pulse. Her actions rough, but she smiles as if that covers it.

"Doesn't the machine do that?"

I gesture to the beeping machine showing his pulse. She didn't like that. I don't care.

"I trust the old way. Machines can be wrong."

I withdraw, remembering she will be the one caring for Lou when I leave. In that split second. She doesn't like me, and I don't like her. It's obvious. The old me and the new me doesn't mind clashing heads. I look around her and make eye contact with Lou while she changes Lou's saline solution bag. There's anxiety in his eyes. Why? The question forms in my eyes. Lou blinks his eyes, signaling to me. I got it.

"Thank you," I say to her.

Surprised, she looks at me. "For what?" she replies.

"For taking care of him. I'm a little on edge, you know. Will he be all right?" I ask her.

"Time will tell. So, who's this kind young man, Lou?"

Her smile looks rehearsed. She takes a pre-filled syringe and injects the contents into Lou's I.V. Lou immediately blinks slowly. Whatever she gave him affects him fast.

"I'm Jimmy, the neighbors' kid," I answer for Lou.

"My mom had a neighbors' kid like that. So sweet, but kids today aren't like that, are they? Well, nice to meet you, Jack."

She smiles, pulling off her blue latex gloves with a snap. She looks like a lioness that just swallowed her young.

"Jimmy."

"Sorry about that. Jimmy."

She's washes her hands in the small sink as if delaying leaving the room. Lou's speech is slurring.

"Like I was say-y-in, I'll be fine. Love you, k-kid."

He's blinking slowly. Something is not right.

"Lou?" I say, but he doesn't answer.

"Just a sedative. He needs his rest."

The nurse walks out of the room, closing the door behind her.

"Lou. Lou. Can you hear me?"

The heart monitor sounds an alarming long beep. The jagged lines once spiking showing his heartbeat falls flat. I hear many feet running toward the room. A medical team rushes in with a cart that bangs the door open. The nurse that was just here is not among them.

"CLEAR,"

My mouth falls open as all the color from the room fades. I drift out of the room. At least it feels that way. One of the staff leads me into the hall. In seconds, the defibrillator is engaged.

"CLEAR,"

Lou's body jolts, rises, falls.

"Again. CLEAR,"

It is violent. His chest rises slightly and falls.

"Calling it," says the doctor.

Lou is gone. I can't stay. I want to stay. But I can't. The doctor calls his time of death. I hear it from the hall. My breath comes back as they leave the room one by one. A nurse puts her hand on my shoulder. My back against the wall. A piece of me died.

"I'm sorry," the nurse says. "We did our best. He's gone."

"Where's the other nurse?" I ask her.

"Which nurse?"

"The blond one. She came in a minute ago! She gave him something!"

"I don't know... we're the only ones on the floor tonight-"

"-she said she was his nurse! She put medicine in his IV."

"I am his assigned nurse." She points to the wipe away board in his room with her name written on it and taps her plastic name badge hanging from her neck with her picture and name on it. "Mr. De'Marco wasn't getting any medicine by I.V. or injection. Pills only. It's an emotional time, son. Maybe, you thought-"

"-I'm not crazy!"

"Didn't say you were. Wait, you must mean Mrs. Harris, the head nurse. She comes in from time to time and administers medication if needed. If she felt he needed something, sleep aids, believe me, it was for the better. Mr. De'Marco was in much pain. Come with me, we have a family grief room. I'll get someone that can help you."

Leaving her standing there, I head for the stairwell. The whole hospital is spinning. That sinking feeling in the pit of my stomach hasn't risen yet. I want to run out of this trapped feeling. I don't feel the snow falling on my long sleeve cotton shirt. I don't feel the cold. I don't feel. Where do I go? What does it matter? I'm wandering. My legs are moving, just to be moving.

"Hey. Watch yourself!"

I bump into something and it yells at me. I know exactly where to go. Guaranteed to be open today too. I shove my fists into my jean pockets and walk as fast as I can. Visions of Lou laughing with me in his office flash in front of my face. I swat them away with anger and rage. Carless, I shove people out of my way as I pass them. Reckless. That's what I am. Reckless. It's enough. Everything is enough. It's now or never. If not, I will lose myself forever.

I tug the liquor store door. The metal cow bell hanging from it, rings. Tony looks up from behind the counter. He's making a good amount of sales tonight. The store has at least ten people stocking up for their little Christmas gatherings in toasty houses with sparkling lights.

"Hey, Caleb, didn't expect you today... what are you doing?" says Leo.

I grab an enormous bottle of whiskey and walk toward the door.

"Hey! You can't just take that!"

"Get off me, Leo-"

I snatch my arm away, but he's still holding onto my sleeve.

"No." I pull back.

Accidentally, my arm bumps a display and glass bottles smash at my feet. The shoppers gasp, and some idiot is filming me with his cell phone. I break loose from Leo's grasp and head for the guy with the cell phone.

"You want a picture! What? You never seen a homeless drunk before? Look at your father!"

I haul my left arm back, swing at him.

"Nice, jerk. Keep talking, you're gonna be famous," he says, ducking my swings still holding up his cell phone.

"I'll make you famous! Come here."

He runs, putting a display between us.

"You'll be all over the news... let me at him, Leo!"

Good! At least my aim is still dead-on. I throw a bottle. It hit him right in the head.

"I'm gonna sue you!" he says, dropping the cell phone. He's holding his head like a sap. Leo's got a good grip on one arm. He's stronger than he looks.

"Joke's on you, Jack!" I throw my arms open. "I got nothing to sue for."

Bustled out the door by Leo, I grab another. Laughing to tears, I free from his grip. He follows me onto the sidewalk.

"I'm leaving, I'm leaving."

"Caleb. What's going on?" asks Leo, with hands extended.

Looking over his destroyed displays and customers walking out shaking their heads. Lou would not be proud. Now I hurt Leo too. The wind just came out of me. I look at the bottle in my clutch.

"Sorry."

Leo will do what is necessary. I know his next move. I count on it. Tapping my pocket, I feel the idiot's wallet. The streets taught me one thing, how to pick a pocket. His wallet feels flat, but you never know. Guys like him have nice new crisp bills that stick together. It didn't take long. I got a few steps away and downed the bottle, shut my eyes and let the alcohol have full control. Flashes of riding in a worn-out police car, down a desolate dirt road replace the dark wet Manhattan sidewalk.

Meadows for as far as the eye could see. An arched rugged wooden gate, then the monastery. Tall wooden doors with black metal locks and hinges with two circle rings in the center on each side for doorknobs. A red-haired lady. The police car pulls up in front of the doors. I'm in the back. My teenage reflection is in the car window. One hand grips the police door handle tightly. The other holds my father's dog tags. I'm finished thinking in my dream. Let it roll. I'm in the monastery hall, being wrestled to the ground. Someone is trying to open my hand. My fist is clenched on my father's dog tags. I feel warm blood dripping down my wrist.

"Can't he just keep them?" says the Police Officer that drove me to the monastery. Determined, the Monk keeps trying to pry the dog tags from my sealed fist.

"Against policy," replies the Monk.

He won. In my imagination, the tags fall from my cut hand. I open my hand and snow gently touches my bloody palm. Eager to see the dog tags, I turn my head but see a bloody disappointment. The broken liquor bottle falls from my palm. Something broke inside. I can't fix it. Alcohol can't fix it either. I hear myself groan uncontrollably, bitterly, guttural. I don't exist. I'm invisible. I matter to no one.

What will happen when the sun comes up? Will I dig in the garbage? Run from the police? No. I can't do that again. It is time. It is now or never. I'm losing myself. My past is clouding my present and the line is so blurred I can't see it anymore. Christmas night traffic zips past. I step off the curb and face the traffic. I probably won't feel it. Not for long, anyway. A few more steps. There. Headlights. A taxi. The one I have been waiting for. I tilt my head upward and shut my eyes. Everything goes black. Finally, it is over.

CHAPTER SEVEN

Jason Jones

Hotel Room, New York

I can't help but pace. My glasses are sliding, and I instinctively flick them into place right above the nose. I never went for those thin flimsy eye glass frames. I favor the durability of thick black ones. What is that sound? Oh, yes, Sam is on the phone in my hand. Deep breath.

"Jason? Are you listening to me?" Sort of. "Director White wants you back in D.C. by morning."

"Why?" I ask.

That is curious. It makes me stop pacing the floor. I still have my suit jacket on. I can hear her chewing.

"You weren't answering your phone, so she called me. She hates me. I can feel it. She didn't tell me anything except that," says Sam.

"It's in your mind, Sam. Who wouldn't like lovable-little you?" I say, seeing her smiling in my mind.

"Where were you? How much coffee have you had?" she asks.

I wish she would stop chewing. I go through my bag and pull out that cheap burner phone I used earlier and check for calls.

"Lost count," I reply, still pacing the floor.

"The police sent the report here," she says.

I stop pacing and sit on the foot of the bed facing the television that is playing the news.

"What does it say?" I ask. Now, she has my full attention.

"What is the likelihood? They searched for Caleb Promise," she says.

I inhale.

"And?"

"Inconclusive."

I exhale.

"So, he has the same last name of the Officer that served with Wilkes. I am an optimist, but there is no record of him, we don't even know if Officer Promise's child was a boy, and not a girl. Did the orphanage mess up?" she asks.

"No, the orphanage had a fire that burned everything just months after this kid turned eighteen, along with every monk that worked there. They died trying to get all the orphans out."

That's the story I had to feed Sam.

"But his employer, wouldn't he have a file on this guy?" Sam asks.

"Nothing. I even checked the diner he worked at. He lived in a dive where no one kept records, for obvious reasons."

"Let me guess, no friends either."

"Yes."

She's smart. That's why I hired her. Caleb is on the street, a ghost. I can feel her thinking while picking over her second serving of Christmas dinner.

"I want every shelter searched in the NY metro area. They sign in. With this storm, he won't be on the streets. He's wanted for murder, I highly doubt he'll go anywhere that may ask for I.D.," I tell her.

"No problem. But you know the Police have probably already done that. It may just be a waste of time."

I need time right now. She'll understand later.

"We have to try," I reply. "Wilkes is on a flight to Brazil. Something is brewing. I can feel it."

"Jason, how does the murder of Elizabeth Harvard tie to the murder of Officer Promise and his wife? I mean, accident. The old Police report states a drunk driver hit them in a rainstorm. They went off a bridge into an embankment and died from their injuries," Sam says clearly having read the file.

Curious, I never used the word 'murder' when referring to Officer Promise's death.

"Who autopsied the bodies?" I ask her, already knowing the answer.

"Locals? I'm guessing."

"Exactly. Locals from a small town that can't afford to lose residents for fear some murderer is on a spree. Request that search for me. As soon as you're done, spend some time with your family."

"Will do. Jason, do yourself a favor in the future, don't ride the subway based on the lyrics of a rap song."

"It worked, didn't it?"

I hear her laugh and then the click of her hanging up. Why did she want him fired? Why would they kill her for wanting him fired? Where are you, Caleb? I look at the little black phone. The hard wind slams snow into my window. Coffee. I need more coffee.

CHAPTER EIGHT

Caleb Promise

Where am I? A lulling rumbling. I can't see, but I can hear muffled voices as if I'm under water. I'm floating on my back, warm and cozy. I can't remember the last time I felt warm. No pain. No hunger or cravings. All past anguishes are gone. For once, I don't have a single care. I am not afraid. Wherever I am, I don't feel like anything bad will happen. My body feels renewed. It is just as I expected heaven would be. I didn't think I'd make it here, though. I'm rising, I can tell. An effortless lifting sensation. I must be going to see God now. I didn't pay much attention in Sunday school. Now, I wish I did. I have a consciousness. I like it here.

The rising stops. More mumbles and jumbles of faint voices. They are comforting because I know I'm not alone. Everything is soft. The floating continues, then comes to an abrupt stop, a slight jostle. Not bad. A hand rests gently on my shoulder, a murmur of words, and a warmth sweeps through me. I'm falling into deep sleep. I let it take over.

"Good Morning."

A male voice. God? I need to repent. That much I know.

"I'm sorry," I say.

"What?" he replies.

I still can't see. The veil seems to have lifted from my ears and every sound is sharp and concise. Maybe they're bringing me in slowly, letting me work in little by little. That's kind. A gentle wipe over one eye. A soft cloth and caring, slow touch.

"Good morning," the voice says again, a little louder.

"You'll be here all day with that."

A harsh female voice?

(BAM, BAM, BAM!)

"RISE AND SHINE!" she yells.

I jump from the shock of it. What is going on? I need to see. One eye works. I look around. Where am I? Is this heaven? I force myself to open the eye that works. No! A hospital. I.V. taped to my forearm, something clamped onto my pointer finger and a beeping machine on a poll over my head. Pain killers. No wonder I feel so good. Am I glad to be alive? I don't know yet. It's just like the orphanage, but worse. There is a television mounted on the wall directly in front of the bed. A bed, that's what I was on. A rolling hospital bed being rolled into the room. On the news, the grand retirement banquet for defense Secretary Wilkes. The reporter's words typed in close caption across the bottom of the screen. This nurse's voice is loud.

"Doc, you got to call him out from under that white lighting. Need anything else?"

She pulls on her gloves and adjusts her scarf around her neck.

"No thank you, nurse," says the soft-spoken middle-aged doctor. "No one knows what you're talking about half the time. You are aware of that?"

The doctor chuckles. The nurse smacks the wall one last time, winks her eye, adjusts her purse strap on her topcoat and leaves. She's noisy. Everything about her is noisy, even her quiet nursing shoes squeak. I can only lift one hand. Handcuffs. I just shut my eye wishing I were dead. I am going to prison. I want the euphoria back. The floating, the muffled sounds. Life was better that way.

"Good Morning... Austin, is it?" the doctor asks, flipping virtual pages on his chart on the tablet.

Austin? The wallet. I'm so glad I'm a thief.

"Can you hear me? You were injured in a car accident. A car hit you. Austin, you are in Mt. Sinai Hospital and I am Dr. Gordon. Do you understand what I'm saying?"

I nod but keep my eyes shut.

"Good. It's a miracle you are alive. One eye is swollen shut, you had salve on the other so if that feels funny, that's all it is. Can you move your legs for me?"

I turn to the window. I don't want people. Not now. Never.

"Okay, can you lift your right arm for me? Mr. Austin Douglas, that's your name, isn't it?"

"Yes." I say feeling sweat bead on my forehead.

"We ran a battery of tests on you last night and aside from some bruises and a slight concussion, you are fine. It's a miracle really. If you saw what you looked like when they brought you in, you would understand. Tell me, what happened?"

I feel him sit on the foot of the bed. Moving in for the kill. I don't want to be bothered.

"Sir. This is how it works. If you don't cooperate with me, they will send in the house psychologist. He'll ask you the same questions I'm asking you now. If you don't respond to him, they will send in the psychiatrist who will gladly give you an injection that will have you staring into space, wetting your own pants for about three days. Now, you are not injured enough to take up this bed much longer so by the time I walk out of this room the ball will begin rolling. Do you understand?"

A nod.

"Now we're getting somewhere. Did you step in front of that taxi on purpose?"

I shake my head 'no' slowly knowing that yes will cost me a trip to the psych ward.

"All right. That's good for now. Your breakfast should come in soon. Please eat. Rest. The day nurse will bring in your pain medication. It'll make you comfortable. We will also give you something to help you sleep."

I drift back to the television. I recognise that scene. It's the bridge. The caption reads...

"BREAKING NEWS... A call to the N.Y.P.D. of shots fired led to the discovery of the body of a man just beneath this bridge. A location well known for its homeless presence. Police urge anyone with information to call the precinct. The man, Caucasian, late forties was gunned down in what the police are calling a professional hit. The man was shot once in the head at close range."

Investigators are all over the scene. It looks familiar. They roll the body past the camera. A sheet covers the body, but the arm falls out from beneath the sheet. That's my jacket. The one the guy stole from me. The one Judy gave me. I didn't kill him. Who did? Oh, the doctor is still talking.

"... and I'll send the nurse to get the handcuff off. My apologies but you were very intoxicated when we brought you in. You tried to bite an orderly. The handcuff was for your own protection. Your belongings are in that cabinet. Any question?"

I exhale. No prison. I close my eye. God is real.

"No."

I just want to look at the television. Nothing stops in this City. Die or not.

"Oh, one more thing, I got one contact out, but the other must still be in the other eye. When the swelling goes down, I will help you get it out," the doctor says as he taps the door post twice and walks out of the room. I feel adrenaline pump through my body so strong it supersedes my pain killers. My breathing increases... I don't wear contacts.

CHAPTER NINE

Caleb Promise

I can smell a new beginning on the horizon. I wasn't crazy and didn't imagine it. Something happened to me, but what? I was abducted and carefully replaced like a fine piece of China in a shop. I've heard people complain about hospital beds not being comfortable. This is my first time and I have no complaints. A great improvement to my old bed. I feel the reason to keep going slipping back into my veins.

For a while, it felt as if everything was in vain. I press the head incline button on the bed. That's better, sitting up. I hate the sound of the handcuffs clanking. I want to get to the bathroom. Two knocks on the door.

"Breakfast."

Purposely, I reach for the tray with the handcuffed hand. The expression on the servers' face was hilarious.

"Breakfast..."
He is staring at me and then the handcuffs as if fascinated.

"Triple murder," I say to him. He puts down the tray and leaves as fast as possible.

Precisely what I wanted.

"Mr. Douglas?"

A nurse walks in dangling some keys.

"Yes," I reply. I'm getting used to the name.

"Your freedom draws nigh." She dangles the handcuff keys in the air.

"Thanks."

I rub my wrist.

"And, your medication. This will help with pain, and help you sleep."

I want to stay awake. Finally, I want to be clear minded. I need to stop her before she pushes the plunger into the I.V.

"UMM, can you...not?" Grabbing her arm. I see her startled response. "Sorry." I lift my hand.

"We don't go in for that stuff here. Do I need to restrain you or are we clear?" asks the nurse.

"No, I'm good. It's just I have to use the bathroom."

"Oh."

She drops her Defenses. The hospital cell phone rings in her pocket and she answers it.

"Yes? Okay, I'll be right there."

I scoot to a seated position and aches return like a bad dream.

"I'll be right back. Remember, call don't fall. Don't move." She pushes the plunger into the I. V. nipple. "This stuff makes you feel wonky. Food helps. Eat. I will be right back."

The pain killers act fast. Oh, that's great. Immediately the pain leaves but I am feeling a little foggy. The more I sit up, the more the room spins. My legs feel numb. Rest would be the best thing, but I don't want to sleep. I need to see. I need to know for certain I'm not crazy. If the contact is in my eye, they abducted me. They threw me into a van and put me back into my room as if nothing happened. If that is the case, I truly have something to live for. All these years weren't for nothing.

I can't see clearly. It's annoying. Wiping the eye helps a little. The room is clearer but not perfect. My hands and knuckles have minor cuts and bruises. There's a gauze bandage around my right wrist. After not eating in days, the food smells wonderful. I'm glad no one was in the room. I scoop the soft scrambled eggs with my fingers and shove it into my mouth and follow with the roll. Runny eggs and oatmeal. A treat.

Out of the bed, I grab the I.V. pole and stand. If I go slowly, I can make it to the bathroom. I shuffle along. Awkward droopy hospital socks sag around my ankles but keep me from sliding. The wheels on the tall steel pole holding my I.V. is awkward to maneuver and bumps something on the way to the bathroom just a few feet away. Another hospital bed with a man in it is just behind the pale curtain. He's asleep. Snoring. He won't mind that I borrow his shaving kit. I slip it under my arm and scoot into the bathroom and lock the door behind me.

It's clean. A toilet, sink and a tall laundry basket. There's a shower. Who is that in the mirror? Even with my vision blurred, I see I'm a hairy mess. My eye is swollen shut. Red and bruised on the lid. Cold water. That should help the swelling a bit. I need to check.

I must know if there is a contact in this eye to be sure that the doctor didn't make a mistake. I dry my face. The cold water reduced the swelling of the eye somewhat, but not enough to open it. Still clumsy, my hand knocks the razor off the pedestal sink.

I lean in toward the mirror and painfully pry my eyelids apart using my two forefingers. Almost there, I lose my balance. I stop, catch myself on the wall and sink. I try again. Won't stop this time. I feel the tips of my fingers graze my eyeball. There, I can see a clear film covering the eyeball. I sweep across my eyeball and a thin contact lens clings to my dry finger.

Suddenly, that night flashes. Being taken. The black hood put on my head. The pinch on my neck. Being tossed around in a vehicle. My room with all things placed perfectly. It wasn't a dream. It wasn't my imagination. It happened.

The lens on my finger is evidence. I have something worth taking. Me. Next question, what did they accomplish? My vision was the same in my left eye, so the contact didn't have any altering prescription. It was skin-thin. It feels like nothing at all but has a swirling imprinted image in it. I need to have it examined by an expert.

It may not be wise to cut my hair and beard with blurred vision and shaking hands, but I can't wear it anymore. Although my hands are shaking, I pick the straight razor up and start. Hair first.

Finally finished, stubbly hair stands only a few inches on the top of my head. My hair and beard is on the floor around my socked feet. I rinse and feel the touch of the towel on my chin and head for the first time in months. I see my true self peeking through the clouds.It's me. Finally, me again. I look like my dad in an old picture he had on his desk. A bang on the door.

"I know you didn't go to that bathroom without help. Mr. Douglas? Are you all right in there? Hello?"

The nurse. I shove the razor and things into the leather bag.

"I will emergency-enter this bathroom in three, two-"

"I'm good. Be out in a minute."

I use a towel to scoop the hair up as much as possible anyway and drop the towel in the laundry bin. No. The contact falls down the drain as I rinse hair off my hands.

"That's it. I'm restraining you again. ROB!" she calls.

"I'm here." I unlock the door.

I open the door still holding the pole. She looks like she sees a ghost when I open the door. She finds her voice.

"Mr. Douglas, you-"

"I - I just couldn't let you see me like that again. You don't need Rob."

I force a smile. I haven't smiled in... I don't know when I smiled last. She smiles at me. Can't remember the last time that happened either.

"All right, Casanova. Back into bed right now. You looked like a sixty-year-old bum when you came in. Now, you just look like a twenty-five-year-old bum."

"Thanks."

"And don't try batting that one eye at me." she jokes.

I couldn't help but want to laugh at that. I feel better. Lighter, now that the weight of the hair is gone. Knowing that I'm not nuts helps.

"Don't quit your day job," I say to her.

She laughs. I can't remember the last time I made someone laugh. She looks like a person you want to hug. Like someone's aunt.

"What's going on here, Joan? You need help?"

This must be Rob. I'm bigger than Rob. She's bigger than Rob.

"I'm fine. I got it."

"They need you next door."

Rob leaves and a man in scrubs appears in the door with a clip board in hand.

"Registrar?" Joan asks.

"Yep, just need a signature." Says the man.

"Quick, okay, I need him asleep, yesterday."

She pulls the covers up to my waist and lovingly tussles my spiky hair. "I'll be back." Joan leaves the room, but a group of student nurses gather right outside the door of my room in the hallway.

The registrar is staring at me. A locked stare. He isn't smiling at all. He looks nervous. I know I'm a mess but get a hold of yourself, man. He flips the page up on the clip board but never breaks eye contact.

"Sir, sign here, please."

His voice is strangely serious for such a simple thing. His goatee is perfectly trimmed. But he's got a tan. It's the middle of winter. 'C-a'...I crumple the paper. I started to write Caleb, but I scratch it out fast and look to see if he noticed. He didn't, he's still staring at my face. "A. Douglas".

"Here."

I turn the board back to him.

"One more spot."

He lifts the page, turns the clipboard to me and puts his finger on a sticky note with three bold letters written in black thick marker.

"Sign here."

I look down at the spot he is pointing to.

"RUN,"

I look him straight in the eyes. He crumples the note, pushes a small vial into my hand and closes it. Adrenaline rushes through me. My heartbeat accelerates. He drops the clip board into the garbage can beside the door. Takes one step out, turns to me and says another three-letter word that raises me from the bed.

"Now."

Standing in my doorway, his back to me, he raises the back of his scrub shirt. The elevator dings. He pulls a pistol out of the small of his back. I hear screams. Screams of terror.

Brakes squeal outside. Four or five screeches. I rip the I.V. out of my arm. I look at my clothes soaking wet and muddy in the clear plastic bag at the foot of the bed. No way.

I open the cabinet of the guy next to me and he's got khakis and a red and blue sweater hanging in it. I pull them on without thinking. They are too short. I pull off the slouchy hospital socks and try to shove my size eleven and a half feet into the shoes. They don't fit at all. Not even in desperation. The screams are getting louder. Closer.

He's not in the doorway anymore. He's crouched in front of the nurse's station. The elevator is on the other side. I can hear the room doors closing. Lock down protocol.

It's my nurse. She shuts my door, but it only closes half-way when the elevator doors open. She walks toward it trying to intercept whoever is on it. A large muscular man steps out of the elevator with three other men in black military gear and looks directly at her. His gun is in his hand. She takes a few steps backward. This is not the Police.

"Where is Caleb Promise?"

I put my back to the wall beside the door to hear.

"There is no patient by the name Caleb Promise here."

She's telling her truth. I am listed as Austin Douglas.

"Are you sure? No one that looks like this."
He holds up a photograph. The old me. Beard and all. She swallows. She knows. Only she knows. Her and the small man crouched behind the desk. Will she give me away? What will she say? I couldn't blame her if she did. She owes me nothing.

"No. You can check the records if you like."

Shaking, looking at his gun.

"You wouldn't be lying to me, would you? The orderly downstairs said someone that looks just like this bit him. He told me, and I believe him, that this person," he holds the photo directly up to her eyes, " came up here. Look again and take your time."

He says it with a strange calm. Almost soothing.

"I haven't seen this man."

He puts his hand on her shoulder.

"All right. Thank you."

He shoots her in the forehead. Her body shudders, then drops. He looks at my open door and starts walking toward it.

A man running across the hall catches his eye. He has a full beard and long hair. As I... had. He shoots him in the leg and approaches the groaning man. The armed small man crouched behind the nurse's station waves me out of the room. I don't think about it. My feet just start running down the hall, barefoot toward the sign "STAIRS".

A few feet away, but the gunfire is going down the hall. A door. The doctors' lounge. I grab a lab coat and pull it on. No shoes. I have to get to the steps. I open the door slowly, see the door for the stairs, I run for it. My hand is on the doorknob then, it opens and a man in black tactical gear steps out. If he sees my face, he'll know I'm a patient. Quickly, I hunker on the floor in the hall. Put my hands on my left hand on the back of my head. My head is spinning, vision blurred and can't see well. The vial is still in my right hand.

"Why not? I've drunk worse."

I flip off the cap with my thumb and discreetly drink it. It's bitter. Immediately, the fog lifts and all pain my pain vanishes. I can feel my swollen eye tingle. The eye is still swollen, but the vision in the open eye is perfectly clear. I feel no pain and no drowsiness.

"Wow. UP!" I say to myself.

He will shoot me.

"Please! I'm a doctor... I'm just a doctor."

"Get out of here!" he yells.

I turn to avoid him seeing my face. He waves me on to pass by. I push the stairwell door open and feel his hand grab my shoulder.

"Hey!" He says spinning me around.

He's looking down at my bare feet. The gun is rising toward my chest. I grab it. He's strong. It fires, aiming upward. I hear two shots. He goes limp and falls. He's hit from behind. The registrar shot him.

"GO." He yells to me.

Shots fire toward him. I run down the stairs and I hear thuds and groans. Was he hit? The stairwell is packed with people running downstairs. A gunman is coming up the stairwell. His pistol lowered. People are rushing down the stairwell past him without even noticing. He's in street clothes, ambling. He holds his cell phone up to his face, looking at every man as they pass him. Just three steps and he will see me.

We are face to face. His eyes, flat black like shark eyes. Emotionless, searching. A hint of characteristic verifying that I am his target. His eyes dart across my face. It is grotesquely swollen. He pushes past me roughly. I turn around to see his cell phone screen. It's me. Full beard and long hair. A grainy photo.

Trying to navigate with only one eye, I am handicapped and vulnerable. Several other men with that same dead glare in their eyes, each one glancing at a cell phone, occasionally stop men, then shoves them along. Which one is the experienced hunter able to see past missing hair and a swollen eye?

The fire alarm is blaring. Finally, "EMERGENCY ROOM" in big bold letters and bright red letters. I drop the physician's coat. Sneakers. Perfect. Left beside a patient's bed. At the foot of a bed and a three-quarter length wool coat. I slip them on. Behind me, I hear a man come out of the patient bathroom.

"My shoes! You must be kidding me?" He says.

I need to get out of here. People crying in panic push their way out the door, then cross the street standing against the half stone wall that surrounds the park looking for loved ones. I go with the flow of the crowd right out of the Emergency Room doors to the sidewalk.

Several black sport utility vehicles dot the perimeter of the building. They are new and judging from their immaculate appearance; they have been kept in a garage. The wailing police sirens in route join the people standing in the worst blizzard New York ever knew.

My eye is still tingling. I can open it half-way. Enough to see the crowd in front of me rush out of the Emergency Room doors in total panic. Some barefoot, sliding on the icy ground wrapped in blankets, crying, banging on the doors of nearby stores that are closed for Christmas. That didn't stop them. Glass breaks. They rush into a closed store, ignoring its blaring alarm.

I go for what is familiar. I head straight for the Central Park wall across the street. There is no opening. I jump the wall. I don't know what was in that vial, but I feel great. My feet land on the ground. I lift my foot to run. I'm stuck.

I entangle my dangling shoelace in a bush behind the stone wall. I try to kick it loose. Nothing. I bend, snatch the lace from the branch and shove the lace in the shoe's side. A blow. I feel myself flipped upside down and land on my side in a pile of snow. This was not a hit from a person. It was a force.

An explosion. My ears are ringing. I roll to my knees. Another explosion knocks me to the ground again. I cover my head. Something tells me this isn't over. Another, then another. I count them. Six blasts, all equally powerful. Then, an eerie silence.

My ears are ringing. The bush that my shoelace was caught in is black and charred. I get to my knees. Rub my eyes. I open them and see a woman's hands gripping the wall as if she is trying to climb over it. Her Christmas red nail polish chipped and scratched. Her hands splattered with blood. I stand to look over the wall to help her stand. I lean over the hands and look down. The runny eggs swell in my throat and I vomit.

Half of her is not there. It mangled her. Her torn torso and twisted legs shoved against the wall.

This can't be happening. I stagger backwards. The building is smoking. Shattered glass and metal rain from the neighboring buildings.

My heart pounding in my chest. This can't all be about me. I can't hear anything except a loud ringing. The hospital has smoke billowing out of a gaping hole in the side of it. The

Emergency Room entrance is destroyed, and debris is littered all over the street. Three white vans emerge from an underground parking garage next to the hospital and drive in line.

I know I must get out of here. I cover my right eye.   The biting cold stings it and I still don't know where I will go. As my hearing returns, it sounds like a war zone behind me. Car alarm, fire alarms, sirens and fire truck horns in the distance get louder as the ringing in my ears subsides. I need to get far away. I can't seem to get away from this park. The further I run, the quieter it gets.   There are people drifting toward the site, mouths wide open. I must be a sight.

"Caleb? Is that you?"   says a familiar female voice. "Whoa- what happened to you? Are you all right?"

Rachel? What is she doing here, now? My father's words are echoing in my head. 'Don't trust anyone.'

"What are you doing here?" I ask.

"I was shopping," she lifts shopping bags, "and saw the explosion and thought someone might need help. I'm so glad I found you." She hugs me.

I may take her up on her offer. I have nowhere to go. But wait. How in the world could she recognize me like this?   I barely recognize myself.

"My car is right there. We can go to my place."

She's leading me by the arm. I stop walking.

"How did you know it was me?"

"What? Caleb, I would know you anywhere. Are you kidding me? It's freezing. I'll make us that spaghetti dinner. Come on."

She threads her arm through mine and starts walking again.

"I'm okay. Really. Thanks a lot though." I pause.

I let go of her arm and create some distance between us.

"Caleb, why are you acting this way? You're injured, you're not thinking straight." Her tone is firmer and so is her stance. "I'm just trying to help."

"I know. Thanks, but no thanks."

She drops her head to the right as if she were looking at something, but her lips move, ever so slightly. She's talking to someone. In my peripheral vision, I see the two white vans that pulled out of the underground parking lot turn in our direction. As they turn through the smoke, I see a flower logo with Rachel's flower shop "Big Blooms" on the side of it.

"It's better if you come, peacefully."

She steps toward me. What? Confirmed. The sun hits her eyes. Trust no one. That's what dad always said, and he was right. She has a contact lens in her eye, and it has the same pattern in it as the one I pulled out of my eye. I let my expression reveal what I have learned. She pulls out a gun.

A helicopter circles above. For once, I want to see the words Police on the side of that helicopter. It's not. In the passenger seat, the tall man in black. If I'm right, I won't even have to take care of her. Let's see.

I turn to run into the tree line. I feel Rachel put her aim on my back. The man in the chopper draws. He aims. A shot. I'm not hit. I turn and watch as Rachel's body hits the stiff snow with a thud. Her blood floods over the snow. I was right. They want me alive. I must make it to the tree line to get any kind of chance. My legs. No, not now. They are feeling weak again.

A screech from behind. The three white vans. These sneakers are too big. I can't keep running at this pace. Great. I think stuff is wearing off. An opening in the stone wall, I need to get to it.

The van driver looks at me and looks at the opening in the stone Central Park wall. It speeds up. The helicopter is landing. No!

The tall man gets out with a gun to my rear left and the van is approaching to my right. My legs feel weak and the wind from the chopper is pushing me. The floor feels like it's moving and the aches from the accident have returned as quickly as they disappeared after drinking that stuff.

I accept it. I can't run anymore. They've got me. There it is. The opening of the path. I stop. A tree, good. I can steady myself. The white vans will turn into the park and will be right in front of me. I close my eyes and rest my head on the tree. This is it.

"GET IN," yells a familiar voice.

I open my eyes. The voice is familiar. A gray car pulls in front of the white vans and blocks them. It screeches to a stop in front of me. Who is it? I think I'm passing out. It's the guy. The guy in the scrubs.

CHAPTER TEN

Things have slowed. Something whizzes past me. There's a continuous clanking. Bullets. Hitting the trunk of the gray car. I fight to stay awake forcing my eyes to open. Things are moving in slow motion. The guy in the scrubs waving, ducking the bullets.

"Caleb! Get in!"

How does he know my name? In the hospital, I was Mr. Douglas.

My body obeys before my mind realizes it. I hear the snow crunching beneath my feet. But my sneakers are slipping. The guy reaches back and pushes the back door of the car wide open. I lunge into the back seat. He hits the gas and the force slams the door shut. The tall man runs toward the chopper.

"Can you shoot?" he asks, waving a gun at me.

My hands are trembling. Laying on my side in the seat, I shake my head 'no'. The truth is, I can shoot. I can't help but hear 'trust no one' in the back of my mind. Aside from the fact that I don't think I can steady my hands enough to shoot, this will tell me a great deal about this man.

I keep my eyes open long enough to see him pull an AK47 out of the front seat, prop it against his shoulder, point it out the window, steady the car and shoot at the chopper's gas tank.

Three shots, the bullets bury themselves into its metal with a clunk. The third shot and it explodes. Throws the tall guy backwards to the ground, the other man slumped out of the helicopter aflame. Plumes of smoke block the van's view. I learned what I needed to. He has been trained. He's not even breathing hard. This man has done this before. The Jacqueline Kennedy Reservoir directly in front of us. The van is on our heels. Fragments of the helicopter blades lodge into nearby trees.

"Hang on! This will be close!" he yells at me.

I can't sit up, but I turn facing the back of the seat and grab the seatbelt strap. The vans speed up in pursuit. He makes a hard-right turn, skimming the perimeter of the reservoir. The van clears the smoke of the explosion. At the tip of the reservoir, he hit the brakes and yanks the steering wheel right. Our rear tire dips into the reservoir, then out again. Behind us, the screech of brakes. The van stops just at the tip of the freezing water. Then a bang.

The second van plows into his back, sending both vans into the freezing lake. The driver puts the AK47 on the passenger seat and reduces speed. Two thumps over speed bumps and we exit the park, heading toward the highway.

He makes a phone call and puts it on speaker. The sound of the phone ringing reminds me of a collectible my mother used in her office. I picture a heavy black classic Crosley Kettle telephone ringing loudly. He pulls on a baseball cap. Someone answers the phone but doesn't speak.

"Sono io." says the driver.

"Che cosa? English, Vinnie." says the man who answered the phone.

"Moving forward," says the driver, hanging up the phone.

Italian.

"Hey, are you alive?" says the driver, Vinnie.

"Yeah," I respond.

He looks at me through the rear-view mirror. He has a friendly face, young; and is probably just a little older than me.

"In the bag, by your feet. Small jar. Put it on your eye, now."

I feel around in the bag and find the small empty jar. It looks empty. I can't steady my hands to open it. I sit up, leaning on my elbow.

"Who are you?" I ask.

"Vincenzo, but my friends call me Vinnie."

"Vin, I think I'm going to die in your backseat. I'm not picky. Drop me anywhere."

He laughs. He must be from New York.

"Put the stuff on your eye."

I look at the jar, center myself in the seat, and look at him through the rear-view mirror. He knows what I'm thinking.

"Gotta trust someone, Caleb. Why not me?"

I scoop out some clear gel and smear it on my eye. A tingling sensation, a pinching sensation, and then heat. I put my right hand on my eye and feel the swelling going down. All the way down. A cool sensation and my eye is back to normal. I wipe away the residue. My vision perfectly clear.

"I need you at full capacity."

"I should put this all over my body."

Vin chuckles again. Although he is talking to me, he is alert. He's checking his rear-view mirrors, his three o'clock and nine o'clock. This man has been trained and trained well. My father used to do the same maneuver in new settings.

"No. You're in detox."

"Vin, ... what..."

"We don't have time.I know you have questions, Caleb-"

"How do you know my name? And why-"

"I told you we don't have time. I'm here to help you."

"I'm just a bus-boy!"

"By now, you know that I know you are more than that." He makes eye contact through the rearview mirror. "You sped it up."

"Sped WHAT up?"

Several police cars pass us. Then, a few black Sport Utility Vehicles that look just like the ones at the hospital. Vin turns his face discreetly away from the oncoming traffic and turns right into a small street.

"We need another ride," says Vin.

We pull into an underground parking garage. Finally. Just stopping for a moment is a relief. Vin turns around in the seat and looks directly at me.

"Can you steal a Can you steal a Porsche?" I ask.

"Funny. Thought we'd never find you."

"We? Nothing you're saying makes sense. How did this stuff work? Where did you get it?"

"You don't have to do that," says Vin.

"Do what?" I ask.

"Act like you have no clue." He says.

"Although I have no clue about what you're talking about?" I say, closing my eyes.

I'm not admitting anything until I know I can trust him. Saving my life's not enough. A clever crook would do that.

Vin smiles. He smiles as if he knows me. I don't like that because I don't know him.

"Let's go. Bring the bag."

He opens another car with a key. We get inside. I get into the front seat. Vin starts it. The doors lock automatically. The windows are tinted.

"Seatbelt," says Vin.

I look at him. He is serious. I buckle my seatbelt.

"Sorry about this." He says.

"Sorry about what?"

Vin has his left hand tucked under his right forearm. I look down and there is a small gun poke out. He shoots me. Things are fade fast...again.

My nose tells me I'm not in the dingy car. A blaring headache is usually waiting when I open my eyes. I'll turn. A squeak? Am I in bed? Was this a dream? You've got to be kidding. Will I wake up to find myself in my room? Is my jacket thrown over the chair and my keys in the night table drawer beside the cheap aspirin? Wait. Even with my eyes closed I know something is definitely different.

No pain. No neighbors are screaming at each other. If all this wasn't real, I'm checking myself into the closest psych ward. It's quiet. Very quiet. Now I know that I'm not in Manhattan.

I open my eyes. The walls are rustic, and the paint is deep mustard. There's a small oval antique mirror hanging on the wall. I look at my hands. Steady. Something's odd. Not a single scratch or scrape. My badly bruised knuckles are perfectly healed. My hands are steady, no tremors or withdrawal. I've seen nothing like this. I feel new.

Exposed natural stone walls, Terra-cotta floors and a rectangular window over my head. The window opens vertically by an old-fashioned crank, confirming my thoughts. A tapestry hangs on the wall beside the mirror with an embroidered scene in deep earth tones perfectly matching the walls. Someone's coming. I hear footsteps approaching the rustic wood door with black bindings. The door opens.

"You're up," says Vin.

He's relaxed. Blue jeans and a pullover.

"You shot me."

"A tranquilizer."

I look down at my clothes. I am in matching pajamas, something I have never worn. They feel soft and good.

"Did you...?" I ask, looking at the clothes.

"No. I would rather save your life than dress you." He hands me a glass. "Water."

Vin sits in a rustic single chair across from the bed as if they made it for him. Reluctantly, I take it. Again, 'trust no one'. But I trust Vin. There is something real about him. He has a small scar above his right eye. He scratches at it. It's the second time he touched it.

"What's in here? Cyanide?"

"If I wanted you dead, I'd have just left you there."

Very true. I drink the glass of water.

"A tranquilizer? Why?"

"The process works," gesturing to my face and hands that are healed, "but hurts, a lot. You're better off unconscious while it runs its course. You are less likely to bite through your tongue."

"I want to know everything. Now."

Vin crosses his legs.

"Calma."

He crosses his ankle over his knee.
"Who do you work for?"

"Work, no. I'm here because I want to be. Let's just say, I protect a scientist that your father trusted... with your life."

I sit up straight, my jaw drops. I have heard no one utter anything about my parents... ever.

"My father. Did you know him?"

He can't speak fast enough. I want to hear more, everything all at once. I'm sitting with someone who can validate a piece of my life and possibly give me the answers they promised me would one day unfold. I'm eager to hear, but afraid of what I will learn. I don't think Vin would hold back information from me. He's looking at me as if he were waiting to see me for a long time. Funny, he's antsy. He was calm under the pressure of being chased and shot at. Here, no fear no threat, but he bounces his leg and moves in his seat as if unsettled. I am as relaxed as a child in his element waiting for the climax of a good story.

"No," with a chuckle, "how old do you think I am?" Vin says tapping his heel on the floor. "Your father is Officer Joshua Promise, of the United States Army, Special Forces. He possessed top secret data. The accident that killed your father, your parents, Caleb... was no accident. There was no drunk driver."

Finally. Confirmation to one question. My chin stays low, but I can feel my eyes rise. Revenge took a seat in my heart. Vin continues.

"The gents, the ones trying to kill you," his tone hardens, "they work for the man that ordered the kill on your parents."

"Who is he?" I sit up taller.

I can feel the muscles in my jaws flex as I bite down repeatedly. My fists form without me even thinking about it.

"I know you're angry..."

Vin uncrosses his legs and leans forward resting his elbows on his knees.

"WHO IS HE?"

"You will find out soon, but not from me. From the scientist your father trusted. He's been watching out for you since you left the orphanage. Like an angel looking over your shoulder. You got evicted, and well, he lost you. He didn't know where you were. But he never gave up looking. You're safe here. He wants to help you, Caleb."

I can hear the echo in my head. Trust no one.

"Why, what's in it for him?"

"He will answer the rest of your questions. A piece of advice: think, Caleb, don't feel, think. If you want to stop this man, move with your head, not your heart."

His words, logical. It was as if someone took a scalpel and cut to the source of my pain. I turn away from him and wipe my eyes with my sleeve. Warm linen. I haven't worn pajamas in years.

"Come with me. Stand slowly."

The clothes slip into place as I move. They are like excellent quality. I don't use fabric softener. Denim jeans and cotton long sleeve shirts are my favorite. I couldn't afford these clothes and they feel too soft for me. I roll my shoulders feeling awkward in them. The floor is cool.

"Put those on." He says.

Slippers. They are leather bottom with wool lining.

"I'm no woman."

Vin laughs. "Then be a man. Catch pneumonia. These stone floors are freezing."

He doesn't know what freezing is. He walks ahead of me. They look comfortable. I step in them. They do feel good. Very different from value-store socks. I match from head to toe. Odd. Vin opens the tall wooden door with a screech and steps aside for me to go first. The smell of fresh spaghetti sauce wafts in our faces. This place smells like a home and memories are gushing from this rustic roost.

A short corridor with the country-worn hall table. An old dial-up phone sits on the table beside a clear vase of fresh-cut flowers. At the other end of the corridor are three simple doors. To my right, facing the vintage phone, the hall opens to a modest living room framed with antique furniture.

The room is neither masculine nor feminine. Comfortable classic with leather-bound books stacked beside a Tiffany style lamp on an end table. Tasteful oil paintings hang casually beneath the high crown molding between two long slender crank windows. A faded fresco looms above on the ceiling, capping off the cozy setting. A man with his back to us turns his head slightly in my direction. His sideburns and full jaw-line beard visibly grayed.

"Well now..." he says to me.

He's seated at a roll-top wall desk. He puts down a heavy monogrammed fountain pen on a notepad, spins around in his chair, then lifts his dark framed reading glasses revealing warm gray eyes.

"You look much better. I'm Richard. Please." He smiles.

He extends his hand guiding me to the single Queen Ann style chair adjacent to the small sofa. Nothing about this man is threatening. He approaches me, placing both hands on either side of my head and maneuvers it like an experienced doctor who had done this all his life. His fingers immediately fall into position examining my lymph nodes.

"Any pain when I do this?" He asks.

Rotating my head gently makes me realize I can't remember the last time I went to a doctor. Well, except after being mashed by the taxi.

"No, but-"
"Say Ahh."

I comply. He tips my head back, looks inside my nose and mouth. I slam his hands down. He can see the distrust in my eyes. I'm letting him see it. Yet, he doesn't seem surprised.

"Good, good," he says, ignoring it. "You may be a little fuzzy later, to be expected. Anything more, let me know. Vin, some tea please." He says smiling.

He gives Vin a friendly pat on the shoulder and Vin leaves the room beneath a exposed stone archway. They must be good friends. They seem that way at least. Hit man and tea maker. Interesting.

"Excuse me." says Vin.

Sitting back on the sofa, he impulsively crosses his legs and lifts a cigar shouldering in a heavy handmade dark ash tray. He doesn't even puff it.

"I'm Richard. And you have questions. Many, I'm sure. This is a horrid truth to learn, son. What you must've been through," He looks down and shakes his head lightly as if absorbing the pain of it.

"How did you know my father?"

He nods. His cardigan sweater is over a light blue button front shirt. He looks me straight in the eye when he talks. His voice is raspy from smoking.

"Your father, an honorable man. The most noble I've ever met. A man of his word. Rare to find nowadays."

"Who killed him? Who did this to my family!"

I can feel myself leaning forward and my hands clutching the arm rests. I'm so close to the truth. Finally. Answers to the nagging questions. It's what initially drew me into this mission.

"Caleb, there is a lot of healing that has to happen here. I have nothing in a bottle for that, my friend. All I can give you is the truth. The plain truth about what has caused you to be here, now. Some, you may remember," he puffs his cigar, "some you may not. This is your story, Caleb Promise."

I ease back into the soft seat feeling child-like, perched for a bedtime story. Shutters on the windows are closed but the sun shoves its way through the wooden slats. In the next room, the clunk of a wooden spoon in a pot is comforting and the kettle screams, sputtering to a boil, warming the atmosphere.

"As Vin may have told you, your father was in the Army, but not just any division, he was in the Special Forces sent on very secret missions. But it wasn't an ordered mission that caused us to cross paths, it was him. His pure character. He was honest, real. The sort of man that could look you straight in the eye and mean every word of what he said. Dependable," he chuckles, "to a fault. He knew your father was a good man. A rare man, Caleb, rare. Most of all, a brilliant man. He was a quiet thinker. A master strategist. The man responsible for your father's death, knew this about your father and knew it well. Officer Promise absolutely loved chess and could think five moves ahead of any opponent. Did you know that? Did you know he played chess?"

My mind lapses back to entering my father's study to the chess board with the pieces placed mid-game on a small circular table. He played himself.

"No, no, I don't think so. It was a long time ago. Every thing's a blur."

Trust no one. Besides, so far he hasn't told me anything that isn't common knowledge for anyone who knew my father. I don't know Richard. Not yet. Why does he use an old land line? Yes, he is an older man, but it's rather convenient to not have your calls traced.

"I know, son, it's all right. Anyway, after your father and his platoon got out of the army, jobs were scarce as for many soldiers, many. But this man never forgot your father's loyalty and when military jobs came open, he would call your father to fill them. Strange loyalty he had. Yes, very strange. It was touch and go, but your father would do anything to keep food on the table and a roof over you and your mothers' head. He even sold his boat, his beloved boat when things got rough. He really loved that boat.

Later, this man got engaged in a project, a big one. Your father was the one he asked to head security. But this project was different." He puts his cigar down. "It was top secret, hidden from everyone. They buried it, as it should have been, deep in a fog-covered forested valley of Brazil. No roads. We had to be air-lifted in and out. I always hated flying."

He coughs raspingly, catches his breath, continues.

"Always have, bloody gut-wrenching it is... anyway, before the crack of dawn we, the scientists, were dropped off. Stayed in that God-forsaken place for weeks. Oh, we had everything we could need of course, living quarters, but, such a lethal place.

Seven of us climbed out of that helicopter. We felt like ants walking to those gigantic arched steel doors painted with anti-reflective paint. I held my bag tight and the women clutching their purses. It was invisible to the naked eye with the overgrown brush purposely left to hang casually over it. Sometimes dripping with poisonous tropical spiders and insects, I got bit once. We stayed inside.

Getting in wasn't easy. There was a two-step key process. Fingerprint matching scanner to unlock the doors. Once inside, you stood in a five by seven steel cage that will not open unless the large arched doors are closed behind you and you pass the retinal scan. They thought of everything. Yes, everything. All of this was to keep the unwanted people out. But we felt trapped like an animal until those steel bars lower into the ground with a beep letting us enter. State-of-the art, that's what he said it would be, and it was, just that. We were all impressed. All excited. All inspired." Richard's eyes light with the memory.

"All I want to know is what his name is and-"

"I'm coming to that. I'm coming to that... please. You must know everything, Caleb."

He's entreating. I will yield.

"We were told we were creating something that would help the world's peace. Six, masterminds from all over the world. Experts in our fields. Together, for the first time tasked to construct something that they promised us would help our countries. The science, perfect. The people, not. So many personalities all stuck together and for so long. Inevitably, we clashed, but never in the science.

We learned to steer clear of speaking politics. We may have burned the bloody place down with that one, you know. So many people, so strongly opinionated about the politics of their countries. So proud of who we were. Anyway...when the project was... well, done, I saw a change in my best friend, the head scientist. Got engulfed in it. Didn't want to leave and spent a lot of time talking alone to the man whose name you want so badly." He lifts his cigar and puffs a few times, looks down at his lap, brushes off an invisible piece of lint.

"I got concerned. We all did. With good reason; soon afterward, my best friend approached me with an offer not to be refused. An offer that would financially set me up for life. We would gain the shares promised to the other scientists. Shares that would be worth millions once our project was revealed to the world. I was told it was inevitable, because they meant no witnesses to this project to remain. But, because of our friendship, a deal was made with the man so I could live. The others were to be-"

"Killed like my father," I blurt out.

"Yes." He looks downward as if he were guilty. "Caleb, I refused. I couldn't live with such a thing. We all had our differences but they, they became my friends. We all came to appreciate our differences. Mostly, we saw our commonality. We all had a family. We all cared about humanity and we knew the power of our data and records. We knew that such data in the wrong hands, could start a war as easily as bring peace. Secretly, I told the others. Secretly, I told your father. The scientists and I agreed to ensure against this. We agreed to record our own data and split it between two external hard drives and none of us would know where both drives were. We wiped the computers.

Before we got the chance to hide the drives, he struck. Without warning." He gazes at the window. "On a simple Tuesday morning. We were just getting started. The prototype worked and was doing well. The very guards that protected us, that smiled at us every morning, stormed the lab." Tears well in his eyes. He is telling me about the moment while living it.

"Caleb, your father-" he turns his gaze to me.

"No, no! You say that and I'll knock your head off! My dad would NEVER-" I stand.

"*Your* father tried to stop them. By himself. I guess that was part of his master plan."

He lowers his eyes to the floor. I sit. Vin enters and places the tea tray on the table sensing the tension in the room. He goes back into the kitchen, whispering to someone.

"Caleb, in the chaos," his voice lowering to a whisper, "I gave your father both hard drives. They tried to make it look like rebels attacked us. I could hear the scientists groaning and writhing on the floor. Officer Promise hunkered over me, protecting me from the shots being fired. Your father got me out of there. I knew he was the only one I could trust. I thought I would be killed even if I made it out of the shooting by that blasted forest. But your father told me he would get both of us out of there and he did. I remember distinctly telling him... 'They'll be looking for us.' I watched all the other scientists murdered. There was no one left but the soldiers that murdered us and I knew that as soon as they realized our bodies were not among the others, they will come. Your father said he had a way to buy us some time.

Caleb, I watched his eyes sadden while he pressed that detonator. The explosion knocked us both off our feet. We hid in that forest for days. It felt like forever. I trusted the man implicitly. I marveled at his survival skills but most of all, his humanity. Saved my life, from a ruddy deadly snake. Then, made it our dinner. We talked. We laughed. He made me forget we were two steps from death. Eventually, he got me here, to this place, and told me I can never return home. He made me promise to monitor you if anything happened to him. But it had to be from a distance. My direct presence would have sealed your fate for certain. As far as your father's murderer is concerned, I died in that explosion. But I had to keep my promise to your father. Even if it meant risking my life. He was that kind of man. What he did with the hard drives, I begged him not to tell me." Richard lowers his eyes and taps ashes from his cigar and continues.

A gap is filling for me, or is it? So far, his story fits into the pieces of what I know. Trust him, perhaps.

"There's no denying that, son. I'm sorry. But your father knew what he was taking on when he took those hard drives. He'd never put another man's life before his own."

"The project, was it that stuff you put on my face?"

"We discovered many things in the course of this amazing project. It was a healing element input into the.... well... just be assured your father did NOT die in vain."

"The what?"

"Some things are better left unspoken."

"All these years? So, why does this man want to kill me? I know nothing about these drives. I assume that's why he's chasing me."

"Uncertainty. It is the poison of the guilty. A father and son relationships are deep, Caleb. Deeper than anything else. Clues, hints to what he was involved in, that may have been passed by the stories of an ex-army man to his son haunt him. He is afraid his dirty secret could get out."

He leans toward the tea tray and pours two cups of tea into clean white teacups. I watch how Richard handles the cup, spins the handles, uses the sugar.

"Help yourself. It will make you feel better."

I imitate it seamlessly. He'll never guess that was my first time drinking from a proper teacup. It is warm and comforting. I settle back into the seat, satiated by all the information. How do I know all of this is true? Why should I believe this man? I don't know. Was he just an honorable man following through on a promise made amid chaos? Was he something else? But, what would he have to gain? Maybe he thinks I know where the hard drives are. I look suspiciously in the teacup. An uneasiness settles in my head and the comfort of the little cozy room slips away and suddenly I want to run. I want to leave this place and forget everything I learned. I can hide from him, start a new life in this new place. The door is there. I see it. I try to hide my dis-ease.

"So," I try to sit back but I feel uneasy. "What now?"

I want to break the awkward silence and eliminate any building suspicion of my planned escape.

"Now, Caleb, you have to decide whether all of this is fiction or nonfiction. You feel like fleeing and are assessing your survival options. You're wondering if I am lying or if you really can trust me implicitly."

Either he is brilliant or there is something in the tea.

"I'm no mind reader, your suspicions are justifiable, a typical side effect of the treatment. But I had to tell you the whole truth because there is an important reason you are here. One you may not want to hear."

"You're right. I don't want to hear it."

Tired of playing civil. I put down the teacup spilling the tea onto the tray. My heart is beating faster.

"I'm sorry... you've been very kind a-and I appreciate you bringing me here and but... I just, I think I just need to be alone for a minute."

I decide to escape.

"Caleb. Your heart is racing. Your thoughts, tracing on self-preservation. It's not you, son, it's just a side effect. You're sweating and will feel nausea shortly if you do not eat soon."

"NO! Get out of my mind... please," I yell, leaning forward.

The truth is, I don't know if I'm fighting side-effects or fighting trusting him. After all these years, feeling the absence of a family and having questions, now, I want to run from the answers. Richard walks over to me, bends and places his hands on my shoulders.

"It will be all right, Caleb. Hold on. Breathe, it will pass."

Half of me wants to push him away. The other half wants to hug him. Something in me wants to rest. Truly rest.

"Breathe."

I take a few deep breaths and the anxiety subsides. I am feeling nauseous but won't say it.

"It's okay, son, you will be okay. You are meant to be here now. Trust me."

My thinking clears and I am still decidedly going to leave. But, not now. Just a little while longer. Just a few more moments in a place with answers. A few more moments with people who seem to want to help me.

New York savvy has makes me look curiously at anyone who says, 'trust me'. I always thought, if you have to say it, you aren't trustworthy. Maybe it's not true of Richard. I almost hope it's not true of Richard. Home. It feels good to be around people who seem to like you, even if it is fake. Nothing about him is threatening. His Italian shoes comfortably worn. His cigar fingers dip where he has continuously held cigar after cigar in the same place and his eyes seem to hold kindness and mystery. The dip in the sofa where he undoubtedly sits repeatedly.

"Dinner is served," calls a woman with from the kitchen.

"Go on, son, steady now."

Richard pats me on the back as I walk toward the arched kitchen door. Vin goes into a room down the hall drinking a glass of water. His shoes are off, and he looks comfortable. Italian sausage in meatballs, the smell rushes up my nose. My mother made it all the time. I would know that smell anywhere. The woman faces the small window above the sink, svelte with her apron bow tied at her lower back. A black satin cap covers her hair and palazzo pants skirting her flat shoes. Long sleeves rolled up and her turtleneck turned down neatly. She reaches upward, her heals lift as she takes dinner plates from the cabinet.

"Vinnie, come when you're ready."

"Two minutes," Vin calls from the room.

He sounds like a brother getting his last few minutes on a video game. A chair is pulled out for me at the rectangular chocolate heavy wood table. The table is set with silverware and a clear crystal goblet chilled and heavy filled with water. Is the table set for me? In a flash, I am in my kitchen, fourteen years old, a humble ranch house on five acres surrounded by trees just off the lake.

A room, long forgotten, hidden in the crest of my memory reappears, dragged to the forefront of my mind. The positioning of the table, placing the stove to the left with a window above the sink. Exactly like home. The mat beneath her black shoes matches her apron with flecks of red in it. It resembles the piece of cut carpet beneath my mother's feet. My father had the house carpeted and asked the carpenter for a box cutter and cut the mat for her.

While she stood at the sink, he picked her up, giggling, tossed her over his muscular shoulder, dropped the cut carpet in front of the sink then placed her on it. 'There, now every time you stand here, you will think of me.' What I see was the back of mom's hair swinging as dad rocks her in a hug side to side. The woman speaks to me.

"Yes, I think that's good for you."

She covers the pot, lifts her right hand, grasps the cooking cap from the front and slides it off. Her hair, it... flows to her shoulders, the same length of my mother's, and the exact hair color of the woman in my nightmares. In my nightmare I never see the woman's face. But now, she's coming toward me with the plate filled with food. I stand watching the horror of my dream play-out before me. The red-haired woman dangles like a desperate creature from her husband being wrenched upward.

In a flash, the red-haired woman's face transforms to my mother's, walking toward me with her hands out as if approaching for an embrace. I don't see the plate of food in her hand. My reality is blending with my fears. What's happening to me? I grab something and hear dishes crash. I feel like I'm falling.

"Rich-art! Come... quickly!"

"Gretchen? Is everything all right-" yells Vinnie.

I hear footsteps coming closer.

"Vinnie, come help." Says Richard.

I'm on my back. I see the plate of food splattered on the floor beside me. Everything goes dark.

How long have I been out? A cool compress is on my forehead with the weight of a resting hand. My eyes are shut but I hear them whispering.

"No, I don't think it is a good idea, Rich-art," says the woman.

Her accent is thick.

"What choice do we have, dear? It must be done," Richard replies.

"But look at him, this boy has been through enough. He couldn't..." she says.

"What is the alternative? Think, Gretchen. Allow that madman to destroy everything our countries have worked toward? To let him kill millions?"

"That is NOT this boy's burden to bear!"

I open my eyes slightly, hearing water trickling from the cloth she is wringing into a glass bowl on the table. She is on her knees beside the sofa I am laying on.

"Gretchen," says Vin, "No one else is in the position he is in. No one else can get nearly close enough."

"Vin is right, we can't be selfish about this," says Richard.

Through my partially closed eyes, I see Gretchen folds the cloth, shaking her head defiantly. Vin walks to the window and looks out between the slats.

"Has it been so long you have forgotten! You know what he will do to this boy if he finds out." She folds the cloth again. "You know what he did to my... only son."

She places the cloth on my head and rests her hand on it, holding it down.

"Gretchen, I know." Richard places his hand on hers and I feel the weight of their hands on my head. "This boy is every bit my concern as he is yours. I promised his father I would keep him safe and this is the biggest risk."

"Then let's do just keep him here. With us, and Vinnie he is safe."

"Your son is gone, Gretchen. He's gone. Now, we must make sure no one else loses their son to this monster. You know I'm right. You know the inevitable."

Silence. I feel her hand lift from my head. I open my eyes slowly. She is standing.

"I'll have no part in this." She takes keys and a jacket. "Make sure he eats, yes? I need some air."

"Gretchen."

Vin goes after her.

"No, Vinnie, leave her. She'll be all right."

The front door closes.

"Maybe she's right, Vinnie. I'm so tired."

I hear Richard's seat creak as he sits back

"International peace is at hand, Richard-" Vin starts.

"SHH!" Richard interrupts.

He doesn't notice my open eyes beneath the cloth. Vin continues.

"It is only a matter of time! We've come this far, and no offense, I didn't risk my life to bring him here for you to back out of the other half of the plan. At least tell him and let him decide. Tell him, Richard, tell him everything. I haven't known him long, but I know him enough to say he's quick. Like his father in many respects, from what you told me. He's capable of making up his own mind, believe me."

"I - I don't know."

Vin gestures toward me. Richard looks at him in wonder about what I may have heard. I take the cloth off my eyes.

"How do you feel?"

"Hungry. Sorry about that plate," I say, sitting up.

Richard hands me a large bowl of spaghetti with Italian garlic bread. I eat it heartily. Other than moms, this is the best spaghetti I have ever had.

"There is something you need to know, Caleb," says Vin.

"Vin! Easy, please let him eat," interrupts Richard.

"No, let him continue." I say taking a mouth full of food. I don't care if they talk all afternoon.

"We don't have time for subtlety, Richard! This is serious. You didn't see what happened in New York! People died, and he needs to know."

"Needs to know what?" I ask. "Vin, just tell me."

He opens his mouth to answer me and Vin freezes. He gets a confused look in his eyes. He looks down at his chest. Blood spreads over his shirt just above his heart. A bullet ripped through the slit in the shutters and hit Vin in the chest.

"NO!" screams Richard, lunging to catch him before his body hits the ground.

I roll off the sofa and crawl to Vin and drag him into the hall. Richard applies pressure to the wound.

"Vincenzo!" Richard yells. Spittle from his shout lands in his beard and his rough wrinkled hands quickly get covered in blood. Vin's eyes are open, staring at the ceiling.

"Vincenzo, hold on, son! Hold on!" begs Richard.

CHAPTER ELEVEN

Jason Jones

I expected something, but not this. This means he's in more danger than I expected.

"Sir," says a well-meaning fire fighter, "you can't be up here."

"It's all right." I flash my C.I.A. badge.

The records stated they admitted only two men that night but only one of them was heavily intoxicated. Possible Christmas suicide attempt. According to my intel, that fits. The room door is still open and bullet holes are all over the walls.

I push the door and see a man dead in the hospital bed. He must be heavily sedated to have slept through all of this until he met his fate. It's not Caleb. The bathroom door is open. Hair, small pieces but it is definitely hair on the floor trailing to the laundry bin. It is easily missed beneath the rubble. I take a pen and lift a wadded towel and clumps of hair fall out.

"He's clean cut! No beard." I say to myself.

I speed dial Sam.

"Yes, Jason." She says.

"I need a new composite of him. Remove beard and hair. Send it to my phone only."

"What happened?" Sam asks.

I hang up. She should be used to that by now.

He got out. I exhale.

Caleb Promise

Vin's eyes slowly slide to me.

"Caleb... keep them safe."

I nod just in time. His stare goes blank. The door bursts open. It's Gretchen. Breathless, hair wind-blown.

"Richard! They are here! I saw a boat in the harbour, we must..."

Richard is rocking Vin cradled in his arms like a father would. She puts her hands over her mouth and her eyes widen.

"We have to go. Richard, Gretchen now." I say.

Automatically stepped into the space Vin just left empty. Richard gently lowers Vin's head to the floor, closes his eyes places his hands on his chest. He stands and pulls Gretchen. She is sobbing and reaches out to touch Vin's hand one last time. Richard roughly wipes his face.

"This way," Richard says to me.

Richard picks up the old phone on the wall table, dials three numbers and the sound of a sliding door opening in the bedroom sounds. He hangs up the phone. We step into a bedroom and through a doorway that otherwise would look like the wall. Richard presses a button and the door slides closed behind us. A steep stairwell. We go down steps, cross a small opening into the next building and come out to a field.

In the distance behind us, the cluster of townhouses dot the shoreline. Beneath a cover concealed by some brush, Richard reveals a classic mint green Fiat. Inside, silence. A moment to mourn Vin. How do you miss someone you just met, so much? He saved my life. He made me laugh. He reminded me, of me. Young with a vision that exceeds him. I don't know how I ended up driving. Richard is pointing me down a long winding gravel road.

"How could they have found us? We were so careful, so long," asks Richard, breaking the silence with what sounds like his private thought.

"They must have followed Vin. It was the chance we had to take," replies Gretchen.

"We're here. Park there." I park the car. "Quickly, inside." Richard says looking around nervously.

It is a stately, two-story country house with vines climbing its side. Inside, it is fully furnished and stocked, despite its external abandoned appearance. The grass overgrown and vines overtake the walls giving it an authentic rustic feel as if abandoned. Richard looks out of the window.

Gretchen slowly removes sheets from the settee, her tears still rolling down her cheeks. Richard uses a box of matches on the mantel, lights the fireplace that laid with logs. It catches quickly and warms the cottage room quickly. Gretchen stands staring into the fire.

"Richard," she whispers.

He holds her and sits with her on the sofa.

"Vincenzo was with us since your father helped me flee. He had a choice to leave, but he stayed."

"Are you all right, Caleb?" Gretchen whispers to me. She goes into a closet and takes out a duffel bag.

"Some clothes, shoes, and bottled water." she says, handing it to me. "You need to drink. You are still healing."

"Thank you, Gretchen." I say.

I look at the clothes. They are exactly what Vin would have worn. I don't think I ever wore a dead man's clothes. I change into the jeans and a sweater. The sofa faces an antique oval table and two single chairs side by side. No pictures on the wall, nothing that made this safe house feel homely. I feel responsible for them. It's crazy, I haven't felt obligated to anyone for years. Like an only son looking after his parents. Vin is gone, their greatest helper and source of protection.

"What did I need to know? Vin was saying that I needed to know something," I ask Richard.

"Caleb," begins Richard, "What happened to you in the kitchen. What did you see?"

"A dream, it was just a dream I have. Often. No big deal."

"What dream?" asks Gretchen, looking concerned. "Is it the same dream?"

"Yes."

"Caleb, start at the beginning. Tell us the dream," she says.

"What's the point? Means nothing."
Guarding, something I've done for years. This dream, my warp companion. Distorted and meaningless. To tell it means letting these people into a part of my life that is private. I'm struggling to break the secrecy of my life but looking into their wide eyes I see they may deem it to be a minor exchange for a friendship. Until this point, they asked nothing of me.

"Okay," I take a deep breath and run my fingers through the top of my choppy cut hair. I ram my hands into my jean pockets. Standing in front of that fireplace, in the warm light, exposes the deepest darkest part of myself feels good. It feels like telling your parents a bad dream. Once said, it strips it of all power. "It always starts the same. Just regular people, but they're hiding in woods and sewage tunnels. Anywhere they can find. Thin and terrified. At first, I don't see what they are running from, but I feel like it was... something. Something God didn't make. There are government cars, two or three, lined up watching it. The funny thing is they aren't criminals or anything. Just regular people living regular lives. The only thing they did wrong was believe, believe in something that the government decided they shouldn't believe in. They were hiding together and praying. Hungry. Sick. Scared. But..."

"But what?" Gretchen asks.

They are on the edge of their seat listening. Gretchen has stopped crying and is astonished. I hesitate, almost afraid of their response, believing I will lose their respect somehow. I'm afraid to let the crazy out. My fists are squirming in my pockets.

"It was some kind of training exercise," I say.

"Impossible," says Gretchen, with a haunted gaze.

"Please, Gretchen. Caleb... continue. Did you see it?" asks Richard.

"No."

I can't. I just can't give it all, not yet.

"Can't be..." murmurs Gretchen to herself. "How could this be Richard? It is impossible, but clearly..." walking in a daze to the fireplace.

"What?" I ask.

Richard answers me.

"What you dreamed was not just a dream. It happened. It's what we fear will happen again and again. The plot of a madman. The prototype created was tested. Over five hundred people died, and it was never exposed to the public." He exhales. "It was indeed an experiment. One that should never have taken place. But there was no one to stop him. No one to stop it!"

"Is this what Vin said I should know?"

"Yes," Richard answers flatly. "The Ex-Secretary of Defense is the man responsible for your parents' death. He is behind all of this."

Quickly, I put all the pieces together. I watched the retirement dinner of the Secretary of Defense, Wilkes on television at the hospital. The man that stole my coat, found dead. They must have realized it wasn't me and killed him. The hospital explosion broadcasted as a terrorist attack on New York City. The media urged people to band together. It was all covered up.

"He won't kill you. You stand to lead him to billions," says Richard. "Vinnie, they had no use for, but you. You they need desperately. Do you know where the drives are?"

"No. I don't." I say.

"Your father was a brilliant man that thought ten steps ahead. It will come to you. You need time. Unfortunately, we don't have it."

Standing, we are eye to eye. My squared jawline and close haircut make me look like I stepped out of the military. Nothing could be further from the truth. My build is lean yet sculpted and my height has always been an asset.

"You look like him. Just like him." Richard embraces me. As if he were holding my father. Gratefully, comfortingly.

The air in the room thickens. He knows this is a death mission. If I find the drives, Wilkes will kill me. If I can't, Wilkes will tie his loose ends and kill me. Either way, I end up pushing up daisies. He sits on the sofa beside Gretchen again.

"The man that murdered my colleagues, your father, your mother, five hundred people and Vin is not finished. I'm sad to say that murderous bastard will stop at nothing. He is using our prototype. As we speak, he is gathering another team of scientists to reconstruct the project, who, no doubt, afterward will not live to see the glory of it."

"How do you know?" I ask.

"Banished, I am, disconnected, I am not. If he finds that hard drive before we do, you have no idea what he will be capable of. Genocide to say the least."

"You think I can handle him?"

"Yes. I do."

"Why?"

"Because you are your father's son. Don't feel, think. He needs you. You are the one person in the world who does not have to worry about being killed, not by him. He needs you to find those hard drives. If he feels you may find it for him, your life is safe. Do you understand?"

"Yeah, yeah, yeah, that all makes sense but one problem. I have no clue where they are," I throw my arms open.

"Caleb, you do! You must, it's in there, son," Richard taps his temple. "You *will* find it. He will help you."

"And what makes you think I won't just blow his head off? What makes you think I will give a damn about this 'thing'?"

"The Beaston," Richard says.

"That's what it's called?"

"Yes. We made it from the BST-10 Project. So, we named it the Beaston. We must destroy the Beaston. Every life in every country is at stake. We are talking about an abolishment of human rights globally. Look at me, Caleb. This was your father's true mission."

I bite my jaw tightly and look directly at Richard. That I believe. He has told me truth.

"Everything you have heard is truth. This is bigger than your revenge or mine or Gretchen's. You don't think I want him dead! They have reduced me, a famous scientist, to living like a fugitive. If we don't get those hard drives first, he may. He represents greed and everything evil that accompanies it,"

I feel trapped in the truth. Walking away with a free mind isn't possible. Gretchen's holding her breath.

"I'm in," I say.

I felt comfortable leaving Richard and Gretchen at the house. It was a long flight and I'm still not sure why Richard insisted I start here. The car he arranged to collect me from the airport dropped me off at this street. It looks familiar. The chatter of children playing gets louder. Loud laughter, then giggling.

"I won, I won! I won!"

"No, ya didn't."

"Yes, I did!"

"No, ya didn't!"

"Yes, I did! I told you he wasn't a friend!"

"No, you didn't!"

"MOMMY, MOMMY, stranger!"

My hands, tucked in my blue jeans pocket, my brown leather jacket feels stiff. It is not *my* jacket. The long sleeve white cotton shirt, perfect for me. The brown Timberland boots are new.

"Thanks, Gretchen," I say to myself sauntering down this wide street.

Strange. I know I lived here, but I feel disconnected. It's familiar, yet foreign.

"There, momma!" they say with a lisp.

"Get back," a woman says.

Something familiar tickles my ear. The sound of her voice found a place to sit down. From behind, I hear it again.

"Caleb?"

I know that voice. County fare. Long walks with ice cream. It is the voice that whispered in my fourteen-year-old ear. My first kiss. I can feel her standing behind me. Her voice quivers and my heart races. I shut my eyes. Instantly, I am a teenager, afraid to turn around.

"Momma, whooz-dat?"

"Go to grandma, baby. Take your brother."

I turn around. Our eyes lock and time freezes. The birds stop tweeting and I can't feel myself breath. I'm consumed and from the look in her eyes, so is she. Rosie. She's a tough cookie. I have seen her cry once. The day they drove me to the orphanage.

"Skip any rocks lately?" I ask her, smiling.

I search her eyes and don't see anger for not having called for years.

"Not a chance. No worthy opponents," she says. Her chest heaving.

Her eyes are exactly as I recall. Deep hazel pools. She looks tired, but it doesn't matter. I can feel my breath floating out of me and a warmth in my heart I haven't felt in years. It's all gone. Just that quickly it disappears. The thoughts of Richard, my parent's murder, the drives I'm supposed to find, all of it. Right here, right now, there's one thing I want. To step back into my life with her.

"I hate you," she says.

Okay. Didn't expect that. She shoves me.

"What? No, let me guess, your hands were broken so you couldn't write me."

She crosses her arms and drops one hip.

"I wrote you," I say. "You're the one that never wrote back. You never came to see me."

I watch her pace while she talks. She hasn't changed at all.

"What? I did. When have I ever broken a promise to you? Tell me." She purses her lips.
She probably won't remember this.

"Ms. Harris' class. You said you'd do my homework, nothing. I failed. I went to summer school and you went to Disney."

She laughs, covering her mouth.

"Don't cry about it like a little girl," she says.

"Father Bolton, it had to be him. He was in charge of the mail and visitation. Bitter soul."

"Fat guy, no hair, flat feet?"

How does she know he had flat feet? He did.

"Yes, that's him," I reply.

"I went there, he told me, you didn't want any visitors. You were in some kind of therapy," she says.

Turning to look up the block toward my house is the best way I can think of to hide my emotions. Two minutes of talking to her and I want my old life back. But it's gone. And I can't pull her into mine. Not now. My present can't collide with my past. I see a man's shadow stick its head out from the trees.

"Is he good to you?" I ask her.

Why is she hesitating? I need to see her response. I look downward at her. She lifts her eyes and looks like she did at fourteen.

"He pays the bills. Gets drunk some. Yeah, he's... good for what's around here."

"Do you love him?"

"No."

That wasn't delayed.

"Why? He's good to you, you have two kids together," I ask her.

"He's not you. It's not... us."

I have to end this for her good. My life could hurt her, and I see hope building in her eyes.

"I'm sorry."

"Sorry for what, Caleb?"

"Sorry I left you alone. Sorry I'm not him."

"You didn't leave me. You had no choice."

I wipe tears from my eyes.

"Rosie, I have to go."

I turn away from her.

"Don't you dare walk out of my life again!"

From the corner of my eye, I think I see a person stick their head out from behind a tree. It pulls me back into reality.

"I just have to take care of some things right now. Rosie, you have to trust me."

She pauses. She sees something in my eyes that no one else would. It's like we can read each other's thoughts.

"Fine. But meet me at our spot... please. Please, Caleb, promise me you will be there in five minutes."

"Promise. That's my name."

I watch her rush inside and pull her ponytail holder out, letting her hair drop to her shoulders. I must focus. The dirt road is empty. Here it is, dilapidated. Sad. I remember every Saturday morning my mother digging in that garden and planting flowers while I cut the grass. Now look at it. Overgrown shrubs and trees. All that work for nothing. The roof barely visible and most of the windows are boarded up or broken out. The walking paths are covered.

Funny, the front door is locked but round back, the door is open. It's frozen in time. Fortunately, people don't see belongings like photos and books as being valuable. Personal belongings are abandoned, like me at that orphanage. The carpet disintegrated to musty dust. The family room is littered with broken furniture and the wallpaper is ripped in many places. I can hear the echo of past laughter in the vacant rooms.

I can smell the home-made pizza and hear my mother humming 'Baby Mine' as she sprinkles the cheese with one hand and rubs her swollen belly with the other. She was four months pregnant. Until that car accident. No one knew but me and my father. My baby brother was taken from me in that 'car accident'.

No autopsy ordered. Not need when you drown in a frozen lake trapped in your car.

Even in a common ponytail, mom was stunningly beautiful. Dad and I raced to the sofa. The winner got the first slice. This place is haunted. Not by ghosts, by memories. It was bursting with them.

The bookcases were once filled with volumes of classics and hand selections from places all over the world. They had beautiful leather bindings. Above it, two brackets that held dad's two-edged sword. He brought it home from a tour he did overseas.

We mounted it above mom's bookshelf that my father built for her, I wish I could see those books. Dad smiled, seeing her curled up in his seat every night, looking eagerly at the pages with a cup of hot mint and honey tea steaming beside her. He often stood in the doorway, holding his coffee and watching her read like a good movie.

Her favorite book was the one she read repeatedly. When it was finished, she put it in a specially made wooden book-box with a latch and used it as a book end for her other books. It was fragile from use and cherished so dearly, but now it is gone. Probably pilfered, broken or sold for a pittance.

Here, I can't escape the rush of memories. I want to. Thunder. A good old country storm is rolling in. For a long time, I hated the rain. Sounds stupid now, but I blamed the rain for their accident. Dad was a skilled driver. His reflexes, faster than most. I always questioned their theory of his death. This is the thunder that scares children in the night.

I wish I didn't remember it, but that night is coming back to me. Standing here looking at the front door, I can see Officer Tom-Tom at the door, rain pouring over his plastic covered Sheriff's cap. He looked more like Santa Claus than a cop. He was the one that took me to the orphanage.

He was torn between taking me to the orphanage and scooping me up and raising me as his own. Tom-Tom was a sloppy widower that drove a police car day and night. His life-habits made him an unsuitable parent. He knew it. He visited me every few months, bringing chocolate and little knick-knacks. Looking back, him being a cop was the only reason they let him into the orphanage to see me.

Now, I realize one kindness Tom-Tom afforded me. Instead of bringing social services with him that night, after he broke procedure, he brought the preacher and his wife to my home. They prayed with me and talked to me, while I sat silently in shock on the sofa.

The first lady is etched in my mind. She made tea, lit a fire, helped pack my bags with pictures she knew someday I would appreciate. It was my last night at home. She knew when to let me cry in private and when to step in and hold me. Because of her, I woke the next day to the smell of bacon and eggs. For that moment, I thought it was all a bad dream and that when I got to the kitchen, I'd see mom standing there turning the bacon and dad in his office waiting for her 'breakfast' call.

I thanked Tom-Tom during one of his visits for doing that. He was sick, but he still came. His shirts always had coffee and crumbs stuck to it. Shortly after that visit the preacher visited me and told me that Tom-Tom passed away peacefully in his sleep. He deserved that. Peace.

The memories are smothering in here. I feel like I can't breathe. I pull the scab back, but for the first time remembering doesn't sting. Finally, it's real. Standing in this house seems to close the gaps and fill the cracks in my memory. It somehow gave me the past I lost. I feel full. Now, I want to get the man that took them from me.

The lake is beautiful, but not as big as I remember. The boat dock and small wooden boat house now decrepit and mostly broken off sunken beneath the river.

We kept a tackle box submerged beside a stump next to the water's edge. A fishing line tied to the stump keeps it in place. My job was to fill it with live bait the day before. Where's that line? There. I pull it but it can't raise the box.

One more tug on the line and... 'ouch'. Cut by dirty fishing line. Suck it up and keep it moving. Dad's favorite saying other than, trust no one. The tackle box is full of water and debris.

What is that? Something, something slippery. I rub my fingers over it and dip it in the water to wash it off. It's a tiny zip-lock bag with a folded piece of paper inside. I have been in this box hundreds of times and never saw this before. I dry my fingers on my jeans and part the small plastic opening.

"Caleb."

Rosie. I'll look at it later. Nope, she doesn't see me push the box back into the water with my foot or slip the plastic baggie into my jean pocket. She embraces me. I feel her exhale in my arms. I would be lying if I said I didn't miss her. She knows me. She's one of the few people my stand-off character doesn't intimidate.

"Rosie-"

"No one else calls me Rosie. Not a soul. I won't let them. It's yours."

She's looking so deeply into my eyes, I'm afraid she will see more than I want her to. I release the hug.

"I have so many questions for you. We can talk later," she says.

Bags? She has a small suitcase on the small hill. My mouth falls open and I shut my eyes because I know what I must do.

"It's okay. Momma said she'll keep the kids for a while at least till we get situated," she says excitedly.

I step backward.

"You came back to get me, didn't you?" I say nothing. "Didn't you? You promised." I look at the ground. "What is this? I kept my promise! I said, I would be here when you got out."

I glance at her finger. The fresh indentation of a wedding ring she must have just taken off.

"Say something," she retorts.

I forgot how hard it is to talk to someone that can read your every move. You can't surprise them. I wish I could let her know I would take her hand and pull her into my world for the rest of our lives if my world wasn't filled with murdering maniacs trying to kill me. I need her alive even if she isn't in my world and I'm not in hers. Knowing she's out there makes me feel whole. I will get rid of her now. I saw the bushes move. They're here.

"I'm engaged," I blurt.

Explains me not having a ring.

"Then, why are you here?" She puts her hand on her hip and tilts her head in disbelief. "Why?"

Saying these words will even hurt me, though they are not true.

"I needed to know I was over you."

I can't read her. Does she believe? That's the one thing that will get her to let go. Not out of bitterness or anger. She didn't exactly hibernate, waiting for me. If she knows I'm happy and truly found love, she would let go. That's how we are.

At the State Fair, I would walk away with the small bear instead of risking going for the big bear. She would push me to try. She will push me now. She looks at my hands in my pockets. Dead give-away.

"Name," she says.

"You don't need to know. I needed to look you in the eyes."

How can I make her believe? I can see her heart pounding. Mine is too. I step closer to her. She can smell the new leather of my jacket. It's not *my* jacket.

"I needed to hold you, smell your hair again and see if it still turned my head. I knew that if I could walk away and not feel what I used to, that she's the one. Sorry, Rosie, I can. I'm over you. It was a childhood thing."

Tears are forming in her eyes and she swallows hard. If I flinch, just a little, she won't believe me, and she'll push for the truth, a truth I can't give her. I have to seal this up. There is movement in the bushes in two places now. I lower my voice to a whisper.

"I moved on and so have you. Wait for me? You didn't wait for me and it's not my fault you don't love him. Sorry I gave you the wrong impression but there is no 'us' anymore. Go home to your kids. What kind of mother would leave her kids, anyway?"

I turn my back to her. She pulls my shoulder and turns me facing her. I expected it. She hits hard too. A slap across the face.

"You're a real bastard, Caleb Promise. A real bastard. This childhood 'thing' was real to me. At least have the guts to face me."

Through her tears, she sees it. I see her light exhale. She plays along. That-a-girl Rosie. Her eyes skip to the right. She caught the movement across the lake too. Funny, she's okay with knowing someone's after me, as long as I still love her. Come on, Rosie. Keep it going.

"I never want to see you again!" she screams.

That one hurt. A right hook. Average girl would have just slapped me. Rosie is no average girl.

"Here! I kept this stupid Cracker Jack ring all these years."

She shoves it in my hand, but it's not a ring. It's a piece of folded paper. I watch her grab her suitcase and stomp through the tall grass back up the hill.

"I HATE YOU, CALEB PROMISE! I WILL ALWAYS HATE YOU!"

I can picture those big brown eyes smiling now. That's my girl.

CHAPTER TWELVE

I pick up a small rock, an excuse to make sure the tackle box sunk, and skip it across the lake toward Rosie's hint. I cast my glance across the lake as if watching the rock. Someone is there, behind the brush. They haven't made a move yet, which means they are watching. Waiting. Waiting to see if I get the hard-drives or not. I don't know what is in this small plastic bag, it may be valuable, maybe not. I'll find out soon.

They had me running. I am turning the tables. I'm setting the pace. Not sure how they found me so fast, but they know I'm looking. Why else would I be here after two years? But they are on my grounds now. The faster I get it, if I get it, the faster they will move in on me. I don't want to leave here. Not yet. Besides, once I leave, I don't think I'll ever come back. Except maybe to see Rosie.

There, just ahead dirt road leading to the orphanage. The old stone monastery and all its memories come back. I don't want to walk there so a quick stop and I intentionally lean on a tree in front of the old church and let my memories roll in. I can still hear Wallie's voice crack. We were teenagers and it was changing. I was born with a baritone voice. It just deepened with time. Something in him bloomed late. All of him bloomed late. He was a fifteen-year-old kid in a twelve-year-old body. I was a forty-year-old in a thirty-year-old body. Somehow, even on a sweltering summer day, we were a perfect match.

"Come on, Caleb! Quick before he comes back," says Wallie, pushing his sleeves up, squatting and opening his hands for a catch.

"I've got work to do, man," I reply.

"Just once, right here, wha'cha got?"

"More than you."

Like clock-work, a monk steps out from behind a tree with his hands held behind his back just as the pomegranate hits Wallie in the chest and splatters its blood red juice on his white tunic. A miracle, all we got was a disapproving glance. The monk turns around, pretending he didn't see what happened. We both just stood there surprised.

"Whew, that may have gotten you a week of kitchen duty. God bless brother Long." Bowing with hands clasped.

I couldn't help but smile at that.

"Wouldn't be the first time you got us in trouble," I say.

"Stop whining. You have to live a little, Caleb. We won't be in here forever. They won't rule us for long. One year," Wallie says.

"One for you, two for me." I say.

"Know where you're going?" Wallie asks me.

"Not a clue. Far, I hope. I know where your going-"

"-don't say it." Wallie says, picking up pieces of the broken pomegranate.

"You know I'm gonna say it, a gigantic mansion somewhere in Switzerland and you'll have servants waiting on you hand and foot saying, 'Would you like to play catch Sir Wallie Davenport? Would you like me to shave your peach fuzz from your chin, Sir Wallie Davenport?'"

"Yeah, right," Wallie laughs.

"You'll go all soft and squishy-like, and you'll forget all about this place... and..."

I stop myself.

"Not everything." He says somberly.

Wallie kicks the dry summer dirt with his sneaker. The dust spins in the sunlight. He enjoys doing that for some strange reason.

"Hey, how come don't you talk to anyone else? You know they all think you're some kind of psychopath waiting to blow. I, on the other hand, disagree. I don't think you're a psycho ready to blow. I know it."

"How did you end up being called Wallie, anyway?"

Two more pomegranate crates to go.

"Long story. I'll tell you when we get out-a here."

"Hey Wallie, you don't have to make promises to me. I get it, they set things up for you and that's good. Leave here and don't look back. There's nothing worth remembering here. You got it."

I hate these tunic pants they have no pockets.

"Stop trying to 'big brother' me," says Wallie, "I'm older than you. Sometimes you act like an old fart. A dusty crusty old fart."

"Say it, 'I won't look back'." I say.

"Not saying it." He insists.

"Say it." I push.

"I've got you by a year, remember that. My mom died giving birth to me, I watched my father suffer to death. I have a lot I want to forget, but here, is not one of them. I'll find you-"

"-no. I don't need promises. Let's just play it by ear as always, okay?"

This is one of the few days I wanted to remember. Leaning on this tree, it happens. Like finally remembering where you put your car keys. I know the exact moment it overtook me. Anger. Wallie's black polished limousine crunches the gravel beneath its new tires as it pulls away from the orphanage and me. I can see Wallie turned around in his car seat, face pressed closely to the rear window until it disappears past the orphanage gates as they shut behind him.

That was the moment my grief transformed into anger. I didn't plan it. It just happened. No one spoke to me for my last year, nor I to anyone. Anger keeps people away that I don't want to talk to, but its benefit was also its curse. It brings wretched loneliness.

Wallie's corny jokes, dreams of starting the biggest tech company in the world, kept me human. They brought light to my darkness. I didn't have any dreams then. They stopped when my folks died. The day I buried my parents, Wallie was the only one I let near me. I can still smell the smoke. There we were under the stars on our hands and knees in our underwear digging a pit in with bare hands. We clawed at the ground, teeth gritted, tears and snot pouring from our faces and fingers curled like animal claws. We grated away the grass and dirt and tossed away the stones.

It was coming out. Pouring out of us like rain. The sorrow, pain and anger of losing the centre of our lives. We cried and dug until we collapsed on the ground, lying on our backs staring at the stars in the dark sky above us. Then we tossed in sticks, leaves and used matches we stole from Brother Long to start the fire. We tossed in our funeral suits and vowed over a spit-filled handshake that those were the last funerals we would ever attend.

Wallie didn't even know he was the gate keeper for my faith in humanity. I often imagined he was the brother I would have had if my mother did not die with my baby brother inside of her. A lot died that day. Our bond survived. I never expected Wallie to keep that promise, but he is the only one who knows every ugly thing about me. I trusted him with them, and I still like to picture him in Switzerland.

The pastor and his wife were gone, but the church still stands, weather beaten as always. The steps still creak. Ignorant, I used to think that it must have helped with collection time to get members to dig a little deeper, but the Reverend loved the look. Later, I learned he kept it that way because it resembled him. Worn, comfortable and welcoming.

I know whoever is following me is outside. Tucked in a bush or hiding behind a tree. I look at my watch. Good, just a few more moments. That's all I need. I'm alone. The church is empty. I take the things from my pockets. Rosie's folded paper. Her phone number. What's this? I didn't know this was in there. A secret pocket in the lining. A passport and money. Lots of money, cash.

I could disappear with this. Richard and Gretchen must really trust me. There is a note inside the first page of the passport. 'In case of an emergency'. I remove the finger-sized sealed plastic bag from my pocket and hold it deep in my lap. The writing. It's dad's handwriting.

"9729,"

The first thing that came to mind was that it was the number to a safe deposit box at a bank. That's logical. Important hard drive, safe, makes sense. Yet, it doesn't sit well. Anyone could think of that and dad was not just anyone.

Wait, it was familiar for the saddest reason. It was the plot number for their grave site. Dad purchased it long before they died, wanting to make sure everything was in order. He showed me everything. He told me planning kills fear and we should always kill fear. I need to go to the tombstone but not with a tail. I look at my watch. In seven minutes, the Pastor will come out of the back room and open the church doors. Crowds of people have formed outside. They will pour in.

If memory serves me, right behind the altar there is a back door to the graveyard. There are two graveyards, the one in front and one behind the church. Mom and Dad's tombstones are behind the church.

The Pastor walks past me with a solemn nod and opens the doors. Now. I slip out the back door. The town people they won't hesitate to pull a total stranger into church on a Sunday morning. I see the two men following me drift into the church pulled by the Pastor himself. They are probably going in willingly out of curiosity because they didn't see me come out. The chatter of the church members fade. I bend down behind the large tombstone. I rub my fingers across their names.

"Well, you got me here, dad. Only you could have gotten me here again."

The tombstone is intact. No flowers. But, footprints. Men's boot prints. They've matted down the grass circling it. There is nothing here. It's a wooden duck. A decoy. Wait. The numbers game! Dad's game. We played to pass the time while fishing. It was our personal game. We made it up. 'Add one, skip two, add three'. The outcome, a set of numbers that made sense somehow. Thinking about it, did 'we' make it up or did dad teach it to me. I had played it so many times I got good enough to beat dad's time. I haven't played it in years and can hear dad's voice talking me through it. Twenty-five, thirty-three, forty-three he says in his head.

I feel like there's a reason he brought me here to figure it out. I can't help but grin to myself. Dad is with me again. His greatest talent was knowing how people think and he knew how I would think. He knew the wooden duck wouldn't trick me. A reason to live fills me again. He must have wanted me to think about mom. But why?

"What about mom?"

What did she love? Coffee and books. Coffee first. She even had a shirt that said that. Where did she go for her coffee?

"I love you, momma and will never forget you."

I disappear into surrounding brush. A shortcut path to my next clue.

That's the benefit of home ground. You know every hidden path that cars can't follow. Every Police speed trap and dip in the road. Mom's spot, a quaint perfectly feminine coffee and tea shop with small round tables overlaid with heavy floral tablecloths matching the drapes around the large picture window. It hosted the women's club meetings twice a month. The few elderly ladies stare shamelessly, putting together their version of my life on a glance.

"Pick a seat, we're not formal here, honey," says the waitress to me from behind the counter.

I choose mom's old seat. The waitress approaches, swabbing her hand on her frilled apron. She pulls out a worn order pad.

"Coffee or tea?" the waitress asks.

"Coffee, please."

"Here-ya-go. New to town, huh? Haven't seen you here before."

Does she have to pop that gum that loud? Sounds like she cracked a tooth.

"Actually, I grew up here."

"Yeah, nice, huh? Remodelled years ago. Who did you say you were?"

Nosy. I didn't. Trying to get the first scoop on the newcomer. Ignore.

"There was a waitress here, nice lady, blond hair. Mi-something."

"Oh, Mildred. She was a real sweetie."

"Was?"

"Cancer. Two years ago. A real shame. She sure knew how to clean a coffee pot. Cat lady. Divorced. Sweet. Why?"

I wonder how long she can go on talking in two-word sentences. It is sad that a whole life could be summed-up in a few words.

"Mildred served her regularly and I just wanted to talk to her that's all."

"What was her name?" she pauses. "Must be a very special lady for a guy like you to come into a place like this."

I couldn't help it. I chuckled. Was never referred to as 'a guy like you' in a positive sense before. In New York, you have to hit a particularly high standard before you can get that phrase. I never hit that standard.

"Mrs. Promise."

Sounds strange. I haven't said that name to anyone.

"Oh, yes. I remember her. A beauty. Extra strong, sweet, natural sugar only and non-dairy creamer. Mildred always served her but when she knew she was, well, going... she told me how her regulars took their coffee. See, Mildred only ever knew service. She loved it, genuinely. Can't say I feel the same. What was she to you?"

"Miss. Excuse me," interrupts one of the elderly ladies from the other table.

"Be right back." Irritated she couldn't get that itch in her ear scratched.

Did I get it wrong? Did I miss the clue? The television mounted to the corner is playing BBC World News.

"The President of the United States is confident that despite his absence, great things will come of the secret World Summit. We expect it that every European country's leader will be in attendance and despite keeping its location a secret, security will make this an 'air-tight' event. The World Leaders Summit is expected to bond the leaders and hold talks on global peace. They have dedicated an entire day to them bonding as a motivational act of unity. They hope this will affect their homelands..."

The waitress rushes back to me almost breathless.

"You were saying?" she says eagerly.

This was a dead end.

"Nothing. How much do I owe you?"

"Never mind, honey, just nice to have a good-looking man in here." She looks me up and down as I reach for the door.

"There you go, Mrs. Finny. Nice and hot." She attends to the other table.

I hear her pouring the coffee. Could it be?

"What brand? Her coffee, what brand was her favorite?" I ask her.

"Same as we use now," holding the pot up, "Cold Ridge, dark brew."

I push the door and she yells; "You can't find it in the store. It's wholesale only. We get it from the warehouse beside the tracks. Ole Billy Baxter's been supplying the town forever."

"Thanks, thank you."

I look both ways outside. Still no one following me. Nevertheless, I walk off the main path to the coffee warehouse. I don't know if this is right, but it's what I've got. I'm here. Dirt parking lot. Fork-lifts, and a huge steel warehouse with a tiny inner office. The door is slightly ajar. The place smells great. It wakes my senses immediately. Approaching the door, an elderly man holding a clipboard calls to me.

"We don't sell to the public. Wholesale, kid. Hey, Ken! Not over there, that load goes inside!"

I walk up to him casually. My jeans and boots get a dusting of dirt in the yard.

"My mother loves - uh, loved your coffee. Please, I'll pay whatever you ask."

The man pulls two yellow earplugs out of his ears.

"Tinnitus. Most of these guys have it. Not me. These babies work. Five bucks a pop but I'll never go deaf. Ken over there, couldn't hear a hammer if it hit him on the head. What were you saying?"

"I said my mother loves your coffee. I'll pay anything for a bag. Just one."

This may not help my hunt for the drive but every time I smell it, it will be as if she is right here. He pauses. What's wrong?

"What's your name, kid?" he fixes his eyes on me, oddly.

"Caleb. Caleb Promise."

He stands up straighter and puts his clipboard under his arm.

"Wait here." He walks into the warehouse ignoring the man yelling after him.

"Hey, Nick! Where-ya going?" yells the forklift driver.

He doesn't have his earplugs in. He goes up a thin steel staircase to an office overlooking the warehouse.

"Come up, kid." He waves me up.

He looks nervous. This must be right. He opens the office door and an older gentleman with glasses seated behind a rough desk, points me to sit at the seat across from him. His thick circular glasses and overalls with a plaid shirt over them reek of tobacco. I've never been around a person spitting chewing tobacco. I have missed nothing.

"You got I.D.?"

"No, Sir, I don't."

"Prove your Promise's boy." He says rocking back in his rolling chair.

"Military man, loved fishing-" I start.

"Not that stuff. Everybody knows that stuff. That fish won't swim, kid."

"When he was a boy, he got shot in the butt with a b-b gun. Told no one. Left him with a scar. He told my mother it was a dimple."

He's laughs. That must be it.

"Didn't know that one," he chuckles. "Nope that's not it. Almost wish I didn't hear that." He laughs. "Try again."

"I - I don't know."

"If you're his son, you know something about him that no one else in the world knows. Something he wouldn't tell anyone but his son. Think."

"He always wanted a boat. His father loved the water but never had enough money to get one. He saved and saved and one summer bought a fixer-upper. Everyone thought it was just because he liked boats. It wasn't. But his father died before he could get it running. Ever since then, he took me out every weekend."

"Of all the stories, why did you pick that one?"

"Because that's the one that made my father cry. He told me on the boat, no one else could have known."

The man smiles. He reaches behind him and pushes a hidden panel behind his desk and pulls out a dusty paper bag.

"That is a special roast. I've held it quite some time for you."

He plops the bag on the desk, completely ignoring the puff of dust. I can't help but just stare at it for a moment.   I got something right.   After years of feeling like the crack in the mirror, I got something big right.

"He told me you'd walk through that door one day-" He spits.

"-he said to tell you, leave at 7:00 p.m.   I don't know what's in there but, son, it's worth dying for."

A loud knocking on the steel door below. He sticks his finger through the blinds, pulls it down and sees the foreman looking up at him shaking his head 'no'. Something is wrong. The man's smile lowers quickly. He pulls a shotgun out from under the desk.

"They're here.   Go.   Through there." He points toward a slender cabinet door.   "Remember, 7:00p.m."

"Wait, I have so much to ask you."

"No time, son."

"Why are you helping me?   You know how dangerous it is, why?"

He spits tobacco into an empty coffee can and cocks his gun like a pro.

"Semper Fi." He smiles with a soldiers' smirk.

A warmth swells in my chest. That bond extended our family to people who didn't have our last name but would give us the shirt off their backs without asking why. They put themselves at risk for one another. Now, I understand dad differently. I grab the bag, open it and take out the small coffee bag. I shove it into my inner pocket and go through a thin door that looks like a cabinet door.

CHAPTER THIRTEEN

This guy's smart. I follow this hidden doorway to a steel opening above my head. I push it open. Great, another roof. At least this one's got a ladder at the end. Gunshots. Single caliber. Then, the boom of his shotgun.

I balance with both arms out on the slanted grooved metal roof. Slowly, I pass the sunroof, and glance down. I couldn't see them until it was too late.

"HE'S ON THE ROOF!"

A few more feet and I'm at the ladder. Again, boom. The shotgun. But then, sadly, continuous rapid fire. Then silence.

"BRING IT DOWN," says the leader.

"The boss wants him alive," replies one man with a gun.

"I don't care if I drag in a corpse," says the leader.

I think it bruised his ego when Vin blew up his helicopter. He was the one at the hospital.

"He won't like it," replies the man with a gun.

The leader looks at him, puts his gun to the man's forehead and pulls the trigger. Afterward, a few explosions shake the building. My balance shakes. The roof is collapsing. I drop, sliding on my side down the side of the roof. The ladder. If I miss it, I'm done.

The building crumbles fast. I grapple for my grip. My hands slip off the metal roof. The descending roof lowers so much, when I reach the end of the roof, the fall off the side doesn't break my legs. I roll in the dirt and stop on my back. I hate roofs. The tree line is about twenty feet away. There are men on the ground. I look at my watch. It's 6:45 pm. This is going to be close. I jump up and run toward the tree line.

"There!"

Lights in the distance beyond the tree line. The Winter Festival. The train tracks are beside the Festival grounds. I hear the train horn blow approaching the 7:00 pm train stop. Dad gave me an exit.

We came here every year. The code. The chatter of the people is welcoming. My long legs got me here quickly yet I can see flashlights waving in the brush behind me. I need the row of lockers. Where is it?

"12, 13...14, number 15. Our locker."

I always chose my locker number to correspond with my age. I worked my way down the row over the years. You bring your own combination lock and the locker rental was free. I find number 15, that was the last time I was here. There's a combination lock already on it. I spin it quickly looking over my shoulder every other number. Here it goes. Nothing. It won't open. The men in black are closing in. I keep my head down. No time. Deep breath.

"Come on, come on."

I tug it. Nothing. Maybe I'm wrong.

"Hey!" says a little boy holding a bag of popcorn.

He's loud. Really loud. I don't need this attention.

"That's my locker! Thief. Dad!"

This guy's huge. Like a tree standing behind me, eating a King Henry the Eighth turkey leg. Great.

"Sorry, my mistake."

"What are you, a freak stealing from the lockers? Huh?" the big man says, pointing his turkey leg at me.

Funny, I'm not stealing anything.

"No, just a mistake, could you please-" I say to him quietly.

I tilt my head to see behind him yet hide behind him.

"Please what!"

"No need to yell, man, it's just a mistake."
I can see the men in the distance standing on benches, looking over the crowd.

"You trying to make me look bad in front of my kid? Trying to tell me what to do?"

Great, ego. I've had enough of this guy. I step backwards and hold my hands up, trying to glance at the lockers while he's ranting. I grab the lock on the locker that matches my age now.

"This has to be it," I say, turning the lock.

"Freak. He's a stupid freak!" he says, watching me.

How could dad possibly know how old I would be when I found this? Worth a try. The green giant is waiting. If it doesn't open, this will get ugly. Turkey leg and all. I turn it, tug it. It opens. I freeze, holding the combination lock sitting in my palm, feeling its weight. I'm holding something my father placed just for me.

"What's wrong with you? I ought to knock your lights-" the big man says.

I had to do it. He fell like a ton of bricks. Dad, the boxing lessons work. The men in black close in. The locker's empty. No false bottom, nothing. I slam it shut. It's not in the locker. I squeeze the lock. Of course. It's in the lock.

Over the music, I can hear the train coming. The track turns just ahead, then the train slows. They're shooting at me. People are screaming. The Sheriffs guarding the fair draw their weapons and head toward them. That buys me time. Running beside the train I hear bullets ping the train. I've got to get to the other side of the train. That means I need to cross in front of it at the slow down point, the turn. If memory serves me right, it's right after the Willow tree. Gravel crunches beneath my feet. Here. I must take my chance now. I need to cut in front of the train now or never. Police lights blink behind me. I can hear the leader yell.

"There! He's going try to cross in front!"

"No way," says one man breathlessly.

I feel a boost like something pushes me in the back. NOW.

"He's gone. Where is he?" yells the leader.

That was crazy! I would do it again any day. Whooo! Holding the metal vertical handles on the train car, my adrenaline is pumping. I feel alive! The police lights are disappearing behind me. Holding on, what time is it? I look at my watch.

"7:03." Can't help but smile.

"Get to the next stop!" yells the leader.

I slide push metal the container doors open, swing inside and shut them. Back against the wall of the car, knees bent with coffee bag in my right hand, I dangle the lock around my finger on my left hand. My heart is still thumping I can't wait to see what I've got. The empty car rattles and has just enough light for me to see. Examining the lock, I don't see any opening marks. It rattles. I hear something making a 'ping' sound inside of it. I bang it on the floor, but it doesn't budge. Think.

I put the combination in backwards and the back of the lock pops open. A small steel box with indents on its side falls out. It was welded all the way around. The indents look like the teeth of an old key. It is safe in the lock. I'll keep it in my jeans pocket.

I pull open the coffee bag. Whole beans. Smells great too. What's this? Glasses. Held up in the light, they look normal. I put them on and a vertical line of light slides across each lens. A retinal scanner. A tiny pinhead sized green light flickers on the arm then holds steady. Then, an image becomes clear. I can't believe what I'm seeing.

It is the inside of dad's workshop. Dad is sitting at the rustic table we worked at more times than I can count. I hear the coffee beans spilling out on the floor. I don't care.

"Son, I knew you'd figure it out. I'm gone. I know. And I'm sorry I left you alone. To survive you need to use everything I've taught you. One day, you'll teach them to your son. Remember, keep God first, obey your parents, and do well in school."

He is exactly as I remember him.

"Focus, Caleb. If you're on the train, from the warehouse you have exactly 12 minutes before the first full stop. This video is

exactly three minutes long. Keep time, just as I taught you." I tap my foot. It's a counter. "If they're on to you, they will breach before that stop. They will take you. Use what I taught you, while fishing, walking, working... it will come back. You will be fine. They won't kill you. You're too important. Know your value. I've combined the data to one drive. They may still think it's on two drives so use that how you want. Here goes. You know I was in the Marine's Special Operations, what I didn't...well, couldn't tell you and mom is, I was also a part of the P.S.D.T. Presidential Secret Detail Team. A handful of men trained to go 'double deep'. We get embedded into U. S. Forces when needed to root out the small foxes. Small foxes hide deep. They embedded me to look into the things that were of direct concern to the President. Some would call me a snitch, some a patriot. I don't care what they called me I just want to save lives. A mission in Afghanistan gave me the Intel they were looking for-"

No! The video's jumping, the picture warped. Finally, it's playing again.

"-is the one responsible. Caleb, everything is on the hard drive. When you find it, and you will, you must do what you feel is right with it. When and where you find it is equally important.

Trust no one. They were making killing machine and the problem is, it has no soul. Son, there's another player, I never found this person. I don't know who they are but it's someone you probably haven't met yet, but trust that whoever they are, they are watching.

That player is more dangerous than the one chasing you now. Hear me. Son, no matter how they made it look, my death was not an accident. I didn't kill myself or anything crazy like that. I would never leave you and your mother. Stay focused. No matter what you feel, you can't make this about revenge. Remember, flesh clouds spirit. When fishing, we used small fish as bait to..."

I mouth the answer while he speaks it.

"... catch bigger fish."

He continues. *"Same principle, son. Promise, no revenge. If you do, your cause isn't pure, and you'll be seeing me sooner than you think. Remember what I taught you in fighting?"*

Again, I mouth it simultaneously with him again.

"Strike once in the right place and you can topple a giant."

"I knew you'd remember."

I feel myself smile. Even as a grown man, I love knowing my father is pleased with me. The video continues:

"We, strike like one sword, a two-edged sword. That's how we leave our mark. Millions of lives are at stake."

Only saw my dad hang his head like that once. It was at the death of his parents. He hangs his head and swallows.

"This is dangerous. The drive, it is in the safest place on earth. It would amaze your mother. Complete the mission. You are not alone. If you don't, they will never stop hunting you. Son, only give it to the one who would have no use for it." He glances at his watch. *"Time to go, Caleb. I love you, son."*

No. Not yet. I don't want him to go, he stands and looks out the door to the work shed. What is he looking at? He looks directly into the camera and smiles pushing his hands into his jean pockets. He turns the camera, facing it out of the open shed door. There is a boy playing kickball in the distance beside the lake. It's me. I'm fifteen.

"Dad, look, I can do it!" My teenage-self says to him through the door.

Dad looks straight into the camera.

221

*"I knew you could do it." He says, then smiles into the camera.
"You are the one thing in my life that is perfect. I'll see you again
one day, my son."*

He has tears in his eyes. He reaches toward the camera with
his right hand. I reach out, to touch him just one more time. I
exhale. Tears? He let me see him cry on purpose. He never let
people see him cry. The image goes black.

I remove the glasses. I know I should destroy them but
something in me can't do it. Not yet. It's the only thing I have of
him. His voice, his face. Suddenly, I appreciate every moment
we spent in that dusty old shed.

He was right. I can hear them coming. The train is still
moving. A helicopter is close. I hear boots on the roof of the
train car, running. I roughly wipe my nose, scoop up the coffee
beans and shove them into the bag and hold it in my hand. I put
the glasses in my inner breast jacket pocket. I want them to
come. I want them to take me. Take me to Wilkes. This will
look real. I take a stance and have no problem clenching my
fists. Full anger rises. I feel my mouth turn down. I will land a
few punches just for them to think they took me unwillingly. All
right, it's to make me feel good too. I am not alone. My father's
knowledge is with me.

It didn't take long for them to breach. Got a bloody lip, but it
was worth it. Through the black hood, I see one guy in black,
holding his nose, blood pouring through his hand. Another
holding his ribs and the guy next to him tapping a cut on his
temple. My knuckles raw, but it was worth it. We arrive at a
building.

They shoved me down a long hall and into an examination
room then zip tie me to a seat. I'm not alone. Only his warped
mind would grin watching a person squirm in pain with tight zip
ties digging to the bone. Is it? Yes, it's the tall man from the
hospital. My hands and feet are numb. He's sitting in a seat
across from me.

"Roger that."

Who is he talking to? He's not on a phone. I don't want him to know I can see him. I move my eyes but don't see anyone else in the room. An earpiece. He snatches off my black hood. I shut my eyes and let my head bob.

"Look at me!"

He hits me on the side of my head. His lip is bleeding. I got him too? Good.

"My work here is finished. He's all yours." He leans into my ear. "If it were up to me, pieces of you would be all over the floor."

He walks out of the room. Then, the man in the corner speaks from the shadows.

"You have something to tell me," he says.

That voice is familiar.

"Dread?"

"Good memory," he says.

Impossible. He was part of my father's platoon killed in Afghanistan. We had a memorial service.

"You're dead." I say.

He's grinning like an old sailor about to tell his favorite sea story. I want to knock it off his face.

"It's a long story."

"No. I mean, you are dead. I will kill you. You being here means you have something to do with my parents' death."

He slides off a table. He never sat properly in chairs. When he did, he sat backwards. I think he came out of the womb butt first.

"Where's the drives?" He approaches my chair.

There was always something about him I didn't like.

"You'll find I don't like to repeat myself," Dread says crossing his arms.

"What made you turn?" I ask him. "Dad was your kid's Godfather? Boy, are you going to hell." He's steaming up. Good. One more little push. "He showed me pictures. Said you were the bad-ass that made everyone feel alive, and kept them on their toes. Why? Why-"

"Enough!" yells Dread.

"Did you do it? Was it you behind that wheel, Dread? You did it, didn't you? Tell me, come on, let it out!"

He hits hard. I think my other lip's bleeding.

"Yes, Sir," says Dread. Speaking to that voice in his earpiece. I saw it in his ear when he hit me. "I'm not family, kid. You are just a job I have a job to do. It is my job to find out what's in that head. You can tell me now, without pain or we'll find another way."

I spit on him. That was fun. Another punch in the face. My blood splatters onto the floor. I can feel my teeth grind when my jaw swung loosely. My heads ringing like a bell from the blow. He's rolls out a stainless-steel tray. Shiny clean scalpels, various knives, mini saws, a cigar cutter and a mini hammer, all carefully displayed.

"Last chance." says Dread.

I shake my head no. 'Know your value' keeps ringing in my head. He picks up the cigar cutter and lifts one of my purple fingers. They are so numb I can barely feel them.

"Touch me and you won't get a thing." I say looking into the camera mounted in the corner on the wall. "Free my hands. I'm not bluffing. I have a cyanide capsule in my tooth. He touches me, I swallow it and you get nothing."

Dread laughs. Then he pauses. He's listening to that voice in his ear. The voice in his ear will tell him to go for the non-existent capsule and I will get a hearty bite into Dread. Idiots.

"Ahhh! You bit me! I'm gonna kill him!" he yells drawing his gun and putting it on my temple.

I'm laughing so hard inside I almost wet my pants. Just in time. Reluctantly, he holsters his weapon, pulls a box cutter from his back pocket, exposes the blade, looking me straight in the eye with a cold calm and cuts the straps binding my feet, then my hands.
The blood flows back into my hands. I wipe my bottom lip using my wrist looking Dread straight in the eyes.

"Now talk. You're dealing with me," Dread says.

"Yeah, right." I say sarcastically.

Staring at the camera again, I address the one I will be taken to see in just a few short moments.

"You want what's in my head. I want what's in yours. That's the price. No negotiations."

Dread cocks and aims his pistol at my head.

"You got some nerve," says Dread.

All I need do is wait. Dreads nostrils flare, itching to take the shot. I can see his finger tapping the trigger. His face red and the veins on his temples are popping. He can't bite his jaws any harder. Weighing in his mind whether it's worth it to satisfy his urge or continue to breathe another day, knowing better than anyone else that Wilkes won't hesitate to purge the dross. Logic won.

Walking through this hall, I can smell Wilkes. It must be him. He appears to be the type of person to wear aftershave and cologne. He probably wears hair spray too. We approach double doors. Two armed guards in a variation of military uniform open the door. I can feel my body shiver with anticipation. The double doors swing open. I'm not surprised. This looks like a room in someone's house, not an office. The lights are soft from lamps, the floor covered with Persian rugs and classic dark wood and leather seating. Ceiling to floor windows behind the stately oak desk reveal snow-capped mountains. Where am I?

He covered the wall facing the desk with over-sized security monitors rotating live images of every inch of the facility including a helicopter landing pad and private airstrip with a private G-650 on it. He's unremarkable. There he is, seated behind a large oak wood desk. He looks the same as he does on television. I want to talk to him, then, I want to kill him. In that order.

"You've been very difficult to find, son. Please, sit," says Wilkes, "help yourself."

On his desk, a suited man pours coffee from a pot into clean white coffee cups. There are several pastries on a plate. Wilkes takes a cup, adds sugar and creamer and drinks it. He doesn't die. He points to the chair facing his desk that looks comfortable. Rich deep dark creased leather. I remain standing. I lock my eyes onto Wilkes' eyes, looking for his soul. Seeing if he had an ounce of guilt, searching for that unspoken information a person unknowingly divulges without even knowing its escaping.

Something in me digs and keeps digging, looking at every gesture, every slide of his hand across the desk, the turning over of a paper, the lifting of his coffee cup with his right hand to his lips. The squint in the corner of his eyes so smugly satisfied with himself.

His moustache finely trimmed and full salt and pepper beard well brushed. I wonder if dad would have been gray by now. His shirt, crisp white and typical navy suit. Every person has a gesture that gives away their true feels. There it is. His habit, returning his hand to the hilt of the cane that leans on his desk.

I want to hear and feel everything in this moment unclouded by human emotions, the total opposite of the last few years of my life. I feel my New York teaching, cool, not revealing amazement, fear, even anger. Never let your enemy see you sweat. It's difficult because I feel the tremors begin in my hands. Side-effects of ending my drinking habit. Thank you, Big Apple.

I put my hands in the pocket of my leather jacket, hearing the comfortable stretch of the leather as the weight of my hands rest deep inside them, feeling that smooth lining. Coffee and pastry would help. I feel a headache starting to form. He hasn't died from drinking the coffee and I don't think he's stupid enough to poison me now that he may have my cooperation.

"And I'm not your son," I say coldly.

"I see," he replies.

He busies himself shuffling things on his desk. Is he nervous or trying to unnerve me?

"I'm not trying to kill you or starve you, Caleb. You had nothing in the little cafe in town. Take one. Do you know who I am, Caleb?" He asks me.

I stand beside the chair with my fists in my pockets.

"I don't know what you've heard-" he starts.

"What makes you think I've heard anything?"

I don't want to allude to Richard and Gretchen at all. They are the only two who could have told me anything.

"You are the son of my best friend. Officer Joshua Promise saved my life-"

"Don't say his name!"

"Okay. You may not recall but, I remember you playing by the lake one day, you fell, hit your head and I pulled you out before you drowned. I saved your life Caleb."

"You know what I remember. I remember the last day I saw my parents alive. Did you do it?"

"Direct, aren't we?" he says.

"I'm no politician. Answer the question."

I watch his head shake 'no' but his eyes say yes. Could it be true? Not enough proof. Will he grab the cane? If he touches it, even gestures in its direction, I will know. The letter opener on the table would do the trick.

"I did not kill your parents."

His hand doesn't move. Not a muscle, a twitch, a finger jerk. Nothing. I feel the approaching closure dissipate and become that unsettling itch again.

"Caleb, I know you have questions. I want to help you get your answers, but you have some very vital information I require, and time is of the essence..."

Why is he staring at me?

"... you are so much like... your dad. That mind is clicking away, isn't it? You won't tell me, will you? Not until you get what you want. The complete story."

He can't help it. He's almost rambling. The eagerness in his eyes, he desperately wants to release his genius. He's almost seeking approval. I have none to give him. I see something strange in his eyes though. He's looking at me the way he used to look at dad. I just want to get information I can use against him.

He said he was he so much like dad, the problem is I don't know how. I can't remember. So many years of pushing the memories away and avoiding truth, I submerged them in alcohol. I don't know if I can get them back. Ironic, the man I want to kill may be the only one to open the door to my memory since everyone else in my father's platoon is dead. Except Dread. But he's a bad egg.

"I've been to your house more times than I can count. I watched you skip rocks when you were no taller than my knee. You want answers, I'll give them to you, but you may want to sit."

I sit. He begins.

"That desert, unforgiving. But life, Caleb is ruthless. In my early stages of being a Captain, I had the benefit of working beside a brilliant man. A man who comprehended a lot about human life and how to sustain it. At first, naïve, I thought him extreme and well, to be honest, a touch crazy. But, after my first tour, I too understood what was necessary. I saw what perplexed him. I saw what it meant for young lives to be taken for nothing.

Absolutely nothing. Homes and families destroyed for generations over nothing more than an order on a piece of paper. Then, I commanded some of those men. My men. I saw them killed, some right before my eyes, some died in my arms. Some, I finished to keep them from suffering. Oh, you can look at me like that if you want to, but you don't understand. Most 'people' don't.

Help, hundreds of miles away, one-hundred and twenty-degree heat, alone, watching from their satellites and you're holding a boy twitching from pain, feeling every gruelling ounce of agony. It's terrible to take a chance leaving him in the enemy's hands for them to do God knows what to him before they string him up like a trophy for his mother to see. So, you can look at me and judge me if you want to. His eyes begged me to do it. So, I did. More times than any human being should have to. Then, I found a better way. A better way to war. Strategic. That madman wasn't so mad. I got on board. I had only been to the lab once and I was all-in. He showed me the big picture. No more Americans dying for nothing. Put in harm's way. On a tour in Afghanistan, ten men died in one mission, one useless mission to find a trigger maker responsible for making the trigger that blew up a mosque killing over fifty people.

They didn't just kill them. That would have been humane. They tortured those men for weeks then hung their bodies like hunks of meat in that sweltering desert for publicity. Did we ever hear about it at home? No. Of course not. They died and were quietly buried under a shroud of honor. But I knew the truth. I had to bear the truth. I knew it didn't have to be so. This weapon. Not a piece of metal that can make mistakes. No, so far beyond that was created to save lives. American lives, and preserve our way of life. Prototype of the BST-10 Project. Otherwise known as the Beaston." He leans forward. "A weapon that thinks."

He's left the room. His mind left. It's no longer here. I can tell by that far-away look. I see the end of the man.

"I'll never forget the day they called me and said it was ready. I was in my office in Washington. They were the sweetest words spoken. Strong. Dedicated. Believing in my vision. The scientists' brilliance surpassed my expectations. It was our creation. They led me to it like a mother to her newborn child. I can still see the smile on their faces even after having been shut away in the laboratory beneath the Brazilian forest.

Skins pale from lack of sunlight, yet they were as excited as I. It walked around on hind legs. Straight up like a man. It even knew how to cock its head and study us, boasting its superiority. Feet like a bear for silent movement, legs muscular like a zebra but as lean as a lion. Its pelt shined and shimmered in the darkness, a black and silvery gray combination making it easy to become nothing more than a shadow. A fete a camouflage man could never achieve."

This was the creature in my nightmares. He continues.

"Its head and face like that of a lioness," he cups his hands as if he were caressing its face. "with eyes of a keen eagle but rounded with a human likeness. It heard me through the foot-thick glass. Ears perked like a cat and arms with hand-like joint structure but tipped with talons. When it spread its arms, it had almost a retractable skin-like cape that comes out making it able to swim, catch wind and hold its weight.

It sensed us from behind its enclosure before it even saw us. I created it to have these capabilities. A sense of smell and sight exceeding animals and intellectual capabilities exceeding most human beings. It deduces quickly and strategises after assessing its surroundings. Perfect in every way." He takes a sip of coffee. "Yet, it gave me a chill that crept up my spine watching it hide in plain sight when I stepped forward, then intentionally revealing itself, sensing the moment my anxiety reached its peak. It knew what an imposing figure it was. Fear mixed with a sense of power stepped into my soul because it was ours."

This Beaston, everything he described, is exactly what I felt and saw in my recurring dream. Foreshadowing? I don't know.

Maybe it was God's gracious way of letting me see it before I saw it in reality. Wilkes goes on.

"It takes orders and will strike its intended targets without prejudice. Adapts to terrain of any kind and was trained in every environment. Remarkable."

He's on a roll. He's purging, so maybe he will divulge more than he planned to.

"How did the platoon die?" I ask.

He pauses and looks at me, almost as if he's trying to determine if he should keep going.

"Ron, more hot coffee, please. Gentlemen, give me the room." He says.

Ron pours the coffee and pauses for the other guards to leave the room then walks out behind them closing the door.

"No one knows what I'm about to tell you. Not a living soul." Wilkes takes a deep breath like a sinner in the confession booth. "It was the maiden trial. It was one week after they killed the ten Americans. The Beaston's maiden mission was to find the trigger maker responsible for the bomb and hold him for questioning. The Beaston found him in record time. It solved one problem but created another. The solution had consequences I still live with."

"Funny," he chuckles, "you're getting free what the C.I.A. begged for just yesterday," he says, turning away from me.

There is a sharp letter opener on his desk. His back is to me. He's gazing over the snow caped mountains and clouds. This is way too much temptation. I need to refocus and listen.

"Caleb, I was unconscious. I don't know how long, but when I woke, I was bleeding to death on a blood-soaked cot.   Your father, he was with me, using strips of his shirt to stop my bleeding. My men were in a cell beside us. Fletcher, Willz, Doc, the package, Dread, I couldn't see them. I had no way of knowing what was about to happen. None."

CHAPTER FOURTEEN

Wilkes Confession

"I can still feel the sand on my face. That stuff always reminds you how far from home you are. We were in the mess hall. Our last meal before we left. I felt like a father watching his kids play. There they were, as usual, prodding each other like kids do. It kept them sharp. I could hear them. I could always hear them. Dread was telling his doom and gloom stories to the new wide-eyed doc that just came aboard.

"You want to die? This is the place to do it, like a man in the hot dirt. Just step outside those doors..." Dread said to the Doc.

"As usual, Fletcher was running interference. None of them were ever crazy enough to challenge Fletcher. He was elite. Martial arts, marksman, and smart. Dread was telling Doc a story about their last mission. Dread kept going with his story."

"... so, I pull the pin-" continues dread.

"Here we go," says Willz.

"-I looked him dead in the eye, then Willz backs into me, I drop the thing and it rolls into the next room and BOOM! I almost crapped myself," says Dread. "Rollie told me it was a dud. I wanted to kill him. My informant bolts, and we're in the dust like 'what the hell!'"

"I thought it *was* a dud," says Rollie, laughing uncontrollably. "I'm sticking to working the computers. Next time you're on your own. I bet someone switched it."

"Let me guess, Rollie, it's a conspiracy," says Fletcher.

"You tell me why are we getting blood drawn, huh, you tell me? Conspiracy," says Rollie.

"Man, nobody wants your blood," says Picker, eating. "They probably want to make sure you caught nothing from that blond you met on leave." Laughs Fletcher.

"Caleb, Picker was our sniper. This mission, he was unusually quiet. I can always tell when a man has too much on his mind. And before this mission, he had plenty on his mind. Just before we deployed, the doctor found his daughter had a brain tumor. They couldn't afford the surgery. It was growing fast. She was going blind.
That morning, his wife called to thank me. She thought I did it, but it was your dad. I heard him on the video phone with your mother earlier:

"Thanks, baby. I know how much you loved the house being paid off," your dad said. "It's the right thing to do. You just come home safe and figure out how we'll pay it back," your mom told him."

"Caleb, your father mortgaged his house to pay for Picker's daughter's surgery. He told him right before we left. I never saw a man so relieved. Your dad knew Picker couldn't pay it back. The truth is, he never expected him to. That was your father. Men like that shouldn't die. We loaded up. Rollie was on communications, Fletcher, Willz, Doc, Picker sniper, and Dread the gunnery and your father with the package. Then the package arrived."

"What package?" asks Caleb.

"A man."

I need to sit. My hip has stiffened again.

"A man?" repeats Caleb.

He's engulfed in the story and now, so am I. I can see it in his eyes.

"Yes. A man with a steel suitcase. He had precious cargo. Our mission was to deliver the case and the man. They made it clear that the case was more important than the man. This to happen after nightfall. I ordered the men to park on one side of the mountain, I made the remaining journey alone. All they had to do was wait for me to return. Everything was on schedule then they attacked the men. Ambushed. Wrong place, wrong time. They held them in a gunfight. They were seen as a trophy."

"What was in the suitcase?"

"The solution to an enormous problem."

I sip the coffee. Smooth, sweet and dark. I needed it. This story takes something from me. I swivel my hip and can feel the grind of the steel pin in it rub my bone. I hope Caleb doesn't see my pain. He's as perceptive as is father was.

"It was the Beaston's maiden voyage. My predecessor confided in me, though it was in a very preliminary state. We were to collect it and the trigger maker that night. When I got to the location; I wish I never saw what I saw. I still hear her wailing. The woman, his wife. I heard no one cry like that. It was from her core. She was on her knees, clutching his bloody sandal to her chest. She looked at me and I could see hate and anger rush in as soon as she saw my uniform. He was a slumped pile of unidentifiable flesh she couldn't even bring herself to embrace. The town people were yelling at me. They thought it was 'Yuz', meaning leopard. She looked at me as if she knew better.

From the mutilated face, I couldn't tell if it was Amir, the Beaston's target. Then, I saw his bag on the ground in the dirt, overlooked by everyone. I grabbed it and there it was. Triggers. Bomb triggers. It was him. Probably coming home from work. He looked like any other man. Then I saw it in his bag. A toy truck, a tiny thing, wrapped in brown paper and tied with string. No doubt for his son and a pair of earrings for his wife, Tirashi. That was her name. The Beaston lured him into the bushes just outside his house, and that's where its flaw manifested.

You see, it yielded its animalistic tendencies. It's thirst to conquer its prey. If that instinct couldn't be suppressed, it was useless. It didn't eat him, it mutilated him and left him for his wife to find. Typical of an animal marking its territory. I got the evidence, the triggers, but no Amir. No answers. I loaded the Beaston into the cargo truck, tranquillised it and headed back to meet the men. That's when things went south. The convoy was under enemy fire. After what felt like hours of a gunfight, with the Beaston in the back, things got worst. It was the only prototype and couldn't risk it getting killed. I got shot. They killed Picker. They captured us. Your father, thinking on his feet, negotiated for our lives. In that rancid cell, I told him about it before I passed out. I knew the enemy had found it."

"There's something you're not telling me," says Caleb.

He was right. I wanted it off my chest. Here, safe, I could release it. Besides, he will not live to tell this story.

"Myself, Fletcher, Rollie, Doc, the Package and Dread and your father were tossed into the worst rusty bloody cells I've ever seen. I won't ever forget the smell of recent death and rotting flesh that hung in the hot desert air. Your father used what I told him it to negotiate for our lives with empty promises, they believed. It was not a secret anymore. Before we could get State side, I had to give the men an ultimatum. I thought they would understand, being soldiers. But they didn't. It was the hardest conversation I ever had."

"Except Dread," says Caleb.

I could only nod at him. I was back in that horrid place again. Suffocating from the heat. Surrounded by the judging eyes of men who looked up to me.

"Caleb, they couldn't leave the desert, son. They just couldn't. But I needed your father. It was all Fletcher's fault. Christian, logic prevailed and the men respected him. I did what I could, promised them money, a guarantee of jobs after their tours. Medical security, everything a soldier could want. But Fletcher's ideals spoke louder than all of that. All they had to do is keep their mouths shut. That's it! Damn Fletcher! His words, they were righteous. They cut to the bone and the marrow. There they were all standing around my cot in that rancid cell. Fletcher's words still make me wonder if it was right. I can hear him...*'It ain't right! God didn't make that. I won't have any part. If we let this thing exist, what else will they make? Next thing you know they'll be trying to clone us!'* Fletcher said.

That's when I saw it, that flicker in Fletcher's eye. He looked at the metal suitcase handcuffed to the thin man's wrist. He had been silent and appeared terrified. When he saw Fletcher's glare, he gripped the handle until his knuckles turned white.

One by one the men looked at the case as if it were calling their names. Then they looked at me. Rollie, the conspiracy theorist, was the first to speak, but even he didn't want to believe it. Not really. *'No, no way, man. Can't be! Cap. Tell him it ain't. You wouldn't let them do that to us! Tell him!'* Rollie kept yelling. I hear those words echo in my sleep.

I watched Rollie back away from that case like it contained the plague. He looked at me like a son disappointed in his father. They trusted me implicitly. Then Fletcher kept pushing.

"One way to find out. Open it." Said Fletcher.

"He can't, you know that. Not even he has the key." said Rollie.

Then your father spoke the words that nailed my coffin.

'Only the recipient has the key.' He was right. And with one gesture, your father pegged me as the recipient. They looked at me. The disappointment in his eyes hurt worse than the gunshot to the hip. I tried to convince Fletcher:

"You're not clear on this, Fletcher," I said. But it didn't work.

"All due respect, Sir," he said, "I'm crystal clear. Now give me the key!"

Dread tried to help me. He wanted the money.

"We don't know he's got it," said Dread.

Your father was smart. So smart.

He said, *"I know one thing. If he's got that key, none of us are supposed to leave this desert alive."*

Then they all paused. In that filthy cell, the loud sound of prayers spoken over a loudspeaker filled the awkward silence and I felt the shock and uncertainty pry us apart. Fletcher... pulled off my boot. The key was in the sole of my boot. I'll never forget their faces when Fletcher opened the case and they saw it.
The vials of their blood, labeled with their dog-tag ID numbers. Each vial contained the characteristics necessary to perfect the Beaston. Your father closed his eyes. I hated myself in that moment. It was clear. They weren't in. I was barely conscious from the pain. They were going to break the vials."

I stop and toss my small white pill in my mouth and drink some water. Caleb's heart is beating so fast I can see his chest rise. Is that anger?

"What happened? How did you walk out of there?" Caleb asks.

"It was the Package, he pulled a gun he had hidden and as cool as a cucumber he killed Fletcher. One shot to the head. Then Rollie. Dread finished Doc. I wouldn't let them touch your father. He saved my life and he was my friend."

Caleb thinks, then asks the obvious. I think he knows the answer.

"Why did they let you go?"

"A promise that when the Beaston was perfected, they would get the data. Told them there was a tracker in it and hell fire would rain on them if they didn't take the deal. Words in the wind. It was the only way they'd let us leave, alive. Also, I agreed to let them take credit for the killing... of my men. At the time, that served me.
The vision is bigger than any one person, you see. The Beaston had to evolve, but it needed-"

"-them," says Caleb.

"Yes, Caleb. Their dedication, their resolve, restraint, loyalty."

"You admired them, then killed them. The Beaston isn't the monster you are. Face what you did!"

"I faced it. They brought her into my cell. Tirashi, Amir's wife with her son. They made me listen to her. We would have been dead, but your father convinced them we would keep our word.
She had such hate in her eyes for me. I couldn't blame her. She told me how she and Amir waited years to have a child.

Now, he had one and he'd never see him grow up. She made me look at the boy. See his tears. I felt for her, I did, but she would have done the same to save her child. Without hesitation.

I explained to your father that this project was to keep men out of the field. So, ambushes like this could never happen. Your father made me believe he was in. I guess I wanted to believe it too. Dread was already in. Now, I know it was just a survival tactic. I should have expected it, but I didn't see it."

"So later you kill him-" starts Caleb.

"I had no reason to kill your father, son." I say.

"I'm not your son."

"Logically, I needed what he had. Those drives. What would I gain by killing him?"

CHAPTER FIFTEEN

Caleb Promise

I listened. I sat still and listened. Resisted the urge to kill him and just listened to him. He was empty. A shell of a man. Telling the story aged him five years. He grabs the hilt of his cane, leaning on his desk. He's confessed to the equivalent of treason and the murder of his entire platoon. Either he trusts me implicitly or he plans to kill me when this is all over. It's probably the latter. Strangely, there was something solvent about Wilkes. If pure, his loyalty could build worlds.

"Caleb. That's it. The piece of your puzzle. Now you know I had no motive for killing your father. None. That's all you wanted to know anyway, right? It's your turn."

I put the glasses on the desk. Wilkes doesn't touch them. I'm surprised. There is nothing on the video that gives away the drives. Its contents canonized his dependence on me thus ensuring my safety. Disclosure for disclosure. It keeps the gate open. He presses a button on his desk and Ron comes into the room.

He gestures to Ron. The message is so personal that I feel invaded. Again. I have no choice. Now I watch while this suited stranger puts them on. The pin-sized light on the arm of the glasses turns red instead of green. His body stiffens and he falls to the ground, face first. Pin-sized holes on each of his temples release drops of blood. Razor sharp wires shot out from the arms. I guess he failed the retinal scan. Wilkes doesn't look surprised at all.

"For your eyes only, huh? Prom, you never cease to amaze me." Looking up at the ceiling. "What did it say?" Wilkes asks, unfazed by Ron's wide-eyed corpse on the floor.

"You trust me to tell you the truth?"

"In good faith. I told you the truth. Yes, it's code of honor among men. You're a man, aren't you?"

The door opens and an armed man removes the glasses, places them on the desk, then drags Ron's body out with blood now flowing out of his temples, with his eyes still open. His new shoes leaving a drag mark in the carpet. Another suited man steps into the room, dressed like Ron, formal, and stands at the door discreetly like a butler. He's expressionless.

"More coffee, Ron."

I look at Wilkes. Did he forgot that he killed Ron?

"I haven't forgotten, Caleb. They are all Ron to me. They come and go so frequently. Why bother to learn a name? They know the risks." he says to me. "I'm waiting."

Cold bastard.

"It was dad. He said his death was no accident."

Wilkes pulls a cigar from a wooden box on the desk, snips one end and pierces a hole in the other and lights it. He takes a long draw as if forcing his patience.

"He said he loved me, and he was sorry he left me. That's it."

"You're breaking the code."

I fiddle with the lock in my pocket. If I don't disclose it, my boots may leave drag marks in the carpet. He probably already knows I have it. This may be a test. Rage is sitting in my chest. Waiting to burst free. Wilkes' impatience is growing. He grasps the hilt of the cane again.

"I thought you were a man of honor like your father. I misjudged you. You have one thing in common with your father. You can't bluff because you're not a liar by nature."

With the cigar clenched between his lips, he presses a series of buttons on a small black tablet. The snow-capped mountains whisk away, leaving a smoky glass wall. I can see something appearing. The glass is clearing slowly. It's clear. I can see it and my heart sinks.

A woman lying in a glass domed incubator with monitor lights blinking, covered by a clean white sheet. There is a nurse, her back to us, washing her hands in a sink. I didn't feel myself walk to the glass. I just sort of ended up there. I pass his desk and look at that silver envelope holder. I am closer. I can see her clearly.

"Impossible-" escapes my lips.

"In my world this is very possible."

Wilkes walks over and stands beside me. I feel the suited man approach behind me.

"How?" I ask.

"No more answers. Talk or she dies, again."

It's my mother. Rage wins. I grab the envelope opener and put it to Wilkes' throat.

"I want to see her!"

"You're in debt, young Promise."

I squeeze his lapel tighter and hear the cock of the gun and feel the nuzzle press into the back of my head. This Ron is faster than I thought. Wilkes sees it. How badly I want to kill him.

"That's something your father always knew how to control. Tsk-tsk, young Promise. It will get you nowhere."

Sharp pain. The butt of Ron's gun at the base of my neck. I'm on one knee near the bottom of his cane.

"Sir?" the nurse says.

I know that voice.

"Do it," Wilkes says.

What does he mean 'do it'? She's filling a syringe.

"Caleb, say goodbye."

It's the same nurse from Lou's room.

"NO!" I yell, hitting the glass.

I stare at her through the glass. It looks exactly like her! He thinks I'm just in shock, but I'm looking. Looking for that tiny scar on the back of her right hand. The one she got on my first fishing trip. I cast the line and hooked her hand. Is this truly her? Mom was an Audrey Hepburn fan. She never pierced her ears. She wore clip-on earrings and never lived in her time. She was made for an earlier time when grace and beauty were in subtly and modesty. Are those piercings in her ears or shadows? I can't tell. So that was not her lying motionless, although part of me wishes it were.

The clincher, a tiny glass bottle of morphine half empty at the nurse's station. Why would you have to give morphine to a woman in a coma? I need him to believe he has something on me. The truth is, I'm not done with him. I want his contacts. There's a bigger fish in the pond.

"Banging won't help you. Think, young Promise, think. You know how to stop this," says Wilkes, puffing on his cigar.

She's looking at Wilkes for the all clear to suppress the syringe into her I.V. tube.

"Do it, Marge."

"Wait! Okay! He left me a clue to where it is, but I haven't figured it out yet."

Wilkes looks into my eyes and holds his hand up, signaling Marge to stop.

"You give me everything and we are the best of friends, you cross me, and I'll dump you and your mother in a shallow grave. My cause is that important to me."

"I get it, okay," I answer.

"Good, sit down."

"That's all for now, dear," Wilkes says to the nurse.

The fake snow-capped mountains re-appear on the glass.

"I value human life, but one life can't stand in the way of a new way to war. Where is my data?"

"Just let me think."

"You have three minutes, Caleb."

He exhales impatiently and sips his coffee. In the back of my head, I can hear Richard's voice begging me to bring the hard drive to him and Gretchen. I know I must backtrack and slow down, to figure this out. I'm fourteen again, hearing the sawdust scratch the rustic wood planks beneath my sneakers. Playing cards with Rose.

Through the open doorway I can see mom curled on the sofa, back propped against dad's chest. His arm around her shoulders, they look at the pages in a book. She turned pages gently with delicate hands and freshly polished nails in her favorite shade of red, just cradling a book with calm and love on her face as if she were looking at a newborn baby's face. She respected books. They took her places they couldn't afford to go. She was finding their dream vacation destination.

"Where!" yells Wilkes.

Wilkes has one more time to yell at me. If I didn't need him, I'd choke him out.

"Where?" Dad asked Mom lovingly.

"Look," mom said, "this one just made number one. Steeped in art history and guess what?"

She turned the page of the book.

"What?" Dad asked.

"It's-" she begins.

I say it with her, "-the safest place on the earth."

I close my eyes to see the book in her hand. A lit dome. Arched bridge. I can't see the name. Wait. I know it. Can it be? Yes. It is.

"Time's up." Wilkes puts his cigar down.

I hear the click. Ron cocks the gun.

"The Vatican."

I could take that gun right out of his hands. But not yet. I'm not finished. Wilkes' sly smile becomes him. Now he really looks like a snake.

"The Vatican." Wilkes repeats it with surprise. "I would never have guessed. The plane. Now."

The tarmac is windy, but we approach the G-650. Wilkes, Dread, the tall man and myself. Two stewardess' are standing at the front entrance greeting Wilkes as "Mr. Secretary."
It's not coach. Butter soft tan seating. Dread and the tall man follow behind us and sit at a table near the door. Wilkes leads us to the table and seats near the rear.

"First time?" Wilkes asks me.

He's kidding, right? Small talk. Never. All the window shades are drawn and a stewardess places two menus on the table in front of us.

"Just like your dad-"

"Why do you keep saying that? 'Just like your dad'?" I blurt.

"Well, the way you talk, soft spoken, observant, always locked in. Your dad was my chief strategist for a reason. He mastered being present, without being intrusive. He could soak in a room and within minutes know the weakness of every man in there, thus, knowing how to defeat them. Do you have 'that', Caleb?"

"You tell me." I reply, looking at him with my chin cocked upward.

"I think you've got these guys figured out. You know, I have no children. Lost my wife to cancer at thirty-two years old. You could say, I always wanted a successor. If your anything like your father, you're a good learner. I'd welcome the chance to work with the great Officer Promises blood-line."

He speaks about me like I'm a breed of dog.

"A few days ago," I lean forward with my forearm on the table and tap on it with my fingertips, "I was a jobless drunk, homeless, robbed, suicidal thief chased by the police and wanted for murder. I have nothing... but my self-respect. Think I'll keep it."

Dread and the tall man are playing cards.

"Get to know me, Caleb, always know your opponent." He fixes his tie and jacket. "I know you. I have been watching you."

"Then you didn't see much!"

The stewardess puts down two cups of coffee and finger sandwiches. I drink coffee from her. It's good. I eat a few sandwiches too. I need strength for what will happen next.

"I saw enough. Your father wouldn't have approved. Your drinking, the toy store... Elizabeth."

"I had nothing to do with that."

I put the coffee cup down and my fists tighten impulsively. I shove them in my jacket pockets.

"That's not what The N.Y.P.D. think. I know you didn't do it, because I did. Your father rammed his fists in his pockets just like that whenever he was thinking hard."

"You knew they'd blame me."

"Not at all. Elizabeth was a problem." Casually stirring his coffee. "She wanted you fired which would have pulled you out my world. It figures, you never take cabs and of all nights-" Wilkes shakes his head and takes a sip.

Things are coming together.

"The florist?" I ask.

"Mine. Though, not professional. Too impatient. Unpredictable. Think she got bitter because you kept rejecting her. She couldn't be trusted. She had to go."

"Joe?" I swallow hard, feeling like a pawn on a board though I had my suspicions. There is one name I don't want to say.

"Mine. Just a set of eyes. Keep going."

He's enjoying this. He would.

"Judy?"

"Mine. Well, not anymore. She put the tracker on the coat. Amateur. Got that poor thief killed for nothing. Cost me clean up. Come on, come on."

"The toy store guy?" I need to be sure.

"No, no, that pathetic creature was definitely real. I couldn't make him up. You're getting warm," says Wilkes.

He wants to hear me say it. I feel my stomach sink because there was only one other person who mattered. I don't want his name to be on that list.

"Yes. Say it. You know you want to know." He beckons with his fingers.

"Lou."

I feel my jaw tighten.

"Bingo. Yes. My first recruit. I paid the mortgage off on that roach-trap diner for him. Unfortunately, he got too vested. He was supposed to act like a father to get into your head. Then, one day, it became too real to him. He began withholding information. Joe let me know. One of our guys visited him to apply some necessary pressure. I was unaware that he had a bad heart."

That explains Lou's attack the night he was taken away in the ambulance. The night Liz began to hate me.

"For the record," Wilkes puts his cup down, "He loved you like a father. That was real. When you quit, I had no further need for his services. In essence, you killed Lou."

I lunge at him across the table and grab him at the neck. Dread and the tall man pull me off him. The tall man puts a gun to the top of my head while Dread forces me down to the seat.

"No need gentlemen. I'm alright." Says Wilkes tugging his suit jacket down. "Are we composed?"

A chill creeps up my spine. The one that only comes when the evil enters a room. My hatred for Wilkes boils.

"You can't grow without facing cold hard facts. I value human life, but one life can't stand in the way a new way to war."

I can feel my breath deepen. I want to kill him, now.

"I *will* watch you die."

I slam the table and Dread and the tall man stand up.

"No. Now, gentlemen, it's all right." Slowly, Dread and the tall man sit again. "Let's stay calm and think. You wanted answers, didn't you? Didn't you? That's why you're still here. Knowledge is intriguing, isn't it? The more you get, no matter how distasteful, how wretched, the more you want, until one day knowledge is not enough. You want power to change things. To be that variable that induces an outcome. Do you want to stop being the helpless observer and become the agent of change?"

"This *thing* is your agent of change?" I grunt sarcastically.

"No, Caleb. I am the agent of change. It is my muse."

Wilkes lights a cigar. A cell phone rings. The new Ron approaches the table cautiously and whispers into Secretary Wilkes ear. He takes the cigar out of his mouth to take the call.

"Yes." Smiling. "As we speak."

He hangs up the phone.

"Minutes to landing, Sir," the pilot says over the intercom.

Wilkes takes out his cell phone and presses in a five-digit code and a red digital clock. He turns the cell phone toward me. A count down starts on the bottom of the screen.

"Swipe right," Wilkes says.

I do it. A live video of my fake mother's encasement. She may be someone's mother. She's just not mine, but a life is a life worth saving.

"What is this?"

"A push."

The clock reads forty-five minutes. It's counting down.

"We land in five minutes. You bring me my data, or every life support system will shut down, one by one and you will bury her. For real this time. Then, I'll bury you."

My jaw tightens and I can feel my teeth bite down.

"Temper, temper, young Promise. I'm the only one who knows the code to cancel the order. Kill me, she dies. Disappear, she dies. Cross me,"

Wilkes holds his hand up to his ear.

"She dies." I say.

Wilkes snips the tip of another cigar.

"Dave and Dread will accompany you. Give me what I want and you two can walk into the sunset to start over somewhere. I really don't care where."

We exit the plane. It's cold. A caravan of Wilkes' goons are waiting for us in compact vehicles. Seeing this place makes me realize I have seen nothing yet. A drive surrounded by a fleet of Wilkes men in cars quickly gets us to The Vatican.

The tall man, Dread and I, ride in a vehicle with a driver wearing black sunglasses. We arrive and get out of the vehicles. It's cold, but the Basilica is alive. An orchestra is playing the Festive Eucharist with a children's choir singing. A part of me wants to experience this and soak in the strings and harmonious music but I can't.

The people look so happy. So, content. They look as if they know they belong there. A bare-faced nun bundled, with a simple smile, hands each of us pamphlet and scurries off distributing them to the next group.

"Christmas Mass, three o'clock in the Basilica. Archbishop Agnoli presiding," it says on the cover.

These people represent nationalities from all over the world. The scope of Wilkes' intentions settles in. What if I can't stop him and the Beaston lives? What if one day, he deems these people to be a threat to 'his' way of life? I can't imagine being responsible for murders.

Just a few days ago, I had no control over people living or dying. Now, I do. There is one life that grips my reasoning. Even if that one life isn't really my mother. Strangely enough, I want to believe it is her. But my eyes know differently. We enter St. Peter's Square, circular, with a large but tasteful stone fountain in the centre. Dad chose this place for a reason. He wanted me to know God is watching over me. I'm sure of it.

The Vatican symbolism is poignantly imposing. It represents the purity and the goodness of Jesus Christ and Christianity as a whole despite man's flaws. The papacy meaningful in its comfort as described by Karl Marx, "the opiate of the masses." My eyes drawn upward to the building's architecture. A mother correcting a boy. He seems to be about ten years old.

"Jimmy! Keep up. Pick your head up, you'll walk into a pillar staring at that thing! Charles, talk to him. That thing shouldn't be allowed. Anyway. Roaming is an art."

The timer is running. I know there is a clue where to go, something. I've got the numbers and this funny looking key thing inside the lock.

"Sorry, mister."

The child bumps into me and his device falls at my feet. On first glance it looks like a video game. It's not. It is a Global Positioning System device.

"Mo-om, you're going the wrong way," the boy says, bending to pick it up.

"Here you go," I say, handing it to him.   Suddenly, I got it. "Can I borrow it for a second, please?"

"Sure. Just don't break it, all right?"

How could I not smile at that? I do the number game in my head. I press some buttons. My hands are trembling slightly. Withdrawal. I can't wait until this is over. I'm not sure it ever ends. It's the first time I've quit. It may affect my personality. One minute I feel happy to be finding out what I'm finding out, the next I want to kill someone. Or, maybe that's just who I really am. If it is, I can live with that. I can barely press the buttons. The timer is counting down in my pocket. Her fate is in my hands.

"Give-r here. Just tell me the numbers," says the kid, wide-eyed. Honest. Pure. Me, so many years ago.

"Thanks." I hand it over. "41, 90, 12,45."

"Sounds weird," he says, whistling through a missing tooth. "Oh, I got it."

"What?" I ask.

"The number's in longitude and latitude are like 'point' something. It's 41.90, 12.45 like that. See?" He holds the device up with a toothless smile. I look at the location. "Got another? This is fun."

"Let's go," Grunts Dread. "Enough games."

"I appreciate it," I say.

I look directly into his innocent eyes. The boy nods and his mother ushers him away.

"Where to?" Dread asks.

"Don't speak to me again. Traitor." I walk ahead of them.

Dread shoves my shoulder. I turn around and face him.
"Wilkes ain't here to protect you. Just remember that. You can find the drives just as well with a bullet in your leg."

"Enough." interrupts the tall man. "Where to?"

"The Vatican Library," I say, almost nose to nose with Dread. Fury blazing in both our eyes.

Walking through the crowd, I needed more information.

"He will kill me, isn't he?" I ask the tall man.

"Probably. You'll be the first to know."

"Think you're safe? You and Dread. You're witnesses to all this stuff. You two are just Rons' without the suit. Government guys always tie their loose ends. You're swinging in the wind, my friends."

"I proved my loyalty. I'm in it for the long hall. What's so funny?" asks Dread.

The tall guy chuckles. This is getting interesting.

"Proved yourself? You're a gun." He says. "That's all you are. Not a brain. Brains are indispensable, guns aren't. You lose one, you buy another. You've learned nothing," says the tall man.

"You know something, speak up," Dread grunts.

Time to throw some dirt throw in the game. Old New York trick. You throw the dirt and see where it sticks.

"All right, just forget it. It's probable that he won't kill you, Dread."

"Shut up, Caleb! Hey," Dread turns to the tall man, "if you know something speak up. I put my neck on the line plenty. What did that bastard tell you?"

The tall guy sets up for the lay-up. Approaches the basket, and... shoots.

"Wilkes said nothing, just rumors from Ron that Wilkes thinks it's time for a fresh face. More... discreet. Ron's his right hand and his right ear."

"Should have known that pencil neck would turn. But you said nothing until now!"

It looks good. Divide and conquer. Now to be the voice of reason.

"Look. We're in this together. He's got my mom, he wants Dread dead, and who knows what he has planned for you?" I say discreetly.

"Caleb's right. Hate to admit it but he's got a point. I'll finish him before he gets to me." Says Dread biting his jaw.

Swoosh! A three pointer.

"Speak for yourself," says the tall man. He taps his ear. "Did you hear that, Sir?" the tall man asks Wilkes. He has an earpiece.

Why didn't I think of that? Oh well.
"That clock's ticking. Let's go!" says the tall man.

Dread shoves me in the back.

"You're on your own," says Dread.

They don't seem concerned about me trying to disappear in the crowd. Perhaps it is because they can just shoot me in the back. In the library, I flip through every book that corresponds to the numbers. Nothing. I can't help but look the digital numbers counting down. Perspiration drips from my brow and my hands shake. I slam the last book shut on the dark wood table and it echoes so loudly, others at the neighboring tables look up.

"Nothing." I run my hands through my short spiky hair. I forgot I cut it for a minute. "I need to go," I say to them.

"Are you kidding me?" says the tall man.

Dread looks at me.

"Let's go," he says.

I walk toward the stalls in the back of the bathroom and the tall man shoves me against the wall. I turn. Fists clenched.

"Are you playing with me, boy?" The tall man grabs my collar. "I don't like games! I've been waiting too long for this! Besides, the longer you take to find it, the longer I have to wait to kill you. Where is it?"

The tall man tightens his choke hold. My veins bulge on my temples. I can't breathe.

A short high-pitched sound and I feel Dave let go. His body drops into slowly. Dread drags him into a stall and sits him on a toilet. He turns, shushes me and pulls the earpiece out of Dave's ear, presses something on it and hands it to me.

"There, you can hear Wilkes, but he can't hear you," says Dread.

"Took you long enough," I say, pulling my jacket down into place. I search the guys military vest and there they are. Three small clear gel-based trackers. They stick to anything and are virtually invisible. I shove them into my pocket. Dread didn't notice.

"I was wondering whose side you were on." I say to Dread who turned around to open the door to the large handicap toilet stall.

"All that mouth, I was giving you a chance to see what you're really made of," says Dread smiling.

"How in the world did you work with that guy?" I ask.

"Wasn't easy. I wanted to kill him like six different times," replies Dread.

"Three minutes," says Dread, taking the tall man's cell phone and checking his pockets.

"What are you looking for?" I ask.

Dread looks at me and answers.

"He owes me five bucks."

"Are you kidding me?" I say.

"Who is she?" I ask him.

"Don't know. But she really looks like your mom." Dread says.

Frustration gets the best of me and I hit the mirror, shattering it into the sink.

"I could have killed him."

"You would have blown it if you did. He's been talking to someone on a cheap phone. Can't tell if he's giving orders or taking them."

"That's not good enough." I say then splash cold water on my face and pull two paper towels out to dry my hands.

"It's all I got, and you're running out of time."

The bathroom door opens. It's the bare-faced nun. Dread and I look at each other. She glances at me, face dripping wet, then at Dread, standing in the doorway of a stall in front of the tall man slumped on the toilet seat.

"What is this?" she asks her hands tucked into her habit.

Great. Dread couldn't resist.

"Keep standing there and you'll look like him." Dread says to her.

Is he crazy? She'll call security. What's she going to do? I can't read her. She looks familiar. She's the nun that handed me the pamphlet in the Basilica.

"I'd like to see you try it, big oaf." She puts her hand on her hip letting the door shut behind her.

What? Wait, is it? It is. I should have known by the big brown eyes. Jean? Otherwise known as the hall prostitute. She looks so different not slathered in cheap makeup. Quite a transformation.

"Did you find it?" Jean asks.

"Not yet," says Dread.

"Caleb," Jean says, smiling at me.

Quickly, she pulls a small kit out from under her habit, opens it on a shelf in the bathroom and turns Dread around. She lifts his shirt to remove his tracker.

"Like my new tattoo?" says Dread to her while she cleans the surgical spot.

"Shut up," says Jean.

"What else do you have under there?" Dread continues.

"You'll never find out. Be still," she says.

She's focused, always focused. I don't think she knows how much seeing her every day squatted in that dank hall made me respect her. I felt less lonely, for a while.

"Jean, we have a problem," I say.

"Speak."

I hold up the phone to her, showing the live feed and large red numbers counting down. She squints to see it.

"You're kidding me. Is that-?" she says, with her eyes glued on the live feed.

"I don't know. But if I don't hand it over to him, she dies." I say.

Jean shakes her head and drops Dreads tracker into a small pan. She puts surgical tape on Dread's opening slaps him on the back signaling he is done. She spins her finger in a circle in the air to me to turn around and waves a long black device over my back and it beeps. I take off my jacket so she can remove it.

"Sh-" she says hearing something.

The restroom door opens again. An elderly man proudly wearing his new a floppy-rim hat with camera swinging from the long black strap around his neck walks into the bathroom. He looks at me, at the sink, Dave in the stall digging in the tall man's pockets and a nun holding a small black kit with sharp scalpels in her hand. Dread looks at him unyieldingly.

This man has age and wisdom. You can have one without the other, you know. He backs out of the lavatory and lets the door shut gently. From inside the lavatory we hear him speaking to his wife.

"What's the matter, dear? I thought you had to go?" says the old man's wife.

"False alarm, let's go. Just, let's go." says the old man.

"But, dear..."

Jean locks the restroom door, then finishes removing my tracker, waves the long black sensor up and down the front and back of me.

"You're clean. Caleb, I know how hard this is, but we can't give it to him. We can't. That's the entire mission."

"I know that's the mission, Jean. For years, I've known that's the mission." I look at her. "That's why you have to get her out. He'll kill her. We let her die and we are just like him." I say.

"What? No." She shakes her head and snatches off her surgical gloves.

"Dread has the co-ordinates. You take care of this, when you're clear with her, we meet at the rally point." I say looking for her confirmation.

She's not on board. She starts taking off her habit roughly.

"No. Caleb, we stick to mission. That's priority. I'm sorry but it is. Remember when we first spoke, look at me, Caleb. Do you remember?"

"Yes."

How could I forget? I see it like yesterday. She played me like a fiddle. I felt sorry for her sitting in that drafty hall and offered her pizza and a night in a bed, alone. I let her into my cheap room and as soon as the door shut, she told me who really sent her and who she was and why she was there. Jean, disguised as a prostitute, said they sent her to protect me and help me get the mission accomplished. She was always watching, gratefully so, especially the night she distracted Jerry for me to enter the building unseen.

To throw everyone off my scent, she had to kick my butt that night she stayed in my room for hours convincing me she was truly sent to help. It was the logical thing to do but to this day, I think she enjoyed it. My bruises, the loud television always running in her non-existent pimp's empty room gave the perfect illusion and reason for her being in that hall all night. But even she couldn't stop my spiral downward. She could only watch.

"Caleb, I made it clear, they sent me to make sure you stay on mission-" says Jean, pleading in her eyes.

"I remember-"

"-and that you keep the big picture first. This is the big picture. If he gets this data, more creatures will be made, and they will use them for genocide and whatever else they see fit. Millions of lives are at stake. Not just one."

"You almost sound like him." I say.

"What? Caleb, what are you saying?"

"I'm saying that if we stop looking at one life as being valuable, it's too easy to see none as valuable. How is her life less valuable?"

"You're not thinking clearly because this looks like your mother. He got in your head. Am I right?" Jean asks looking at Dread.

"She might be right, Caleb." Says Dread.

She drops her hands and tilts her head. She makes her point, yet I will not budge.

"We got new intelligence." She says. "Something big is in the making. We believe Wilkes is looking to cut a deal for the data. We don't know where or when, but it will be soon. All the chatter points to it. He can't get the drives, Caleb."

I hear her. Every word. But he told me that I have the lead.

"This is the plan. Jean, you get her, I get the drive. You let me know when you have her and that you're clear. Then, only then, we will turn it over to the President as planned."

"And if I can't get her?" says Jean in frustration.

She looks at Dread. I know her. She's looking for a mutiny. I expected it.

"Either of you think of crossing me, I'll drop you both. We rise together or fall together. That's the deal." I turn to Jean. "You *will* get her. I know you can." I gently place my hand on her cheek.

There goes those eyes again. Finally, Dread speaks.

"We need to move."

He touches his ear, listening in the earpiece.

"They're coming."

Jean shoves her costume in the garbage. Dread pulls his favorite pistol out and hands it to me.

"You will need this," says Dread.

"Thanks." He hands me a handgun. I tuck in my jeans' waist in the small of my back.

"Here." I hand Jean a phone. "When you have her, call me on this."

I put my hand on her shoulder. All those days seeing her in that hall. I couldn't touch her. If there's anyone I trust with this, it's her. Time will tell if I've made a mistake.

"Thought we lost you in New York. I know that look. That, living-out-of-a-bottle look. You were losing yourself in your cover."

Now, my eyes are clear and so is my head. I look into the broken mirror. It fragments my image. Distorted. Just as I was these past years. I lost myself in grief and self-pity. The only thing that kept me on mission was the promise that seeing it through may uncover what really happened to my parents. It is the question that plagues me. It helped me hold my tongue while listening to Wilkes' long tale yet drives my fists to clench. I feel my inner battle coming to a close. I step to the right and look in the next mirror. Perfect. Whole. No cracks.

"I'm back."

CHAPTER SIXTEEN

Jason Jones

I couldn't do anything else in New York, so I went back to D.C. storm and all. At least I couldn't fall off the sofa. It is impossible with the deep dip in it. I just sunk in at about three o'clock in the morning and pulled my blanket over me. My phone. What time is it? There goes the lamp. It hit the floor. Ah. The phone.

"Great 8:17 a.m." I say out loud.

I need to see Director White. I pull myself together and go to her office. Paused in front of the door I hear her speaking.

"Not going to open itself. Just go in."

"You are?" I ask.

"None of your business. Going in." She pushes the door open and Director White hangs up her phone quickly.

Director White scribbles her signature on some papers the woman hands her, shuts the file and hands it back to her quickly. She looks disheveled.

"Agent Jones. I thought you would be half-way home by now."

The young lady shuts the door behind her as she leaves the office. The window in the office reveals a cloudy snowy sky.

"No," I point to the window, "the storm isn't over yet."

"It's not as bad as it looks." Director White says, standing catching my pun.

"It's treacherous but you know what I like about storms?"

"What?" she asks.

"It shakes things up and causes everything loose to fall. When the snow clears, then we will see everything dead under it. All the hidden things."

"I assume you have something to tell me. You didn't come here to give me a weather report. What happened in New York?"

"Nothing worthwhile. I wasn't sure, so I checked it out. Nothing."

"That's two 'nothings' in one sentence. That spells something."

She gestures to my shirt. It is buttoned wrong. I knew it. I just didn't feel it was relevant to fix. Until now. She's observant.

"Not at all," I say.

"Well, I have something to tell you." She opens her office fridge and takes out a pre-packaged sandwich. "The case is closed."

She sits down at the desk with a large television mounted on the wall playing CNN and begins watching it while opening the sandwich.

"Closed?   Something fishy happened in Afghanistan. His entire platoon dead? Everyone except him and his first Officer walk out of there without a scratch on them from the Afghans? He's retired. People relax when they retire. They get sloppy. This is exactly when we need to look. That's investigation 101."

"This conversation is irrelevant. I haven't forgotten your stunt at the inquisition. I almost lost my job because of that."

I step in front of the chair in front of her desk to sit.

"Stand. You won't be here that long," she says, stopping me mid-bend.

I hate that she didn't even look my way when she said that.
"He purposely beat the storm, flew out on a private jet." I say.

"He has substantial stock in companies in other countries. Gee, I don't know, maybe checking on his investments to insure his nest egg. This has too many holes in it. We can't justify spending any more money on hunches."

I look at the burner phone in my pocket. Still no calls. No news.

"The case is closed."   Director White bites her sandwich. "This is for the best, Jason."

I had my suspicions that there was someone on the inside. Someone with enough pull to curve the facts. They want him to retire clean. That's what they push for. Was Director White the keeper of Secretary John Wilkes' secrets?

A phone is ringing in my pocket but it's not the right phone.

"This better be good, Sam."

"You're chipper. There is movement, Jason."
"Speak," I say.

"John Wilkes and three others arrived in Italy."

I grunt in response. I can hear Director White put her coffee cup down on the desk from behind the door. I don't want to speak here. To the sunken sofa. I turn the corner and see a man, suited, turn the corner talking on a cell phone.

"Do you have an I.D. on the other three yet?" I ask, reaching for the doorknob.

The door is ajar. I pause. I know I closed it. I always close doors. A slight push on the door. The room appears untouched.

"I'll call you back." I hang up.

I walk in a straight line to the coffee table where the files are. The ones I pulled this morning are in their stack, but one file was hastily pushed back into the line-up. It's one at the bottom. The most important one labeled "TOP SECRET" in red faded lettering. I slide it out and open it and on the first page, it's his file.

Even reading it cover to cover, it reveals little of his identity despite the photo. The hall. No one, to the left or right. I check the burner phone again. Still, no call. I won't just wait. Someone is on to me. I dial one of the few numbers I made myself memorize.

"Have you heard anything?" I ask.

A male voice answers and replies.

"Nothing."

I grunt.

"Just keep me posted when he contacts you." I hang up the call.

Waiting has never been my strong point. Unfortunately, I have no choice but to wait.

Caleb Promise

The earpiece is excellent. I can hear Wilkes.

"Move in," Wilkes says.

He must be alone. I hear a phone ring and Wilkes answers it and puts it on speaker phone.

"Good Day, Mr. President," says Wilkes.

"John, I have conferred with the others. Tolerance is short. The climate, volatile. I pray your product is as marvellous as you claim or you will lose what little respect you have from the leaders," says a man with a heavy accent.

The voice is not that of the President of the U. S.

"You may care to watch your tone. You don't want me as an enemy. Not now. Remember, I have no leash. This dog is free. And you can tell the others that my bark isn't nearly as powerful as my bite." He hangs up.

"Ron, where are they?" Wilkes says.

"In pursuit, Sir. Closing in."

I turn to Dread and Jean who are ready to leave. I look at the red dot on my hand-held device: a team approaches from the left of the bathroom door and another, approaches from the right. A group of tourists are approaching. This is our opportunity. We slip in and disperse.

I follow her to her Fiat. I give her the cell phone device showing the live feed. Jean plugs it into her computer with a U.S.B. cord. A few taps on her keyboard and a hologram map rises from the device showing the globe. She spins it and a red marker dot flashes on, co-ordinates appear.

"Got it," she says.

She hands the cell phone device to me through the window. I reach to take it from her, but she holds it, making me stop and look at her.

"Caleb. You know me," she says.

"Promise me you will get her," I say to her.

"I promise," she says.

I race toward the Vatican Archives. About ten of Wilkes' men see me. They are approaching. Wilkes is not crazy enough to start an international incident in the Vatican. Or is he? The Swiss Guard will descend. The Archbishop is about to begin the Mass.

"Dread, I need a distraction. Now." I put my left finger on the earpiece.

They are coming toward me quickly. I put my right hand on the pistol in the small of my back when a group of children run between us. Suddenly, in the distance, gunshots. It must be

Dread. My distraction. Screams from the crowd and everyone runs frantically.

"There! Get out that way!" I yell, pointing them toward Wilkes' men, forcing the distance between us to increase. This is it.

I must get to it now before they shut down the square. People run full steam out of the Archives. In the blink of an eye Swiss Guard are marching into the square. The guards in the perimeter are watching for movement. Dread is in the wind, I'm sure.

I slip into the Archives just before the metal gate shuts. Approaching the reading room stirs the memory of our visit. It is quiet in here. I sit in the same seat I sat in when I was just eleven. Dad is precise so I must be close.

"Where is it, dad?" I say aloud.

I can hear the excitement in my mother's voice. I remember it like yesterday.

"In here, you must ask them for what you want to look at and they will bring it to you- "Mother whispered in my ear, "-but some treasures, hide in plain sight," I recall mom saying. She points.

I look in the direction she pointed in. The echo in the room muffled, absorbed by the books. The time is winding down. I walk to the shelf, skimming the titles. Nothing stands out. Boots. I hear them coming. No. Not now. I just need a little time. Think, think. I feel my pocket. The mysterious metal box key.

There, right where mother pointed, an ornate shelf marker. In the decorative metal, a box shape. I lean in then slide the metal box key into the grooves. Wait, what was that. The tile beneath my feet lowered about half an inch. I turn the metal box and the shelf releases and a section of it swings open like a door.

Something it could not do if the tile beneath my feet was in place. The men are here. Right outside the door.

I step inside the open hidden doorway. It swings easily, and creaks. In front of me, an old stone wall. Ancient, dusty. The Archives seem to be a room inside of an old stone room. In front of me, a circular stairwell with a black metal railing descending into darkness. There is no light. I pull the door shut. A soft click and it seals and a light comes on. They are here. I hear them bang on the bookcase that just closed. They are pulling out the books and throwing them onto the floor. It won't do much good. The back of this door is steel.

The further I walk down the stairwell the darker it gets. I have never been afraid of darkness. I have only ever been afraid of meeting the dark side of me. That side that is fearful, angry, jealous. Descending in this place makes me face more of myself than I expected. Above, I can hear them pressing forward.

"He's in the wall, Sir."

"Tear it down," says Wilkes.

The signal stops. I can't hear them anymore. I must have gone down at least two floors already. The steps are steep. The timer stopped on "00:03:47".

The tunnel is dimly lit by small flickering lanterns. No soot. They were recently lit. But, by who? Why? Someone knew I was coming. Are they for me or against me? The dirt floor corridor is dotted with arched stone openings. Some arched openings have ancient steel doors, some, open. The answers are close. I can feel it. The hair on my neck is standing up.

Wind is whistling through openings in the stone. Is that a man? It's too dark. I can't see. Perhaps a woman, yes, it must be, I see a dress skimming the floor. A few feet away, the person is standing purposely between lanterns, in the shadows. I am wrong. It is not a woman. It is a man. I stop a few steps away from him. I am not easily intimidated. There is a first time for everything. Immediately, I'm intimidated. Not by his title, represented by his garb. I learned something useful from my time in the Monastery. He has an air about him that commands respect in its paradox.

He's a Cardinal. His Ferraiuolo, I mistook it for a dress. Second to the Pope. Cardinals are nominated by the Pope. How could my father possibly have had anything to do with this man? He's not here accidentally. He looks as if he were waiting for me. Patiently waiting in this abandoned place. What if he's not what he seems?

"Caleb Promise." he says.

His voice is deep, bold, but smooth and clear as a bell. Every letter of my name pronounced perfectly. He declared I was Caleb Promise. He didn't ask if I were. By habit, trust no one. I touch the gun in the small of my back with my fingertips.

"You won't be needing that. Not with me." he says.

His hands clasped behind his behind his back, he turns around slowly looking at the fifteen-foot ceilings looming above them. The lights flicker and a breeze flows through the corridor we are standing in, swaying his Ferraiuolo.

"Remarkable. Old but still standing. Just like me. I am equally unyielding, so I've been told."

"Who are you?" I ask.

"Not important." He walks. "Follow me."

I pause. How do I know it's not a trap? Yet, I trust him.

"Your father thought you would have reservations. He told me to tell you these words. He said by them, you would know he sent me."

I swallow so hard I think he will hear it. This journey has been wrought with many things, comfort is not one of them, until now.

"Keep God first, obey your parents, and do well in school." He looks at me long enough to catch my response.

Never thought something could hit me this way. I don't know why but something inside broke like a cracked cistern. I've been looking for a drive and found closure. I'm on my knees with dirt beneath me. All of my years and pain from losing them rolls out of me. Not in bitterness, just clean sadness. Finally, I grieve.

Something unspoken about this man is disarming. His words so few but his presence powerful. Now I can admit it. I got lost. The mission swallowed me. Pretending to be an alcoholic became real. Pretending to be wandering aimlessly through life, became me. I needed alcohol. I never even felt the need to admit it addicted me to drink, but here, somehow, it felt right. To purge. Let the old totally go.

That night, the last night in New York, I grabbed the wrong bottle on purpose and Leo knew it. The one intended for me to grab, the fourth one, was always filled with water. Leo, an agent, replaced it every day.

Here, with minutes to go, I'm facing the shame of veering from those three things. I stopped keeping God first. I disobeyed my parents by drinking, and well, I could have done better in school.

"It's all right, Caleb," he says.

"I miss them so much. I never told them. There's so much I wish I told them."

"From the sound of things, they know."

The Cardinal takes something out of his pocket. He holds his hand open. It is the hard drive.

"If you become the man God intended you to be, this journey is worth it. He told me, if I found you wanting, to withhold it."

His shoulders slouch humbly. His eyes pierce to my soul. He's weighing me, I can feel it. But something bigger was happening. It confirms my purpose. I know who and what I am. Whether or not he gives it to me, I know what I must do. Then it happens. He extends the drive to me in an open palm. I take it.

"God bless you, Caleb Promise. Do what God has called you to do. With this, and always."

I take it and look at it and turn it around in my fingertips. So small but so much.

"Is there any-?" I start. I look around but he has vanished.

In the distance, there is the lit outline of a doorway.

I push it open and I'm standing in the sun, in a field. In the distance, The Vatican wall and my problem with drink. My mind feels new. I didn't expect this new beginning. My enemy, Wilkes pushed me to my freedom. The real me, the whole me came out in this place. I reconnected. It's easy to get lost in a character played. If it's played long enough and it embodies one, like it or not. The sun shines on my face but the mission isn't over. '00:01:13'. My phone rings. It's Jean. I answer it and speak to and hear her through my earpiece.

"Did you get her?" I ask looking at my phone.

"Do you have the drive?"

"Yes, I do. Do you have her?" I press.

"Sorry, Caleb. I tried my best."

Wilkes' caravan is approaching from my left in the distance. I am disappointed in her answer. Two things died today. That woman and my trust in Jean.

"Jean, I was thinking, you're right, he'll probably kill her, anyway. I may as well destroy it," I say.

"Caleb! I'm near. I can get you and we finish this mission." She says.

Her helicopter approaches behind me.

"Did you at least get to her?" I say, looking my device.

"Yes, yes, but the place is like Fort Knox."

"Really?"

"Destroying it won't help. See it through. Give it to me, and we will turn it into the President of the United States together." Says Jean.

"Seems he's not the only one I can't trust." I say.

The red dot on the tracking device in my hand, she circled in the distance and returned. I stuck a clear tracker to her shirt when I touched her shoulder in the bathroom shows she never left the area in the chopper.

"Who do you work for, Jean?" I ask her.

She doesn't answer. Wilkes's is here. The timer "00:00:03" At least twenty of Wilkes' men exit the vehicles a few yards away. To my right, the other vehicle approaches. Jean's chopper appears hovering behind me.

"What are you talking about?" she yells.

"Behind your left shoulder." I say.

"You tracked me."

"Answer me Jean! YOU came to ME. You told me they sent you to help me and knew about it all! My contact at the orphanage, everything." I retort.

"Caleb, it's not what you think. We'll talk and sort it out later. I need that drive."

"Caleb!" yells Wilkes exiting his vehicle a few yards away to my left. "Your time is up."

I see Jean's chopper. The wind blows everything on the ground.

"Caleb, I'm MI6," says Jean.

I feel my jaw drop and I look at the helicopter.

"I'm not your enemy, Caleb. I'm your sister. I'm sorry." She pauses then yells, "GET DOWN!"

Her helicopter raises, but not fast enough. It's hit. I drop to one knee, my arm raised to block flying debris. Pieces of metal hit the surrounding ground. Did she jump? Did she get out? No. The helicopter is a ball of fire burning on the ground. Nothing. Jean is gone.
    The debris settles, Wilkes approaches me. One of his goons puts the launcher in the back of their truck. The new Ron hands Wilkes the tablet. He punches in numbers.

"Wait!" I throw my hand up and get to my feet.

My jaw won't release. Jean had to be lying. She had to be. Don't trust anyone. Dad said only give it to someone who doesn't want it. She wanted it. Badly. The tracker showed she never left the area. She was a liar. She could've been lying to get me to trust her again. Too many ifs.

"Caleb!" yells a man exiting the vehicle to my right.

What? Richard shouldn't be here. He walks toward us. His chest held high like a peacock trying to appear larger than he really is. Still, his soft casual apparel gives him away. Wilkes stiff creased suit and shined shoes are bold.

"Well, well, look who came to visit. I thought you would be dead by now," says Wilkes, adjusting his tie approaching Richard.

Face to face, Wilkes is smiling smugly.

"Yes. I lived! It's over, Wilkes." Says Richard.
Richard looks resolute but I can tell he's scared. Gretchen walks up behind Richard and puts her hand reassuringly on his shoulder. He's not made for this. He's made for a sofa in Italy in a cozy villa. Her loose warm shawl flaps in the wind and her hair pulled back and tied with a decorative gold hair clip at the nape of her neck. Her signature palazzo pants skim the tops of her black flats. Richard pats her hand.

"Seems quite the gathering. You know the only reason I don't kill you right here and now is because of my promise to your father," Wilkes says to me. "I will spare yours. Time to choose, Caleb."

Richard looks at me and I toss the drive to him. He catches it and squeezes it tightly, backing up from Wilkes with Gretchen. Richard's armed man keeps his gun aimed at Wilkes.
You killed her. He presses a button on his phone and holds up his device showing the woman heaving and then expiring. Something's not right. Wilkes looks too calm. Too content. He's not looking at Richard. Wait, he's looking at... Gretchen. How did I miss this? It's her. She is the one. Gretchen was the lead scientist made a deal with.

"RICHARD!" I yell to warn him.

Too late. Gretchen puts a small pistol to Richard's head. In disbelief, he slowly turns to face her. The pistol now at the center of his forehead.
"My love? I did everything you asked." asks Richard.

I can't bear the look in Richard's eyes. The pain.

"You are not *my* love." Gretchen pulls the trigger.

"You chose poorly, Caleb." says Wilkes.

Richard's body falls forward with his fist clenched. Gretchen kneels, opens Richards hand and takes the drive, holding it up like a diamond to the sunlight. Nothing. Not a tear, no remorse, nothing.

"Doctor, so good to see you again," Wilkes says to Gretchen.

She takes his hand and steps over Richard's body. Ultimate insult. The new Ron's gun is aimed at my head.

"Looks the part, doesn't he? He *was* one of them, but she was the mastermind.

Gretchen steps toward me. An icy breeze blows between us. I've never hit a woman but hey, today may be the day.

"You look puzzled, Caleb," says Gretchen.

"About this, no. I'm not puzzled. You murdered Vin, didn't you? You were the only one outside at the time he was killed. You rush inside, hysterical, knowing what Richard would do. No one was after us, were they?"

"You are a clever one, aren't you?" She clasps her hands and tilts her head walking toward me. "Your little emotional crack-up almost wrecked everything. Suicide, really! So pathetic. Turning to drink. Tell me, do you still feel your stomach knotting for it? Hands shaking lately? If we didn't need your services, I would have let you drink yourself to death. Vincenzo's role was over. Yours wasn't. I knew Rosie would bring you back to her senses."

I bite down and tighten my grip on the handle of the gun Dread gave me. She shouldn't have said her name. I aim it right at her face. I hear several guns cock. I grab her turning her around using her as a shield. She doesn't even struggle.

"Was it you?" I ask.

"You mean did I kill your parents? You will just have to keep looking." She says.

"Then your role is over. I pull the trigger. An empty click. What?

"Know your subjects," Gretchen faces me.

"I thought that was Dread's gun. I just had to get a tad closer to see for certain. Let me guess. You thought you could trust him. You can trust no one it seems."

"It's time to go." Says Wilkes puffing his cigar.

I could have grabbed her and snapped her neck, what good would that do? One of Wilkes men would just shoot me here and, the mission is over. I look at Dread standing in the wings. He was there all the time. Policia sirens are blaring around the exploded chopper. They're coming closer. I can see the lights.
"Goodbye, Caleb. I have paid my debt to your father." Says Wilkes.

Dread steps forward, the traitor. He hit me hard. I buckle to my knees. I grasp at the dirt at Gretchen's feet. I grab her ankle.

Dread kicks me in the ribs. I need to know where, when and to whom he is planning to sell this data too. That person is the biggest enemy to all countries. Wilkes steps into the black vehicle with Gretchen and their men. They drive away passing the approaching Vatican Police cars.

"It's over," says Dread.

He pulls his handgun. The view is not as comforting staring down this end of the barrel. I step backward. I wonder, is he waiting until Wilkes car is out of sight before we make our escape? Did he turn? Wilkes' vehicles are out of sight. He still pointing it at me. I see. My fists clench and my brows drop.

"Sorry, Caleb. Just doing my job."

"Me too."

A jolt. It's awake. That part of me I hid so well all these drunken years. I step forward. My technique rusty, but now, the gun is mine. The Vatican police lights approach. I don't want to kill him but if he lives, he'll never stop hunting me. One head shot. Dread drops face forward in the dirt. It's done.

The keys are still in the ignition of Richard and Gretchen's vehicle. It starts and I head up the street toward the town. I toss the earpiece and put my phone on speaker. I know he's been waiting. Watching. He's probably boiling mad at me by now. I haven't seen him since his last visit to the orphanage. He came faithfully. Disguised as a monk therapist to nurse me through my anger issues and help me break my silence.

It was then, that he recruited me. He told me about my father's double deep cover and how my life would be in danger. He had Chen, also known as Father Long to secretly teach me martial arts in the centre of the monastery's elaborate maze garden. defense moves, tactics and Wing Chun. We studied my father's Top-Secret files. I learned his strategies, how he thought. That was the side of him I never knew.

He gave me Leo, the liquor store guy who was my contact agent. My drinking problem justified me going to the liquor store every night. It was a check-in. Leo sees me, as usual and all is well. If I don't show up, or seem off kilter, Leo was supposed to call him. My scene at the liquor store was my signal to him. I knew Leo would act accordingly. The toy store owner, poor sap, he was ours too. He was a toy store owner and was really married to that lady. His job, to make sure I was there every night sitting on the curb outside of Central Park. I had to ask Wilkes about them because, well, trust no one. But Leo and the toy store owner proved true. After all, I'm still alive. You must trust someone when you tell them to hit you with a car. Driving in Italy on this narrow street, finally I am alone. I dial the number I have memorized. It's ringing.

CHAPTER SEVENTEEN

It rings in Washington D. C.

"Hello."

I remember that voice.

"It's me." I say.

Silence.   What is he doing?   It sounds like he's walking outside.

"First, are you safe?" asks Jason Jones.

"Yes, Jason. You?" I ask.

I hear him stop walking.

"There are footsteps behind me," Jason says lowly. "I can't see over five feet in any direction. This snow. I'm going to my car. You're wanted for murder."

"At least it's not for murdering you," I say.

"Funny. So, you know."

"I do."

"I can't clear your name right now without risking this mission. Was that you on the plane with Wilkes?"

"Yeah." I say, "how are things on your end?"

"Funny you should ask. It's gotten complicated. Listen, I know I told you when we first met that your only job was to find the drive and get it to me... but... we've got a mole and I don't know who to trust. Right now, you're the only one I trust. Are you 100%? Suicide, Caleb? You should have called me. Remember, the little gold key. The safe deposit box... the phone was in there all the time. That's what it was for, emergencies."

"It wasn't real, Jason." I ease his mind.

"Follow directions. That's what I told you. If you needed help, you had Leo... what did you say?"

"It wasn't real. It was Leo driving the taxi. I set it up to happen when our guy closed the toy shop to make sure he was outside and could call the ambulance. The Mt. Sinai Hospital explosion was not a terrorist attack."

"I know. I was there." Jason says.

"Wilkes has those resources. The explosion and manipulation of the press." I say maneuvering through the narrowing road. He's quiet. He's thinking. That's good.

"Leo was derelict in duty. He should have given me a heads up."

"I gave him no choice, Jason. He was following my orders."

"Last time I checked the orders come from me." Jason grunts.

"It worked." I say lightly.

I can hear him pressing the cars key fob. It doesn't beep.

"What's wrong with this thing? The batteries must be dead. Great." says Jason.

"Hurry and get out of there, Jason. Something doesn't feel right."

"What? Great, I dropped the fob in the snow. Figures." says Jason. "Got it. Thank God for this key inside the fob."

I hear him open the car door and toss something big onto a seat, start the car and pull out with wheels spinning in the snow.

"By doing that, you stirred the nest. Hang on while I put you on speaker." he says.

"Jason, I had to. It was killing me."
"That, Leo told me. He knew something was wrong when you started grabbing the wrong bottle a month ago. Why didn't you use the reserve? You were never poor."

"Yeah and blow my cover by using mysteriously appearing money. Besides, how better to validate suicide and get checked for whatever they did to me when I was abducted without raising suspicion that I knew." I say.

The town is quiet and I'm following my guidance device to the river side. I keep glancing in my rear-view mirror to see if I'm being followed.

"Smart. All right you improvised. I need that drive in my hand or destroyed. One or the other but…"

"Spit it out Jason, what is it?"

"You're not fully trained for this kind of thing. It could get messy and you'll be alone. But I have no choice but to ask it of you. I need you to do whatever it takes to find out whose behind this and who the buyer will be if we can't contain the sale."

"Done." I say. "Jason, do I have a sister?"

I hear his brakes screech.

"A sister?" Jason asks.

"All right, all right!" Jason yells. Car horns are blowing on him. "What makes you ask that?"

Jason doesn't deny. He is fishing or knows the answer. I thought we were past this.

"Caleb, it's vital I know everything that's happened. No games."

I look in my rear-view mirror and in the distance; I see Policia lights getting closer. The town is small the streets are slim. Thankfully no one's outside. I speed up.

"I do not know of a sister and that's the truth. When I first approached you in the orphanage, I told you everything I knew. I knew something stunk about Wilkes, but I didn't know what. This case has spread into something bigger." Says Jason.

"I know what happened in Afghanistan," I say.

He's quiet. I expected as much. I'm almost there. I can see the waterline.

"Now we really need to talk." I hear his tires screech from a fast turn. "Did you find it?"

"Yes. And I'll get it back." Through the phone, there's a loud bang and Jason uses every explicative he knows.

"What was that?" I ask.

"I got hit from behind. This guy just rear-ended me."

"Jason! Don't get out. GO! NOW!" I yell.

I can hear his wheels spinning. It must be the snow.
"Why am I listening to you?" he asks.

"Are they gone?" I ask increasing my speed. The Policia behind me are getting closer.

"No. Still behind me." says Jason.

"A girl claiming to be my sister knew everything about the mission. Everything. She embedded two years ago. She's not Wilkes', not Richard's, not yours. She said she's MI6. Find out who she was."

"Was?"

"She's dead. Jason, whatever Wilkes has been planning, it's happening tomorrow."

"Where? We got no intelligence on this." His voice is anxious.

In my rear-view window, two police cars on their sirens. I floor the accelerator.

"Yes, you do. You know what, you just don't know where. It's the World Peace Summit."

"Are those sirens?" Jason asks.

"Not that I hear," I say, tearing around the corner clipping the curb with the rear tire and the Policia sirens blaring behind me.

I hear him skidding around turns as well.

"Get off my tail!" Jason says to the vehicle following him. "No one knows its location."

"No one? Really... hmm." I say.

I think he heard my sarcasm.

"Even if you know that, how will you get in?" Jason says.

I hear what sounds like a bullet piercing Jason's window. I'm all too familiar with that sound. Three more shots sink into his trunk.

"You still alive?" I ask, swerving to the left on my winding road. The Italian Policia Sirens still close to me.

"Yes!" yells Jason.

"Run a light!" I yell.

"What! Are you crazy?"

"Run one, Jason. Do it!"

I hear him speed up then car horns blare at him.

"I did it! But he's still there!" Jason yells.

I'm running out of time. I have to go through the town. The streets are skinny. Only passable for two compact cars. Slowly. But this is not a compact. I can't slow down now. What is that? A truck coming from the right. If I can pass it in time, it will block the police. Almost there.

"Out of the Way!" I yell at a man stepping off the curb in front of me.

"Move!" yells Jason.

I can hear the gunshots behind him. His engine racing. A few feet more and I'm free of the police.

"I can't get this car off my back," says Jason, more glass breaking.

"Is your seatbelt on?" I ask him.

"It is now!" Jason says. I hear the click.

"BRAKE!" I yell speeding up.

I hear Jason's tires skip then a crash. I swerve around the truck. Startled, the truck turned to avoid hitting me and wedges between the buildings. Just in time. It blocks the Policia behind me. I make a hard left and a right toward the water. I look in my rear-view. I have lost them.

"Are you there?" I ask. Nothing. "Jason, answer me. Are you there?" Still nothing. "Come on."

I hear something scrambling over the cell phone mouthpiece.

"I am going to kill you when I see you," Jason answers finally.

"Look in your rear-view. Is he still there?"

"Yes. But his shooting days are over. He's hanging out of the windshield. Well, part of him."

I pull over and park the vehicle in a side alley, cross a grassy field to the water and step into a motorboat tied in the River Tiber. I used that little gold key once. The perfect opportunity arose when I was homeless. I went into the bank with my wonderful little gold key. That safe deposit box held cash, passport and a cell phone. Emergency run gear Jason stashed for me. I used the phone in the bathroom and set up for the next stage of this mission. It was evident that they stacked the odds against Jason. I called someone that I knew had the resources I need.

This became necessary when I saw them pull that hospital shooting and explosion off as a terrorist attack, I knew I might not be able to rely on his resources to extract the drive without becoming collateral damage just like my father. So, I made other arrangements that I can't tell anyone about. Not even Jason. I put the phone back into the safe deposit box and made sure the bank security guard gave me a hard shove out of the door so suspicions weren't raised for any of Wilkes men who may have been watching me.

"Jason-"

"-Stop talking. I hate you right now. I think we call this fleeing the scene."

I hear him slam his car door. I get out of my vehicle at the shore, shut the door and step onto the boat.

"What have you been doing all these years? Big Agent." I say mockingly.

"I work at a desk, Caleb. A desk. This back… I'm going to need therapy I can feel it." Jason mutters.

"That's obvious."

"Shut up… okay, just… skip it. I need to know who that was." He says.

"You've got a picture of his face."

He's quiet.

"The traffic camera when I ran the light." says Jason.

"Yes." I reply.

I climb into the boat and start the ignition. It has a distinct gurgle.

"What is that? Are you on a boat?" Jason asks.

"Ditch your cell. Don't go home. You know this stuff, right?"

"If you recall, I trained you." says Jason.

"Pull that footage and get back to me. Our big fish sent him." I say.

"You need to tell me where you are going. Where is the World Peace Summit?"

"I will. As soon as I'm sure. Oh-" I say looking at a blinking dot on a tracking device. The dot is moving.

"What?" asks Jason.

"Don't get killed."

"Shut up."

I think Jason truly enjoys hanging up on me. I don't feel alone anymore. Strange how things changed. He was there all along, but it wasn't him I lost. It was me. The dim view I had of my life just a few days ago. I will bring this guy down. We, my father and I will strike as one sword with two blades and bring this to an end.

I can breathe here. It feels good to feel like myself again. Shedding that skin of grief wasn't easy. Embracing new things. This is the first time I drove a boat since I was a kid. Funny, it's like riding a bike it all came back to me. I look at the tracker. It looks like I'm going to Switzerland. Twenty minutes ride to get to the station.

The train announcer is speaking in Italian. Thanks to Wallie, I understand most of it. I can't help but smile to myself. His father was very specific in his Will. I guess when you know you're dying for a year in advance you have time to think about all these things.

He set up the trust for Wallie. Specified his living quarters in the remote Monastery for Wallie's safety, which Wallie hated, and chose his diet. They brought in all the furnishings from his room at home. I guess like any father, he wanted him to feel at home. How could he know? He couldn't have guessed all of this isolated him. Being called the golden boy, never picked for teams, nothing. Maybe that's what drew me to him. In the orphanage, Wallie was the crack in the mirror.

Every week without fail his three tutors came in. While me and the other orphans learned masonry, and helped repair broken stone walls, Wallie disappeared into the garden or a classroom with a tutor toting books and charts. He always looked as if he wanted someone to rescue him. I would have, if I could. One of those tutors was his Wing Chun master so the teasing only went so far. I guess his father knew he'd need it behind all the other things he gave him. Wallie taught me the languages he learned. Thanks, Wallie. I still can't find my compartment. Pushing through people, I see this girl staring at me across the room. I pass her to get to the next car.

"Excuse me, Sir," she reaches for my shoulder but I discreetly pull it back avoiding the touch, "do you know where the service desk is?" she retracts her hand.

"Non parlo inglese." I say.

I push past her. She smells like food. The service desk was right behind her. She has no luggage. Looking at her in the marque reflection, she's still standing there, and she has asked no one else. As I thought. Her eyes lock on me again. The long corridor on the train has windows on one side and the other has a series of identical slender doors. I'm looking for my cabin and purposely pass it twice to see if anyone is following me.

All looks clear. I duck and step into the door to my cabin and lock the door behind me. Finally, I can exhale. Basic. Clean. But that window is a view into another world. It feels good to slouch down in the seat and stretch my legs out. It's only supposed to be a forty-minute ride.

Once, in New York, I fell asleep on the F train in Manhattan. Strange. I awoke feeling just as tired as when my eyes shut. I wonder if sleeping in this chamber alone and feeling somewhat secure will be different. The truth is I don't want to sleep. I want to absorb every moment of this beautiful place and its views.

This mystery has unraveled well. I have gotten many answers but not to the biggest question of all. I know why my parents were killed, but not who. The who is as important as the why. For me at least. Right now, I need to rest my mind. The scenery passes quickly. Lately my life is as adventurous when my eyes are open as when they are closed. I shut my eyes, but I can't shut out the flashes of the past few days.

I must have dozed off because the intimidating figure of the Archbishop with smoke rising behind him jolts me awake. Where am I? Oh, yes. The hum of the train calms me quickly. I can see the heels of someone standing against my door. What is that noise? Teenagers. They're getting closer. I can tell from their laughter that is getting louder. The shadow from the person's heels is still there. Standing outside the door.

"Excuse us," says a giddy teenager.

Whoever it is, they didn't move. The girls are scooting past them. But one girl's shadow is large. She stops.

"Buddy, this will not work."

So, it's a man. He steps to the side and she passes him.

"Thanks," she says sarcastically.

The train announcer speaks, and I can hear a conductor shouting 'biglietto', (ticket). What's that? Just outside the window. A crowd of people stirs. I'm done running. I open the door and pivot in the direction he went toward.

"Biglietto, Signore," says the ticket agent.

The person is gone. There's no one in the corridor as far as I can see in either direction. Arriving in Switzerland is invigorating. The training in the Monastery prepared me to think and plan but it didn't prepare me for the enlightenment travel brings. Jason couldn't have trained me for how going to these beautiful places would stretch my thinking. Break my borders and parameters. I can never be content in the one room hotel again. I couldn't be taught how it would make that little room in the cheap hotel feel like a prison. That moment of being homeless made me feel grateful. Very grateful. I chose this hotel for practical purposes. I am, by nature, practical. It was in the right location. It has every amenity known to man. I couldn't help but visualize myself on that balcony.

All right, it also served a whimsy. I figured, if I lived long enough to get to this stage, I wanted to treat myself as well. Besides, when this is all over, I'll probably be staring at the crack in the mirror in my old room again. I walk up to the hotel desk to check-in.

"There you are, Mr. Driven, your key," says the reservation agent at the desk, "we will have your luggage collected..." she gestures to a bell hop to come, "... and help you unpack."

"No luggage. I'll be shopping. Have the concierge call. " I have always wanted to say that.

She looks impressed. Mr. Driven is Jason's creation. The fake passport and identification all tucked neatly in that safe deposit box. I could have taken it a long time ago compliments of that little gold key. I could have vanished and never looked back. But that wouldn't bring me any closer to the answers I seek.

"Well, Mr. Driven, if you require any help with your packages upon your return, please let us know." She smiles as I walk out.

She's flirting with me. Funny what money prompts. I wonder...would she still be smiling at me and fluttering her eyelashes if I were dressed in my bus-boy uniform? Frivolity gets put aside when struggling to survive. I haven't shopped in years but needed to look the part to get into the event. The Bradutt's Palace in St. Moritz is just up the street. It was the secret location of the World Summit.

Chen was very thorough in the report he sent to my phone. They dispatched him there when the Secretary of Defenses actions came to light. Chen doesn't leave things to chance. His report stated that the hotel's regular staff were weeded out. Everyone employed within the last three years got a paid vacation leaving senior staff for the event. From chefs to valet, scouring background checks were completed months ago. They denied all requests for personal chefs because of a conflict of interests.

One kitchen, multiple chefs stringently loyal to their leader may offer temptation that can't be prevented. Like curious reporters, I did my homework. I got suspicious when the entire hotel showed 'booked' on-line for months in advance.

The shops across the cobblestone street remain open. Michael Kors, Louis Vuitton, and a few others offer a semblance of normalcy for the dignitaries with their staff subject to the same scrutiny as the hotel. I window shopped needing something more than this leather jacket and blue jeans for this event. Up in my room I sit on the bed and no sooner there is a knock on the door.

"I am the hotel concierge. I was told you may require clothing. I brought the in-house tailor for measurements. How may I serve you, Mr. Driven?"

I could get used to that name. Jason's idea. I don't like it but it's common. Forgettable.

"I need a black suit, black shoes, two white long sleeve cuff-link shirts, platinum cuff-links slightly decorative but modest."

"Excellent, Sir. Will there be anything else?" she says with modest eyes.

The tailor takes out his tape measure and begins measuring me.

The concierge's shoes are freshly polished, but I can see deep scuff marks beneath the polish. The tailor circles around me, measuring jotting down numbers, then repeating.

"Yes, one more thing. Laderach, The Pralines and Truffles eighteen count box from their Masters Collection. Three of them," I say.

"Excellent choice, Mr. Driven." She smiles, knowing of the Laderach.

"One is for you, the other for you, Sir." I look at the tailor. "Charge it to the room," I reply.

Her pause and his smile made it worth it.

"Sir, I'm flattered, however, we're not permitted to accept gifts from the guests. I do thank you though. I have heard it is quite a treat."

It does something to you. Being in service. You do allot of work with little of gratitude. A luxury like this would set you back for months.

"I understand," I say.

"We will deliver your items within the hour, Mr. Driven. It is my pleasure to serve you." They leave.

She looked past the leather jacket, jeans and dusty shoes and saw a human being. No doubt sophistication is stifling this hotel but so far, kindness makes it feel like home. The balcony is calling me.
The air is crisp. Leaning on my elbows on this balcony rail feels just like standing on a New York balcony to me. Both views, unforgettable for different reasons. Snow-capped Swiss Alps are beautiful with clouds drifting past them. I could stand here forever.

My phone rings.

"Are you secure?" asks Jason.

"Yes. You?" I can see my breath in the cold air.

"There're more hands in the pot than I thought," says Jason.

"I not surprised. Who is or was our shooter?"

"A ghost with a Russian tattoo. That's all I know so far. Someone inside had to do this."

"What's your plan?" I ask.

"For now. Stay alive long enough to find out who burned me. I have a good idea though. What do you need from me?"

"Nothing. Send me a picture of the tattoo," I say.

I receive the picture of an image on a hand, clasped around a steering wheel.

"Where are you?"

"Knowing that won't help right now. I'll keep my eyes open for this tattoo. Oh, Jason, when this is over, I'm treating to dinner. I'm loaded, you know."

In my mind, I can see him smiling.

"I don't want to eat with you. Two guys, alone. That's just sad."

"Pool?" I ask.

"I'm in. Listen, Russians are not a people to be played with." he says.

"Trust no one," I reply.

A pause.

"Is your man in place?" Jason asks.
"Yes," I reply.

Jason is quiet. Too quiet. He is always spewing instructions or advice.

"If you don't hear from me by morning, Caleb, you know what to do," Jason says.

"You've got to see Italy. It's a beauty. I'll buy your ticket."

"All right, Caleb." Jason says exhaling.

I hung up on him this time. He gets why. Just as the concierge stated, the clothing arrived all neatly packaged, pre-pressed and smelling brand new. For those prices, they should have come with someone to dress me too.

Dressed from head to toe, I sit on the side of my hotel room bed. This hotel is everything it advertised. I will miss it after tonight.

CHAPTER EIGHTEEN

Hotel Room of U. K. Prime Minister
Chen, Head Butler & Agent

"Lord, help me serve to the best of my ability and-" I mutter pressing the elevator button to the Penthouse floor.

"Who did you pay off?" asks Thomas.

Answering a prating fool is a waste of words. Thomas is full of words. He'll continue without me. He usually does.

"I know you paid someone off! Until yesterday, they assigned me to the top two. The Prime Minister of the U.K. and the President of France. Suddenly, I'm your rutty assistant. And for God's sake, stop mumbling," says Thomas agitated.

For God's sake, I am mumbling. He depends entirely on his physique. Wearing a king's crown doesn't make one a king. Only someone playing dress-up.

"As soon as you leave, I'm going to the director. I'll have an investigation put in. You did something. Smug little Chinaman. You and your smart sayings can go to hell. This was my opportunity to get out of here. But you don't think like that... no, it's beneath you to think of advancement. I want to finally work for someone important. They would have seen it. I'm sure of it. They would have seen how keen I am and hired me if it weren't for your scheming." continues Thomas fixing his suit for the third time.

I focus my eyes on the floor. No audience for the court jester. He continues. I look upward at the elevator numbers rising.

"See those jets they flew in on? I would've bloody well been on one with them flying all over this world. I will get you. Believe me, whatever you did, I will find out!" Thomas says, straining his whisper. His face is beet red.

My word bank is still full. I haven't answered him once. The elevator doors open. There are fingerprints on the number panel. Not for long. I polish it quickly with my handkerchief and re-fold it so it sits flat in my trouser pocket and is not a distracting bulge.

"Forgive me, Lord, for the interruption. And grant me grace to finish my race. In Jesus' name, Amen," I say aloud.

Thomas turns angrily toward me. The elevator dings. We are on the penthouse level. I lift each of the heels of my shoes twice, making sure my new shoes don't squeak. My routine is, I pat my three pockets, feeling for the items. A pen and small pad, in case those I serve should need one. Small polishing cloth. Mobile phone. Keys to the rooms. Check. The doors open. I pause. Few do. From left to right, I look. The hall floral arrangement is perfect, frames and hall tables are sparkling.

Top to bottom. Light fixtures, clean. Floor, well vacuumed. I've mastered it. Completing my check before the elevator doors close behind me. I lift my pocket watch hanging from my polished chain. Three minutes to arrival. I'm in place. Three feet away from the opening elevator doors with prattling Thomas to my right. The guards nod at me acknowledging my presence.

My height, a gift. Born a discreet figure. I disappear easily. The art of an excellent servant is to serve without imposition. The elevator is moving. Still rising. This must be she. It dings. Inhale. Pause and let her examine myself and the hall. Now.

"Madame, Prime Minister, I am Chen, your butler. Please this way."

I can't help but smile as I turn the key to her room. The Prime Minister of England received the Helen Bradrutt Suite. Door doesn't creak, good. Elegant three-room suite with center sitting room. It suits her. But something tells me she's frazzled.

"I'll need you to fetch it from the plane. I get one assistant, just one." Madame Prime Minister of the United Kingdom says.

She's not happy. Oh my. The rules are strict. Strangely strict. Each dignitary was assigned a room and was permitted one companion.

The gift package I placed in her room is lavish. Wilkes' generosity cost him over five thousand dollars alone. She looks at it, her jaw tightens. It doesn't win her cooperation.

I have found dignitaries don't like rules and the affluent are not impressed with things they can buy on their own. They are accustomed to making the rules, not following the rules. They remember their restrictions more than the Champagne gift baskets.

"My apologies, Madame Prime Minister, but I can't leave you." Replies her assistant.

Her assistant is physically fit. Her movements smooth and thoughtful. She studied a martial art. Her body moves as one. She is more than just an assistant, I perceive. I feel there is something more, troubling Madame Prime Minister. Her assistant can't see it. It's not about the bag. She doesn't want to be here.

"I forgot. An MI6 agent that can't remember a bag. Bloody rules... one assistant." She exhales. "My apologies. It isn't your fault. None of this is your fault." says Madame Prime Minister.

"Madame Prime Minister, if I may offer a solution. I can arrange for your bag to be brought to you within the hour."

She's wondering if she can trust me. I can see it in her eyes.

"Mr. Chen, is it?"

"Yes."

She exhales and smiles.

"I appreciate your help. Thank you."

I nod to Thomas who is standing near the door trying his best to be seen. The silent go-ahead to retrieve the bag from the private airport miles away. Thomas' smile drops and Madame Prime Minister notices. Thomas leaves the room.

"Chen, it seems your hands are full."

"Madame is observant. A good leader knows the best place for each person they lead." Madame Prime Minister smiles.

Odd. The media frenzy drew a halo of unity around the gathering, successfully masking its true purpose. This Summit was soaked in hope for peace. So why does it seem that no one wants to be here? She was here once before. She doesn't remember me. If do my job well, they don't remember me, they only remember the hotel. Then, she was calm and charming. She speaks to her MI6 Assistant.

"Confirm the delivery, then get my son on the phone." She says, pulling the fingers of her gloves, she places them on the sofa table and glances around the room.

The assistant presses the buttons on her smart watch in a specific combination and points the face of the watch as she walks through the rooms. A green light flashes followed by two high pitch beeps sound.

"He'll never forgive me." She seems to be speaking to herself. "Miss his fifteenth birthday for this bloody meeting. Ostentatious, isn't it?" she says, looking over the Champagne, gourmet chocolates and bouquets that dot the room. "You would think we wished to be here."

"The room is clear," says her assistant, "delivery received. Your son is on the line." She says handing her the phone.

"John?"

The Prime Minister removes her suit jacket, lays it carefully on the back of a single Queen Anne chair and sits gently on the settee, crossing her legs as if she were in a Parliament meeting. Gracious and kind-natured, her heart consumed with the good of her land and her people. Her decisiveness would be admired if she were a man, but twice as tough as one standing against the harshest criticism and judgment. Study those you serve. Only then, may you serve effectively.

In an article, I read that family became more important to her than ever during her campaign. Her husband died before the final vote. He supported her, stood beside her, and pushed her forward when her own doubts got the better of her. Maneuvering around their special days became mandatory in her sight.

Now I know why she is so troubled. This meeting breaks her rule of family first. It made her leave her son on such an important day.

I remember the first time I met Caleb in the monastery. As an agent of the Central Intelligence Agency, Jason thought I was the perfect candidate to dress as a monk and visit Caleb as a therapy counsellor to help his depression. He wasn't speaking to people. He was the perfect prayer candidate. I watched. Mostly, just watched and prayed his heart would heal. Deep in the garden maze we practiced him Wing Chun. The other monks thought it was a way for him to dispel his anger. Now, he's fighting something evil and vile. The stony hearts of men. I'm praying for Caleb, again. I lift my watch discreetly. The time is approaching.

"Happy birthday son. Do you like it?"

There is a knock at the door. The MI6 Assistant nods, permitting me to answer it. A tray with a Fortnum & Mason tea set with full English tea. A three-tiered server with sweet, scones and savory sandwiches on the bottom, perfectly made and humbly delivered.

"We didn't order that." says her assistant halting his entry.

"I learned that Madam Prime Minister had a flight delay. I took the liberty of ordering it." I say.

The Prime Minister smiles while looking at the tray and nods at her. The assistant lets the server enter and place the tray. Giving someone what they need before they even know they need it is a skill set that I take pride in, not shame. That she may enjoy the tray and won't have to call for a single utensil or condiment, thus refreshing herself for her meeting, makes me happy. It frees her to focus on the larger tasks before her. Her MI6 assistant looks at me suspiciously. And I her.

"When I get home, I have another surprise for you," says Madame Prime Minister.

She looks at the tea tray and leans forward in her seat, makes her tea and takes a sandwich from the bottom tier. The assistant looks at me. No gloating glance returned.

"If you require anything, just press this button."

My hand-held device is vibrating. They have requested me in the suite of the President of France.

Hotel room of the President of France

I approach the door of the President of France and hear a loud conversation in progress. I must interrupt. I knock and hear 'Enter' shouted from within. I open the door.

"Mr. President, I am Chen, your butler. How may I be of service?" I say.

He completely ignores my greeting. At least I thought he did, but then, mid-sentence, he looks at me and nods.

"I don't understand you." He continues speaking to his wife. "It was *you* who insisted upon coming despite the instructed protocol that I come alone, and you complain! I want you here, my love, you must believe me, but I won't have you questioning my political decision making."

He sits at the left end of the sofa, legs crossed. His wife pauses from pacing behind the sofa for a moment, acknowledging my presence, then dives in again. They are comfortable with whom they are. I feel a part of a family standing here. Not an unwanted intruder. She is elegant. Beautiful and clearly passionate about her point. She speaks.

"I must question when it makes no sense. This man insults you, berates you and you come when he calls! You don't even do that for me." The First Lady throws her hands when she speaks.

"I did what is best for France. I don't have the privilege of letting my ego get in the way," Mr. President says.

"In this meeting, you must show your strength! You must let him see that you are not-" the First lady says.

"Stop, Ines," says Mr. President.

Ines sighs in frustration and pivots to the window, crossing her arms tightly. He is expert at drawing in his emotions at a moment's notice and composing himself, leaving no crumbs for a searching mouse to pick up. Ines seems his polar opposite. Though they quarrel I see she realizes the depth of their dynamic. Expressing what he cannot. Wearing her feelings on her sleeve and not trying to hide them.

I read that the President's advisers have stopped trying to cultivate her into the stoic-faced perfect picture of neutrality. This trait serves her well. The people of France admire her. They see truth in her and like knowing she is not a polished politician but that most of what she feels displays what they feel. Now, I admire her.

She's a significant tie of the people to her husband. Strong, educated, opinionated. She is his greatest asset because he never has to wonder if she is telling him the truth. She doesn't have to bite her tongue for his favor in fear of losing her job. The papers misjudge their squabbles, inexperienced ears see them as the ending of a marriage, but I see so much more. They know in their hearts that if they are free to be themselves together and voice their opinions without condemnation or refrain, their love breathes. They live and their marriage is alive and healthy.

"Mr. Chen, I hear you are a trustworthy man."

"I am humbled by the compliment, Sir."

"I would like transport arranged. This is to be between you and me, only. My wife-"

"Alexandre-" the First Lady interrupts.

She pivots and drops her arms. He stands facing me as Mr. President continues.

"My wife will be taken to our plane and returned to France. Toute de suite. You are not to leave her side until she is seated and safe."

"Her baggage, Mr. President?"

"It remains here." Mr. President says, looking firmly but calmly into my eyes.

We establish an unspoken understanding between us. He wants it to appear that she is still there.

"I can arrange a garment befitting the circumstances. I will bring it personally." I say.

"Bon." says Mr. President. "Chen, if you need anything, let me know directly."

He nods, lowering his head slightly. A gentleman's sign that he is finished speaking.

"Very good, Mr. President."

I turn to leave.

"Chen."

"Yes, Mr. President."

Facing him fully. My arms comfortably by my side.

"Thank you." says Mr. President.

"It is my privilege to serve you, Mr. President," I say.

"I am NOT leaving!" Ines, the First Lady says firmly.

I avert my eyes as the President gently places his hands on her shoulders, leans his head back slightly, pulling on their deep understanding of one another.

"Ines, I feel it, in here." He touches his heart. "There's evil at work here," says Mr. President, placing his forehead on hers, "and I need you to go. With you safe, my senses are sharp, my eyes keen. With you here, you have that part of me. And, you know I cannot leave."

I couldn't help but hear. The rationale, indisputable, his gentle words cutting her defense but paramount was the fact that there is no possibility of changing his mind. She trusts him implicitly. It's obvious. Her fire quenched by his love. She exhales and surrenders her will. He embraces her as I did my wife.

"Say it." Mr. President says.

"So said, so done." she replies. "I will pray for you, my love."

He looks settled, as every leader should be.

"I have no doubt." Mr. President says.

She turns and nods at me, an indication that I will get no struggle. For that moment, they let me into their world. I'm grateful. Ines, the First Lady, is the opposite of my wife in every respect but their connection reminded me of why I loved waking up every day for forty-five years. That warm foot I lay mine across in our bed every night. They made me miss that foot. I went quickly. The Abaya fit her well. It surprised me, her willingness to wear it. There is concern in her eyes all the way to the airport. She steps onto the plane with a warm cape covering her. She hesitantly steps onto the plane. I enter behind her.

"First Lady." says a female crew attendant that served earlier.

"First Lady, I thought perhaps it would bring you comfort to have a familiar face." I say.

She smiles.

"I wish to keep my word to your husband."

She sits and puts on her seatbelt.

"It was my privilege to serve you. Safe journey to you."

I walk to the exit when she stops me and holds out a card. Her personal card with the phone number on it.
"Chen, should you see cause, call me?"

"I shall."

On exiting I hear her speak to her personal assistant.

"As soon as we get home. I want you to pay all of this man's debts and secure his retirement fund."

"Yes, First Lady."

From the car, I see her glance out of the plane's window, lift off the head covering, close her eyes and pray.

The drive back to the hotel is swift, gratefully so. I was summoned to the room of Ex-Secretary of Defense Wilkes. I only met him once since he checked into the hotel. Him, I could forget. Her, I will never forget. An ungodly coldness follows her. It enters rooms with her yet doesn't seem to bother her. She sees things in and about people they don't want to divulge. Perhaps she will look at me and see I'm a servant of God first and then of this hotel. I can't help but wonder if her eyes will see through my intent. If she does, so be it. However, I am much more useful to Caleb alive.
The cold, perhaps I'm the only one who feels it. Now, I must feel it again. I pause outside of the suite door. I'm in no rush to be in the presence of such evil. I can hear Wilkes speaking to Gretchen through the door. I'm sure Caleb may need what I hear.

Wilkes Hotel Room

"They all checked in. Snug as bugs in a rug." says Wilkes.

"You sound like a father talking about his children," replies Gretchen.

I can hear the rustling of her gown as she walks across the floor.

"You couldn't resist," she says, "the Hitchcock Suite."

I can smell her perfume seeping from beneath the door. I can picture him sitting in the firm cushion of the golden yellow armchair beside the balcony door, flanked by the royal blue drapes with golden decorative inlay.

"My dear, you look lovely," he says.

"Thank you, my sweet. My fingers just can't do the latch," says Gretchen.

"I will gladly do your latch for the rest of our lives. There, all done. Your hands, so delicate. Your pale nail polish, so tasteful for the occasion. I can't help but notice everything about you. I spent years imagining, now here you are. My reality. I will spoil you to chase thoughts of Richard from your mind."

"No need. They are already gone. There was nothing but business between us," she says. "Now, tell me, what have you been rehearsing in that little brain of yours? Now, my dear, tell me your master plan." she says.

I hear her kiss him. Someone is around the corner. I can't stand here much longer listening. I will have to go in but hopefully, I hear something Caleb can use.

"I intend to keep the Beaston. It will be the U. S.'s peace-keeper. They will see its capabilities and we will use it as a compliance to peace incentive. That tool against tyranny. My dear? Are you ill?" he says.

"No, no. It's just that the agreement was to sell the Beaston."

"I'm concerned with peace for the United States. It's about us now. We've meddled and toiled, trying to create peace among other nations for decades. Time after time proving useless. Then being dragged into it by humanity issues. It's our turn to look out for us now. When they see the stealth of the Beaston and realize the threat to them if they don't make peace, they will be the ones creating the peace-treaties." replies Wilkes.

"My love. The first idea suites both of our desires. After all, we are a team. You and I having created this wonderful creature. We're like parents, so I propose-" Gretchen says.

No, not now. Guests, coming up the hall, looking directly at me. I bend, taking hold of my shoelace purposely putting my back to them. Finally, they pass. I caught them mid-sentence. The beauty of this hotel, from the hall, you can hear everything in each room.

"Gretchen," Wilkes interrupts, "I'm afraid you've mistaken your position. You are my love, my inspiration, the one I trusted to realize my dream, but the Beaston is not our child, it is mine. The entire project wouldn't have existed if it weren't for me. I withstood the inquisition for its birth, not you. I masterminded the funds, not you. You did what I commissioned you to do, and gratefully so, but it was a piece of the puzzle, certainly not its entirety. I explained that to you when we first spoke. Do you remember, dear?"

"Yes, but I thought, after all this time, and after my role with Richard-" she says desperately.

"Richard was my friend. He was just blind to the truth." says Wilkes.

"I reeled him in. Kept him on the project-" replies Gretchen.

"But failed to get his data." I hear a lighter flicker and smell cigar smoke coming from beneath the door. "Really, what are we doing? Disputing after all this time. Where is that butler?"

I'm out of time. A few more moments.

"Gretchen, I am grateful. Sacrifices were made by both of us. I betrayed the loyalty of my President. A man I truly respect, but who didn't see what I saw on those battlefields. A man who may one day thank me for this. I could have gone to prison. The United States needs this. We need a new way to war." he says.

I knock on the door.

"Enter." Wilkes says.

I open the door.

"Good evening, Sir, Madam. I am your butler, Chen. How may I serve you?"

He sits in the chair beside the balcony door beneath the glow of a soft lamp and puffs his cigar. She picks up her mobile phone and speaks to someone quietly then hangs up.

"How are my guests?" he asks smugly.

I can feel Gretchen's cold stare creeping up around my feet. She's examining every thread on my uniform.

"Sir, I am not at liberty-"

"I see. I had to try."

Her smooth makeup and immaculate hair can't cover the darkness inside of her well enough to fool me. Her gown is pure white Italian silk with black swirled embroidery. It hugs her petite waist then, flares and flows to the floor. Her paleness suits her. Hair drawn back into a decorative bun at the nape of her neck.

"Is there anything I can get you, Madame?" I ask, looking directly into her eyes. She smiles with her mouth only.

"No. Chen, is it?" Gretchen asks.

Her eyes intentionally piercing. She looks as if she recognizes me. Wilkes is in his own world, puffing away on his cigar.

"Yes, madame." I say purposely breaking our stare.

"Gretchen, let's not ruin the evening with this needless chatter. We'll be in the Fiji Islands before afternoon."

"You're right." She smooths her dress. "It doesn't matter as long as we're together." Forcing a smile coated with pretense.

There is no sincerity in her answer. There is a knock at the door.

"Get that will you... Mr. Chen." says Gretchen.

I turn to get the door.

"I've ordered a little something for us. You haven't eaten all day." says Gretchen.

She disappears into the bedroom.

"I'm not hungry." says Wilkes, tapping ashes from his cigar.

From my vantage point, I see her pick up her new shoes placed beside the others. She still doesn't see the tiny black tracker stuck to the instep of the other shoes Caleb told me he placed, when on the ground near her feet outside the Vatican. His training proves profitable.

I close the door and examine the uniform of the server bent over the cart. Two plates covered by ornate lids with cutlery perfectly laid. He is not from the hotel. The fit of his uniform is off. They tailor our uniforms to fit. Perfection at every turn. His hem is too high and his hands, rough. Those of a tradesman. He purposely diverts his face from view.

"May I assist?" I ask him. Trying to prompt a response. I want to hear his voice.

I lift a water glass and purposely spill it on his gloved hand.

"My apologies, Sir," I whisper to him, taking a spare pair of white serving gloves from my breast pocket. He nervously removes his glove. The same hand Caleb told me may bear a tattoo. He looks at me, noticing that I see it. His eyes are ice blue.

"Really, dear, I'm not hungry at all." Continues Wilkes.

"You need this." Gretchen says, walking into the room.

The server turns to Gretchen with a pleasant demeanor.

"Is everything satisfactory, Madam?" the server asks.

"Oh, I'm afraid not, you've forgotten the cream for my coffee." She says.

"I shall return with it." he says exiting quickly.

Wilkes can't touch that food.

"Looks good, Gretch. I think I may have some." Wilkes says lifting a roll to his lips.

Her chest beginning to heave with anticipation. He lifts the roll and notices the time on his watch.

"Oh, dear! We must get going." Wilkes drops the roll. Gretchen exhales deeply.

"Please, allow me." I say, opening the door for them.

"You need to re-think this," she whispers to him as we walk down the hall. "They won't see it your way. Perhaps diplomacy is not the best tactic."

I press the elevator button and face the doors as we wait.

"Diplomacy got me you." Wilkes smiles.

They enter the elevator. I step in standing closest to the doors. I press the button to the lobby. I hear him kiss her. The doors close. Wilkes continues.

"I can't wait for you to see the house in Milan, I told the decorator that if she is not done by tomorrow for our move in, she'll never work again. Everything is perfect. I've decided something, Gretchen. I want you by my side tonight. I know you don't like the fanfare. You've been behind the scenes all this time, but I want the world to see you by my side." He says.

"I'd really rather not, dear, I-" says Gretchen.

"For me?" he presses.

"I can't. I love you but you know how I hate attention."

"Okay, all right."

The elevator doors open. The lobby is elegantly lit. A few hand selected photographers approach the elevator. I step aside, for Mr. Wilkes have his long-awaited moment in the spotlight. If Caleb is capable, it will be Wilkes' last.

I wish my wife were alive to see this. The glitter of the night. My butterfly. She fluttered through our small flat. Toward the end, she was small, frail. I promised her better days but failed to give them to her. I miss her. I couldn't give her the finery she cooed over in the society magazines. We dreamed of making a better life as far from Liuzhou as possible. The day I was breathless from running up the steps to our flat with our traveling papers in my hand, and the good news that I got this job hung on my tongue then, I saw my butterfly flew away without me. Her wings lay on our bed.

Today, my butterfly is here. Watching these dignitaries pose for photos in the elegant vestibule of the hotel. Handshakes smiles and pats on the back. The flash of cameras immortalizing them in magazines and newspapers. Do they really know the power of their decisions?

Through the front glass doors, a commotion is brewing. Guards with wired earpieces in their left ears stand firmly facing someone. It's him. He is taller. He looks well. His tie is crooked. No handkerchief. He sees me. He pauses and grins. I push the large glass door open and clear my throat.

"Sir. The Prime Minister asked for you. Please come with me."

"Stop," says a guard to Caleb. "I need his identification."

"I am Chen, the head butler. They have requested him-"

"I'm not speaking to you." says the guard.

We don't want this attention. More guards are approaching. Caleb casually puts his left hand in his pocket, embodying his attire as if it were his norm.

"I left it in my other trousers. I'll gladly get it. If you don't mind explaining to the Prime Minister; why I will be late." says Caleb.

Caleb was very believable. The guard looks at me. I glance boldly at my pocket watch, my hand still holding the door open.

"I will gladly do so. She'll appreciate that I did it to protect her." says the guard.

This may get ugly. I recall Caleb doesn't like obstacles. The guards' hand is on his side arm. The other guards are following suit. I got here just in time.

"Are you certain?" Caleb says, turning around.

If I recall, that is one of the first moves I taught him before striking. This would blow our element of surprise. Just then, someone walks through the door I am holding open. An Archbishop. I feel a warmth following him.

"Thank you," says the Archbishop to me.

It's funny. To challenge him is like challenging God. The guards must feel it too.

"Good evening. Sir. We are all waiting," says the Archbishop.

The guards look at each other, then step aside, lowering their hands from their guns, letting Caleb pass.

"I should take this guy to Jerry." Caleb says to me.

"Who is Jerry?" I ask.

"Never mind." Caleb mumbles.

I lead them to the special elevator and press the coded sequence. The elevator doors open. There are two seats two bolted to the floor is in the elevator.

"Please have a seat," I say to Caleb and the Archbishop.
"Thank you. Chen, it's good to see you," says Caleb.

He embraces me. In his eyes, I see a man in transformation. He still needs prayer. The elevator doors close but neither he nor I release our gaze until the doors seal. My work here is almost done.

CHAPTER NINETEEN

Caleb Promise

Alone in the elevator, I seize the moment.

"I saw you in a dream." I say.

"And I, you." the Archbishop replies. "What will you do, young David?"

"David and Goliath. Are you testing my Bible knowledge?" I say.

"I kept it simple. Be grateful it wasn't Habakkuk."

"Yes, that would have stumped me. The eighth book of the twelve minor prophets. His personal struggle to understand injustice. Fitting to the occasion but that would have stumped me." I say.

He's smiles.

"I'm impressed."

"I learned something in that monastery."

The elevator descends, then stops. The rear wall lifts, our seat turns around and move smoothly down a sterile white corridor for a few feet, then enters another elevator. A panel closes behind us and a small sign flashes 'Stay Seated'. An infrared scanner does a body scan panning over us. It is probably searching for weapons. Then the small sign flashes again. 'Exit' and the elevator doors open to a corridor. At the end, two large open double doors with two guards on either side. We step out of the elevator. To our right, a steel door with a small square window opens and a young man walks out, holding his cell phone up to the ceiling and several assistants sit uncomfortably close in the waiting room.

"Damn. No signal," says young man. He notices the Archbishop. "Excuse me, Father."

He walks back into the room.

"What do you think I should do with the drive once I get it back?" I ask the Archbishop.

"Destroy it, Caleb. It holds no good thing. Remember, you can't fight spiritual warfare with carnal weapons."

"You think that will help against real bullets, or that thing they created?" I ask.

He leans in discreetly and whispers in my ear.

"Oh, ye of little faith. Your father believed for you despite the doctors. Born three months early. Now, look at you."

I can't help but relax when I talk to this man. We saunter to the large double doors. The closer we get I see the back of a row of seats.

"Your world must be so simple," I say.

"My world stares down the face of evil every day but holds hope. There is nothing simple about that."

I can't tell just how far the elevator descended. What trickery, manipulation or threats did Wilkes used to get these diplomats to agree to come here. The few we pass do not look pleased to be here.

We walk through the doors. The domed room is dwarfing. Immediately, I look upward. The Archbishop doesn't. He must be used to grandeur. Lights shine from the ceiling illuminating the centre of the room and a semi-circle white shiny stage putting the perimeter in the shadows.

It is dim with leather seats set facing the stage. Heads of state from all over the world are seated with no formality. They sit where they chose and most of them sat in the front around the stage, no doubt to get the best look possible. Three large screens hover above the stage. The Archbishop and I sit as close to the doors in the back as possible.

At exactly 7:00 p.m. The doors close automatically and the lights dim further. A single large spotlight illuminates the stage. Centre stage, the curtain parts. Wilkes. He's a centre stage kind of man. He steps out, trying his best to look serious. I can tell he's desperately trying to hold back a smile. He walks into the centre of the round stage. The seats form a giant 'C' around the stage. It's cold. Basic seats and no windows. There is tension in the room. I don't know everyone's name or what country they rule, but I know angry when I see it. And they look angry.

I recognize the Prime Minister of the United Kingdom. I've seen her in the news. That looks like the President of France, I recall him congratulating the President after the elections. What is that? A slight rumbling above. That's not what you want to hear when you are near snow-covered mountains.

"Welcome. There is no pretense here, only truth." says Wilkes. "Every leader knows what it is like to watch your people die in war. Die for your country at your own requests. I know this feeling. Ladies and gentlemen, the United States has created a new way to war. We will be the peace-makers of the world."

"You say 'we' yet, your President is not here." yells an irate leader from his seat in the front.

"I speak for the President. You know my position. We have worked for decades at world peace, and I've seen first-hand that it's a waste of time. There is one thing you all understand. Fear. But instead of using it for war, we will use fear for peace."

Wilkes takes a small fob-sized black remote out of his pocket. Just before he presses the button. Then the sound of high-heeled shoes walking in the shadows across the shiny white stage is heard. Gretchen? She stands beside him. Why does he look surprised?

"Ladies and Gentlemen, we call it, The Beaston."

"Please, my dear, may I elaborate?" Gretchen asks.

Wilkes slips the black remote into his tuxedo jacket pocket.

"Of course. Ladies and Gentlemen, a scientist responsible for the project. My Gretchen." Wilkes says.

He embraces her briefly then steps back leaning lightly on his cane.

"What does every war have in common? Death. It is inevitable in war. The Beaston is a new way to war. It is dedicated to its master. Impervious to atmospheric changes, not given to emotional irrational actions."

She walks forward to the front of the stage with her toes just touching the edge. I can see the flicker of passion for this in her eyes. This is a birthing moment for her. One I desperately want to end. But not yet. Also, our big fish may be here or watching. There are cameras discreetly mounted on the room's perimeter.

"It follows instructions implicitly," she says, "but holds the capability of deduction, thermal sight, and examines structures and can strategically plan its own attacks, predicting its prey's behavior. Remarkable really. These skills are best appreciated in real-life circumstances out in nature. But it would be interesting to see it practiced here."

Wilkes looks at her, bewildered, but holds his composure. Everyone looks at one another. A sense of vulnerability just filled the room.

"Secretary Wilkes and I agree that we need a new way to war. However, I believe the problem is not with power, it is with who holds the power. It's with the leaders."

Chatter rises from the crowd. The Canadian President seated in front of me turns to the German Prime Minister.

"How dare she." says a leader. "I'm leaving."

She turns to Wilkes, removes the small black device from her pocket and holds it up for him to see. It is just like her to dangle it in his face. Wilkes taps his right suit pocket and his mouth opens slightly in shock. She must have taken it from his pocket when they embraced.

"My love, you didn't recruit me, I recruited you. You gave me the one thing I needed. Resources." Gretchen says to Wilkes.

She presses the button and a glass sphere rises from the stage, trapping Wilkes in the middle of it. He rushes to get out of the sphere. His cane slips and he falls. The glass sphere rises quickly trapping him inside. He struggles to reach his cane. He can't stand. He crawls to the glass and beats his hands on the glass. Surprised. A few leaders stand.

"Behold," She continues, "A brilliant contraption customized to contain the Alpha Beaston. You are safe, for now." She says to the audience. "The cylinder glass is impenetrable. In the centre, the opening to–well, for lack of a more sophisticated word, the pit. If I press this tiny button, the floor slides open within the cylinder and well, you can deduce the rest."

"Dear God," I hear the Archbishop murmur.

Wilkes' leg weakens, his balance gives way. He leans into the glass.

"I'm leaving too." Agrees another President.

Gretchen presses another button and the click of large bolts seal the doors behind us.

"Gretchen, what are you doing?" yells Wilkes.

She ignores him. I adjust myself in my seat. Gretchen walks back and forward on the stage with ease.

"You are in no danger. Your cell phones won't work, don't bother. You don't really know who I am. But, in time, you will."

Wilkes is beating the glass desperately. He looks like a forgotten bug on the inside of a window.

"Gretchen! Let me out of here! You hear me..." yells Wilkes. She continues as if he is nonexistent.

"This is just a demonstration," says Gretchen. "I am offering you the tool to rid you of your problems and ours. The ones who disrupt our peace and pull on the earth's resources. Christians, Jews, your impoverished, whoever takes without giving. Anyone who won't bow to your authority."

"Intolerable!" yells a leader in front of me, standing. "Who do you think you are? I'm leaving this atrocity."

"Dear Prime Minister, if you please, reach beneath your seat, something I think you'll be quite interested in. Please. All of you, beneath your seats. Indulge me. Your right thumbprint unlocks your personal live video." She pauses as they take them out and place their thumbs on the devices screen. The Archbishop does not reach for it. Direct your attention to the large screens above. Your video will appear in a section on the screen. You will know it when you see it."

Her gown swings as she struts across the stage, confidently. A leader standing in front of me pulls out the device. Initially, he stood to leave but what he sees stops him in his tracks.

"Go ahead," says Gretchen, seeing reluctance in some of them. "DO IT. You will not be disappointed."

"Take a good look, ladies and gentlemen, at a new way to war." Says Gretchen.

Wilkes looks frail. He searches his pockets. Gretchen walks to the glass cylinder separating them and pulls his little silver pill box from a pocket in her skirt.

"Looking for these, my dear?" she shows it to him. "Consider it a favor if you die before it gets to you."

Wilkes closes his eyes. She played him well. The look on his face is the same as the one Richard had. Just before she killed him. She turns her attention to the audience again.

The Prime Minister in front of me looks at her with a rage in his eyes.

"I will kill you for this!" he says.

I lean to my right peering over his shoulder to see the live-feed video of a body camera inching close to a sleeping child. He's about four years old. Tucked in his bed, teddy bears beside him, alone in his bedroom. It must be his son. The leader is trembling from rage. The leaders that stood, sit down.

The Archbishop seated beside me has clasped his hands and shut his eyes. He looks like he's sunbathing on a beach without a care in the world. I believe he is praying.

On the large monitors, individual videos begin to appear. Live videos projecting what is on every leader's hand-held device. Now I know why they sat.

"You do not know what you have done." he snarls. His hands tremble the longer he stares at the monitor.

"I know exactly what I have done. I have the attention of the world." says Gretchen.

"You have just started war," he says. "Remove your man now and I may forgive you!"

"Man? That is not a man." She says.

Their eyes widen. It is the Beaston. Many of them.

A leader to my left holds his device, seated, wide-eyed, helplessly watching a body camera approaching his wife from behind. She can't see it. She's reading in a chair in front of an ornate bedroom fireplace, holding a glass of red wine. But it is not the presence of the approaching danger that drops his jaw. It is the presence of another man in the room also holding a wine glass.

The Prime Minister of the United Kingdom closes her eyes, her hand resting on the device she placed face down in her lap. She opens her eyes and turns it over. She presses her thumb on the device. Immediately, the image appears on the large screen.

In her image, a moving body cam leaps from tree to tree avoiding infrared security beams on the manicured lawn. It softly lands on the ground beneath a window. Her son.

There is a birthday party. He's talking and dancing with a girl. Birthday balloons whirling around the room filled with smiling friends. He takes her hand and leads her outside through French doors onto the balcony just beside the lurking Beaston. The Prime Minister closes her eyes and a tear wells beneath her lashes.

Wilkes' turns his anger to the crowd.

"YOU IDIOTS! SHE'S MAD! STOP HER! Gretchen, stop this madness, I-" yells Wilkes.

"You are a dead man," Gretchen says to Wilkes. "You think they will help you? It is because of you they are here. Be silent."

"It's not real," the Italian President says. "Falsified recordings. They must be!"

The British Prime Minister has tears in her eyes.

"No. It's live," she says.

Another speaks out.

"It can't be. You dare threaten all of us. It is suicide!"

Gretchen ignores them. She pressed the device and a circular trap door on the floor beneath Wilkes slowly slides open. Then, a sound that silences the room. A deep-animals growling. The room falls silent. Wilkes shuts his eyes, his hands still on the glass, he turns his head, afraid to look backward. He has scooted onto a short ledge beside the glass to keep from falling into the dark hole enlarging as the floor slides open.

"This weapon has a unique gift given to it by its genetic composition. It can tell who its enemy truly loves and can hunt that person, and only that person."

A leader seated in the row in front of me watches the large monitor. His eyes fixed on the image of a body camera emerging from water beside a young woman laughing. She is swimming playfully with a man. A large diamond engagement ring glistens on her finger. It must be his daughter, just beginning life.

It descends, the camera submerges under water and it swims around their feet effortlessly. Her giggles muffled. His rage is building. I can hear him breathing heavily. However, like everyone in the room he is helpless to stop it. He watches while comments of outrage fly from the leaders toward Gretchen.

One particular leader, a few seats away from me, is watching a camera walk through a woman's apartment, with boxes of baby items scattered on the floor, delivered by mail. Over six months pregnant, diamonds and gifts trail across her dresser, she prepares a bath, humming and rubbing her belly lightly. There are photographs she and the leader on the night table, but there is no wedding ring on her finger. However, the hand holding the device is wearing a wedding ring.

"... unlike the public, it can't be fooled," says Gretchen.

"You can't do this," says the Prime Minister with the young son, "they are innocent."

Gretchen casually glances at a ring on her finger and answers him.

"The unique characteristic of genuine leaders is that they are always willing to die to protect others but won't let others die to protect them. They are leverage to me. Nothing more. You will make your choices now. Are you a genuine leader? If you can put aside your political ideologies, together, we can cleanse your regions, if not, others will take your place."

"This is outrageous! Let's get out of here!" yells the leader.

He heads toward the doors, but he stops at Gretchen's words.

"Look at your image now. All of you look at the result of your decisions." She says holding her hand up to the screen above her.

On the large screens, all the other images disappear leaving that Prime Minister's image alone enlarged on the screen.

He looks at the screen. It is his bedroom. A warm glow of an enormous stone fireplace warms the room with flickering light. His wedding photo in oil painting hangs above with fresh flowers beneath it on the mantle. The body camera turns from the fireplace and the snorting breath of the hunter is heard whiffing the room, detecting her scent, like a dog smells the air.

The camera jostles and the view of the camera is high, taller than any man would be. Its movements methodical, smooth. It's high against a corner in the ceiling gripping the walls in the shadows. Prime Minister's wife's robe lays across an ottoman at the foot of the bed. Then, the Beaston reaches for the robe. Hooks it with one talon. Gasps rise at the sight of its mutant claw fill the room. I didn't gasp. I've seen that claw every night in my dreams. Suddenly, I remember the preacher talking about how God will never leave you ignorant of the devil's devices. I guess it is true.

The Beaston's hand is larger than a man's hand. Covered with a shiny black-gray course hair. It sniffs the robe, snarls with a deep prehistoric rumble. The woman rolls over, still asleep.

"You want to know if this is real-time? Call her," says Gretchen.

A guard hands the leader a satellite phone. He dials quickly. The phone rings. Gretchen smiles. That's not good.

His wife's foot moves and the Beaston extends its claws reaching for her ankle. She stretches to reach the phone drawing her foot beneath the covers. Gretchen makes two soft clicks with her tongue detected by the clear earpiece in her ear and immediately the Beaston withdraws its claws. We all watch as the Beaston silently leaps and clings to the corner on the ceiling in the shadows, it darkens its color like a chameleon and blends into the shadows. It is undetectable.

The woman gropes for the phone, her eyes still closed.

"Answer!" he says hoping to warn her.

Finally, she answers it. Her satin cream gown elegant and long.

"Hello?"

"GET OUT! Get out of the room!" he yells.

"Hello? Paul? Is that you?"

"RUN! ANGELINA, RUN!"

He's perspiring, seeing what she can't.

"What are you saying? Do you know what time it is."

She sits up in the bed, swipes her brown shoulder length from hair from her face. Her lips flush. She has dark brown eyes and gentle features. One of the spaghetti straps on her nightgown slips off her small shoulder. Then Gretchen does it. She clicks her tongue once. The Beaston drops. She still can't see it. Not all of it. I know the feeling. In my dream I only saw parts of it until it revealed itself. I sit forward in my seat. Like in my dream, I strain to see all of it. My heart is pounding. I am living my nightmare and can feel the pain of this leader who watches the unthinkable. There it is. All of it. I close my eyes. A shrill.

"Angelina! No!" he yells.

"Help me! Pau...Paul!"

Her screams fade to gurgles. Paul is still. Helpless he lets the device fall from his hand. This man, that holds power over an entire country is helpless. His world, completely different from mine.

I drop my chin and look at Gretchen. I feel myself biting down and my fists find their way into my pockets.

The Beaston steps back. The camera is speckled with thick red blood. The picture is veiled but the outcome obvious. Tearing sounds, gurgling cries. Archbishop's eyes are still shut. The leader closes his eyes.

"Your entire country will pay! Her blood is on the head of your President," he says through his teeth.

"Yes, well, we shall see. Now that you all know that this is no bluff, let's get started." says Gretchen.

I can feel their brains thinking frantically. The President of France glances at his watch. He is the most composed. Why? He hasn't placed his thumb on the device until now. A circle spins. Buffering. He exhales. Then, before his next breath, an image appears. A woman calmly peering through the window of her plane. The image is upside down. She unbuckles her seatbelt and gets on her knees in front of her seat, praying with her bible open before her. He shuts his eyes. The image shifts to the night sky filled with stars.

"If you refuse to comply, I will erase every semblance of your existence along with your lineage. Agree to comply with my conditions stated in the contract making me your one-world ambassador to rid you of your unwanted, or ..." she raises her arm toward the screens.

Each person's hand device beeps twice and the screen shows a long contract with fingerprint signature box.

"It is an agreement bonding us for the cause," she says.

Wilkes is sweating profusely, clutching at his heart. Gretchen turns away from him. It's odd, seeing evil and greater evil together. I feel a value for human life. I'm no judge or jury. God knows I'm no saint. But there is something inhuman about watching another person die and doing nothing to help. The leaders look at one another. Then. Hope. The man stands.

"I will not sign," says the Israeli Prime Minister.

He throws the phone to the ground and stamps it. Two guards walk up to each side of his row. He ignores them. Gretchen turns to him.

"Ah, the religious," she says. "I expected as much. Willing to die for the sake of righteousness."

"I will NOT consent to this evil being loosed in my land. I will NOT partner with darkness. God will prevail, snake! Just like in the garden. I will NOT have it named of me and my family. The fate of my land will never be handed to you. Do what you will," says the Israeli Prime Minister.

"Think wisely, Mister Prime Minister. You are not Abraham and there is NO ram in this bush. I'm offering you-" says Gretchen.

"-the world and all its kingdoms? As you did to Jesus in the desert. It didn't work then, and it won't work now. Don't fall for her tricks," he turns to the leaders. "Though our religions are different, we are leaders. If we stand together, this... thing loses." He turns back to Gretchen. "You might take my life, my family's lives, but not our souls. They belong to God."

"Shut up!" Gretchen says.

She drops her hands and walks to edge of the stage. Interesting, her composure is shaken.

"Hear!" he continues. "In my region, just as in many of theirs," he waves his arm over the leaders, "the threat of death is ever present. We live with a readiness to die. My family and my people are grounded. God first. We will fight evil as we have in times past. You are no different. You have nothing to threaten us with. We are leaders! You cannot bully us! What say you?" he yells to the leaders.

One leader stands, smashes the phone. Then another, and another. The Prime Minister of the United Kingdom stands, smashes her phone with tears in her eyes and defiance on her face. The President of France stands. The President of Spain, the Prime Minister of Italy and countless others stand. My heart swells, hearing the phones smash on the floor. This *is* a World Peace Summit.

"Woman," says the Italian Prime Minister, "it seems you have accomplished something remarkable." says a leader. "You have unified us." he says, holding his arms out. The entire room is standing.

CHAPTER TWENTY

The room jolts. What was that?

"Noble. I must admit the camaraderie surprises me. I knew there may be one willing to take such a stand. How long lived will this unity be? It may surprise you at how hated the treaty-breaker can be. Let's see."

She walks to the center of the stage, removes the hard drive from her pocket. It's small, the size of her thumb. She holds it up.

"A decade of perfect scientific research at your fingertips. Look around this room. It is the key to ultimate power making your country the leader in military weaponry. The blueprint for the Alpha Beaston. Let me show you. Though I think Wilkes will see it first." She turns to him, still trapped behind the glass now half conscious.

For the right price, dear leaders, you will leave here owning the Beaston and all its genetic secrets. The opening bid, ten billion dollars. A small price to make your enemies go away and to become the most powerful country in the world. You leave this room with victory over century old struggles." She smiles.

A tension rises in the room as heads turn and the leaders look at each other to confirm solidarity. Don't do it. I look over the leaders. They appear resolute. Steady. If they stand together, she has no play. Peace has a chance. No one is even breathing. Then... No.

One leader in the back lifts his hand. His Rolex drops into place on his wrist. Was it the fear from the Beaston that ominously crept into his bones or was it the thirst for power? Whatever it was, he bowed. Coldness permeates the atmosphere. It drives away the warmth of the bond. The others turn to him.

"Don't do it," says the leader seated beside the man with his hand raised.

"Ah, a taker," Gretchen says.

"TRAITOR!" yells another leader.

The crowd yells at him. One by one the dispute grows. The man beside him shoves him. The one behind him too. He bursts back. This is it. I must move now.

"Call me what you want! I'm not ready to watch my family murdered and die for what? You? You train your people to hate mine." he yells at his regional adversary. "For what? Nothing!" says the Leader who took the offer.

"I'll kill you myself! Selfish coward." roar the leaders.

"Get HIM!" they shout.

The leaders charge at him. The guards go to the chaos. Gretchen stands watching. Smiling with a cold calm. She wants to watch them tear themselves apart. On my way out of the aisle, my leg bumps the Archbishop. He opens his eyes, hands still clasped. I watched long enough. He nods and closes his eyes again. My plan was, first, kill the Alpha Beaston. Second, get the drive from Gretchen and reveal the big fish.   Now, whichever opportunity comes first. I ease past Gretchen who is standing on the stage distracted by the chaos ensuing; staying close to the wall in the shadows.   The stage door is a few feet away.

Wilkes. No. He sees me with my hand on the doorknob. He is pressed against the glass gripping his chest. He's just staring at me. His eyes are moist. Will he alert her? Has he erased all feeling for her? He's opening his mouth. Then, he closes it again. He makes the shape of a square with his pointer fingers discreetly. He knows what I will do. Gretchen turns toward us. Everything in me wants to kill here now, here on this stage. But she had help. I'm sure of it and it wasn't Wilkes. If I kill her, I may never find that person.

If I can kill the Alpha Beaston, the foot soldiers will go into the fold. That's the way prides work. Wilkes lowers his right hand to his side and makes a fist. A military sign-language meaning 'hold' or 'wait'. He looks at Gretchen. She sneers at him then turns away. Wilkes opens his hand, with closed fingers pointed toward the door. I push the door open. The noise draws Gretchen's attention. She quickly turns. Wilkes shuffles to his feet and bumps the glass with his cane intentionally.

"Gretchen, please… my love. I'm begging you not to do this." Wilkes says.

It gives me the chance to get through the door unseen. It closes slowly behind me. Standing in the hallway I hear the circular platform in the centre of the glass cylinder that Wilkes is in, rising slowly. Curiosity wins. I push the door open slightly, and peek through the slit.The leaders stop arguing and stare.

"Welcome, the Alpha Beaston. See what ten billion can buy you." Gretchen says.

The rising platform jams but with one leap upward, there it is. A manifested nightmare. It hooks its foot talons onto the ledge Wilkes is balancing on. The circular pit beneath him, opened. It looks directly at Wilkes. The room tremors at its weighted landing.

Wilkes flattens himself against the glass. Just as in my nightmare, its head is that of a lioness, its body stands at least eight feet tall with large muscular arms like that of a gorilla. The claws are as a bear and legs, thick muscular like a zebra. It is covered in a shimmering fir that lays down perfectly. The eyes are piercing eagle eyes and it dominates the room. Disputes stop and everyone stares. I let the door close. Wilkes' screams fade behind the thick steel door and I turn to the sterile white corridor. Doors are on either side.

Four guards come around the corner. They look at me and realize I'm not supposed to be there. They draw their guns. It happens faster this time. My reflexes.

They approach, I pretend to surrender. One reaches out to grab my arm. Instinctively it releases Chen's lessons like a coiled spring. Another two guards engage. When it is over, two lay twisted on the floor and one, is slumped with his own knife through his throat. On his wrist, the tattoo.

Gretchen is our mystery man's puppet. Dedicated to the cause and no doubt enjoying her moment in the sun. Wilkes led me this way for a reason. I push a few doors, they locked most but this one opens. A laptop is on a table. That was the rectangle Wilkes drew. Stuck in its U.S.B. port, a hard drive. Probably a copy. I pull it and stick it into my pocket. I need to find the control panel to the pit. No! A sting. I can't feel my body.

"Rat. I thought I squashed you at the Vatican. Apparently, Dread wasn't as effective as thought."

Gretchen. How did she know?

My legs are shaky. How many volts was that? Stun gun? Why not kill me?

"Your genes are more valuable than you are." says Gretchen.

My satellite phone rings. No. Not now, it's Jason. Can't blow his cover. Gretchen steps aside, letting four more guards come at me. The big one pulls the phone from my jacket pocket and hands it to Gretchen. Stiff boots pummel my gut. I receive the blows helplessly on the floor. My body still numb, I don't experience the pain; but the damage is being done and I will feel this later. Gretchen holds it up to me.

"You can give me the code, or I can chop your finger off. I know you didn't get this far on your own." Gretchen says.

Jason is worth a finger. No answer.

"I will find better genes. Take him to the pit. He will be a late-night snack." she says.

"How will your boss feel about that? You better check with him first." I say stalling until my circulation comes back.

She stops walks out of the door, places her hand on the door post and pivots seductively, but her smile falls at my question. Pride is making her wonder what flaw in her performance revealed her incapable of this planning.

"Small mind. What makes you think I need anyone else?"

"You're evil, not constructive. Whoever did this is a builder at heart," I say. "What are you going to do with them? Not much time before the world's armies descend on you."

Finally, I'm starting to feel my body.

"What will you do with them?" I ask.

"Release them. Unharmed," she says.

"You never intended to kill them, did you? You will let them kill each other. War. That was your objective. You knew someone would take the offer. And even if they leave here united, they will never forget the one who betrayed them. Then, you hold the Beaston and you are the new biggest arms dealer in the world. Smart. Too bad you didn't think of that. You're too, what's the word I'm looking for... shallow. So, what's his name? Who's the mystery man, Wretch, I mean Gretch," I say.

She's trying to hold her composure, but my taunting is getting to her.

"War is good for the economy. Good for my economy. They don't think far enough down the line. Now, they have a target and a reason to war. Men are simple. They go for what is in front of them. Funny, you never considered the one person who is here."

She steps closer to me. She can't be right. But my gut never lies. And it sank in, the one who is not here is the President of the United States. Is it possible? If she is telling the truth, his scrutiny of the BST-10 project was to cover his secret involvement. Is it possible that the President had men, like my father embedded in double-deep cover to obtain the data and let Wilkes take the fall?

"I see your wheels turning. To the pit," she says.

The guards pull me toward the door.

"You didn't have to kill Elizabeth," I yell as they pull me to my feet.

"I'm sorry, that name is insignificant to me-" replies Gretchen.

"The waitress at the diner I worked in. She was no threat."

"Oh, yes, that."

She turns around and sweeps back her hair, uses her finger to touch up her lipstick.

"Annoying little creature. I had to kill her." Gretchen sneers.

I hear it. A beep from the wall behind me. I drop to the ground. The blast blows the furniture around the room. Wood and debris blow past my head and open the wall behind me. Steve Harvard's men, dressed in black military attire, swarm the room, shooting AK47's. Shots, precise shots. They kill Gretchen's guards. Steve Harvard's lead man touches his ear, he's listening to Harvard.

Gretchen is getting away. The smoke clears and she's pushing open the doors going to the stage. Steve Harvard's men are there. They grab her arms and drag her through the opening they just blew out in the wall. I pick up the laptop and walk toward the stage door.

"He wants to talk to you." Harvard's lead man hands me a phone.

"It's me," I say.

"I heard." He says.

"I told you. I didn't kill Elizabeth."

"So, you did. You were smart to contact me."

I stuck the last of the clear gel trackers to myself and sent Harvard the signal algorithm. Since we couldn't trust anyone in government, I needed to secure back-up. Reliable back-up. Revenge is reliable and Harvard wanted revenge.

"Your warrant in New York will be taken care of. You're a free man, Caleb Promise." says Harvard.

"I didn't want Liz dead. Sorry for your loss." I say.

"Thanks. Where is Wilkes?" he asks.

"Dead." I say.

"You?" Harvard asks.

"No. Fate. I need Gretchen alive. She's got information to the big fish," I say.

"I'll try to convince Giovanna to leave something for you. Caleb, how did you know I wouldn't kill you?" asks Harvard.

"I believed you recognize the truth when you hear it. You didn't get where you are being blind," I say.

He's quiet.

"Don't know what it is about you, Caleb Promise, but I like it. A gift. Tell your friend he has a rat in his office." says Harvard.

"Friend?" I deflect.

"I know you won't confirm or deny. I have a name," he says.

By this, I will know if he's lying or not.

"Sam." Harvard says.

A chill runs up my back.

"What about Director White?"

"She's clean. Quirky, but clean."

"Are we squared?" I say.

A term a New Yorker knows. It means even.

"We're squared." says Harvard.

I think I contacted him to free my name and give him closure. People deserve closure. I'm still waiting for mine, so I know what it feels like. Harvard's men disperse. I must warn Jason that Sam is the mole. The Beaston is not on the stage. From the blood marks inside the glass cylinder, it dragged Wilkes' body into the pit beneath the stage. The small black device controlling the cylinder and stage door is in pieces and the glass cylinder is halfway down and still descending. A roar from beneath the pit. The leaders move to the exterior doors to get out of the forum room. They are bolted. I consider taking the leaders through the entrance Harvard blew open when an explosion rocks the building and collapses the doorway and hall I just stepped out of. We're trapped.

A few of Harvard's men are on the stage. I look down at my hand. That's it! The laptop. Wilkes wanted me to find the entire laptop not just the drive.

"Shoot anything that comes out of that hole," I say to Harvard's men as I open the laptop.

Somehow, I know that bullets won't stop it. It certainly won't stop the ones deployed. A loud screeching cry like an owl shrill. Password? Great. What would it be... 'Beaston'? I can't type. Gunshots! 'B-E-A-S-T-O-N'... enter.

"Incorrect Password entered. SELF-DESTRUCTION WARNING," the computer says.

A minor explosion shakes the room. Harvard's men must have dropped a grenade. The Beaston must be moving closer. What could it be? War? "W-A-R", enter.

"Incorrect Password entered FINAL DESTRUCTION WARNING in 10...9...8...7..." says the computer.

He is military. He thinks military. It must be this... "BSTN-10 PROJECT"... I inhale. Enter.

"...2...1," says the computer. "ACCESS GRANTED. Hello, Captain Wilkes."

I exhale. I found it. The self-destruct file. wouldn't have arranged this without an emergency kill-switch. My guess is that the pit is wired.

It reads:

"1. Enter code 82-A76842Z-CD on main panel.
2. Stage door seals.
3. Exterior doors will unlock.

If the stage door does not seal, the exterior doors will not unlock.
4. Pit Explosives will detonate"

I search the stage wall for the control panel. That remote was short-wave so it can't be very far away. There! Behind the curtain. Gunfire is rapid. Squeals and thumps are heard in the pit.

"82-A-7684, Z-CD, 82-A-728..." I repeat.

I lift my hand to type in the numbers on the panel when I see it. The glass is down. Instantly, the Beaston's claw, snatches one of Harvard's guards. His body lurches forward with such a force, we hear his back crack. His yell is gut-wrenching.

"No!" the guard beside him yells, unleashing a slew of bullets into the pit.

Only two guards are left.

"I'M OUT," he yells to the guard on the opposite side of the pit.

"Here!" He throws a cartridge to him across the pit.

He reloads and starts again. It may be futile, but it is a deterrent.

The sounds of tearing flesh and bones crushing seeps between the gunshots. The leaders are against the sealed exterior doors. I hold my hands up to them to stay there. I finish putting in the code. The pit door begins to close. It's working! Wait, what is wrong? It slows then a grinding sound. It stops. No! What's wrong?

"IT'S NOT EVEN HALFWAY!" Harvard's man yells to me from across the stage. His gun still aimed down the hole.

"No kidding!" I yell to him.

I punch the code in again.

"DOOR JAMMED." it says.

I punch it in again.

"DOOR JAMMED." it says again.

"Can we still blow it?" he asks. I look at him.

Why hasn't the Beaston come out? It is calculating. It's waiting for me to override the doors. It wants out. All the way out." I say.

"Is there an override code?" yells a leader standing beside the doors. "I used to be an engineer."

Harvard's man looks at me. He sees the answer in my eyes. He knows that if I say yes, the leaders will want me to use the override which leaves the stage doors open and releases the locks on the double doors. We can escape but can the Beaston. Alternative, I don't use the override and detonate the explosion, we kill the Beaston and all of us. Everyone. I have to let them know. It's a decision we all must agree on.

"Yes. There is an override code." I say.

I explain the circumstances. The leaders look at each other.

"They are running out of bullets. We are running out of time."

They know others will die if it gets out. What did Gretchen say? True leaders will die for others but not have others die for them? Let's see if this is a room of leaders. They confer.

"We agree. Blow it." says the French President. "Do it quickly."

The leaders nod and some pray.

"We're good." I ask Harvard's men.

I'm glad I made peace with my life. That I saw Rosie one last time. I type the code into the panel.

"OVERRIDE ACCEPTED. EXPLOSION IMMINENT IN 5...4...3... " says the main panel.

I shut my eyes and pray.

"Lord, I repent from all my sins. I accept you into my life. Forgive for not letting you in sooner but receive me now,"

"2..."

What's that? Is it? Yes, it is. The stage door motor. It's started. It's grinding but the stage doors are closing, quickly! It is almost sealed. I look among the leaders for the Archbishop. He is still seated with his eyes closed. The Beaston leaps. It's hand grips the stage. It prevents the door from sealing.

"NOW! HIT IT!" I yell.

Harvard's men throw every grenade and flash bane into the hole. We dive for cover.

"...1." says the main panel.

The small grenades blow first. The floor shakes and cracks. The leaders hunker against the door. The big explosion hits. The room shakes violently. The domed ceiling cracks and large pieces fall crushing the chairs. The explosion rocks the room and cracks the stage.

One of Harvard's men is sliding toward the crack. I run toward him and dive grabbing his hand before he slips down into the crack. Fire and smoke squeeze through the slit in the stage pit doors.

The monitors crash to the floor beside us. Thick dust and smoke swirl around us. A horrible screeching sound and the smell of meat burning, and crackling fills the room. Then silence. A distant rumble, then eerie silence in the dust blown room.

CHAPTER TWENTY-ONE

The sound of steel bolts unlocking and the release of the air pump locking system of the double doors brings exhales. The doors swing open freeing us into fresh air and an undamaged hallway. The leaders rise from the floor slowly and look at the stage.

Harvard's men stand. I finish pulling Harvard's man up. We stand and look at the pit.

"Thanks." He says.

I nod. On the stage, the rest of the claw is burning on the stage wedged in the pit opening. I jump off the stage and walk out of the forum room to the leaders into the long corridor. They compose themselves as they approach the elevator, one leader looks up and realizes he's walking behind the leader who wanted to purchase the Beaston. He shoves him from behind.

"You don't belong here! You're not getting on this elevator coward! You should die with your precious beast."

The leader's suit is ripped and his glasses broken. He's sweating profusely but standing by his decision for trying to buy the Beaston.

"My people suffer for not having a strong defense. You fault me for wanting to better our position! Then hate me." he says with great conviction.

This must stop. Watching from the forum room door, I am angry. I'm angry at Wilkes and Gretchen. They pulled the thread of already torn relationships. They can't leave like this or war is imminent. Gretchen's mystery man will swoop in to profit from it. Something should be said. How can I say it? I live in the shadows. A busboy. A fired busboy. Homeless without a penny to my name but somehow, the strengthened 'me' feels passionate enough to speak. The elevator is here. I rush in front of the open doors, reach in and push the 'hold door' button. I open my mouth and the words fall out.

"The world can't know what happened here tonight. They can't know. Your families are safe, Wilkes is dead, and we destroy the Beaston. So, what is left? The bitterness they sowed. If you let this build contention among you, evil wins. You united in there." I point at the forum room. "Do it again."

"Who are you?" asks Madame Prime Minister of the United Kingdom.

I didn't expect that question. I push my fists into my pockets. Suddenly I feel under-dressed. I feel like that scruffy kid in blue jeans, sweat shirt and worn brown leather jacket.

"Caleb, Caleb Promise."

"Your name is Hebrew." Begins the Israeli Prime Minister, "it means faithful, devoted, whole-hearted, bold and brave."

"You lived up to your name today." The President of Mexico says.

"But," says the UK Prime Minister, "You sound American. What country *do* you represent?"

This question defined me. It helped me realize what everything I went through was for.

"I represent mankind and what is fair."

"Then you are Caleb... the fixer." The UK Prime Minister says smiling. "What is your plan, Mr. Promise?" she asks.

A graceful polish flows out of me. It's a part of me I never used before. It's fake, just refined. My mother would be proud. But I'm still blue jeans and leather jacket kind of guy.

"This was a peace summit. Let's make it one. In every way," I say.

"That man is a traitor!" says a leader from behind. "He shouldn't be allowed to live! He was willing to put all our lives, our people's lives in danger for power."
The President of France turns to the crowd of leaders.

"What would you do for love, Monsieur?" The President of France turns to the shouting leader. "What would you do to protect the ones' you love? Your people? I did everything to protect my wife. That man lost his wife before his eyes. I'm not saying what he did was right, but we all feel this burden from time to time. We have all done some things we are not proud of to run our country. When we feel safe, we drop our swords."

The entire group turns silent. They understand the weight of being responsible for a country. It is something they all bear. Funny, I don't see their titles right now. Some of noble birth. Some were elected, others, took it by force. But they all bore the scars of living their lives open to public scrutiny daily. Yet they rise.
I see men and women with families like mine. People with something to protect. To me they are no different from Lou or the chef who would slip me a fresh roll, seeing me staring at the

food when I hadn't eaten all day. I had to serve platters of meals I couldn't afford to buy. These leaders are just people. I wonder, would any of them even slip me a roll? Here they are, wide-eyed, some of them having found a new reason to hate the United States because of Wilkes.

"You need to leave here united." I say. "The other issues can be sorted out later, when the world is not watching.' I say, gesturing to their dusty clothes and disheveled hair.

"Forget what happened in there. The future may hold things worth going to war for. This is not one."

They look hesitant to agree, despite my words. They don't seem convinced. I run my hands through my hair feeling this may all fall apart. Then, he arrives.

The Archbishop steps up beside me. It's nice to see I'm not the only one that he has a profound effect on. They look at him from head to toe. His calm. His steady character. He clasps his hands behind his back. Walking forward, he speaks to them.

"To truly see what is in a pot, you must stir it. Today, you saw what is in yours. It is not any man's place to judge. Do not be the first to cast the stone. This will give no place to the devil. Go in peace." says the Archbishop.

I feel them concede. He has a calm presence that is identifiable. Slowly, the Israeli Prime Minister extends his hand to the leader who tried to buy the Beaston. One by one, the others follow suit and even embrace.

"No country can effectively standalone. We all need allies." Says a leader to the disheveled man.

"My apologies, ladies and gentlemen." He says. "At the time, I..."

"No need." Says the Archbishop.

I look them over.

"You need clothes," I say.

The leaders look down at their clothing, then at me. I open the door of the room where their assistants are waiting. Wide-eyed oblivious to the cause of the tremors.

The Archbishop and I step away from them. They begin exchanging jackets, shirts, and ties with their assistants. Madame Prime Minister of the United Kingdom is using her assistant's makeup. We stroll to the elevator.

"Did you ever ask yourself why of all people, your father trusted me with the drive?" asks the Archbishop.

I glance over his shoulder. The leaders are calmly entering the elevator. Each leader is accompanied by their assistant.

"No, I figured it was because you were a priest or something. God fearing and all that." I say.

"I was in seminary when your father and I met. He saw something in me I struggled to see in myself." says the Archbishop, pausing, going into a long stare.

"Tell me about it." I ask.

"Not today." he says, smiling.

"What if I failed?"

"No good father gives his child a task they can't complete. Is your father a good man?" he asks.

"Yes. Of course, but-" I say.

"The task was for you to become everything you were destined to become. Somehow, he knew this would break your shell. Have you changed?"

"Yes, I have." I say.

"One can't fight something out here, if one has not first defeated it within ourselves. It is hard to attack something that we embody." says the Archbishop. "That's why they could not kill the leader who offered to buy it."

I run my hands through my hair and put them back into my pockets. He turns and his long robe brushes the floor. He walks toward the elevator. The leaders are gone. We enter the elevator and it takes us to the lobby.

"You may call upon me, in your time of need. You know where to find me, young Promise." says the Archbishop stepping out of the elevator.

"Thank you for everything." We shake hands.

I step outside in front of the hotel and take a deep cleansing breath. The phone rings. It's Jason.

"Why haven't you picked up?" Jason asks.

"I was a little busy." I say.

His television is playing loudly in the background. He does that intentionally to muffling the sound of our call.

"BREAKING NEWS, an earthquake was felt in the Swiss Alps town of St. Moritz. It shook a large local hotel, The Badrutt. Dr. Thomas, how rare are earthquakes this time of year?" asks the News Anchor. Extremely..." says the Meteorologist.

"Jason, I know who your mole is. It's-" I say.

"Hang on Caleb, Sam's calling." says Jason.

"Wait, Jason!"

He comes back on the line.

"What? What did you say?" Jason says.

"The mole. It's Sam," I say.

He is quiet.

"How do you know? Can't be." he asks.

"Trust me." I say.

"She's been with me forever, Caleb. Who is your source?"

"I can't tell you. Trust me. It's valid." I say.

He's quiet. Jason doesn't know the meaning of quiet.

"I'll get back to you." says Jason.

Ten minutes later he calls me back. I can hear him a door lock click in the background. Other than that, silence.

"What's going on, Jason?" I say.

"Tell me you have nothing to do with the so-called earthquake in Switzerland."

"I can neither confirm or deny. I still don't know who our mystery man is. Whoever he is, he has a connect with the tattoo." I say.   A loud bang like a door being kicked in and gunfire.

"Jason!"

Nothing. He's silent. Was he shot? Is he dead?

"Say something." I say.

I stop walking and listen. Heavy footsteps running. Several of them. I picture Jason's face blank, and him lying dead on the floor. My stomach feels like there is a rock in it. Then, I hear a door slam.

"You were right." Jason breathes.

"Where are you?" I ask.

"In the room across the hall. I called Sam and gave her this address and the number of an empty room across the hall.   I watched her, Caleb.   They shot the stack of pillows I stuffed under the blankets. She walked in calmly behind them and pulled the blanket back like she was unwrapping a burrito.   I can't believe it. She called someone."

"It wasn't Director White. She is clean." I say.

"Oh, so she really does just hate me." Jason scoffs.
Glad to hear him joking again. I know how close he and Sam were.

"What's next, Agent Jason Smith?"

"Chen will take you to the Airport."

"Airport?" I ask.

"You've done your bit." he says.

I must be going back to New York. That's home for me. In Manhattan, jobs aren't scarce for someone willing to work. I got fresh start. Italy did something to me. The feel of Europe is different. I can't stay out here though I would love to. I have no roots here. At least in New York, I can start over. The bearded drunk is gone. I won't touch alcohol again. The new Caleb promise can survive in that roach-ridden cheap hotel at least for a while until I can afford somewhere better.

"What will you do?" I ask.

"I'm going dark for a while. Then, I will get my wife."

"Your ex-wife you mean. You said she caught you cheating and walked out."

"Things aren't always as they appear, Caleb. If anyone, I expected you to know that. Find Chen. I will be in touch," says Jason.

"Jason... thank you," I say.

He hangs up on me. But I know he heard it so can't help but smile.

Jason Jones

I am rather disappointed. I need to be still. I think best when I am still. I sit on the chair in the corner of the hotel room. It's firm. No one has probably ever sat in this seat. I don't like to sit on beds. They are for sleeping. What intel did I feed Sam our mystery person over the years? How much of my own information ended up working against me? If I continue along this line of thought, I will grow bitter, paranoid. I will stop now.

Caleb made one miscalculation. This is not over. When people such as the person behind this scheme find their plan thwarted, they find another way. They don't see it as a failure. It becomes just a learned experience to improve the next plan. He's young. He will be fine. But he needs time to heal more than he knows. I've got him by a few years physically, but by decades, mentally.

I can't wait to see my wife again. I never lost the love I felt down on one knee in the sand on Long Beach holding that tiny diamond ring up to her. It has been two years since Amber left, or rather, I made her go. Most agents aren't married. The ones that are, have horrid marriages. We forget how old our kids are and live in a world where time moves based on case progress. We plot entire false lives. So, faking our separation was easy.

We finish one another's sentences and I've learned to love sitting beneath her chenille throw watching action movies. A paradox. I knew she wouldn't need much prompting. Two years ago, on a sunny spring Saturday in the kitchen of our townhouse in Washington D. C., I sat at the kitchen table and just finished paying off all our credit card bills. Amber had the job of her dreams and we were trying to have a baby.

The day before, I got the call offering me this case. I took it. I closed the wallet filled with paid off credit cards and stood up. I looked into her eyes standing right in front of the stainless-steel refrigerator and hugged her. She put down the pitcher of fresh squeezed orange juice on the cabinet behind her. Sinatra playing loudly, as usual, I whispered in her ear,

"We need to pretend to break up. Smile."

They bugged our home with video and audio, we were aware of the invisible intruders in our lives. Beyond being beautiful, she is intelligent. She smiled as I instructed. We danced slightly and I further whispered...

"Stick your hand in my jacket pocket and go with it."

After a few moments of chit-chat and giggles, she does it and pulls out a pair of women's red underwear that is not her own. I purchased them the day before to ensure her response could be authentic. A woman knows her underwear. The rest of the plan spun into action and she never even asked me why. The next morning, I hint to her to walk out on me and grab the wallet of credit cards. I knew she was thrifty, but fifty thousand dollars ensured her security.

My teary drama scene for the cameras begging her forgiveness with promises that it would never happen again validated things. The drama, though an act, had one genuine part to it. Our tears that fell at our last glance just as she turned back from me with her hand on the doorknob of our dream home was real. She knew I wouldn't have done it if it weren't for our betterment. Immediately, I missed my best friend. Now, I'm closer to having her back. One step closer.

Caleb succeeding in eliminating Wilkes and Gretchen was progress, but the unknown player seems a larger threat. He or she is the one Sam is working for, at least I think so. Amber's safety depends upon me cleaning this thoroughly. My instinct to get her as far away as possible at the inception of this case proved right. Thank God I never told Sam that the separation was a hoax. In her eyes, I hate Amber and Amber hates me. I could, would, never unite with my dear Amber until I stamp 'CASE CLOSED' on that file. For now, I go dark.

CHAPTER TWENTY-TWO

New Beginnings
Caleb Promise

In the distance I can see a private plane. We are approaching the tarmac in Switzerland. Who would have guessed? I'm not in a rush to leave.

"Chen, you drive like a madman." I say.

He laughs.

"Only for you, Caleb. Are you whole?"

Small power-pack of wisdom. That's what Chen is. The Swiss Mountains in the distance remind me there is still a grand world to explore. When I get home, I intend to work hard so I can see the rest of it. Life feels purposeful with a vision.

"That's a trick question. Yes, I feel whole," I say.

"No more drink?"

"How did you know?"

He smiles and whips the car into a full stop beside the private plane.

"You look terrible." says Chen.

My hands are bruised, and I have some scrapes on my head and behind my neck. My ribs feel like they rattle when I breath thanks to the guard with the new boots. But overall, I feel better now, than I have felt in years.

"You know, you don't have to be honest about everything." I say smirking.

I'm back in 'my' clothes. Blue jeans and leather. That's me. I left the two boxes of chocolate on the bed when I checked out of the hotel with a note on each. It's not a gift anymore.

"What's this?" I ask, referring to the private plane with the steward standing beside it.

"Jason said to bring you here. That's all I know." Chen says.

"You're getting into heaven, Chen, for sure. Do me a favor and give him this." I reach into my pocket and hand him the little gold key and a stack of money. "That's what's left over." I say.

Chen takes them and I know he will get it to Jason. Even when Jason goes dark, Chen is the one person he divulges his location to.

I ascend the steps of the large private plane. The engines are running, and I'm walking slower than normal trying to relish every moment. This is probably the last time I'll ever experience such luxury. A broke boy from a small town on his way to a rat-trap hotel. I will get used to Jean not being in the hall, eventually. I want to take in this moment.

This airplane is more personalized than Wilkes plane. Newer too. I step into the plane.

"Welcome, Mr. Promise," says the steward. "I'm Edwardo. If there's anything you need-"

The seating format in the plane is like that of Wilkes plane. I choose a reclining captain style seat with a table beside it.

"Ed, call me Caleb, and lose the Sir. Okay?" I say.

"Yes Si-, Caleb," says Edwardo.

He looks uneasy with my instructions. He turns toward the kitchen.

"Whose plane is this?" I ask him.

"My apologies. I am not authorized to give that information. I was instructed to make you comfortable. Have you eaten, Caleb?"

Through the window, I see the dignitaries boarding their planes eagerly but composed.

"Have *you* eaten, Edward?"

"Excuse me? Um... no, Caleb. I was called to duty rather unexpectedly."

I look down at his shoes. Those black server's shoes. Just like mine.

"Bring us two sandwiches," I say, "ginger ale for me, get what you want."

"Yes, Caleb. Thank you." says Edward.

He's surprised. I lean back in my seat. The television is playing BBC World News silently. I turn it up. It is coverage of the World Peace Summit. The sandwich is good. Turkey with spicy mustard on rye bread, lettuce and tomato. This would cost at least seven dollars at the deli in New York. I wash it down with the cold ginger ale.

"It was a prosperous meeting. One we should have had sooner." says the President of Spain.

"I agree. A bond has formed that we pray will never be broken." says the President of France.

News clip after clip shows of the leaders offering positive feedback about the meeting. One after the other smile, posing for photographs. Eagle eyed critics may notice that some of them are wearing their assistant's ties because they don't match their suit. That is completely explainable because of the 'earthquake'.

I close my eyes while the plane ascends and quickly fall asleep. For the first time, I sleep soundly. No nightmare. No dream control. I don't even try. It is a calm comforting sleep.

My dream, simple. My parents and I are in our usual picnic field. They sit, happy and smiling. I am as a little child. I can feel the warmth of my father's hand on my head tousling my hair. Suddenly, I'm a grown man again.

"Well done son," my dad says. "Keep doing the right thing, Caleb. Be good. Be pure. Be you."

I feel a hand on my shoulder and feel my body jostle slightly.

"Caleb... Caleb, we're landing. Please, buckle your seatbelt." says Edwardo.

I open my eyes. Ed is smiling kindly and there is a blanket on me, pulled up to my chin. Edwardo clears his spot where he was eating. We land. The doors open, sunlight pours into the cabin. It's cool, but not cold. This is not New York. Where am I? This is a private runway. A custom Maybach is on the runway with a capped driver seated behind the wheel. Standing at the open plane door, I lean over to Ed.

"Where am I?" I ask.

"Biarritz." says Ed.

I walk down the steps of the plane and realize Ed is not with me.

"Are you coming?" I say over my shoulder.

"No, Caleb, I am only the plane's steward."

I stop, mid-descent down the steps and look Ed directly in the eyes. I ignore the pilot standing there, and the driver waiting Maybach.

"You are not 'only' a steward," I say, extending my hand. Something in his eyes ignites. That's what I wanted to do. Send him on another trail of thought about himself. Just as this mission did for me.

What did Jason do? I call him.

"The number you have dialed has been disconnected. Please check your number and try your call again." a recording says.

The drive is quick. The Maybach takes me to a sprawling stone mansion extending three stories upward. Long slender windows with heavy drapes like the ones in the windows of the Manhattan apartments I stood staring at. We turn onto the long stone driveway flanked with enormous potted evergreens perfectly trimmed to a point.

The car stops. The driver steps out and opens my door. A cool breeze blows over me. Two large ornate black iron gates swing open revealing two equally impressive solid dark wood doors that are also open. The doorway is at least five feet deep. There is a man standing in the doorway. The tips of his form-fitting brown leather shoes touch the sunlight, but his body remains in the shadows. He is holding something in his hand.

I get out of the car and walk toward him searching for a clue as to who this man is. Then, he draws back his hand and tosses something at me. Perplexed, I catch it. It's round and cool. I strain to see him then he takes one step forward into the light. Something about him is familiar but I can't place him. I open my hand and look at what I caught. Now I know. Until now, I don't think I have ever felt joy. But I feel it now. I look down at it and squeeze it in my bruised palm to confirm that it is real. Every ache and pain melts into its red skin smeared with a tear that escaped the old stone monastery.

It is a pomegranate. We smile.

Read Book 2 now. " CAPTURED"

https://buy.bookfunnel.com/jp7i2tbhxa

Or Visit
https://www.kabryant.com

CHAPTER TWENTY-THREE
BEYOND THE BOOK

Monthly Newsletter Book Promotions Pre-Release Offers New Book Release Deals & Give-aways. Unsubscribe any time.

Type the link below into your browser:
https://www.kabryant.com/join-mailer

Jumping into that another world while curled on the couch with coffee is priceless. Hot cup in hand, I started writing for the love of writing and can't think of anything I would rather do for the rest of my life. Once a writer, always a writer. A vision grew to draw a leisure reader, confined patient, or a child on summer vacation with their feet twirling in the grass, into a new world between two covers. I want to invite you to join the K. A. BRYANT Book Readers Club to stay informed of all the new upcoming promotions and book give-away.

Non-Fiction, True account, inspirational, informative with fillable charts and logs. 8"x 11"

Two books in one. "Hope on the Other Side" with "The Workbook".
Perfect for a patient or caregiver. Designed as a useful tool for someone facing a long-term illness, long-term care, or short-term care. An inspirational thread is woven into the fabric of the book with its roots based in Christianity.

Fiction Espionage, Thriller-Mystery, Easy Reading, Page-turner

Caleb Promise Series Mission 1
First book in the Caleb Promise Series, Mission One. A deep 450 Page meaty thriller, espionage, and political mystery novel. There is a dystopian thread through the book with a literary hand. Bursts with suspense, emotional rides, and espionage at the highest levels of government.

Fiction Espionage, Thriller-Mystery, Easy Reading, Page-turner

Caleb Promise Series Mission 2
An attack on United States soil can't go unanswered. One captured man's rescue could prevent war, but only if Caleb Promise denies his instincts. A government coup is in flow. His orders, to extract the CAPTURED man but leave the man's wife, Tempest Bleu. The problem is, he can't.

Online Courses & Podcast

World events have caused many people to take on additional roles. The online courses and podcast, <u>K-Today</u>, delivers the content you need. A monthly newsletter and blog are delivered to your email box. <u>Live Your Life With Kay</u> delivers solutions for success. It guides you to find the strategy to unlock your creativity.

Work at your own pace and review the areas you want to focus on. Priceless, for the peace of mind it will bring. Also, I will teach you how to homeschool using the supplies you already have at home. If you want to go-pro and purchase items, I tell you what to get and how to use it.

Get your online course on the K.A. Bryant's official

Websites : Liveyourlifewithkay.com and kabryant.com/ktoday

Parents have become teacher/caretaker while juggling work as well. You don't have to feel your way through it. I took over a decade of teaching and management experience and put it into this course using audio and video features.

Join the Team

FOR READERS, BLOGGERS, POD-CASTERS, YOU- TUBERS AND BOOK REVIEWERS

SPECIAL OFFER:

Influencers, your voice is valuable. nd it would really help me reach my writing goal if you would write a quick review. Your feedback tells me what you want to see more or less of.

I can write it, but I need you to push it. If you are a Blogger, Pod-Castor, You-Tuber or Book Reviewer, I invite you to join the street team. A vetted influencer can get pre-launch peeks at books.

I believe we never stop learning. It's a lifelong gift to grow and change.

Type the link in your bowser:

Https://www. kabryant.com/street-team-sign-up

CHAPTER TWENTY-FOUR

Letter from the Author

K.A. BRYANT, Author

Letter from the Author

I still remember how warm it was in Mrs. Harris's English class. She liked it that way although she wore a sweater. I don't know why I was always distracted by her long bead necklaces she pulled on habitually. That was when teachers wore silk blouses, long skirts down to their mid-calf with stockings and shoes that clicked when they walked.

She was a retired play-write with her passion for the written word

evident in her detailed critique of every short story scrawled by the twenty children in the class. She was the catalyst. The pointed finger saying, 'go that way'. All I knew was it was fun. Oh, the simple thinking era.

Life, time, and the Internet soon showed me that there was so much more to writing. The wonderful thing was discovering a world of wonderful people with either a love of reading, writing, or both so willing to share their opinions and be a pointed finger.

Much time has passed since Mrs. Harris's class, but I'm still going in the direction of that pointed finger.

My hope... is that my journey in writing will find my books in the hands of readers all over the world and inspire someone to reach further, write more, or just explore their dream. Hope can be lost when you are going through a long, seemingly endless difficult time, just as the main character Caleb Promise experienced. In the book, keeping focused on his mission pulled him out of the pit- experience he was in. An experience that was draining him of his strength and willingness to live.

You and I... can propel a vision beyond expectation by taking three easy steps:

1. Sign-up to stay informed.
2. Write a review online after reading a book.
3. Tell your friends.

You can stay in touch with me by Twitter @kabryantauthor, Facebook @kabryantbooks. I am also on Instagram, GoodReads and WordPress. If you enjoy the books and blogs, you can show your support on Patreon.com.

Thank you for reading the book!

CHAPTER TWENTY-FIVE

Sneak Peek of a Book

CAPTURED

Tempest Bleu

The champagne-soaked hotel carpet, cold and matted beneath my bare feet. What day is it? I feel as though I have been here forever. How long have I been standing? My heals ache. I release my grip and feel my fingernails pull out of my palm and his handkerchief falls to the bed. I need to sit.

What was that? My foot bumped the empty champagne bottle on the floor, and it rolls and taps the platform beneath the beige bed. I shouldn't have drunk. I haven't since our wedding day twenty-five years ago today, so head is spinning. I can feel my smeared mascara dry and tight on my face. My eyes sting and are so puffy it's hard to keep them open. Where is it? I just had it last night.

The card from the embassy agent. Crooked toupee. That's all I remember. It hung too far left… what was his name? I toss the covers on my side of the bed. Nothing.

Christians' side of the bed is still made. I won't ruffle that. I smooth my hand over his cool pillow. The pillow where his head would lay last night if I didn't do what I did. There is blood on the back of my hand, and everything is such a blur.

"Why hasn't the Police called yet? He said they would call… or come by… something." I mutter aloud.

Finally, the phone rings. "Ouch!" My fake nail popped off as I grab the telephone receiver.

"HELLO! Christian?"

"Mrs. Bleu, this is Janet from the front desk."

"Oh."

"I'm calling to let you know that the last evacuation bus is leaving for the airport in five minutes. It has been highly recommended that all Americans- "

"NO! I'm not leaving!" Conviction. Immediately I feel it. I should not have yelled at her. She's only doing her job. I take a deep breath. "No, I'm sorry..." I rub the back of my neck, and strands of my hair, now droopy curls fall over my right eye, "... I will stay, thank you." I hang up the phone agitated.

Gunshots. Still more? I jump with every shot. My top is moist with perspiration and my right sleeve is torn. My body-shaper undergarment is squeezing me terribly. Secondary to my other problems.

Someone should have come by now. Douglas's toupee leaned while he said he'd send the Police. How can they let this go on?

Our passports are still on the bare desk beside my broken perfume bottle. Christian would put them in the safe. I grab them, throw them into the open safe and slam it shut and hurry back to my position on the bed beside the phone. I feel safer here. Close to where he would have lain.

Our suitcases still stand in the corner side by side. We didn't even have time to unpack. I can't help but feel guilty. Why did I do it? Why! I rub my eyes and feel fresh tears slip between my fingers.

Two Days Earlier

I open my eyes. It's bright. Without question, this is my favorite place in the house. The octagonal glass sun-room warm from the sunlight pouring in and the view of the garden seems to go on forever. The tall ceiling to floor windows are impressive. I see the callous handed gardener pruning the rose bushes. With the press of a button, I lower a shade blocking light falling directly on my freshly made-up face. I raise my warm cup of tea to my lips and the sound of water running from the indoor fountain is remarkably relaxing.

When Christian first brought me here, I thought it was too much for us. Too much money, too much space. What would Christian and I do with nine thousand square foot house with greenhouse, indoor and outdoor pool and tennis court and no children?

It's hard to believe that just a year ago our greatest comfort was knowing we could pay the light bill and electric bill at the same time. Our thirteen hundred square foot cape style house with galley kitchen was a blessing. Though one of us had to step out of the kitchen just to open the oven. The dirt, and I mean dirt could never grow grass.

Sitting here in the conservatory, my conservatory is something I only dreamed of. I make it a point to sit in here at least once a day. I had some exotic plants brought in. They bloom reminding me of the wonders of God.

In the past, our sofa-talks started with 'what would you want if…'. Mind-stretching conversations over baked chicken and salad on our matching card tables exposed our deepest desires and wildest imaginations.

Mine, a conservatory and greenhouse. Christian's, a work shed for his construction projects. We watched movies filmed in places we dreamed of visiting and now, we don't have to dream anymore. We just go.

I smile when I think of that day. The day Christian came home with the keys to this house. Purchased with cash for a fast closing, I did what any good Christian wife would do. Faint.

I opened my eyes still laying flat on my back on our worn-out oriental rug we got from a store close-out deal and Christian was still sitting beside me dangling the keys with the most amazing smile on his face.

We had been in this one-bedroom rental for three years and it was wearing on me. I tried not to show it until I just couldn't hide it anymore. It felt dark and small and that feeling grew greater day by day. I'm not a complainer, I know how the Lord feels about murmuring and complaining but still, in my mind, I couldn't wait to leave this place.

We didn't buy furniture because we knew it was a temporary situation. Although we had no exit in sight, we believed that this was not our end. Christian had keys in one hand and the deed in the other.

That was when I realised he found it. He found his niche. After searching for so long for what he wanted to do, to the pleasure of millionaires and billionaires willing to pay for his services, he clearly found it.

His profit margins leaped suddenly when word of mouth about Christian's product design capabilities became the buzz at high society parties. It wasn't just the product though. It was his trustworthy character that spoke volumes. People with massive amounts of money are often leery of who they trust, and Christian is the man that would take a secret to his grave. Not out of fear, rather, integrity. He has always had that. Always.

It is natural for him to be personable, engaging. We are the opposite. He touches the world and I touch him.

Every morning, the sun pours into the conservatory and my tea tray is perfectly set with my favorite tea biscuit's and my aqua mint tea set. I angle my favorite chair to face Christian's office.

Through the glass wall, I see Christian in his office following his morning routine. He's on his land line which means he must be speaking with his business partner.

"Mrs. Bleu, which luggage would you like to use?"

"The Louis Vuitton. Set them out, will you Doris, I'll be up in a second. Have you arranged the outfits I requested yet?"

"Yes, Mrs. Bleu. But you still need to select your personal items."

Doris is a dear. Though only a few years older than I, she thinks like me and I thank God she has a sense of humor. She is discreet. By personal items she means my girdles and shaperwear.

"If it snaps like a slingshot put it in the suitcase, Doris. I need all the help I can get. And Doris, no swimsuits. Let's spare mankind of that one."

Doris takes a tissue from her white apron pocket, dabs her nose trying to hide her smile as she walks away. I found having a sense of humor a natural buffer when I grew to my voluptuous size.

I can't blame it on childbirth, though I've had my share of being mistaken for being pregnant. I don't have children. We wanted them. After our wedding, I was convinced that it would happen on the honeymoon under the clear Mexican sky laden with stars while I watched the palm trees sway.

We thought for certain it would, but it didn't. Nor the next week, the next month or two years later. We were so convinced it would happen in Gods time. I still think if it were His will, I will have them. I still believe, despite the onset of menopause. I have started to have hot flashes. If it is His will, it can happen. That's faith. It's what we build our lives on. Besides, I have started menopause early for some strange reason.

Christian and I were young, newly married and just trying to pay our rent and ate dinner by candlelight quite a few times because they cut the electricity off, but we smiled through it. We had everything because we had each other. Expensive fertility doctors were out of the question, so we marched on like good little soldiers.

I'm glad he gave in and settled on Mexico for our second honeymoon. Christian wanted Singapore, and to stay in that hotel with the pool on the roof but I'm feeling particularly sentimental. We will stay in the same hotel we stayed in on our first honeymoon. It may be the onset of menopause, but I wanted to go back to where it all started. Mexico.

Besides, this time we won't have to sit through a time-share presentation. It was a special offer Christian found that got us free tickets on a boat to an island along with a bunch of other freebies. Clever. That's what he is, clever.

I feel the smile on my face lower. His conversation must be heated. He's standing and walking while he talks, within the limit of the coiled land line telephone chord. He only talks to confidential clients or his partner on that phone.

I tilt my head and watch him take his hand from his pocket and his hand gestures are overt. Christian and his partner have been at odds more than usual lately. I don't like him getting stressed. It's not good for his heart. That's another reason I'm looking forward to this vacation. He needs it. I never know a time when he doesn't think. He slams the phone and hangs up. That's not like him. What now?

I put my teacup down, look at my laptop and take one last look at our reservation confirmations. Shut it, slip my feet back into my slippers and go to Christian. I pause in the doorway. He's so blustered, he doesn't even see me. He's pacing the floor.

"Are you all right?" I ask.

He looks at me, takes his hands out of his pockets. His troubled look melts away as I walk into his open arms. Eyes closed we exhale simultaneously. My face in the chest I've rested on for over thirty years. He's a full man. His arms strong and larger than most men. He's always warm. I feel his entire body relax.

"Now I am. McLean." He says.

"Will he sign?" I ask.

"Your hair smells great."

"You're changing the subject. All right I'll go with it. Two glorious weeks in Mexico. Are you sure giving up Singapore does not upset you?"

"You want Mexico, you've got it." He says kissing me on the forehead.

I kiss his cheek and see large papers on his desk.

"Are those the alternative plans?" I ask.

"Preliminary ones, yes." Excitement fills his voice. He walks to the desk and lifts the corner of the over-sized paper with mathematical dimensions scrawled on it and the details of a brilliant architect.

"Christian, it's amazing. This is beyond our time." I say seeing excitement dance in his eyes. "Can you say who? Let me guess-"

"It's better for you not to know." He says. "I can tell you, this safe is by far my most complicated and revolutionary design. I finished his panic room and he said, 'the sky is the limit' and thus, the idea was born. It hit me like a ton of bricks."

"Come on, show me, or no dinner for you." I tease.

He leans over the desk and pulls draft papers out of the pile laying them on top.

"Tempest, if my calculations are correct, we can launch it. My friend from the National Aeronautics and Space Administration is set look at it when we get back to confirm. This will be the first safe," he looks directly in my eyes, "in space. Unheard of, special permissions and retrieval not a problem," he chuckles, "not for this client. It has never been done."

"Christian, what would someone need to hide... in space?"

His smile drops slightly, and he closes the draft paper.

"I never ask that question." He places his hands on my shoulders tenderly. "That's probably why I'm still alive. I know the gravity of what I'm working with and who I work with. I know you don't want to hear this, ever, but know that I have put things in place should anything ever happen to me."

"I don't want to have this conversation. Not now. Not ever. All right?" I turn away from him and face the window. "You do what you think you must, but all of my plans involve you. If this thing," I point at the sketch," is a risk to your life, get rid of it. I would rather live in a rental with you than in a beach house here in the Hampton's without you. So... no-no more-" I swallow.

"All right, all right." Christian calms.   "Just so you know," He turns to the window and looks outside.   "McLean knows we've gone as far as we can, but the company is his meal ticket."

I turn to face him.

"You do all the work. It's you who the clients request time after time. He's become bitter, Christian. I saw it when we had him and his *girlfriend* over for dinner. I don't like the way he looks at you and you know-"

"-Yes, 'you are usually right'. I think you started hating him when he broke up with Terry. She left him you know."

Christian puts his hands in his pockets. I like those khaki shorts on him. And he's finally wearing the loafers I bought him three months ago.

"Your legs are sexy." I say lightly.

He looks down at them.

"You're bias." He says.

"So?"

"He's my college buddy-"

"-was your college buddy. Now he's a bitter, jealous man who you can't trust. See him for what he is, not what he used to be."

"You're smart."

"Your bias." I say.

"True." He says.

I take his hand and squeeze it tightly.

"You shouldn't have kept him after he tried to steel that other client." I say.

"I know. But we he doesn't exactly work for me. We started this together. At the time, we couldn't buy him out." He says flatly.

"We can now. Many times over." I say.

"I know." He says.

"No one could blame you."

"I know. But-"

"people sometimes need second chances." I finish his sentence.

He nods and those deep brown eyes lined with dark lashes just pull me into his world. His goatee is perfectly trimmed, and the corner of his eyes slightly creased from years of smiling. His hair is lying flat, cut low for the trip and his nails shine from the manicure we both got in our salon room.

"If you embrace a snake, you can expect a bite. He had the papers for over a week."

"He said he'll sign when we get back from our trip. Remember, tell no one where we are going. For security reasons." He says as I walk out of the room. "I already registered the trip with the United States travel Department. Can never be too safe."

"My man." I throw him a kiss as I leave the room and do my happy dance humorously. "The car is ready. We leave for the airport in twenty minutes." I yell back at him hurrying to see what Doris has packed.

I hear him laugh. I've done my job. The phone in his office rings. Why isn't he answering it?

Present Day

Wait, that is here, now. I grab it eagerly. Suddenly, I'm afraid. What if it's the detective with some hideous news? Wait, what if it's Christian?

"Christian?" I breathe.

— —

KEEP READING "CAPTURED" By K. A. BRYANT

Read CAPTURED:

https://buy.bookfunnel.com/jp7i2tbhxa

Available on your favorite reading platforms.

More books: kabryant.com

Printed in Great Britain
by Amazon